Courageous

Books by Dina Sleiman

VALIANT HEARTS

Valiant Hearts ◇ Book Three

Courageous

DINA L. SLEIMAN

BETHANYHOUSE

a division of Baker Publishing Group
Minneapolis, Minnesota

© 2016 by Dina Sleiman

Published by Bethany House Publishers
11400 Hampshire Avenue South
Bloomington, Minnesota 55438
www.bethanyhouse.com

Bethany House Publishers is a division of
Baker Publishing Group, Grand Rapids, Michigan

Printed in the United States of America

ISBN 978-0-7642-1314-4

Library of Congress Control Number: 2016930773

Unless noted, Scripture quotations are from the King James Version of the Bible.

Epigraph Scripture quotation is from the Holy Bible, New International Version®. NIV®. Copyright © 1973, 1978, 1984, 2011 by Biblica, Inc.™ Used by permission of Zondervan. All rights reserved worldwide. www.zondervan.com

This is a work of fiction. Names, characters, incidents, and dialogues are products of the author's imagination and are not to be construed as real. Any resemblance to actual events or persons, living or dead, is entirely coincidental.

Cover design by Paul Higdon
Cover model photography by Steve Gardner, PixelWorks Studios, Inc.

Author represented by The Steve Laube Agency

16 17 18 19 20 21 22   7 6 5 4 3 2 1

To my readers:

My prayer is that you will be strong and courageous. Follow
the path God has laid before you, wherever that might lead.
Be a doctor, a lawyer, a professional athlete, a wife, a mother,
or even a president.

Chase after your dreams, and if a handsome knight in shining
armor should happen to come alongside you, headed in the
same direction, and you should happen to fall in love . . . then
join together and become partners in your quest.

But please remember—you are complete, you are beautiful, and
you are dearly loved by God just the way you are.

But he said to me, "My grace is sufficient for you, for my power is made perfect in weakness." Therefore I will boast all the more gladly about my weaknesses, so that Christ's power may rest on me. That is why, for Christ's sake, I delight in weaknesses, in insults, in hardships, in persecutions, in difficulties. For when I am weak, then I am strong.

—2 Corinthians 12:9–10 NIV

Prologue

I commission thee, Rosalind of Ipsworth,
Defender of the Holy Cross
And crusader of our Lord Jesus Christ.

Soon I will hear those sacred words, and there will be no turning back. My mind swirls with possibilities. I can barely focus on the grand Cathedral of Edendale as I file down the center aisle behind a stream of knights in armor, glinting with an array of colorful lights from the many stained-glass windows surrounding us.

Arched ceilings seem to tremble and radiate high over my head. Walls painted with biblical scenes take on a special sort of glow this day. The marble floor whispers up holy echoes with each step I take toward the altar. Incense wafts over and all around me, flooding my senses with divine presence and keen delight.

With both great honor and the utmost humility, I wear my surcoat emblazoned with crosses in the North Britannian colors of black, ivory, and crimson. Perhaps with more humility than most, for of this crowd, I alone know my greatest sin.

The one for which I am desperate to atone.

At that thought the waves crash over me, as they always do. Waves of pain, of loneliness, of regret—yet followed by a new wash of warmth. The warmth that came with this decision to travel to the Holy Land. The warmth offering a hope that somehow I might find redemption, and that this crusade might open the way.

As I reach the front, I dip a knee before our esteemed duchess, Adela DeMontfort. She smiles at me with warm familiarity. Then I likewise bow before her cousins, the Lady Honoria and the young Lady Sapphira. Sapphira, whose eyes shimmer like the gems for which she is named, with some otherworldly light. With a sense of passion and intensity that has brought us all to this place.

Indeed, that special light inside Sapphira has sparked this crusade. And soon hundreds of men and dozens of women—along with a handful of specially chosen children—will sail away to the Holy Land inspired by Sapphira's divine vision, Honoria's stalwart leadership, and Adela's funding and support.

A true woman's crusade to surpass even Eleanor of Aquitaine's.

Only, ours shall be far more successful, or so we all believe. And unlike the doomed children's crusades of not long ago, this one will match sacred passion and visionary guidance with sound reason and proper planning.

As I join the ranks of crusaders lining the front of the cathedral, my heart speeds, tingles ripple up and down my arms, and my knees quiver as if they might give way. The glow, the radiance, the power of this moment threatens to engulf me. Then the bishop presses his hand in a downward motion, and I thankfully lower myself to my knees along with the many others. The cold, smooth floor is solid beneath me, and I anchor my hands to it until I catch my bearings.

"We are brought here today," says the bishop with holy fire

crackling through his voice, "by the direction of God himself. For He has spoken through the pure, young Lady Sapphira, giving her a vision to inspire us all. A vision of the Holy Land, and a clear call to set the captives free—captives like Lord Richard DeMontfort, the duchess's beloved brother, with the hope that he might be returned safely home to us as our rightful Duke of North Britannia."

As the bishop continues in his inspiring tones, I glance about for my friends and partners in this endeavor. I search out my beloved mistress, the Lady Gwendolyn. She had been just behind me. I feel certain of it. And yet I find her nowhere. My chest tightens. I turn to look for her husband, Sir Allen of Ellsworth, but he is missing from the ranks of those being commissioned as well.

I attempt to maintain subtlety as I peek over my shoulders, but I do not spot them in the throng beyond. Nor my mother. Nor my siblings. Although they are my reason for living and breathing, for working, and even a large part of my reason for pursuing this crusade, I did not invite them this day. The sight of their faces yet brings back too many haunting memories.

I continue to scan the crowd. Of course I see many I know. Knights in the duchess's service, a handful of barons, several ladies of renown—all of whom I met during my time at the grand castle serving Lady Gwendolyn. The duchess herself, who shares my feisty nature and sharp wit and always brings such joy. But I do not spy the two people who matter most to me.

Sir Randel Penigree catches my gaze and grins reassuringly, as if noticing my frenzied search. Sir Randel, so good-natured and calm. A faithful friend to both Gwendolyn and Allen.

"*Where are they?*" I mouth Randel's way.

"*Never fear,*" he mouths back with a wink. "*All is well.*"

And somehow I believe him.

Just then the ladies around me stand to their feet and move

toward the bishop. I follow suit. One by one they kneel before the duchess. Then the moment is upon me. The one I have so desperately dreamed of during this past year of regret and despair.

I fall to my knees before the duchess, who is flanked by the bishop, Honoria, and Sapphira. She taps the flat edge of her sword to my right shoulder and then my left. Heat radiates down my body. I imagine it burning away the darkness. Burning away my sin. "I commission thee, Rosalind of Ipsworth, defender of the holy cross, and crusader of our Lord Jesus Christ."

The wonder of it sends my thoughts reeling once again.

Then the bishop swipes my forehead with holy oil in the shape of the cross. It seeps into my skin, into my very mind, settling deep into my heart. "I anoint you for this task in the name of the Father, the Son, and the Holy Spirit."

As I stand to return to my place, a lightness, a cleanness, swirls about me. I feel as if I just might float away.

After the ceremony I stand in a sea of well-wishers, still searching out my mistress. At last, I squeeze through hugs and pats of congratulations to Sir Randel, a typical-looking soldier with his short-cropped dark hair and crusader surcoat. Though not as broad as some of the knights, he is well muscled, and easy to spot due to his attractive crooked grin.

"Where are they? What do you know?" I scan the crowded cathedral yet again.

He lifts my hand and presses a quick kiss upon it.

Although I no longer relish flirtatious attention from men, have in fact avoided it this past year, the chivalrous and sincere gesture heartens me.

"As I mentioned, all is well," he says. "Come. They await you outside in the courtyard."

His dark eyes sparkle with a secret knowledge as he tucks me under his arm and fights his way through the crowd. This day has left me in a daze. Although I am well trained and able to defend myself with weapons aplenty, for once I am happy to let a knight in shining armor come to my rescue.

As I step from the shadowy cathedral into the bright winter sunshine glaring off the snow, all goes dark for a moment, but Randel continues leading me forward. Soon this snow will melt, and we shall set off across the sea.

When my eyes clear, I spot Gwendolyn waving to me with her handsome husband at her side. Both wearing everyday attire.

"There you . . . but . . . what . . ." I stutter, aware that I am making no sort of sense at all.

Sir Allen wraps his arm about Gwendolyn in her woolen cloak of dark blue.

My young mistress's bright smile nearly outshines the shimmering snow. Though now a married lady, she is a mere seventeen years of age, same as me. "We did not want to tell you before the ceremony, but Allen and I shall not be going on crusade this time, for a very good reason."

What reason could possibly keep the bold and daring Lady Gwendolyn from this grand adventure?

Allen presses a hand to Gwendolyn's flat abdomen. "It seems we are about to undertake our own crusade of epic proportions, especially if our little one has the spunk of its mother."

"Oh!" Gwendolyn swats his chest.

A child! How had I failed to guess? But my mistress's cycles always have been irregular, perhaps due to her strenuous training at the warrior arts. Still, this was Gwendolyn's dream long before it was mine. To go on crusade. To fight for the innocent. "But we discussed this possibility. You said you wished to go no matter what."

Gwendolyn shakes her head in a beatific sort of wonder.

"I know, but motherhood does such odd things to a person. Strange particles seem to flow through my blood. As soon as I realized my condition, all my instincts turned to protecting this tiny creature." She encircles her belly with her hands. "I cannot put him . . . or her in danger. Perhaps if we had already started along our way . . . but we have not."

"And I shall stay with her and oversee the palace guard." Allen pulls Gwendolyn tighter to his side. "I do not want to miss the big event. And the duchess needs good warriors here with so many leaving."

"Precisely," Gwendolyn says, "and I shall attend the duchess until the babe is born."

I struggle to collect my thoughts. So much has happened this day. A baby . . . Of course I am happy for them, and yet, it stirs such memories. . . .

"Well, I for one congratulate you. And I think you have made a most excellent choice," Sir Randel says, rousing me from my speechless stupor.

I glance from him to my friends and back again. "Of course. Congratulations to you both. But I still do not understand. Why did you not tell me?"

"Because if we had, you would have insisted upon staying here. And I know this crusade means the world to you." Something in Gwendolyn's gaze suggests she suspects more than I might wish her to, yet she speaks with compassion and understanding.

"You are going, my friend," says Sir Allen, reaching out to give my shoulder a shake with a lordly sort of authority. "You have been officially commissioned. And do not make excuses of your family. We shall care for them well, precisely as we promised."

"But I was to attend you, m'lady. What shall my role be now?"

"You shall be attendant to the young Lady Sapphira. She

is the heart of this mission, and the duchess wishes her to be well protected."

Sir Allen nods to me. "We all know that after my wife's training, you have ample skills to watch over her."

"That was to have been . . ." I cannot even finish the statement. That was to have been the Lady Gwendolyn's own role. A great honor. One I doubt I deserve, yet I will do my utmost to live up to it. I will protect Lady Sapphira—body, mind, and spirit—and I shall aspire to be an admirable role model who shall in no way lead her astray.

"Yes, you shall go in my stead." Gwendolyn hugs me tightly to her chest with her strong arms. Not so long ago, Gwendolyn nearly beat her champion husband, Sir Allen, in a tournament—although to this day, few know that secret. "And it has been decided that young Sadie of the Farthingale ghosts shall go along on crusade to fill the emptied slot. You will need to watch after her as well. Once we get home, we shall show you the cottage and plot of land we have chosen for you and your family. We want to make sure you have good incentive to return to us well and whole."

I cling to her woolen cloak to keep from stumbling as I breathe in her comforting scent of wild herbs and imagine my own cottage upon their lands. My family will be so happy there.

Perhaps Gwendolyn does understand me, more than I ever realized. How else would she guess that nothing would make me happier than my own home, which might safeguard me from having to marry?

Marriage. A dream I gave up on a disastrous night over a year ago. A dream I will no longer suffer myself to indulge.

This crusade does indeed mean the world to me. Despite Gwendolyn's wish that I return home safely, in truth, nothing would please me more than to offer my life in God's service— and prove myself worthy of His almighty love once again.

Chapter 1

May 1219
Near the coast of the Holy Roman Empire

"Come, Garrett. Your turn next." Randel beckoned the hesitant lad who reminded him so much of himself at that age.

Garrett pushed up from the deck of the huge sailing ship and reached to take the blunted practice sword from the hand of the much taller and far more arrogant Jervais. At the last moment possible, Jervais swiped back the sword and chuckled as Garrett missed it.

But he gave Garrett a friendly pat on the back when he finally handed it to him. Though the two boys were both thirteen years old and spent much time together, Randel always marveled at the differences between them. Garrett's even, young features turned bright pink beneath his wavy brown hair, but he pressed forward, determined despite his embarrassment.

As Garrett lunged before Randel and prepared his sword, a natural dexterity overtook the lad that belied his youthful awkwardness. If only Randel could help him find his confidence and his competitive drive, the boy might make a fine knight someday.

Randel bandied swords with Garrett, thrusting and parrying, dodging and striking. They both made proper adjustments for the slight to-and-fro sway of the ship. After two months at sea, it had become a second home.

He intentionally swung at Garrett from a weak angle to see if the boy would properly respond. Sure enough, the boy ducked low and came up to catch a blow against Randel's side.

"Excellent!" Randel shouted, not bothering to correct the lack of thrust behind the strike. Garrett was strong enough for his small stature, but he hated to inflict pain.

Again, Randel empathized with the young fellow. He had once been small and timid, had hated to hurt a soul. Thus his parents had trained him for the church. Yet a desire for battle had always burned somewhere deep inside of him. So he had snuck off as oft as possible to train with his friends Hugh and Gerald and their sister, Gwendolyn, in secret. And in the end, he had achieved the knighthood he desired.

They continued their match, Randel testing and baiting more than actually fighting. If faced with a true enemy, with true danger, all of this skill and technique would come back to Garrett, and he would do what he must. This Randel knew, for though only nineteen, he himself had already faced the situation many times.

He turned his sword arm to an incorrect position, and surely enough, Garrett took the opportunity to swipe Randel's sword from his hand. It flew through the air and clattered upon the wooden deck.

"Ho! Huzzah! Garrett wins again!" he cheered.

Garrett let a shy, crooked smile slip forth. Although the boy often retreated into a still and stoic sort of mode, not unlike a tortoise in its shell, Randel loved to bring out Garrett's enthusiasm. Each of these children needed a special sort of touch. Some put in their place and taught a healthy bit of fear, and others, like Garrett, needed the encouragement of a win and a heaping dose of praise.

The other four boys, ranging in age from eleven to fifteen, ruffled Garrett's hair and slapped him on the back. Jervais scooped him up around his waist and tossed him upon his shoulder in a celebratory sort of romp—no doubt actually intended to remind everyone that he was the larger and stronger of the two.

Garrett seemed pleased nonetheless.

When the fairylike Lady Sapphira—whose vision had launched this entire crusade—called over, "Good job, Garrett!" he bit his lip and scurried down from his friend's shoulder like a frightened squirrel.

Randel chuckled. How he loved to watch the interplay between those two. They had been raised side by side, as Garrett was the son of Lady Honoria's head knight. Sometimes they appeared to be the closest of chums—siblings, almost—and other times Garrett looked as though he wished the floorboards of the ship would open up and swallow him whole just to escape her. Much as he did right now.

Randel flung an arm over Garrett's shoulder and turned him from the young lady's appraising eye. "You boys go and get a drink. The bell shall ring for your lessons with Father Andrew soon. After our midday meal, you shall work with Rosalind at daggers."

"I still don't understand why we must learn from a stupid old girl," Jervais said with a snicker.

Randel shot Jervais a quelling glare. "Perhaps when you can actually hit the target such a statement shall not sound so ludicrous."

"I for one am happy to work with the lovely Maid Rosalind. Night and day, if need be." The adolescent Lord Humphrey, an entitled and pompous young pup with his head of black curls, winked their way. At fifteen, he no longer pretended to find girls troublesome. He was more than happy to explain the wonders of the fairer sex to his companions.

Randel reached over with his free hand and gave Humphrey a playful thump against his head. "What have I told you about showing respect for the ladies. They are your comrades, and you must treat them as such. Why look, they are training as hard as you are."

They all turned back around to watch.

The young Lady Lillian, in her kirtle of girlish buttercup yellow, let the dagger fly from a limp wrist. It loped several circles through the air before clattering to the deck short of the target.

Jervais stifled a chuckle. "Oh yes, they are quite skilled."

Sapphira, dressed in a kirtle of cornflower blue, shoved her friend aside in frustration. "Goodness, Lillian, they shall think us all a bunch of ninnies. Straight and sure. Like this."

Her white-blond hair wisped about her as she threw the dagger with admirable technique. Still, the weapon merely caught the outer edge of the target. The girls clapped and bobbed up and down like a bouquet of wildflowers in the wind. Only Sadie stood by nonplussed in her earth-toned tunic and boy's leggings.

But Sapphira was never one to be satisfied with less than perfection. She huffed and stomped her slippered foot upon the deck. "'Tis these insipid shoes, I tell you. I cannot keep my grip on this tilting deck."

Rosalind shot her a glare similar to the one Randel used with the children. "No excuses, Sapphira." They had all given up on the tedious lord and lady titles weeks ago. "Your job is to rise above whatever complications you might face."

"But if only I could practice in my bare feet. . . ."

Sadie grunted in annoyance and flipped her own knife in the air, catching it neatly. "You cannot fight in bare feet."

"Enough with the bare feet," Rosalind said. "Your sister would have my neck if I let you traipse about like that. Although, you are more than welcome to wear your 'ugly old war boots.'"

Rosalind fetched the fallen dagger and handed it to the red-haired Lady Issobelle, who looked no more excited to throw it than Lillian had. She took the knife and held it awkwardly away from herself as if it might bite her. Randel really must find a way to rally these girls.

Continuing to watch the comic display, Jervais whispered. "Thank goodness they shall never go near an actual battle."

"Nor shall you," Humphrey said.

"Hey," Jervais elbowed him.

"Hey, hey, hey!" Randel cut the bickering short. "If all goes well, you youngsters will be kept safe on the back lines to support us through prayer alone. But matters do not always go as planned. We are headed into enemy territory, and we must be prepared for anything."

These boys were old enough to serve as pages or even squires to the regular knights, but they had all been placed on this ship and in his care for a specific reason. They, along with these girls, would be Sapphira's special troop.

"You might be called upon to protect the young ladies," Randel said, "but you never know. They might need to protect you. I for one would happily trust Rosalind with my life."

"Oh, most certainly you would." Humphrey's voice dripped with innuendo. As the heir of the Earl of Haverland, the ranking nobleman on this crusade, Humphrey was far too quick to speak his mind.

"I imagine you would trust her in all sorts of instances." Jervais wiggled his brows, emboldened by Humphrey.

"Enough of that. Rosalind is my friend."

"Right. Your *very* good friend." Even Garrett dared to tease. Now Randel suspected his own cheeks had flushed. Of course he admired the strong and beautiful young woman, but he was not interested in romance. "Keep that up, young buck, and I'll have you spar with Sapphira next time."

Garrett's eyes grew wide with horror. His mouth gaped, and they all laughed.

"Go on with you now. Get that drink while you can." Randel shooed them away.

He leaned against the rail of the ship and took a deep breath of the chilly sea air. When he had signed on for this holy crusade, he had not fancied himself involved in child rearing. But he had been chosen because of his own youth and his love for children. He must admit, the energetic youngsters had turned what otherwise might have been a tedious two-month journey into a rollicking adventure and stirred up his own youthful enthusiasm.

Randel would do everything in his power to keep these children safe and to prepare them for any contingency. He had lost men before, which had been terrible enough, but he could not bear losing even one of these young lives. Many thought taking the children along nothing but a foolish whim, but Randel understood. Though he himself had not yet reached two decades in age, already he had seen far too much heartache and tragedy.

These children brought a sense of purity to their cause.

He watched as frothy waves rippled along the side of their Frisian ship, which stretched to a length of one hundred feet and a breadth of thirty. They were moving at a good speed for such a large vessel, as they had for most of their journey. Often crusaders were waylaid by storms or skirmishes. But God had showed them favor all along this trip. Sails full of wind, minimal rain, and not a single impediment. It seemed almost too easy.

They had left North Britannia with the first breath of spring, and if matters continued on this course, they would arrive at Tripoli in a few weeks. He lifted his face to the sun, relishing this calm moment.

The last year had been a difficult one for him. First being dismissed from the grand castle by the council for helping Sir Allen with his short-lived rebellion, then being rejected by his parents for his continued resistance against joining the church, and finally his stunning defeat at Gravensworth Castle just a few months ago, from which he had not yet completely recovered.

But he did not wish to relive those days. He wanted to move forward into a new season. And he prayed that, once in the Holy Land, he would at last be able to join his own desires and the desires his parents had long held for him. If all went well, after helping with this mission, he would join the Knights Templar as a warrior monk.

A bell rang, jerking him from his quiet contemplation. The children rallied in a circle and sat cross-legged on the deck before Father Andrew. Even Rosalind sat upon the deck alongside them, face upturned, awaiting today's lesson. Her eagerness made him smile. Much like the children, Rosalind had broken the tedium of this trip for him and helped to chase away that darkness that hovered always at the edge of his awareness.

Being a warrior monk might mean that he would have to relinquish certain aspects of life, like any hopes of a future with a fair maiden at his side, but he could bear that. Though he had briefly pondered wedding the Lady Gwendolyn to save her from a brutish husband, he had been reared for a life in the church and a tonsured scalp.

Rosalind shook out the loose locks of her long silky black hair that fell from a braided circlet atop her head. She giggled at something the priest said with her rosebud lips contrasting prettily against her ivory skin. Her blue eyes mirrored the clear sky overhead.

But such enchantments would never deter Randel from his goal.

Chapter 2

Rosalind sat forward to better heed the words of Father Andrew. Though a part of her wished to tip back her head to the warm sunshine and watch the sails ripple above her, she could not let this rare opportunity to better herself slip by. While her own education had focused on the skills required of a lady's maid, she was yet young and curious and wished to learn.

"Who can name the crusader states of the Holy Land, also known as the Outremer?" asked Father Andrew with his tonsured hair surrounding the shaved spot at the top of his head like an upside-down bowl and his protruding gut finishing off the roundish effect.

Sapphira held up her arm and bounced almost violently, but Father Andrew knew her too well to fall for her antics.

Finally Lillian raised a hesitant hand.

"Yes, Lillian."

She stood and twirled her soft brown hair about her finger. Looking to the sky as if for answers, she said, "Edessa, Antioch, Tripoli, Jerusalem, and . . . and . . ."

Rosalind had not been familiar with the geography of the

Holy Land before this trip, but along with the children she had learned that the Europeans had divided the area into feudal states when they conquered it a century earlier. French lords now ruled the area of Tripoli, to which they were headed.

Lillian mumbled as she struggled to remember the final state.

Sapphira could no longer contain herself. "And Cyprus!"

The typically cheerful priest shot Sapphira a frustrated glance, then turned his attention back to Lillian. "Very good, Lillian. No doubt you would have gotten the last one had you not been interrupted."

Lillian offered a slight curtsey and sat back down.

"And what might one find surprising about the Kingdom of Jerusalem?"

Jervais's hand quickly shot into the air.

"Yes."

"The crusader state of Jerusalem no longer holds Jerusalem itself."

"Indeed," said Father Andrew, "although the crusaders held the holy city of Jerusalem for nearly a century, it was lost to the famous Saladin in 1291. But the crusaders still hold much of the surrounding area, including the new capital of Acre, and they remain determined to take back the entire region for the glory of God."

"If we achieve our goal in freeing the imprisoned crusaders in Tripoli," Jervais said, "perhaps we can rally them and come at Jerusalem from the north, meeting with the other European forces, which shall no doubt overtake Egypt soon and head to the holy city."

The young Lord Humphrey stood to his feet and shook a fist at the sky. "And victory shall be ours."

All the children cheered.

Father Andrew smiled. "Most excellent thoughts, boys. But let us not get ahead of ourselves. Crusades are a tricky endeavor."

"But God is on our side," Sapphira said, crossing her arms over her slight chest.

"Of course He is. But has He not been on the side of the crusaders all along? War comes at a high cost. There is no avoiding that, holy vision or not." He swallowed hard, and a shadow of sadness flickered across his face.

Rosalind recalled that Father Andrew's young brother had been killed in a skirmish against the Scots, along with most of his troop. Father Andrew understood the cost of war more than most of them. Yet he stalwartly supported their cause.

The priest continued to quiz them about the types of Moslems they might find in the Holy Land as well as their prophet Mohammed, their Allah, and their holy book, the Quran. They were about to enter a whole new world. He reminded them how the Moslems had swept through that region in the seventh century with their reign of terror, taking much territory that had formerly been held by Christians, and even daring to capture parts of Europe.

"I know why we wanted to retake our land in Europe," said Garrett, "but I still do not understand why we are so determined to rule the Holy Land."

"It is an important piece of earth." Father Andrew spoke reverently of the place. "Our Christian roots lie deep in the Holy Land. Christ himself was born, died, and rose again there. We cannot leave it in the hands of Moslem infidels."

Rosalind searched out Sir Randel to note his opinion. However, he was gazing at the sea, as he so often did during the lessons.

Perhaps he found her silly for wishing to learn with the children. No doubt he had been provided an excellent education as the son of an earl. But he never made her feel foolish. Instead he treated her with the greatest respect as they worked side by side. Initially her job had only been to watch over the Lady Sapphira and young Sadie, but knowing of her skill with weapons, he had recruited her to assist him in training all of the children.

Movement caught Rosalind's eye as twelve-year-old Issobelle scooched closer to Jervais. She batted her copper-colored lashes a few times before sliding her hand so that her knuckles grazed his. His eyes popped wide with surprise, but he did not withdraw, rather leaned in closer to the lovely young Issobelle.

"Issobelle!" Rosalind whispered, but the girl paid her no heed.

Ugh! Keeping their childish affections in line might well prove the hardest challenge of the entire crusade. Forget pirates and tempests. Battle with the Saracens would seem a playful romp after this. Rosalind scrambled to her knees and reached over Lillian to tap Issobelle on the shoulder.

Issobelle turned to her and bit her lip, snatching her hand back to her lap.

Rosalind shook her head and indicated the empty spot next to her. "Now," she whispered again, trying unsuccessfully to avoid causing a distraction.

Sadie and Sapphira, neither of whom had much use for boys, both giggled.

Contritely, Issobelle stepped over her friends and settled next to Rosalind. A tear slipped down the girl's lightly freckled cheek. "I'm sorry," she mouthed.

Rosalind patted Issobelle's hand. She did not wish to shame her, but a little sting might serve as a reminder. They must stay focused upon their mission. They were a troop, and they could not risk their unity by forming romantic liaisons.

Matters could get messy with women on the journey. But they were not the first crusaders to include women. This holy cause drew all sorts of people. Male, female, rich, poor, fit, and sickly alike. Sometimes whole families. She had even heard tale of the blind and the lame heading off for crusade. Twice in the past decade, hordes of children had followed visionary young adolescents on crusade. And although neither campaign succeeded, the stories had struck the fancy of would-be crusaders throughout Europe.

Rosalind sighed. She would not struggle over romantic distractions on this trip. She had made too many mistakes in that area and would not allow herself to fall into those sorts of temptations ever again.

She had learned her lesson the hard way from Sir Hugh, Gwendolyn's brother, who had used her so casually, then tossed her to the gutter when she needed him most. If her sins were known, some might consider her unworthy of leading this group of innocent young girls, but Rosalind would guard their virtue with more fierceness than the most stalwart Mother Superior.

Despite her failings. Or rather because of them.

But still . . . a part of her did not understand how parents could risk their children on crusade, when she would do anything in her power to bring her own child back.

She had let her thoughts linger around the murky waters too long. The awful waves began crashing over her again. Regret, despair, pain.

A bright red stain of blood . . . that awful night when she had taken the potion at her mother's prompting and selfishly chosen her own well-being over the life of her unborn child. Except that she had not saved herself. She had nearly destroyed herself along with her child. She pushed the images away and stumbled to her feet.

Unable to focus on Father Andrew's lesson, she moved toward the rail of the ship and gulped in fresh sea air, focused on a single bird soaring overhead.

Though sixteen might be considered by most to be fully grown and well old enough for marriage and childrearing, in that difficult moment last year she had felt so young and helpless. Far too young to make the weighty decision herself, and so had leaned on her mother's wisdom. But Mother had led her astray, and now she was hundreds of—or was it thousands, by now—miles from home and all alone.

A gentle hand came from nowhere and brushed her whipping black hair from her face. As she turned toward it, Randel's crooked grin bolstered her.

"Shh, no crying."

She hadn't even noticed the tears that trickled down her cheeks, but now she awoke to the cold bite of the wind against them and gripped tightly to the rail of the ship.

"Push back the shadows. Forward, ever forward!"

Precious words he had spoken to her often during the trip. Randel did not know her secret pain. At least she hoped he did not. But he always noticed when the darkness washed over her—and was quick to offer encouragement.

Likewise she knew he carried some heavy burden, although she never questioned him about it. Perhaps someday they would share their tales of woe. But for now, just being there for each other was enough.

She swallowed back the pain. "Yes, forward. Ever forward." She gave his hand a quick squeeze where it rested against hers along the rail.

He chuckled. "Did you not just reprimand Issobelle for a similar gesture?"

She bumped him with her hip. "*We* are not foolish children." They had both done far too much living for their ages. "I know not what I would do without your friendship aboard this ship."

"We shall make it, you and I. Never fear."

She turned her face back out to the sea. To the salty mist and the slight scent of fish. To the haze of land at the distance. Having skirted varying coasts along their journey to insure safer passage, they would next follow the shoreline down to Tripoli, and there the true adventure would begin.

As she turned to look back toward the bow of the boat, an odd sight met her eyes. Shadowy blotches upon the horizon. She had yet to see anything like it along their voyage. Pointing that way, she said, "Randel, quickly. What is that?"

He jerked to alert. Shielding his eyes, he studied the anomaly. "Ships. A fleet of them, I would guess. Moving this way on a course to overtake us. And look, that one is approaching even more quickly than the others."

"What in the world? Why has the lookout not alerted us?"

"He is probably asleep on the job again. We have had little enough action along the way." Randel hurried up to the higher, defensive deck over the cabins and took it upon himself to shout the warning. "Invaders! To the northwest!"

Sailors and soldiers alike began to dash about as the word spread.

And that is when the situation fully registered. Rosalind's stomach tied into a hundred small knots. Her shoulders tensed.

She rushed up to join him and catch a better view. "Pirates?"

Randel's hand instinctively went to his sword. "Let us hope not. The threat of excommunication has kept most of them from attacking crusaders, but I do not like the speed with which they approach." Something flashed through his dark eyes, not quite fear, but certainly great apprehension.

As the ships approached—at least seven vessels to their four—Rosalind could better make out the distinctive sails. Soon the ship leading the way would be near enough for them to read its flag. "We must be prepared for anything."

"I agree," Randel said. "Move all the ladies and children to the armory below deck, and place two guards outside the door. All the men will be needed above deck for a show of strength."

"The Lady Honoria will never hear of hiding away, but I shall do my best with the others."

"Of course. And, Rosalind . . ." Something about the way

he said her name broke through her haze of fear and tugged at her heart as if it were a string.

"Yes."

"Take a care for yourself as well."

Heading off to gather the children, she smiled reassuringly but made no promises. So many crusaders were thwarted along their paths. She was not so important, and would gladly offer her life if it meant the others might reach the Holy Land safely. Some might consider that courage, but she was not so sure.

"Come! All of you." She gathered the frightened youngsters like a mother hen, and they huddled about her.

Randel would offer his life if needed as well. She knew that, but as she considered the possibility, the string at her heart pulled tight once again.

Randel located Lady Honoria and her fellow commanders. She, along with the two earls and her chief knight, conferred on the doubly raised castle deck at the stern of the ship. The lady stood with her feet wide and braced. Her firmly set shoulders and the tilt of her head bespoke a natural-born leader, although once in the Holy Land, Lord Haverland would be the official spokesperson of the group, and Sir Ademar, a seasoned crusader, would make most of the military decisions.

"What do you think?" Randel nodded to the ships as he approached.

Lady Honoria took a deep breath. "For now we wait. Are the children secured?"

"Yes, I sent them to the armory as we previously discussed. And your ladies?"

"They should be there as well, although no doubt some of them shall dawdle to fetch their jewels and trinkets."

Lady Honoria wore only her crusader surcoat over a simple

tunic and black leggings. Her thick brown hair was pulled into a severe twist at the nape of her neck. This woman would never be distracted by trinkets.

'Twas for the best, he supposed, to give an appearance of the men being in charge. Especially since Sir Ademar assured them that the Saracens were even more determined to keep females in their place than their Western counterparts. While Randel would be willing to follow Lady Honoria, most of the soldiers would not tolerate a female at the helm.

Even in North Britannia, many still grumbled over the widowed Duchess Adela holding too much power. Thus the citizens had been more than happy to fund this crusade that might bring her brother, Lord Richard DeMontfort, back to serve as their rightful duke.

Lady Honoria laid a hand to the hilt of her sword, much as Randel himself had upon first spotting the vessels. "If they are pirates, we can fight. But the more subtle threat could lie in crusaders from hostile lands, or a fleet from Rome, which might try to deter us."

The truth was, North Britannians had little respect for the corrupt politics of Rome and disagreed with the official church on several issues of doctrine. But rarely were such sentiments spoken aloud.

"Perhaps we should have stopped for the Pope's blessing after all," Sir Ademar said, rational and calm as always.

"We do not take orders from Rome!" A fiery young lord, the Earl of Rumsford, spat the words toward the ships. He shot a glare Randel's way, for the two had never much liked each other. Although Randel could not recall what had begun the offense.

Lady Honoria held up her hand to halt any further tirades. "I believe we made the right decision. The Pope would have tried to send us to Egypt to join the crusaders there, and the duchess did send word of our intentions."

The man offered a slight bow of respect, as the lady's very demeanor demanded. Lady Honoria had earned her strength. She had ruled her region for the past six years in the absence of her husband, who had been lost on crusade. Her only child had died years earlier of the pox. The one joy now left in her life was her orphaned young sister, the Lady Sapphira.

"They are coming upon us fast." Concern etched across Lady Honoria's austere features.

"No doubt the new Genoan *taridas* we've been hearing about, elsewise they could never outrun us." Ademar rubbed his bearded chin. He looked much like his beloved son, Garrett, only taller, older, and beginning to grey.

"But our ships are huge and sturdy. And full of soldiers and weapons," Honoria said. "We will manage."

Randel turned back to ascertain that the children had been safely stowed away and spotted Rosalind running toward him. Much like Honoria, she wore a simple tunic slit over leggings. But she did not belong here.

He jogged to meet her and caught her shoulders in his hands. "Rosalind, what are you doing? I wished you to stay and watch the children."

"They are settled with the women and their guards. I will return to them once we have assessed the threat."

Randel looked to the safety of the hull, to Rosalind, and back again. Truly, he wished to see her tucked away below deck, but her reasoning made much sense. "Fine, but if they are enemies . . ."

"I shall run like the wind. You have my word."

For a brief moment her bright smile chased everything away. But problems like invaders bearing down upon them could not be forgotten long. Realizing he still gripped her shoulders, he finally let go. "Soon we shall know what we face."

As the ships approached, his senses spiked to high alert, as they so often did during a battle.

31

A flash of sword. A splash of blood. A body crumpled against the battlement . . .

Rosalind clasped his wrist and gave it a tug, pulling him out of that dark place.

He blinked the impressions away. He could not afford to dwell in the past. There would be enough trouble to face this day.

Chapter 3

Mama!

A scared little voice called out from somewhere inside Sapphira as she stood in the dark and shadowy hull surrounded by whimpers and anxious murmurs. But her mother was long gone, along with her father and so many others she had loved. And her sister, Honoria, who had cared for her these past years, was needed elsewhere. Sapphira must do the right thing despite her churning emotions. She must be brave, on her own, as she so often seemed to be.

There was only one thing to do at a time like this. Unwilling to be overcome by doubt, she turned toward the corner of the armory to shut out the others, to block away their fear for at least a few moments. She knelt and clutched her crucifix tight, lifting it to her lips for the briefest kiss.

Pressing her eyes closed, Sapphira sought out that inner kingdom, that peaceful place deep within that she had visited so many times. Likewise, she shut her ears to the sobs and whispers. She must pray. Not merely hurl worried requests at her heavenly Father, but truly seek His guidance and His face.

Though she knew herself to still be a foolish child and a failure in so many ways, this one thing she could properly do. "Jesus, Jesus, Jesus," she whispered under her breath for a while, focusing both her heart and her mind upon her Savior—until all the sounds around her melted away. After a few moments of quiet contemplation, she felt herself sinking into that place, that holy sphere.

The swirls . . . the lights . . . soft heavenly strains surrounded her. Astounding music from some ethereal place. She relaxed herself into God's almighty arms.

Gazing into His ever-loving, all-consuming eyes, she awaited her instructions, knowing not how much time passed. Indeed, she suspected time did not exist in eternity.

Finally they came. Three simple words whispered to a place deep within.

Strength in unity.

Nothing specific. Nothing detailed. His messages rarely were. Yet as the words penetrated her heart, she understood what to do.

Opening her eyes, Sapphira stood and scanned the small dim room, fortified in the hull of the ship. Honoria's ladies also prayed, except for a few of the flightier young ones who huddled together near the stockpile of swords.

Humphrey held Issobelle tightly under one arm and Brigitte beneath the other. In normal circumstances, Sapphira would suspect he was enjoying the moment far too much, but his clenched knuckles and the terror in his eyes suggested otherwise.

Lillian and her twin brothers curled into their mother, for their whole family had come together. Not surprising on this trip that was as much about religious pilgrimage as it was about warfare. Several of the others had fathers along, but they would be among the knights or soldiers, preparing to ward off this threat.

Only Sadie, Jervais, and Garrett stood with swords in their hands blocking the others from the doorway.

Would they all die along the trip as thousands of other children and countless crusaders had?

From the very beginning, fear that her vision might not be true had tormented Sapphira. Had she made a tragic error? She had not dared even to speak of the calling until her sister, Honoria, knowing her far too well, had dragged the weighty secret from her.

She could not help but wonder. What if it had not been God at all? What if the infamous boys who had led the children's crusades on the continent a few years ago had been tricked by the devil, luring hordes of pure young souls to their demise? And what if she had followed in their footsteps?

Peace. She heard the whisper in her heart. *I am with you.* Then again, *strength in unity.*

Pushing aside her fears and doubts, she grabbed a sword from the stockpile. She was not yet skilled with the weapon. But anything she attempted, she did with her whole heart and with all of her might. At least the children had been training in swordsmanship, unlike most of the women who had focused on healing and manning the launch weapons from a distance.

Striding across the room, she took her place next to Garrett, whom she had recently passed in height by several inches. Never had she seen her timid friend so determined, but he always had been one to put others before himself.

As she was left-handed, yet another of her many odd and scary quirks, she linked her right hand to Garrett's free one. He looked down, surprised, but then gripped it tightly. Noticing their joint stance, Sadie clasped Garrett's sword hand by the wrist, then Jervais did the same to her.

Together they formed a wall of protection. The four brave thirteen-year-olds, side by side.

No one would pass this way unchallenged.

At once Sapphira felt the energy of the room shift. The sniffles and whispers ceased. Again following the prompting of her heart, she began quoting the Lord's Prayer aloud, and other voices joined her one by one, until they all prayed in unison. Yes, joint prayer. That was their mission. These women and children were brought along to battle primarily in prayer, and now was their chance to train, just as they trained to protect themselves with weapons.

A thud and swish met her ears from beyond the ship's hull. The clatter of men climbing up the sides.

They started their prayer anew. "Our Father which art in heaven, Hallowed be thine name." But no screams sounded above them throughout the entire recitation. They repeated it once more as Sapphira clutched yet tighter to her sword. Only words, whispers through the boards of the deck, made it their way as they prayed again and again. And again, time lost all meaning.

Until footsteps approached.

But she knew several guards stood in the passageway beyond, and she heard no struggle, no grunts or clangs of battle.

Finally, the door opened and Rosalind stepped through. She smiled as she registered their unified front.

"Sapphira, please join us above deck. You are needed."

Rosalind gripped tightly to Sapphira's hand as she led her across the deck to the clergymen from Rome. The group dressed in ornate gilded robes scowled at them as they approached. Only the man in a simple brown flaxen cloak with a rope for a belt gazed at them in a welcoming manner.

Brother Francis, the bishop had called him. Honoria seemed to know the name, but Rosalind had never heard of him.

"So this is the girl who has stirred up so much trouble," the bishop snarled from beneath his tall, pointed cap.

Pulling Sapphira tighter to her side, Rosalind wrapped an arm around her. Initially Rosalind had been relieved to see the papal flag rippling in the breeze—rather than some enemy country or no flag at all, denoting pirates—but Lady Honoria had remained wary.

Lady Honoria had been right.

Though Honoria had tried to explain their mission and their calling when the churchmen first came aboard, this bishop clearly did not believe a word. He insisted that all decisions must go through Rome, and that they had been remiss not to stop for the Pope's blessing. If only their group had left England a few days earlier . . . or later. They would not have come across this random contingent miles off the coast of Europe heading toward Egypt.

The poorly dressed Brother Francis took a step forward. His soft brown hair fell appealingly from his tonsured scalp to match his well-trimmed beard and warm brown eyes, which brought to mind the kindly monks at the monastery near Rosalind's home village. Her shoulders unclenched for the first time since she had first spotted the shadows upon the horizon.

"Perhaps you will allow me to question the young lady. I know a thing or two of visions," said Brother Francis with a wink. Though he hailed from Italy, his French was flawless, suggesting he had enjoyed a privileged upbringing despite his simple attire.

"Of course." Fortunately Rosalind's own French had improved significantly from spending so much time with nobles these last years. She loosened her hold, and Sapphira met the man halfway.

He held out his two hands, and Sapphira took them with no hesitation.

"My Lady Sapphira, I am Brother Francis of Assisi."

Sapphira gasped. Clearly she had heard of him as well. "Good brother, I am honored." She curtseyed before him, though no one had suggested he might have noble blood. "I too dream of someday giving up all worldly pleasures and joining a convent like your Poor Clares. You are an inspiration throughout Europe."

He smiled warmly. "And it seems you are an inspiration throughout North Britannia."

Sapphira fluttered her whitish lashes and bit her lip, but she held her silence.

"I am sure you have heard of the visions of the young shepherd boys on the mainland, Nicholas of Cologne and Stephan of Cloyes, who inspired the children's crusades not long ago."

Everyone knew of the stories. Hordes of youngsters streaming toward the shore, inspired by holy visions, longing to bring a new fervor to the crusades. Yet they had failed so desperately. To Rosalind's knowledge, not a one of them had even reached the Holy Land.

Brother Francis said, "We know such visions can occur. I have seen a few myself. But could you please describe your experiences for me."

"Of course." Sapphira swallowed.

Rosalind longed to run to her but instead clasped her hands tightly together, moved closer to the North Britannian contingency, and whispered up a petition for the child.

If appearances counted for anything, Sapphira just might convince them, for she appeared every inch the angel with her ethereal white-gold hair, pale skin, and delicate features. "I was praying in the garden outside my sister's castle. I oft go there in the afternoons, as I feel ever so close to God in nature."

He nodded for her to continue, while the bishop and other clergymen looked skeptically on.

"I had sunken into that holy sphere deep within, but still my eyes remained open to the beauty and colors of God's creation.

Of a sudden, came a sharp flash of light. And then the world went dark and shadowy, as if I were watching some other place layered over top it."

"Describe this place, please."

Sapphira's face took on an ethereal look. "It was nighttime, and I flew through the sky to a destination far, far away. I soared across the sea and to the area north of Jerusalem. I am not quite sure how I knew that, and yet I did. Then I saw it as a shadow against a fiery backdrop. Tall buildings and a spire I had only ever seen before in the pictures of Moslem mosques, with the shape of the moon at the top."

The bishop snickered. "Anyone might have imagined that."

Unmoved, Sapphira continued. "The flames flickered all around it. I heard cries and shouts. Then above the din came a deep, strong voice. The voice I so often hear during my prayers."

Now her face took on an otherworldly glow. "It said, 'Set my captives free!'"

A chill ran up Rosalind's spine.

Brother Francis gazed deep into Sapphira's eyes. For a moment, they seemed to be locked in some communal sort of rapture. Then he blinked and turned to the bishop. "She speaks true."

The bishop tugged at his tight collar as his face tinged red with barely concealed rage. "But that could mean anything—or nothing at all."

Sapphira shook her head and blinked a few times as well. She appeared to return to the worldly sphere. Rosalind had often seen the youngster lost in prayer, but she had never witnessed anything quite like that in her whole life.

"I rarely get many words," Sapphira said. "But the vision was more clear and vibrant than anything I have ever experienced. And the meaning settled deep into my heart, as is often the case. I understood in an instant that I was to help lead a crusade to rescue the captives in the Holy Land."

"But why to Tripoli? You said it was not clear to you how you knew the area," said one of the priests.

"I just knew. The certainty became clearer as the vision faded."

"Perhaps this is just childish wishing." The bishop stepped forward as well and at last attempted to appear friendly, although he did not quite succeed. "Your sister mentioned that some of your family members were lost in that area. And that your parents have been long dead. No one would blame you if you misunderstood."

"I did not misunderstand." Sapphira was solid, a rock despite her fragile appearance. "In fact, I did not even share the vision for some weeks. I do not relish violence. My sister at long last pried the secret from me."

The bishop swiped a hand down the side of his face in frustration.

"Allow me to ask one more question." Brother Francis cupped Sapphira's cheek. "Do you ever doubt? Do you ever wonder?"

A flash of emotions crossed Sapphira's face. "I . . . well . . ."

Rosalind knew Sapphira would speak nothing but truth. No matter how it hurt.

"Of course I doubt. I am but human, and hundreds will go into battle at my word. A part of me hates that." She pressed a delicate hand to her breast. "But deep in here, I believe it is true, elsewise I would never allow it."

Brother Francis stood tall now. "I am fully convinced. The child has a pure heart and believes every word. She has sight beyond the veil. Whether or not this crusade will prove successful, I cannot say. As we know, visions can be fickle, and they do not always equal victory. But I believe we should allow them to continue on their way."

The bishop's shoulders slumped. He turned his attention to Lady Honoria, and the earls flanking her. "And you say that you did in fact send a dispatch to Rome."

"Yes. Months ago." Honoria was a rock as well. Perhaps that was where Sapphira had learned it.

"These things do take time. And sometimes the messengers never arrive." The bishop shook his head. "I hope you will forgive me for trying my hardest to recruit you to our cause. Troops are desperately needed in Diamatta if we hope to capture Egypt and head to Jerusalem from there. The route from Tripoli proved a failure just two years past. We must try a different tactic."

"We do understand your desperation." Lord Haverland inclined his head. "There is nothing to forgive. And if we succeed and find enough soldiers alive, who knows, perhaps we shall rally them and meet you from the northern front."

"But warfare alone shall not change hearts and minds." Brother Francis's voice now took on a new sort of authority.

Rosalind felt it reverberate to her very core.

"We are commanded to proclaim the kingdom of heaven wherever we go. Your call to free captives is a righteous one, but perhaps it has more meanings than the one you presumed. There are many souls in the Holy Land bound by a false religion that keeps them from falling at Christ's mercy. Remain righteous. Be His witnesses and examples in a place that has gone mad with hatred and ambition."

Sapphira stared up at him, clearly fascinated, as was Rosalind herself. "Is that why you travel to Egypt?"

"Indeed. I hope to speak to the Sultan and to convince him of the love of Christ. It is the only way we shall ever attain lasting change."

Again, Sapphira curtseyed before him. She took his ringless hand and pressed a kiss to it, as if he were the Pope himself. "Then I shall aspire to do the same."

"With good people like you involved, Lady Sapphira, there might yet be hope for this crusade." Brother Francis patted the girl's head and began to turn, but she grabbed his sleeve and tugged him back.

"Have we done well, to bring the children along? It seemed fitting for me to go and for a group of children to surround me, to fulfill the call that failed on the continent, but I saw nothing about this in my vision. Is it wrong to put them in such danger?"

Rosalind had wondered the same. Yet each of the children claimed to feel the call, and their parents had seemed so sure that this was right.

"Though visions can serve to stir us, in the end, it is best to follow God's still small voice that leads us day by day. There is nowhere safer on earth than in the center of God's will. Rest assured in that." Brother Francis smiled. "We should be off. We have delayed long enough, and we have a lengthy voyage yet ahead of us."

"Yes, we must continue," the bishop said. "We wish you well on your journey."

The Earl of Haverland nodded. "Thank you, and you also."

The group dispersed, and the men headed to the side of the ship to be lowered back to their small rowboat.

What had Rosalind just witnessed? A wonder to be sure. She had known Sapphira was special, but now she headed toward the girl with a new sort of awe.

She reached out her hand as Sapphira returned to her and then paused.

"For the love of all that is holy, Rosalind, do not look at me like that!"

Rosalind chuckled, relieved to see the normal, strong-willed Sapphira returned to her care. "Like what?"

"Like I am some sort of ghost who might whisk away."

Rosalind poked at the girl's sides playfully. "I see that you are quite solid."

Sapphira squirmed and giggled. "Truly, I am not so special. My gift comes through God's grace alone."

That struck a chord within Rosalind. She and her mistress, Gwendolyn, had often debated the subject of grace. Was salvation a free gift offered at the cross, or must one continue to earn one's own way through good works, confession, sacraments, and penance? Gwendolyn firmly fell upon the side of grace, but Rosalind felt safer with her rosaries and candles.

"And please," said Sapphira, "whatever you do, do not tell the others what you watched transpire between Brother Francis and me today. They think me freakish already."

Rosalind took Sapphira's hand. "Come, we must let them out of the armory."

"Must we, really? Jervais has been such a pest today." Sapphira grinned at her as they headed that way.

How odd life must be for her. Rosalind knew her well enough to realize that on most any given day, Sapphira merely wished to be a regular girl. Yet she was not. Because of her they were all headed once again to risk life and limb in the Holy Land.

Chapter 4

From across the decks of their small fleet of ships flickered bon-fires and came the distant sounds of music and merrymaking. Randel tapped his toes to the stately tune a small band of the children played aboard his own ship.

This ship carried all of the women and the children deemed worthy of Sapphira's special troop, along with the most trusted noblemen and esteemed knights. The other ships crammed in the rest of the knights with their retinues, horses, and armor, as well as the foot soldiers, archers, and of course the sailors they had hired. Over three hundred in all.

And all on their way once again, thank the good Lord.

"Ah, there you are." A young woman named Jocelyn, brazen as ever, draped herself against Randel's side. "We had wondered where you were hiding."

Three of her close friends surrounded him like a battalion. The prettiest of the women on this campaign, or so they clearly thought themselves. Most of the females were widowed or married. The convent-bound Anna and Margaret kept quietly separate from the others, and Rosalind stayed with the children much of the time. But this pack of she-wolves was always on the prowl for trouble.

Randel cleared his throat. "Not hiding. Just enjoying this lovely evening." He grabbed hold of the rail and turned away, hoping to make his message clear: he meant to stay there, alone.

Though many of the men aboard this ship were married, surely she could find someone better and more titled than himself to flirt with. Yet somehow he seemed to draw the enticing young woman like an annoying lodestone everywhere he went.

"Oh fie! 'Tis not fair that you rob us of your company." She fluttered long dark lashes over her flashing black eyes. But flashing with what? Lust? Ambition? He could never quite decide.

He kept his own eyes firmly upon hers, for he would not wish to give the wrong impression by glancing down at her tightly laced scarlet kirtle with its low-dipping bodice. He wished she would have a bit of self-respect.

As he was yet concocting an escape from tonight's ambush, she took his arm and tugged hard. "Come and dance with me. The children will think you do not like their music." Her bottom lip pouted so exaggeratedly that it nearly grazed her chin.

At that he sighed, for she was right. He surveyed Lillian on the pipe, Issobelle on the lute, and Garrett tapping along on a small drum. All nobles were expected to be able to play or sing for occasions like this. But the children were still young and unsure of themselves.

And with Jocelyn's friends staring his way, he did not wish to make a scene. "One dance. Only one!"

"Huzzah!" She gripped her hands to her chest and bounced. The girl had an appalling ability to draw the eye to that part of her anatomy. Although he knew Jocelyn to be beautiful in an aesthetic sort of manner—with her plump lips, dark wavy hair, and hooded eyes—in all practical ways, she repulsed him.

His glance flicked to Rosalind. A true beauty inside and out.

She laughed at the sight of him caught in Jocelyn's snare. But then, studying his face more closely, she offered him an expression of sympathy.

At least the tune was elegant and courtly, requiring him only to take Jocelyn's fingertips. They began moving through the shapes and patterns. Forward and back. Around in a slow promenade.

"So, tell me of your exploits. I long to hear a story of glory and triumph. And what of Gravensworth Castle?" Jocelyn's chuckle was deep and throaty, unnaturally so.

Why must she always interrogate him? He was tempted to speak the truth and shut her up for good. "I have told you. Warfare is a sad and dark subject, not suited for amusement."

"You think my ears are not fit to hear it because I am a woman. But I shall soon be involved in such exploits myself."

Randel highly doubted that. Jocelyn had not bothered to pick up a sword the entire voyage. She would be left to pray, serve, and tend the wounded. Some of the women might be trusted to fire launchers or even join the archers from a distance . . . but never Jocelyn. "Do you truly wish to hear about battle?"

"I do."

Continuing the dance, he took a deep breath. "It is horrible. Limbs are torn from bodies, and you would lose the contents of your stomach to see what remains. Men tinge to a greyish sort of blue as they die. Their screams and the fear in their eyes would cause you nightmares for months. And the smells . . . I cannot even bring myself to describe them."

Jocelyn tinged a pale shade of grey herself as she listened. She swatted him as they turned, but she was not so playful anymore. "Good gracious, Sir Randel. You are no fun at all."

Regret washed over him. He should not have said that. Randel knew little of her family, as she was from the merchant class.

What if she had lost a family member to war? Then again, she would be forced to face reality soon enough, and he had grown sick of her manipulations.

She tucked herself closer than the dance demanded. "So then why do you fight?"

"I do not do it for glory or adventure. I do it because I feel called deep within my heart to protect and defend those who cannot fight for themselves."

Once the words were out, he wished he had not shared even that small piece of his soul with this temptress. No doubt she just wished to find more ammunition to trap him with, so that she might marry a knight and go home the daughter-in-law of an earl.

But why was she so set upon him? There were at least three men on this vessel in line for baronies of their own, not to mention the handsome and fiery Lord Rumsford. Perhaps she imagined Randel was more within her reach.

She spun a circle under his hand. "I have heard a rumor that your parents wished you to join the church."

He would not give her one more bit of himself. "You should not listen to gossip. It does not become you." He shot her a hard look, and she grimaced.

Just then, the song ended and the young musicians transitioned into a new piece, this one a rollicking country tune like those he had heard coming from the other ships.

Jocelyn frowned. "How crass."

He chuckled at her uppity merchant-class airs, amused by the ridiculousness of the statement coming from such a false and impertinent woman.

She latched on to his arm and began tugging once again, not toward her friends but toward the dark and shadowy hull of the ship.

"Absolutely not!" he said, digging in his heels.

"Never fear, Lady Honoria is sequestered in her cabin with her maps and her stodgy old matrons again. No one need ever know."

Of course she was. These troublesome young ladies never flirted or cavorted under Honoria's watchful eye. But as yet no one had told tales to their leader. Perhaps the time had come that he must.

Jocelyn licked her plump lips, then stared at his own, making her intentions all too clear. She dug her nails deeper into his arm.

"There you are! I have been waiting for that dance you promised."

Randel, overwhelmed with gratitude, turned and nearly stumbled into Rosalind's awaiting arms.

But Jocelyn yanked him back.

"We are busy right now. Perhaps later. Or never." Venom poured from Jocelyn's eyes.

Rosalind lifted her chin and stared back without wavering. "I believe that is Sir Randel's decision."

"Why would he wish to dance with a mere servant girl when he could spend time with someone like this?" Jocelyn ran a hand down her amply curved body.

Again Randel restrained a chuckle, for the girl seemed to have no idea that a cloth merchant's daughter would be little better in the eyes of his parents, as they had no need of her substantial wealth. Besides, Rosalind was highly regarded by both Duchess Adela and Lady Honoria, which put her a far cut above the average lady's maid.

Rosalind raked her gaze up and down Jocelyn's body. "How nice of you to put your assets on such clear display. Must be your background in matters of business. I hear your father could, and would, sell a painting to a blind man."

Now Randel nearly choked. Though a childish part of him wished to let this argument play out, his more honorable side would not allow it. "I do indeed owe Rosalind a dance." He finally managed to pry his arm away from Jocelyn and offered it to Rosalind instead.

Rosalind took his arm and they turned to the open area of the deck.

He fancied steam pouring from Jocelyn's ears but did not turn back to check. "Thank you so much for rescuing me."

"My pleasure."

They faced one another. He held up one hand and one open arm.

She raised a brow. "You know this style of dancing?"

"I have not spent my whole life trapped in a castle. Fourth sons have much freedom."

She took his hand and allowed him to pull her close, as the fast-moving and spinning dance required. While they hopped and twirled with the wind whipping at their clothes, they both began to laugh. How much prettier Rosalind appeared in her simple tunic and mantle than Jocelyn ever could dream to be. Her slender figure fit nicely in Randel's grasp. He was thankful to have her as a friend.

Rosalind tipped back her head and smiled at the sky, which glittered with diamonds of light against a backdrop of black velvet. "Oh, we needed this."

"A good romp to chase away our doldrums."

"Absolutely! For a moment let us pretend there is only here. Only now. And all is perfect."

He could not have agreed more. They continued to skip and spin and laugh. He noted some of the children had joined in for this dance, and they likewise frolicked and giggled to the driving beat.

Rosalind sang along with the rousing tune in perfect pitch. "'A merry time we're having, all is bright and gay. Joy is for the having, come grab ye some today,'"

"You have a lovely voice. I never heard you sing before."

Rosalind lowered her lashes. "I have never been trained at music the way the nobles are, but I have always loved to sing."

"Perhaps someday I shall teach you to play the lute."

"That would be fun. You know, I've been thinking," Rosalind said. "We should do more fun activities with the children. Perhaps that would help to rally the girls. Sir Allen offers agility training for his men. Tumbling skills mostly. The children would enjoy that. I have only learned the basics, but young Sadie is quite skilled and could demonstrate. That is why she was visiting Sir Allen, to help train his men."

"Excellent idea. I would have never thought of it."

"I did not wish to overstep my place. But we have been getting along so well of late." She took a deep breath as they continued to bounce about.

He tugged her yet closer. "I do not want you to feel that you must hold anything back from me, Rosalind. I consider you my partner in this mission to train the children."

She blinked up at him. "Thank you . . . although . . ."

"What?"

"In many ways I feel I know you like an old and cherished friend, but in other ways I believe you hold much back from me."

"Ask me anything you like." Wind rushed about him as they continued to spin and romp.

"What about your family? You never speak of them." She clung tightly to him as they danced.

He sighed. He had avoided the subject long enough. "I was somewhat estranged from them for a time. They wished me to join the church, but I was determined to be a knight."

Rosalind nodded for him to continue.

"My mother can be quite rigid and demanding, and she is very devout. She wanted to be a nun but did not get her way and had pinned so many hopes upon me. But this decision to go on crusade has appeased her for now, and I promised to find a Syrian serin for her, which she is quite excited about."

"A Syrian serin?"

"A bird, similar to a finch, native to the area of Antioch and Tripoli. My grandfather was a crusader and kept extensive journals of the local birds, complete with drawings. I cannot tell you how many evenings my mother and I spent poring over them. Mother was always especially fascinated with the serin, for some reason."

"A bird, you say, similar to a finch?" She quirked a brow, clearly repressing a smile.

Wonderful, now she would think him an addlepated bird lover. "I do have a serious and intellectual side, you know. Which was precisely why my parents thought me suited for the church. My father did not consider me warrior material."

"So what shall you do with this serin? Capture it and bring it home?"

"I had not quite thought that far. Perhaps." He did not wish to mention that he would not be returning home. Perhaps he could send it to his mother, although the thought of the bird in a cage and under his mother's rigid control irked him. "Enough about me. Your turn."

"Me? My father passed away several years ago," she said.

"I'm sorry to hear that."

"It was hard for a time, but we're past all that now. I have had a bit of a falling-out with my mother, though, not that we've ever discussed it. She pressured me into a decision that I came to regret horribly."

Tears welled in Rosalind's eyes, and those dark shadows he had oft noted upon her seemed to be closing in again. He pulled her tighter into the dance hold and spun her in a looping circle. "Ever forward, remember."

"I'm sorry. We were supposed to be enjoying the here and now." Rosalind forced a smile.

"Well, you started this discussion." He grinned in return.

"Well, I'm stopping it. Let's just dance and be happy."

And so they did, staring into one another's eyes, finding joy and strength in each other. By the time the long and repeating song finished, they were both dizzy and out of breath.

"Ho!" shouted some of the sailors, thumping the deck to show their approval.

Rosalind fell against Randel, panting. "And here we are supposed to be well-conditioned fighters, taken down by a single dance."

"Do you truly enjoy fighting?" He had always gotten the impression that she had trained mostly for Gwendolyn's sake.

"I wasn't sure in the beginning, but I like being able to defend myself. 'Tis quite empowering. I wish I could convince more of the girls."

He wiped sweat from his brow. "Come, let us get a drink." Still holding one of Rosalind's hands, he led her to the barrel of water.

As they passed by, Jocelyn huffed and stormed away with her friends. The she-wolves would have nowhere to head but to the partitioned section of the hull where they slept, so he just might escape them for the rest of the night.

"Whatever are you going to do with that woman?" Rosalind's eyes twinkled with a mischief he had not seen there since his early days of knowing her.

"I have no idea. Perhaps the time has come that someone should speak with Lady Honoria."

She pressed her lips together tight. "That does not sit well with me. We must all learn to work as a team. I think we should deal with this between ourselves."

"Then what do you suggest?"

He offered Rosalind the first ladle of water. She drank deeply, without ladylike refinement, yet still feminine in that honest and fresh sort of way so typical of her. She had a graciousness that came from within rather than an outward affectation of manners.

She stared out into the sky as he took his own drink, contemplation thick upon her features.

"Well?" he asked.

"I have an idea, but you might not much like it."

Somehow Randel suspected he would like anything this girl suggested. "Try and see." He awaited her response with all eagerness.

Chapter 5

"In truth," Rosalind said, "I have avoided such impishness this past year, but something about the fresh sea air and the rocking of the ship brings out my feisty nature. Not to mention that awful woman."

Unable to resist, he tucked a flailing wisp of silky black hair behind her ear. "I think you are coming back to your true self. This is the girl I first met hunting in the woods with the duchess. Feisty, funny, and free. And I for one am happy to see her. Tell me your idea."

"Well, you are tired of fending off Jocelyn . . . and I've grown equally weary of hiding from Lord Rumsford."

"Rumsford?" He cut in before she could continue. Although Randel did not wish to speak the words, a young earl like Rumsford could only want one thing from a common girl like Rosalind—and it was not marriage. "Has he approached you? I will not stand for that man toying with you."

Rosalind patted his arm. "Settle yourself. I am a grown woman and quite smart about such issues. I can ward off his attentions, but I have become weary of them."

"So what is your brilliant suggestion?"

"I think we should fabricate an attachment to each other."

His mouth gaped wide. "What? Whatever will Honoria think? And the children?"

"Honoria seems rather obtuse to the romances brewing aboard the ship. And we could tell the children our plan and let them in on the fun. Then if Honoria does find us out, we will have witnesses that it was merely a ruse."

Randel considered that. He would not want people to think he was toying with Rosalind as he had just assumed of Rumsford. But their stations were not as far removed, and perhaps faking an innocent attachment would be just the thing to keep unwanted suitors at bay.

Which would certainly help him in his goal of becoming a warrior monk.

"But what if you meet a man you might actually wish to wed? I am certain there are many appropriate suitors for you among the lesser knights and soldiers."

"I could be coy and say that men always want what they can't have." She struck a sultry yet humorous stance, then returned to her normal relaxed posture. "But the truth is, I do not plan to marry. Ever. And you?"

"I have no intentions to marry either."

He wanted to know more. He wished to understand what heartache had changed her since they first met at the grand castle. Perhaps it had something to do with his friend Sir Hugh, who had once mentioned his intention to compromise the girl's virtue.

But if Randel asked too many questions, she would want to know about his troubles in return. Although he knew he could trust her, he liked their relationship as it stood, and did not wish to weigh it down with the burdens of the past or with his secretive plans for the future. He preferred to keep their friendship light and playful. And her plan seemed perfect for maintaining it.

"So . . . what shall we tell the children?"

"You what?" shouted Issobelle into the shadows of their cramped cabin in the ship's castle area.

"Shh! Everyone will hear you." Sapphira had been shocked as well when Rosalind spoke the words, but they did not need to alert the entire ship.

Rosalind sat up upon her pallet. "We merely plan to give the appearance of an attachment, to fend off unwanted suitors. Our duties keep us in close proximity anyway. I see no harm."

Sapphira ran the reasoning through a number of mental and spiritual calculations.

"Only this afternoon you chastised me like a child for sitting too close to Jervais." Issobelle huffed and crossed her arms over her chest.

"You *are* a child," Sadie said. "And I saw the way you touched his hand, you brazen little hussy."

"Uh!" Issobelle squealed as the girls dissolved into giggles.

All except Sapphira, who did not wish to listen to their bickering after her long and draining day. Her nerves still tingled and snapped as if they had been held too close to a fire. But of course the others did not understand what she had been through. She hated the way she oft felt so lonely and isolated, even among these girls who were supposed to be her friends.

"Sadie, that was uncalled for." Rosalind clearly held back her own giggles.

"Sorry," Sadie said, but her voice did not ring sincere.

"Your cause is hopeless, Rosalind." Issobelle leaned closer. "I am certain our most holy Lady Sapphira shall never allow it."

"I am right here! Do not make assumptions about me."

Sapphira adjusted her blankets, for the evenings grew quite cold at sea. Generally her perfectionistic nature would cause her to demand a stop to such antics as Rosalind suggested. Yet in truth, she and Sir Randel had always seemed quite fond of each other. Sapphira could not see any real deception in the plan.

"And you should take a care, Rosalind," Issobelle said. "Though he is not his father's heir, he is still quite above your station. I hope you do not hold out any secret ambitions in his regard."

"Wait, who has a secret?" asked the oldest of the bunch, Brigitte, who was generally lost in her own silly thoughts of jewelry and flowers and several steps behind the others. She continued to comb her yellow-blond hair, though the rest of them were tucked tight in their beds. The place still smelled of the lavender cream she had rubbed into her hands and face. It was no secret among the girls that despite Rosalind's ban on romance, Brigitte intended to hook the young Lord Humphrey before they returned to England.

"I assure you I do not have secret ambitions." Rosalind's voice resounded with authority throughout their small dim cabin.

"I would." Lillian, who preferred the fun of sleeping with the girls to the company of her mother, sighed and stretched dramatically. "I did not see it at first, but I have come to notice that Sir Randel is quite handsome in an understated sort of way."

"Young lady, you are treading on dangerous territory!" Rosalind's warning held a trace of playfulness. "And it is for just such a reason that we must all work together to protect our dear Sir Randel."

Sadie's hearty laughter rang out. "He would hate it if he knew we thought him in need of protection."

Yet perhaps he was.

Sapphira clearly saw the need to help protect Sir Randel's virtue from that sly serpent of a woman. Many thought that only the clergy were called to live holy lives, and Jocelyn's designs on Randel were anything but holy, as were Lord Rumsford's attentions toward Rosalind. Generally only a young noblewoman's virtue was guarded, for issues of inheritance, but Sapphira believed that God expected every one of His children to live by His righteous commands.

"I hope to marry a handsome man like that someday," Issobelle whispered dreamily.

"We know!" the girls said in unison, then fell into giggles again.

"What!" Issobelle protested. "Do not you all?"

"Not me," came Sadie's muffled answer from beneath her blankets.

"I don't think I shall marry." Rosalind sounded wistful but firm. "Besides, now is not the time for any of us to be thinking on such matters. We should focus upon our mission."

Sapphira wondered if Rosalind hoped to join a convent as well, but despite her admiration for the young woman, she could not quite picture that. She continued to wait and search for the clench in her gut that would tell her God was displeased with Rosalind and Randel's scheme, but it never came.

"I think we should do it," Sapphira said.

Randel lay back upon his pillow and breathed a sigh of relief. The boys packed about him on their pallets in their cabin opposite the girls' had all taken the news in stride and seemed more than willing to play along with Rosalind's plan. He hoped it would keep Jocelyn at bay. But if nothing else, it had returned the twinkle to Rosalind's eye.

"So when *do* you plan to marry?" asked Jervais, seemingly out of nowhere. "Most nineteen-year-old men are already wed."

Randel should have known the boys would not let this pass

so easily. But at least by bunking with them, Randel had escaped the masses sleeping in the hull of the ship and was far away from Jocelyn. "I do not really see myself as the marrying type."

"Will you be a priest?" Garrett asked. A reasonable question, as many younger sons not due to inherit turned to the clergy, but Randel had little patience with the corruption and politics involved in being a priest. "No . . ." was all he said, for he did not want the boys to fear he might desert them for the Templars.

Humphrey sat up and rested his elbows on his bony knees. "I am most certainly the marrying type. I cannot even imagine life without the enchantments of the fairer sex. Ah, with their delicious curves and . . ."

"Enough, Humphrey! There are young lads in the room."

"They shall learn of such things soon enough," the troublesome, fifteen-year-old persisted.

"Perhaps, but not under my watch," Randel said. Again it occurred to Randel that Humphrey might be better off with the squires and knights, but having an older boy about did help at times.

"If you do not plan to be a priest, why not marry?" Jervais asked again.

"Perhaps because he does not wish to be a romantic dolt like you," Garrett said.

Jervais jumped onto Garrett's pallet and began tussling with him.

Garrett managed to fling the heavier boy off of him in an impressive evasive maneuver.

Which gave Randel an idea. In such cases it was best to change the subject, and quickly. "I say, boys, what think you of trying some tumbling maneuvers in the morning as part of our agility training?"

"Like the traveling tumblers who visit our castle?" One of the eleven-year-old twins piped up. "I can do a roll." He

demonstrated right there on his pallet in the dim starlight peeking through the window.

"And I can turn like a wheel on a cart," said the other twin.
He hopped out from under his covers and tried to perform the
trick, bumbling it entirely and landing on his matching brother
in the process.

"Ouch!" complained the first.

Truly Randel wished he could tell the blond-haired duo apart
to know who to scold, but even in the sunlight he had difficulty
knowing one from the other. "Both of you, back to bed. We
shall have a big day on the morrow."

He more than any of them. His stomach did an odd flip at
the remembrance of his new "attachment," which he feared
would be all too easy to feign.

Chapter 6

Rosalind leaned against the side of the ship as she and Randel watched the children hard at work. She jolted for a moment, surprised to discover that Randel had rested his arm along the rail behind her, but then she relaxed into his touch and the warm stroke of sunshine against her cheek.

He was better at this ruse than she had imagined. If Lady Honoria walked by, naught but a slight shift would make their position appear casual and accidental, but if Rumsford or Jocelyn came their way, he could easily tug her close to his side.

She held back a giggle, unable to fend off her delight at besting their adversaries at this game of love. Not only that, but Sadie had taken over with the children today, and she and Randel were quite happy to stand back and allow her to shine. Sadie had been trained in battle as one of the infamous Ghosts of Farthingale Forest, who had survived on wit and cunning, though the evil King John would have seen them all dead.

"Be still and press into the stretch!" Sadie barked at the twins in their upside-down arches, who could not control their wiggling although they both had taken to the trick quite well.

Meanwhile, Jervais seemed unable to imitate the shape. "You need to work on your flexibility, Jervais. Elsewise you shall never get it."

Moving down the line, Sadie said, "Lillian, quite impressive."

Surely enough, the girl formed a high and sturdy arch with her limber body, even as her long brown braid pooled on the wooden deck.

After mass, Rosalind and the girls had spent most of the morning adjusting simple tunics for today's activity. Shortening and adding slits. The boys had supplied the extra leggings, completing the ensembles. And the effort had proven well worth the while.

"Indeed. I would have never expected it of Lillian," whispered Randel from so close that his breath tickled Rosalind's ear, sending a pleasant little shiver down her back.

But Rosalind ignored the inconvenient side effect of their scheme. "She is quite graceful. I knew this would be good for the girls."

"'Tis nice to see them succeed at something battle related."

"And many of these tricks can be turned into evasive maneuvers. Some of the girls might never master weapons, but at least we can give them skills to escape an attack on their persons. Honestly, I doubt many of them could ever run someone through with a sword."

"Sadie could," Randel said. "Sapphira would want to if she deemed it right, but she is so compassionate."

"It would be hard for her."

"And what of you?"

Randel's gaze boring into her caused Rosalind to turn toward his close scrutiny. Her throat felt oddly dry of a sudden under the perusal of his dark eyes. "Me?"

"Could you run a man through? Deliver a death blow?" He seemed to gaze deep into her soul, searching out the truth.

Randel had a special way of looking inside people and discerning their needs.

She swallowed and focused her attention back to the children. "There is a reason we leave the warfare to men. I admit I am more comfortable with distance weapons. Throwing daggers and archery."

Then she imagined pressing her sword into flesh, even the flesh of an enemy, and winced. "For myself, I am not certain, but for one of my girls . . . I believe I could."

Glancing quickly from the side of her eye, she saw him nod. "That is good to know. It might come to that someday."

"Have you . . . ever had to?" she asked.

He took a deep breath and sighed. "'Tis hard. Harder than I imagined. But sometimes a warrior does what he must. Your training takes over in such moments."

She could not resist turning to him again. This time he locked his gaze to the children, who were attempting to stand from the arched shape, and she watched a flash of pain wash over his features. Much like her, he seemed to have some secret pain, which he barely held at bay. While she longed to shoulder some of his burden, she did not wish to open her own humiliating past, and so let the issue drop.

His hand pressed into her waist and he tugged her closer, although she saw no one about. It felt nice there. Right. Different from and yet similar to Sir Hugh, the only other man who had ever touched her so before.

The few times she had seen Hugh since he had tossed her aside had been trying indeed, and she had found not a single scrap of affection left in her heart for the jovial man she had once known—recalling only the bitter attack of their last conversation, which yet echoed through her mind at the most inopportune times.

But she did not wish to relive any of those awful memories on such a lovely day. Tilting her head just an inch to the side, she was able to rest it against Randel's well-muscled shoulder, and found it fit quite nicely.

A giggle caught her ear. Issobelle pointed their way.

Rosalind stood back up straight, raised a sharp brow, and snapped, "Stay focused. All of you!"

Lillian pressed up to the arch and then rocked to standing with ease. "I did it!"

Jervais tried again, but from his barely arched position, crashed back to the deck. "This is not fair. Why can we not work on the joust?"

Garrett rocked back and forth, then stood as well. "Because the horses are on the other ships, you dunderhead."

Jervais swatted at him, but Garrett stepped away and laughed.

"This is good for you, Jervais. Keep it up," Randel said.

"Good for both his body and his arrogance," Rosalind whispered for Randel's ears only.

"Why do you not try it?" Jervais shouted. "'Tis not as easy as it looks."

"Perhaps I will." Randel pulled away from her and jogged over to the children.

The cool breeze at her side took her by surprise, making her feel suddenly alone. She trotted after him and decided to join the fun as well. They must make the most of these carefree days aboard the ship, for they would not last long.

From the dusky shadows of the hull, I stared out into the bright sunshine upon the deck. There he was. Once again cavorting with the children. Playing as if he deserved any happiness in this world.

Randel deserved nothing. Not happiness. Not the honorable position he had been granted in this campaign. Perhaps not even life itself.

Not when my brother, the only person who ever really mattered to me, the only person who truly cared about me in this world, lay rotting in his grave. Seventeen. The boy had been a mere seventeen years old. He should not have even been a soldier, except that he was so desperate to escape our parents. Certainly they had never loved either of us. He and I had planned to someday meet again, when both of us were free of their clutches, but it had not turned out that way.

Dead. Gone. After all these months, I could still hardly believe it.

And it was all the fault of Sir Randel Penigree.

The church could harp about forgiveness all it wanted. But I would never forgive Randel. He had become my very reason for drawing breath. My reason for embarking on this campaign. My reason for enduring this blasted sea voyage and the leadership of that awful shrew of a woman, Honoria.

I never had been one to support these wretched crusades. They had brought England naught but trouble, stealing away our taxes and even the honorable King Richard. Leaving us in the hands of that tyrant John, until our own region of North Britannia had managed to break away. Besides, while I hid the fact well, I found the entire Christian faith far too restrictive and had long incorporated my grandmother's pagan beliefs.

I could not care less about this ludicrous cause.

That fool Randel positioned himself on his head and attempted to press his feet into the air like some idiotic court jester. I would knock him down from his precarious perch easily enough. The only joke here was the fact that Sir Randel led these children while my brother lay dead. He was not a man of honor. He was a coward and an imbecile. He had been my brother's commanding officer, and it was his fault that my brother had died under his watch.

I hated him. And my hatred fortified me like a strong wine. It flamed my blood and blurred my vision of all but him.

Sir Randel tumbled down and grabbed for the maid, Rosalind. The two of them laughed and clung to each other longer than might be considered mannerly. Rosalind, whom I grudgingly admired despite her lowly upbringing. The girl had spunk, no matter her poor choice in companions. But if she stood in my path, she would topple alongside her friend. Nothing would get in my way.

My hand twitched against the dagger, hidden within my clothing.

How I would love to run him through this instant, but I did not desire to destroy my life along with his. I yet had all the time in the world, not to mention a vial of poison hidden away with my belongings. I would continue to watch and wait. Soon I would discover his weakness, and I would bring him tumbling down for good.

Sir Randel would never return to England. I would see to that.

Rosalind scurried up to the highest deck for a rare moment alone while the girls beneath her in their cabin preened for dinner. She stretched out upon the smooth wood, propping her hands behind her. The air was already taking on a nip as the sun dipped low to the west, a hovering bright orange ball against streaks of purple and pink. A bird soared overhead, an arching silhouette upon the sky's rich palette, and then settled itself atop the highest mast to the center of the ship.

For a moment she could almost forget that nearly every muscle in her body screamed at her for the punishment she had forced upon it today. Sadie's training had proven quite challenging, but Rosalind did not regret her involvement.

Her limbs felt somehow more attuned to her mind, more under her control. She had always excelled at activities that involved coordinating the hand and the eye, but she had lacked the requisite strength to fight with skill. She had a feeling—a rather dull aching feeling—Sadie would remedy that soon enough.

Though she could not see over the sides of the ship from her position, she could look across the decks and out over the sea to the horizon beyond. As someone who had grown up inland, sea travel had surprised her in many ways. Not only the mammoth size of the ship and its three sails, but the construction itself.

Having only seen small river vessels, she had never imagined a two-story hull, nor the towering "castle" structures at both the stern and bow of the ship, which offered not only above-board cabins for the more esteemed passengers, but also provided tall, crenelated defensive structures not unlike a castle wall. Had the small Italian *taridas* they encountered yesterday been enemy ships, they could have rained down arrows upon them with ease.

Other things had surprised her as well—like the dried meat and hard bread she had grown weary of within days, the birds miles from the land they skirted as they traveled, and the fresh scent of the sea that seemed to wash all her troubles away. And the outdoor nature of their lives, for no one wished to be crammed in the crowded cabins or dreary hulls for long.

She rolled her neck against the stiffness that was gathering there and stretched her aching back. Leaning forward, she reached for her toes and wiggled her body in a manner worthy of the twins in an effort to relieve the pain.

"That is what you get for tumbling about like a court entertainer."

Seemingly from nowhere, Lord Rumsford sprang onto her private hideaway.

Rosalind quickly straightened her tunic to better cover her leggings. "Lord Rumsford, you should not sneak up on a girl like so."

He wiggled his brows over an admittedly handsome face. His chin-length hair and neatly trimmed beard framed his strong cheekbones and sea blue eyes to perfection. "And how should I sneak up on her?"

Rosalind grimaced. "Not at all."

He tipped up his chin and chuckled, and then plopped down beside her so close that their hips grazed. "I saw you up here alone, and I could not let this moment pass. Is it my imagination, or have you and Sir Randel grown quite attached lately?"

"I cannot account for what you imagine," Rosalind said coyly, although she was pleased he had taken note so soon. Or perhaps . . . they had been spending too much time together all along.

"And I cannot say I much like that fellow. He once took something quite precious from me. I know Lady Honoria trusts him, but perhaps you should not."

Rosalind just twisted sideways and shot him a glare.

"You know, I have more to offer you than Sir Randel." Rumsford adjusted himself so that his arm brushed Rosalind's back.

She scooched forward an inch on the slick deck. "Like what? A ruined reputation?"

He grabbed at his chest. "You wound me, dear Rosalind. I had meant to suggest something far more pleasurable, but you spoiled all the fun. You certainly are a tough nut to crack."

"Well, thank you. That is the first truly nice thing you have ever said to me." She would not wish him to know how much her tough exterior had cost her. She had learned the hard way from her old admirer, Sir Hugh, not to let a nobleman dally with her.

He chuckled again, for they both knew Rumsford had spent ample time and compliments attempting to charm her. "I am not generally one to approve of women being involved in battle, but I have to admit, you actually looked quite lovely out there with the children today. You have a natural grace and a fine form."

"And you have a flattering tongue. Do you ever choke upon it?"

But he would not be deterred. "Please, Rosalind, do not give up on me. Time passes so slowly on this ship. You have a sharp wit, and I can think of no one I would rather converse with. Say you will have dinner with me tonight. Surely you tire of the ship's bland provisions. Sup with me in my cabin."

"'Tis not yours alone."

"Ah, but as a ranking nobleman on this crusade, I think I can persuade the others to allow us some privacy." He winked at her. "I have some lovely treats. Fruits, sweetmeats, cheeses. You will find no others like them on the Mediterranean."

The girls had a few of their own treats hidden away for late-night conversations, but Rosalind would not tell their secrets.

"So what do you say?" Lord Rumsford placed his hand over hers, and she tugged it away.

Sitting up and crossing her legs before her, she adjusted her attire once again. "Perhaps I have not been clear." She turned and looked him straight in the eye. "Sir Randel and I have established . . . an understanding." There, that was true enough.

He shifted farther away from her. "I see. Perhaps I should alert the she-wolves."

"That would be quite helpful." Their plan was going perfectly!

"So you trust his motives, but not mine. Do you think that is wise?"

"I have known Sir Randel for some time. He is a close friend of my employer and quite honorable."

Rumsford nodded slowly as he took in this new information. Then his up-and-down motion switched side to side as he shook his head in the negative. "I would not be so sure if I were you."

"For now we shall remain friends only. This mission is too important to us. We have much time still to see if this shall work, or if we shall even survive."

He winced. "True enough. Which is why I am sure that you shall not blame me for seeking out a companion during these last peaceful days."

She relented and smiled. "I do not blame you, but you shall not succeed with me."

"Fine. I surrender, then. But if you ever change your mind, you know where to find me." He sprung lithely to his feet. "I bid thee adieu, fair maid Rosalind."

So it would be dried meat and hard biscuits again for her tonight, but some pleasures just were not worth the cost. She understood that truth more than most. Rosalind stood to her feet as well and went off in search of Randel before the crashing memories could wash over her once again.

Chapter 7

"We are nearly to our destination." Lady Honoria pointed to the coasts of Armenia and Antioch, which they had been skirting for the last few days, then slid her finger slightly south along the map to the area of Tripoli. "The captain believes we will reach Tripoli sometime tomorrow or the next day at the latest."

Randel pressed his head close with the other leaders gathered around the table in Lady Honoria's cabin. He felt honored to have been included in this meeting alongside Lord Haverland, Lord Rumsford, and several other leaders. It seemed his failure at Gravensworth might not haunt him to the grave as he had once feared.

Nearly there. He both tingled with excitement and went cold with fear. The day they had both awaited and dreaded during their months at sea.

These past weeks had gone by in a pleasant, sun-drenched haze, especially since they had added the tumbling training and since Rosalind had helped him hold Jocelyn at bay. They had not been entirely successful on that front, as the girl was quite persistent, but the situation had improved. And having

Rosalind always at his side had proven even more pleasant than he had anticipated.

She felt right there. Like a natural extension of himself. She did not leave him confused or nervous, like some beautiful women he had met. Instead, she brought him comfort, joy, and peace.

This entire trip felt so right. All those years when his parents had forced him to stay indoors, studying, preparing for a priesthood he had no interest in, this is what he had longed for. This is why he had snuck out again and again to train. And it had proven well worth the while.

Sir Ademar leaned closer to the maps. "We shall land near the main city of Tripoli where the local lord resides. Some Bohemond fellow. He is French, I hear, so we should communicate well enough."

The Norman nobles in England yet spoke their native French, although their ancestors had dwelt in their new land for over a hundred and fifty years.

"Yes." Lady Honoria's brow furrowed. "I have done my research, and it seems that there have been problems with crusaders from differing countries working at odds with each other. Breaking each other's treaties and what not. We hope this Bohemond will be agreeable to our cause and help to guide us."

"So where do you believe the prisoners are being held?" Lord Rumsford asked.

"We have only rumors to go on at this point," Honoria said. "But we believe this area just south of Tripoli, which has been wrestled from Tripoli's grasp by the infidels."

"It shall be a challenge." Sir Ademar's hand clasped the hilt of his sword. "But we must have faith."

"Which brings me to another issue." Lady Honoria took a step back to better see them all. "I expect every one of our crusaders, down to the youngest page and lowliest foot soldier, to behave with the utmost honor to represent Christ well. We will use force only when force is required. And we will show respect to the basic humanity of our enemies to the greatest degree that we can. You all must support me in this matter."

"Of course." Lord Rumsford tipped his head, and the others followed suit.

"You have my full agreement," said Lord Haverland. "Sir Randel, you and Rosalind will continue your leadership of the children. They are coming along quite well under your care. My Humphrey seems to be improving in both skills and attitude."

"And Garrett has a new sense of confidence," added Sir Ademar.

Randel's heart warmed at that. Their statements about their sons confirmed his own belief. He was meant to be a warrior, meant to be a leader. "Rosalind gets much credit. Especially for the girls. She understood their needs much better than I did. We have equipped them with lighter swords and focused their training more on archery and defensive measures."

"Very wise." Lady Honoria nodded. "My compliments to this Rosalind. I am glad we chose young energetic people to work with the children. I do not think many of us could have handled that job. But do you think she can serve as a leader in the field as well, or does she seem likely to grow rattled under pressure?"

Lord Rumsford laughed. "Oh, our Rosalind is not easily rattled."

Though Randel appreciated his support, he did not like Rumsford's familiar tone. He had thought the man had relinquished his pursuit, and he eyed him warily.

"That is good to hear." Lady Honoria seemed to be considering the issue further. "And do the children respect her, though she is not titled?"

"She has won their respect," Randel assured them.

Sir Ademar took the map and rolled it up. "We should gather the ships and make some sort of announcement. Lady Honoria, perhaps a speech is in order."

"Indeed. A speech and a special mass. You will see to it, Father Andrew?"

"Of course, my lady." Father Andrew wore the syrupy smile he always did, although Randel had often wondered what deeper sort of emotions must hide behind it. His gaze slid to Randel, causing a fleeting sense of discomfort to wash over him. But surely it was only his own guilt over his failures. Father Andrew knew far too much of the occurrences at Gravensworth from Randel's time spent in the confessional.

Lady Honoria eyed her men keenly. "There have been too many failures in the Holy Land. Let us remain righteous and honorable. North Britannia shall lead the way to a new era."

Randel drew from her strength. How he longed to live up to her esteemed expectations. Once he had proven himself on the battlefield, he would feel confident to pursue his dream of becoming a well-trained warrior monk with the famed Templars, and joining them in their quest of protecting pilgrims to the Holy Land.

Rosalind adjusted Lillian's hold on the bow by just a hair. "There, do you see? The slightest shift makes a difference, especially when the arrows are aflame."

"Yes, I think I am finally getting this." Lillian let the arrow fly. It whooshed through the air straight and sure and planted itself in the center of the target. "I did it! I did it!"

"Three out of four. Excellent work." Rosalind gave her shoulder a pat.

"Me next!" Issobelle hopped excitedly with her red curls bouncing about her in the breeze.

Rosalind smiled to see these girls finally growing so confident in their archery. Today she worked extra with Lillian, Issobelle, and Brigitte while Sadie and Sapphira practiced at advanced swordplay incorporating tumbling maneuvers with Randel and the boys.

All of the girls now wore practical tunics and leggings on a regular basis and had adjusted to the weight of their sturdy protective boots. Rosalind had turned her considerable skills acquired while sewing gowns for a noblewoman to the task of helping these girls to dress in a way more suited to defending themselves. Though a part of her missed delicate needlework and creative design, truly, she had never put her expertise to such good use before.

They were becoming a real troop. And just in time. Soon they would trade these simple tunics for the crusader ones adorned with crosses in crimson, ivory, and black. Already their ship had slowed its course, and the others were moving closer for this afternoon's meeting.

Issobelle took her turn and hit the target with no assistance whatsoever from Rosalind. Yes, they were ready.

What would Rosalind's dear mother think? All that time spent teaching Rosalind to tend a noblewoman, to create her elaborate hairstyles and paint her face. Rosalind had loved the artistic aspects of her duties, yet they had never quite fulfilled her in the way training these children did.

The pack of she-wolves sauntered past. Jocelyn swiped at her shoulder, as if their hard work and determination might be catching if she walked too close. As she continued in Randel's direction, Jocelyn swayed her hips so violently that Rosalind feared she might displace them. What a pity that would be. She repressed a giggle. But as usual, Randel paid Jocelyn no heed.

"Rosalind, could you please join us for a moment?" Randel called over to her.

"Of course. Issobelle, make sure Brigitte properly positions her elbow." Sometimes it still felt odd not to put *Lady* in front of their names, but they had chosen expediency over propriety early in this voyage.

"What is it?" she asked Randel.

"We are holding a bit of a tournament. It seems our Sadie needs more challenge than the younger boys can offer her. But perhaps less than Humphrey or I can. How about a battle between the two of you?"

"Oh, I don't know." Rosalind felt shy of a sudden. Swordplay had never been her forte, and although she had been learning the tumbling maneuvers that could be adapted to battle, she had not yet tried them in a real fight.

"Come, Rosalind. Are you afraid of a little girl?" Sadie crouched into a battle stance and prepared her blunted practice sword.

Rosalind's stature was above average, and indeed Sadie stood inches shorter, but Sadie had a tough, compact form and an intimidating demeanor. At thirteen, she might be close to her full height already. A determined girl with simple but pleasing features and light brown hair pulled tight.

"Ros-a-lind. Ros-a-lind," the children began to chant.

The archers abandoned their bows and came to join the group.

"You can do it, Rosalind! Take her down once and for all," called Issobelle, who never lasted more than a minute against Sadie.

"Yeah, show her she's not so tough," Jervais shouted.

Sadie raised her brows as a challenge and tested the weight of her small sword.

Finally, Rosalind saw her advantage. "I will do it. But give me a real sword, not one of those little girlish ones." She raised her brows back at Sadie and smirked.

Randel grinned and handed her the longer, heavier practice sword he and some of the larger boys used. Gwendolyn had never allowed Rosalind any quarter, and had always demanded they train with the same swords the men used.

"Fine then. I was just trying to play fair with the others." Sadie tossed her sword to Randel, and he exchanged it for a larger one as well.

"Yes!" said Humphrey. "A girl fight."

Randel reached over and thumped him on the head.

Meanwhile, Rosalind and Sadie squared off. They both crouched low and began to circle one another. Rosalind thrust a few times, testing the weight of her sword. Then, out of nowhere, Sadie surged at her so quickly that she stumbled backward.

Rosalind's training took over. With little thought, her body responded in a backward shoulder roll, returning her neatly to her feet with sword at the ready. Delight overtook her as she executed the new skill. But Sadie would not allow her to enjoy it long.

The fight began in earnest. Thrusting and parrying, dodging and striking. Just as Rosalind thought she would land a blow, Sadie flipped to the side, evading her. She struck again and again, but Sadie fended off every attack. They clashed and tangled to the elbows. Rosalind, being the larger of the two, managed to shove Sadie away.

Sadie stumbled now and fell to her back, but in an instant she flung her legs over her head and in one neat move sprang to standing, an impressive trick Rosalind had not yet learned.

They continued their battle. Sweat now coursed down Rosalind's face. She hoped she would never truly have to fight like this, but if so, she must be prepared.

She pulled back a few steps to assess Sadie. To search out any weakness. To use her head as much as her arm. Then she saw her moment. If only it would work. As Sadie briefly adjusted her sword to her side at an odd angle, Rosalind tumbled her way and kicked at the sword, a trick Sadie herself had taught them.

But apparently Sadie had not expected Rosalind to attempt it, for as if by magic the sword flew from her hand and sailed through the air to clatter back to the deck ten feet away. Rosalind swung back around and lightly pressed her practice sword to Sadie's chest. Sadie lifted her hands in surrender.

The children went wild.

"I did it! I did it!" Rosalind cried, jumping and cheering and doing a little jig. No amount of flair with the needle could compare with Rosalind's newfound confidence at the warrior arts. The ability to defend one's self was truly priceless.

Randel cleared his throat. "Um, Rosalind, warriors do not dance about like so."

"And why not?" came a sturdy voice from behind them. Lady Honoria. "That was an excellent job. Both of you. It shows you what a woman can do when she challenges herself."

"Thank you, m'lady." Rosalind curtseyed, and Sadie followed her lead.

Rumsford, standing at Honoria's side, just smirked. Rosalind already knew he did not approve of women fighting, and she paused to wonder how he felt about treating Honoria as an equal in leading this crusade. "Come, Lady Honoria. Father Andrew awaits us."

They walked off to join Father Andrew just as he rang the bell. The time had arrived.

After Father Andrew finished a stirring service and every last member of their company was administered the Lord's Supper, Honoria took the center of the deck once again. The heady taste of the body and blood of her Lord yet tingled upon

Sapphira's lips. The soothing warmth of His presence still traveled through her veins.

She hoped her sister was not about to switch to matters of logistics, for she was not yet ready to wrap her mind around practical issues.

In inspiring tones, Honoria began to address the crowd aboard her own vessel as well as the three other ships gathered closely around. She exuded such confidence. Far more confidence than Sapphira felt. Of course she had spoken nothing but truth to Brother Francis. She believed her vision was from God.

Yet typical of Honoria's battering-ram nature, her sister had taken the initial call and run with it, turning it into something far larger and grander than Sapphira had ever imagined. Women, children, a fleet of ships. The dear sister she needed much more than she admitted locked away over battle strategies each and every night.

And who knew what the morrow might bring.

What if Sapphira had made a mistake? What if she had not seen a vision, but rather dozed off that day in the garden and experienced a dream? But she must believe. She must keep the faith and trust that deep inner sense of peace in her heart.

Something in her sister's demeanor altered and caught Sapphira's attention.

"And now I would like to invite the young woman who has sparked the flame of this crusade to come and address us."

A surprised little gasp escaped Sapphira's mouth. Her sister should have warned her. Then again, her sister knew her well and would have expected her to demur. Now she had no choice. She must be tough, as Honoria the esteemed battering ram demanded that she be. Over three hundred sets of eyes looked expectantly her way.

She reached to raise her skirts but realized such niceties were no longer required in her practical attire worthy of a soldier.

Her surefooted boots allowed her to make the climb with ease, and her tight braid kept the wind from whipping her hair in her face.

Once in place next to her sister, Sapphira took a deep breath and surveyed the mass of faces. She planted her feet wide and noticed, not for the first time, how strong and connected her body felt. She was a warrior now.

A warrior for Christ. He had sent her a special message, and she would rise to that calling. A warm pressure stirred in her chest and rose up through her throat, and the words came.

"Six months ago, I had a vision, which I am sure you have all heard many times now. It has become a matter of legends and of rumors. But on this day, I charge each of you to search your own heart."

She pressed a hand to her chest. "Allow God to speak to you of His plans for this crusade and of your place in it. None of us will leave the Holy Land unchanged. You can grow bitter and jaded. You can grow evil and opportunistic. Or you can remain righteous and develop an even deeper reliance upon God's Holy Spirit."

The words came from somewhere deep within Sapphira without fully forming in her rational mind. But as they felt true and right, and as all eyes remained focused upon her and glowed with a new-found fire, she continued.

"Along our way I had the pleasure of meeting the famed Brother Francis of Assisi. He reminded me that we must fight for hearts and minds, as that is the only way to bring true change. This land shall be full of captives."

She gestured to the coast at a distance. "Captives of the body and captives of the spirit. Let us do our best to bring freedom wherever we set our feet. May God go with you all."

Silence stretched out over the Mediterranean. Only the swish of waves and the cry of gulls met Sapphira's ears.

And then the crowd burst into cheers. Men took hands and embraced. Tears streamed down faces.

But Sapphira's fellow children gazed upon her as if they had seen a ghost.

As Honoria closed the meeting, Sapphira took her place beside the children once again, yet she felt further apart from them than ever before. Once they were dismissed, they all filed past her with eyes wide. Rosalind and Randel each offered her a gentle pat and a smile, but even they seemed to be a bit awestruck.

Garrett glimpsed at her and nodded abruptly. They had been so close at one time, but now they seemed always to be divided by their genders and the new shyness that had developed between them along with the budding curves upon her chest. He followed close at the heels of the others as they walked away.

Then Sapphira was left alone.

She dropped her gaze. She should not be surprised. Should not be disappointed. She had God, what need had she of men?

Then Sadie looked her way, and she turned back. The normally tough and undemonstrative girl reached out and took Sapphira's hand. "You did well."

"Thank you." Despite the fact that she had longed for company, Sapphira now knew not what to say. She nodded to the other children. "I have scared them all away."

"'Tis surprising to be reminded, I confess. But I'm not easily frightened."

Sapphira grinned. "Yes, I rather admire that about you."

"You're the next best of the girls, you know."

"But I shall never surpass you."

"Probably not, but I'm made for warfare. You're made for prayer."

Sadie was always a girl of few words, but a depth of meaning and understanding flowed from her hazel eyes. Sapphira supposed she should not expect to be the best at everything, and it would be acceptable if Sadie continued to surpass her at swordplay and archery. She had earned the right through years of practice.

As if uncertain about whether to say more, Sadie pressed her lips together. Then finally she spoke again. "I have a young friend who sees angels. And I believe I witnessed God heal her when she almost died. Wren. Her name is Wren."

A cascading warmth flowed through Sapphira, the likes of which she typically only experienced in prayer. "So I am not so odd to you."

Sadie chuckled. Letting go of Sapphira's hand, she gave her a playful shove. "Oh, you're odd enough, but not for that reason."

Bubbling laughter escaped Sapphira, catching her by surprise, as she did not laugh often. "Have you . . . ever seen . . . well, you know?"

Sadie grew serious. "Angels? Not quite, yet I became so accustomed to Wren seeing them that I began to sense a certain crackle and shimmer in the air when she did. 'Tis hard to describe."

"I know precisely what you mean."

Sadie linked her arm through Sapphira's. "Come. Let us ready ourselves for supper."

For the first time, Sapphira felt she had a true friend amongst the girls. And somehow that strengthened her for whatever they might face on the morrow.

Chapter 8

Randel looked back over his shoulder at the children pressed close to Rosalind along the rail of the mammoth wooden ship. A few of them waved and smiled hopefully. Rosalind blew him a kiss.

Though he did not catch it in the air, surrounded as he was by so many esteemed knights and noblemen crammed into the small rowboat, he mentally secured Rosalind's sentiment to his heart. With Honoria at the bow and two sailors steadily propelling them forward through the crashing waves, they headed toward the rocky shoreline of Tripoli.

The beach itself could have been almost anywhere in England, but the water was a stunning crystal blue, and as he gazed beyond the rocky coast, he noted a city of beige stone buildings sprawling before him, accented by fanlike palm trees, colorful silken awnings, and even a domed building—as Sapphira had seen in her vision.

The landscape rose in terraced intervals, with a sturdy castle rising above it all. Though the surrounding hills were mostly arid and dusty, beyond them snowcapped mountains speckled with green trees grazed the sky.

As they fought the ebb and flow of the water, a noble-looking procession followed by a huge contingent of guards made its way down the hillside before them. No doubt the watchmen at the castle had noted the arrival of their fleet, had likely been tracking their progress all day.

Honoria, flanked by Rumsford and Haverland, held high a banner featuring both the crusaders' cross and the English Plantagenet coat of arms with its three golden lions. He hoped whomever they were about to meet would recognize the symbols and consider them friends. Although tensions often flared between the French and English back home, they should be welcomed as neighbors in this land so far away.

As the group on the hillside moved closer, Randel spotted their banner, red with a golden cross, which he assumed must denote the County of Tripoli. Near him someone expelled a *whoosh* of air as the unnamed fear that the native Saracen troops might have taken over this region since the time they last received word was dismissed by the Christian emblem.

But as Randel watched the banner swaying in the breeze, haunting memories washed over him. In an instant he was transported back to his shadowy castle at home in North Britannia.

"Do you see this crest?" his father, always stiff and meticulously groomed, had pointed to their family symbol of a mythical griffin holding three golden arrows in its claws over a background of dark blue.

"Yes, Father," Randel, still recovering from his many wounds suffered at Gravensworth Castle, had mumbled weakly.

"If you wish for the Penigrees to remain your family, your heritage, you must play your role. Cease this foolish nonsense of battles and knighthood. We already have two knights in this family, both of whom far surpass you in skill. You have disappointed me for the last time, and I shall tolerate your arrogance and rebellion no longer."

Though Father esteemed warriors high above clergymen, he had never believed Randel worthy of battle, and so had chosen him as the sacrificial lamb for the church.

Randel's equally stiff and proper mother had shaken her head in despair. "I am so ashamed. You are the child I wished to dedicate to God's service, yet you have followed your own path."

He had swallowed down a lump in his throat, unable to bear his mother's shame. It stabbed him in the gut with more ferocity than any blow he had suffered during his recent defeat.

"Promise us that you shall join the church, and we will allow you to stay in our home and heal," Father had said.

"Otherwise?" Randel had pressed a hand to his bandaged and throbbing head.

"Otherwise we shall disown you. You shall be a man without a family."

Nineteen had felt far too young to be a man disowned. Willing to do anything in that desperate moment to be accepted back into the fold, Randel had agreed. The bitter recollection stabbed him in the gut yet again.

Only later, after he recovered, had they struck this bargain for him to go on crusade and join the Templars as a monk—if, of course, they would have him. He supposed he could yet resort to the Knights Hospitaller or the Teutonic Knights, both religious orders as well, but the Templars with their reputation for military excellence had always been his preference.

So here he was, thousands of miles from his family in order to keep his family. Sometimes life made little sense at all. But at least his parents were satisfied, and he felt a sense of honor in this new path.

Until he glanced to Father Andrew and experienced the wash of guilt he always did in the man's presence.

Randel shook off the troublesome thoughts. Finally the oarsmen fought their way to the shallow waters near a patch of sand. Likewise, the retinue from the city was just reaching the beach.

Lord Haverland stepped out into the Mediterranean first, and then carefully, one by one, the many knights in ivory crusader surcoats, trimmed in crimson and covered with a black cross, followed suit. The warm frothing waters welcomed Randel, tumbling over his calves, soaking his boots and leggings and skimming the bottom of his long tunic, as they all made their way to the shore.

Again Lord Haverland took the lead. "Greetings," he said heartily, in impeccable French. "We come in peace from the area of North Britannia in England."

"Welcome, Englishmen." A middle-aged man in bright silk robes with an eye patch stepped forward. "I wondered what excitement might be looming along my coast and simply had to come and take a look. Allow me to introduce myself. Bohemond the fourth, Count of Tripoli."

An exotic-looking young man, bedecked in loose pantaloons and a tunic, stood at his elbow. "Might I add, formerly—and given any bit of justice, soon to be again—the Prince of Antioch as well."

Bohemond frowned. "Yes, but not at the present time."

The crusader states, including Tripoli, had been established by the crusaders in the Holy Land a century ago, and these French feudal lords had been rulers in this region for generations, but Randel still did not understand the intricacies of their politics.

"We are pleased to make your acquaintance." Lord Haverland offered a small polite bow.

"Do not be too pleased just yet." Bohemond planted his feet wide in the ground and adjusted his belt and long curving sword. "We are not looking to stir up trouble with our Saracen neighbors, for we have only recently regained stability after the last well-meaning group of crusaders tramped through our region."

He brushed something from the sleeve of his robe. "Perhaps you should continue south to our current crusader capital of Acre. I imagine you would be better received there. Or perhaps to Egypt, where soldiers are desperately needed."

Lord Haverland inclined his head. "I understand your hesitation. But would you meet with us and allow us to plead our case?"

"My people care not about your case. They only wish to live in peace and rebuild our city and our trade."

The muscles in Randel's neck tightened. Would they be turned away so soon? This Bohemond both looked and sounded more like a native of this land than a French lord. Randel had not expected that.

Nor the astonishing group surrounding him dressed mostly in Eastern garb, in some cases even wearing the Saracen *kaffiyeh* wraps around their heads. Their skin tones were varied, spanning from pale European shades to that of a tall man with an open vest and a sculpted ebony chest peeking through.

"I am Lord Haverland, and this is Lord Rumsford and the Lady Honoria. I promise that we do not wish any harm upon your city or your people."

"Then give me one good reason why I should allow you to stay," Bohemond said.

"That I can do. Have you heard of the children's crusades in Europe?"

Bohemond's good eye flashed with interest. "The failed children's crusades. A pretty legend, that, but it proved ineffective."

"Our crusade has similarly been inspired by the vision of a pure young maiden. Lady Honoria's sister, Sapphira. Based upon that vision, our goal is unique. We hope to set captives free from Saracen prisons."

The young exotic fellow nudged Bohemond with an elbow.

"If God wills it," added Father Andrew, "perhaps even the man who would rightfully be our duke."

Count Bohemond pulled at his beard. "I am intrigued. But what has this to do with the children's crusades?"

"The Lady Sapphira is a mere thirteen years of age. And we have brought along a group of children to support us in prayer, and women as well," Honoria said.

"How fun!" An even younger man with the smooth skin of a child and typical Western attire pushed his way to the front of the Tripolian retinue. "I should like to meet them. We never have visitors from Europe, Papa. Please let them stay, at least for dinner."

Bohemond took a deep breath and let it out with a low grumble. "Philippe is too quick to speak his mind, but he is correct. I think my new young wife and the rest of my family would enjoy meeting you. Sup with us tonight, be our guests and enjoy our famous Outremer hospitality. We shall discuss logistics later."

"All of us?" Rumsford asked with surprise.

"Those of you gathered here, and the children you mentioned. Are there many ladies among the group?"

"Almost two dozen women, several of them titled," Honoria said.

"Well, choose a handful and meet us back here. And change out of those tedious crusader tunics into something more festive. We shall feast at sunset!"

With that proclamation, Bohemond and his contingent departed up the hill. Randel scratched his head at this odd turn of events. Already this land was proving a surprising and exotic place.

"I hate this stupid kirtle," Sadie complained, tugging at Issobelle's finely woven gown in lilac, which the girls had stuffed her into back on the ship. "And I have no idea how to behave at a feast."

"That is not true," Rosalind corrected her. "You have eaten in the great hall at Sir Allen's castle many a time."

Rosalind clung to Randel's strong arm as she attempted to climb up the uneven stones in her dainty slippers. At least the oarsman had dragged the boat safely to the sand and saved them from getting drenched.

"Perhaps, but never as an honored guest," Sadie persisted. "And never dressed like this."

"Just stick close by me," said Sapphira, who walked nearly hip to hip with her new friend Sadie. The two were an odd yet fitting pair. Sapphira wove her elbow through Sadie's. "We can do this together. You shall be tough for me, and I shall be mannerly for you."

"I suppose so."

They crested the rocky hillside and stepped onto the dusty streets of the exotic city of Tripoli. Rosalind attempted to note every detail as they made their way past spiky trees and an ornate fountain trickling water into a thick-stone basin, sending a spray of cool mist their way. Many of the flat, multi-storied stone dwellings featured odd pointed windows, the likes of which she had never seen before.

Randel had spoken true when he told them all of the varied peoples he had spied. Even during their brief trip she had spotted women covered from head to toe in white cloth, with only their eyes and hands peeking out; a dark-skinned African; and what appeared to be the typical tan-skinned natives with their black hair, thick beards, and colorful attire.

She was thankful she had chosen her most festive gown, a pink castaway from Gwendolyn, which Rosalind had adjusted long ago to fit her slighter frame.

After months at sea, she had grown accustomed to the subtle

shifts of the ship, and now on solid ground she felt strangely disoriented, as if the land moved beneath her feet, although she knew it did not.

"What is that strange creature?" Sadie whispered, as if it might hear her. She pointed to the golden creature, similar to a large horse but with a squarish jaw and a huge hump upon its back.

"I think it might be a camel," Sapphira answered.

"It is most definitely a camel," Jervais said with authority. "My tutor showed me a drawing in a book one time."

"Is it, Papa?" Garrett asked Sir Ademar, who walked just ahead of them.

"It is indeed, son, and just one of many wonders you will find in this place."

Rosalind's mind still swirled with new sights and sounds as they made their way through the gates and across the court-yard. For a moment she thought things might have been about to seem more like home, but the instant they entered the castle with its tile floors like multi-colored artwork and swathes of bold silk draping the walls, she realized she had been mistaken.

She clasped tighter to Randel's arm and nodded to the children in encouragement, but her heart sped with anticipation. As they passed through an archway into an ornate room, she felt as if she had been transported back to some biblical scene. The tables in the room sat low to the floor and cushions piled about them.

"Welcome to our home!" bellowed a man with an eye patch, who must be Count Bohemond, stretching his arms wide.

Chapter 9

The earls and Honoria greeted Count Bohemond as Rosalind and the others hung back. She gaped at the room with its huge marble pillars and large windows open to the fresh sea air and the low-streaming sunshine. Scents of exotic spices wafted through the air.

"'Tis beautiful," Rosalind whispered to Randel. "I don't know what I expected. Perhaps something more rugged and utilitarian."

"I have heard that these crusader lords are more Oriental than European. I suppose it must be true."

As if to prove him correct, musicians began to play from the corner upon instruments that appeared similar to their European pipes and lutes yet had a distinctive melancholy wail.

Bohemond spoke up again, drawing all attention to himself, and began to introduce his family. A young lady blushed prettily beside him. No doubt his second wife, based on the ages of Bohemond's children, who appeared to range from about ten to fifteen. The count presented a few nieces and nephews, as well as relatives of his wife from Cyprus.

Rosalind would never remember them all.

At ease in this welcoming environment, Lady Honoria stepped forward to her rightful place as leader and introduced her own people, starting with the men and moving to the women.

"And this is Rosalind of Ipsworth, one of the leaders of our children," Lady Honoria said.

Rosalind curtseyed. She was beyond honored to be included in this elite group. Most of the she-wolves and the devout Anna and Margaret had been left aboard the ship, as well as about half of the other women. Thank goodness for once she would not have to perform to keep Jocelyn at bay, although she continued to press close to Randel for the mere comfort of his presence.

Finally, Lady Honoria introduced each of the children by name. Rosalind had not realized that she knew them all, for she had spent little time with them on shipboard.

"Lady Sapphira, come forward, please," Count Bohemond said.

Sapphira did as bid, and the count took her two hands in his own. Considering the way he held court so grandly, Rosalind could picture him in his rightful place as Prince of all Antioch.

"A pretty little thing, are you not? My son Philippe has been anxious to meet you. After dinner, I wish you to tell me of your vision. But first we must enjoy our meal."

The host family began mingling among the guests, leading them off to the surrounding tables. A young nobleman grasped Randel's hand and began to discuss matters of politics in Europe. The count's children dispersed among the English youngsters.

Rosalind glanced about. She decided she should stick tight with the children to ensure their good behavior. But before she could follow them, a young man swept up her hand and bowed before her.

"The fair Rosalind of Ipsworth." He pressed his lips to her hand. "I am happy to make your acquaintance."

Though she was surprised he had recalled her name, she attempted to remain casual. "Indeed, and please remind me who you are, for there are so many people here tonight."

His smile lit his dark almond-shaped eyes, which contrasted strikingly with his tan skin. He pushed wavy brown hair away from a handsome face. "I am Leo of Cyprus, beloved cousin of Bohemond's young wife. And by far the most entertaining member of the family."

Rosalind chuckled. "That must be quite a feat, for they are an interesting lot."

"Ah, but how many of them can claim an illegitimate ancestry and a Saracen mother." He wiggled his heavy brows her way. "They are all from the same boring inbred European stock, but I can tell you tales of the desert and Arabian sheiks."

She believed him, for he looked as if he could be a young sheik himself, and she noted a trace of foreign accent to his French. "By all means. I did not come all this way to hear the same old legends of Europe. In fact, I have been curious about the Saracens' religion." She hoped her English accent was not too appalling, nor her French grammar too childish.

"Ah, it is quite complex. There are many different groups and factions. I confess, since my father took me into his home when I was five, I have been raised in the church like any good Christian. But perhaps I can tell you some stories of the Prophet Mohammed while we dine." He held out his arm to her.

Rosalind glanced about. Randel had settled in with a group of young men, and the children were already scattered about in clusters. This Leo seemed a fun sort, if a bit of a rake, so she threaded her arm through his and followed him deeper into the room.

Leo took her hand and helped settle her onto a purple cushion, then sat beside her on a golden one.

She adjusted her long skirts and flowing sleeves and took a deep breath. Her intention had been to come on crusade and offer her life in Christ's service. Not to sup with attractive Arabian sheiks in a hall fit for a king while exotic music floated about them.

Yet here she was, and the night was only starting.

"Is this typical of your land?" Rosalind asked her charming escort, sweeping her hand to indicate the cushions spread about the cool marble tiles.

"Indeed," he said. "Some of the crusader lords still hold with European traditions, but most have settled in over the generations. We have never even seen our—as you might think of it—'homeland.' This is home to us. Much as England has become home to your own Norman nobles."

"And that accent I hear?"

"Arabic. We all speak it, although I am one of the few who learned Arabic before French."

At that moment servants marched into the room carrying huge platters covered with food as colorful and varied as everything else in this land. Fruits, nuts, cheeses, and vegetables, but types and varieties she had never before seen.

Once the first platters had been set before them, Rosalind noted Leo staring at her and jolted. "What?"

"You are just so charming. Like a little child beholding all of our wonders."

She snickered. "Trust me. I am not a child, but I confess, this is all so new and overwhelming."

"Allow me. Olives," he said pointing to a bowl of small black and green orbs. "Figs and dates. And this is a pomegranate." Snatching up the larger red globe, he tossed it into the air and then broke it open, revealing white flesh and hundreds of juicy red seeds.

"Might I try it?"

"Of course." He picked out a single seed and reached toward Rosalind's mouth.

Taken off guard, she opened her lips and was surprised by the sweet tartness that met her tongue as she bit into the seed. "Mmm, delicious."

At that moment, Lord Rumsford caught her eye over Leo's shoulder and shot her a disapproving glare, gesturing to Randel and then frowning her way. Then he shook his head and smiled to let her know he was only jesting. Thank goodness. It seemed he had finally given up his suit, although he did not seem opposed to having a bit of fun on her account.

Rosalind turned her attention back to Leo and pointed to the orbs he had called olives. "These are fruits?"

"I suppose, although they are not very sweet. Here, try one."

This time she held out her palm before he could attempt to feed her again. His wry grin said he noticed, but he capitulated and placed the moist olive in her hand. She examined it and took a whiff of its pungent scent before nibbling off a small bite, which she was not certain she enjoyed.

"You shall get used to it," he assured her, "for they grow everywhere here."

That is when it fully hit her. Rosalind of Ipsworth, born a simple peasant, had traveled halfway across the known world. This journey was more of an adventure than she ever dreamed.

"So tell me something I do not know about the Moslems," she said. "Other than their god and prophet and holy book, I understand very little. What are their values? What are their beliefs?"

"They value family, hospitality, and purity. And they are a prideful people." A hint of pain echoed in his voice, but she did not probe further.

"That is not so terribly different. We Christians claim humility, but few truly live by it."

"Perhaps. You shall have to see for yourself." He shrugged. "They believe in one God, Allah, and by their thinking we worship three, which they find greatly offensive."

"Three!" Rosalind had just taken a bite of cheese and nearly choked on it. "Why would they think a ridiculous thing like that?"

"The trinity. Three in one. Or as they choose to see it, three gods."

"That is rather unfair."

"And yet a glimpse into the minds of a very different sort of people."

"My goodness, they must think we are the infidels."

"Yes!" he said, and pumped his fist to the sky. "One of these crusaders finally gets it. That is precisely what they call us, in their own Arabic language, of course."

"But do they believe in Jesus? In the Ten Commandments?"

"They share many of our biblical stories. But they believe Jesus was merely a good man and a prophet, and they have their own five pillars instead of our commandments."

"Interesting." She tested one of the dates, which proved soft and incredibly sweet. "Tell me something else about them."

"Hmm . . . They are forbidden to eat pork or drink alcohol."

"No." She pressed a hand to her mouth. While she seemed to recall that Jews did not eat pork, wine was a common drink throughout Europe. Although, having watched Gwendolyn's mother almost destroy herself with drink, Rosalind could see the wisdom in refraining.

"Yes, they think us quite dissolute for enjoying them. If I had ever felt pulled toward my mother's faith, that alone would have dissuaded me."

She giggled, thoroughly enjoying his company now. "Are you trying to tell me that the allowance of multiple wives would not balance that out? Have you not felt drawn to the Moslem ways at all?"

"I have not." He raked his hair away from his dark eyes. "All joking aside, they can be ruthless when crossed. And they have no Savior. No assurance of heaven, no matter how hard they work to please Allah."

"How sad," she said, but Rosalind was struck with the realization that she had spent the last year trying to please her God and earn her own redemption. Perhaps she had never quite believed the fires of hell awaited her, but she surely did not feel worthy of His forgiveness nor His love.

"It is indeed sad." He rested back upon his elbow. "Although, they are promised paradise if they die in a holy war."

"No wonder they fight so fiercely."

A servant slowly circulating the room passed by, waving a palm branch to battle the sticky heat, and Leo's wavy locks danced in the cool breeze.

Rosalind turned away from the charming sight to try a fig and was surprised by the rough texture of it, although she enjoyed the taste. "Delicious. This is all so amazing."

"You know, Rosalind," he said, placing his hand over hers and gazing deep into her eyes. "Many crusaders grow to love it here. Some decide to never go home. Perhaps before this is over, I shall convince you to remain with me as my wife."

She tugged her hand away and pressed it to her chest. "Leo! We have only just met. Do not be ridiculous. Is this part of your Oriental ways as well?"

"We never know what the future might bring. When we want something, we go after it straightaway. I have always dreamed of marrying a fine European lady with snapping blue eyes." He grinned indolently at her, not in the least perturbed by her resistance.

She understood seizing the moment. Even back home in England an entire village could be taken out by a pox or a band of marauders with no notice. Or one's father might pass away, changing the entire course of one's life. But though Leo's point was well taken, his reasoning was yet skewed. "You have misunderstood. I am not a lady, but a mere lady's maid. I am attendant to the young Lady Sapphira."

"I do understand. It is you who fail to see that you are so much more. I am certain Lady Honoria brought you along for a reason. Why, look at you." He trailed a finger down her long silken sleeve. "Fit to dine with princes. And as I mentioned, I am not of the purest stock myself. But my uncle, the King of Cyprus, adores me, and has set me up quite well with land and a position as liaison to Bohemond."

She did not know whether to respond to his compliments or to this new discovery that he served as a governmental liaison. And so she held her silence and took a handful of fresh grapes, popping them into her mouth one by one as she collected her thoughts.

"I have overwhelmed you," he said. "I apologize."

"You have only been honest and welcoming and quite complimentary, but, yes, in the short time I have been here nearly everything has overwhelmed me."

"So might I hold out some hope . . ."

"Oh . . . that." Finally she managed to untangle the many thoughts running through her mind. She did not deserve to wed this roguish man and take off on exotic adventures. Not when her tiny child lay in a cold grave in England. And even if she ever forgave herself enough to marry, he would not be her type. "I hate to disappoint you, but I have an understanding with one of the knights in our group. Now is not the time for romance, but if we both make it safely home, we intend to pursue a relationship."

"Which one?" He frowned and scanned the room. "The fellow you were standing next to when you arrived?"

"Precisely. Sir Randel."

"Ah, well, I am sorry to hear it. But as nothing is yet settled, I will not let that stand in my way."

He tossed a date into the air and caught it in his mouth—much as he no doubt intended to catch Rosalind.

Chapter 10

Since Sapphira still was not certain what she thought of the pleasant-looking blond lad beside her, she focused upon her food instead, taking another bite of the fresh, colorful medley of raw vegetables Philippe had called *salade*. That, she knew for certain she liked.

However, the excess and extravagance surrounding her were not to her personal liking. Especially not when they were supposed to be on a religious crusade. How she wished to trade her elaborate blue gown for one of her utilitarian tunics.

She took a piece of soft flat bread and dipped it into a tan mushy substance, which was surprisingly tasty. The food in Tripoli nearly burst upon her palate with bright and bold flavors. Not to mention the rich, aromatic spices sprinkled across the chicken and rice. Perhaps she was just tired of dried meat and hard bread, but she suspected even the best English food would taste bland next to this decadent spread.

Her curiosity got the best of her, and she spoke to Philippe once again. "What did you say this was called?" She nodded to the mush.

"*Hummus.*"

"What is in it?"

"Um . . . it is made of a small tannish bean, which we also call *hummus*, but I am not certain what else is in it," he said. The sun had set as they supped, and torchlight now flickered across his pronounced cheekbones.

"What is that bright, sour sort of flavor that I noticed in so much of the food?"

"That would be lemon. After dinner, I shall take you to the orchard and show you a lemon tree, if you like."

Sapphira decided she would indeed like that, although she did not wish to be alone with this boy. "Perhaps we can all go."

She grasped at Sadie's sleeve to the other side of her and then nodded down the table toward the rest of the children. Philippe's younger brother entertained the twins, Garrett, and Jervais.

Meanwhile Humphrey sat across from Philippe's sister and stared at her wistfully with his chin in his palm as she chatted with Issobelle. Good thing Brigitte and Lillian were at the next table with one of the cousins.

"So are you your father's heir?" Sapphira asked.

"No, my older brother, also named Bohemond, is in Cyprus right now."

"I see." Sapphira nodded. "We long to learn more about your land."

Philippe chuckled.

"What is so funny about that?" Sadie asked. She seemed uncomfortable in this elegant setting and had spoken little all night.

"Please do not be offended." Philippe pressed a hand to his heart. "It is just that I want nothing more than to hear stories of Europe. I have been begging my father to let me visit our relatives in France for years."

Sapphira had noted that he was the only member of Bohemond's family dressed in purely European attire. "I am afraid you would find it quite drab and boring."

"Never! That reminds me. I have a surprise for you." He scrambled to his feet and took off toward the musicians in the corner.

In a moment he was back, and the music transitioned to a familiar European carole. Philippe held out his hand to her. "My lady, might I have this dance?"

"Oh." Sapphira sank deeper into her cushion. "I am not really much of a dancer."

His face twisted in concern. "But you have learned the carole, have you not? Or are we desperately behind the times?"

She offered him a smile. "The carole is a classic, although there are many variations. I hope to join a convent someday, but my sister still insists I learn to comport myself as a proper lady."

He sighed. "Good. Then humor me with a dance, if you will."

Compassion stirred in Sapphira's heart. She did not wish to disappoint this kind boy, who so badly wished to be European, though the night had proven that clearly he was not. "I suppose."

He led her to an open space, and before long other couples joined their circle as they moved through the patterns and steps. She spied Issobelle bouncing prettily next to one of the nephews. Rosalind danced with an exotic-looking fellow, although she kept glancing over to Randel where he sat engrossed in an animated conversation with some of the young Tripolian men. And it appeared that Humphrey had gotten his fondest wish, for he now danced with Philippe's pale, sylph-like sister.

While Sapphira attempted to keep the dance light and friendly, Philippe stared at her in a way that filled her with buoyant little bubbles. For some reason she did not find him a pest, as she did the boys on the ship. Mayhap because he was several years older than her. When she settled her hand into his once again, she noted the way they fit so nicely together.

Odd thoughts for a future nun. She was not at all certain that she liked them.

For a moment she considered cutting the dance short. But having been trained as a noblewoman, Sapphira understood the value of currying favor with one's allies. She must not offend Philippe or his powerful father. And so she stiffened her spine and attempted to complete the steps without falling back under this boy's confusing influence.

After the carole, the music shifted again to the more Oriental tones. Philippe taught her a repetitive stomping dance native to the area, and most of the children joined in. They seemed to enjoy the driving romp about the room far more than Sapphira did.

When the second dance finished, she rushed toward her seat at the table but was stopped short.

"Lady Sapphira," boomed Count Bohemond from the front of the room.

"Yes, my lord." She turned and curtseyed, once again using her best manners to please her sister and win favor with their host.

"Come and speak with me."

"Of course."

Philippe followed her to his father's table.

Upon a mere nod of Bohemond's head, several people left the table with a bow. Sapphira and Philippe took the seats across from the count.

"Looks as if the two of you are getting along quite well." Bohemond winked at Sapphira.

"Your son has been taking very good care of me. There is so much to learn here."

As they spoke, the room quieted, and all eyes turned their way.

"Ah, you can see my people are as curious about you as I am. If you would indulge an old man, please share with us about this vision of yours."

Sapphira sucked in a sharp breath. Everything was happening far too quickly. The dinner, the disconcerting dance, and now this. She glanced to Honoria, who nodded calmly her way and then to Father Andrew, who smiled his support.

Yes, she must gather herself together and do this thing. In an odd turn of events, she had become a spokesperson for their crusade. She must show courage, even when she did not feel it.

Standing to her feet, she sought to find that wellspring of strength that resided deep within, attempting to allow the words to flow from her spirit, not merely her carnal mind. Much as she had done on the ship with Brother Francis, she recounted her vision.

But the result was quite different this time.

"Set the captives free," Count Bohemond scoffed with a swipe of his hand. "I know what I would wish to free. My captive princedom, which my detestable nephew, whose name we do not speak in this place, has stolen. Can you assist me with that?"

A pit formed in the center of Sapphira's stomach. Oh, how she hated to fail at anything, but she could never bear failing at this mission, especially not after bringing so many people all this way. Under her breath, she began to whisper prayers heavenward.

The exotic-looking fellow Rosalind had been dancing with spoke up. "Good count, if you will allow me to speak."

The count nodded his assent.

"This cause is different than that of most crusaders. I think we should hear them out."

Philippe rose beside Sapphira and took her arm in a show of support. "I, for one, am quite moved by the Lady Sapphira's holy vision."

Sapphira looked up at the tall boy with grudging respect, for he did not seem in the least intimidated by her odd spiritual gift.

"Of course *you* are impressed, Philippe." Bohemond chuckled. "I believe that is apparent to us all."

Bohemond's young wife patted his arm. "Now, dearest, do not embarrass the boy."

But Philippe did not appear disturbed. Rather, he grinned impishly at Sapphira, filling her with that bubbly sensation again. "Allow me to support the Englishmen, Father, even if you will not."

Bohemond sighed and rubbed at his temple as if vexed by them all. "Can we not talk about silk? We have the best looms in all the crusader states. Let us load your ships with fine fabrics. You can return home unscathed and we shall all be rich."

Lady Honoria stood as well now. "With all due respect, good count, you cannot expect us to be deterred from the call of God so easily."

"Sadly not." He frowned. "You crusaders never are. But I fell for the persuasion of the Hungarians a few years back, and it nearly saw me destroyed. I will not make such a mistake again."

"What can it hurt to free a few prisoners?" The exotic fellow stepped forward to join Sapphira and Philippe. "Many of the prisons are not even well guarded." He turned now to Honoria. "Do you know where your husband and your cousin, the rightful duke, might be held?"

"We know only that they were taken by the Druze in the area that used to be part of the County of Tripoli."

"So perhaps in the Shouf Mountains or in Beirut," Philippe said. "Father, I hear the mountain prison at Jezeer has only a small troop and one village nearby. They hold many of our own men as well. We should have attacked them long ago, except that we have been so busy rebuilding."

The exotic fellow, who she thought had been introduced as being from Cyprus, though she did not remember his name, stepped closer to the count. "My lord, I think it would be wise to join with the Englishmen, at least for a time. The Maronites have been asking for help to free their soldiers from Jezeer. They will join us. And if your wife agrees, we can lend you the support of the Cyprian forces as well."

Count Bohemond pulled at his beard, as if he were considering it.

"I would be agreeable," the count's young wife said. "Although I defer to my husband's judgement in such weighty matters."

"The Maronites have been your staunchest supporters," Philippe added. "We should aid them in this."

Sapphira had no idea who the Maronites might be, but she would take any assistance offered. "So many languish." She gripped her hands together in petition. "So many despair. My uncle and my rightful duke might well be among them. Please, allow us to pass peacefully through this land, even if you cannot join us in our quest."

Count Bohemond glanced at his family members who had come to Sapphira's defense. "It seems you have won over my people with your impassioned speech, young lady. I admit that I am impressed." He leaned forward with a scowl. "And I am not easily impressed."

He sat back again and appraised Sapphira, then Honoria, then the English earls. "Yes, perhaps we should join together in an attack on Jezeer. Strength in numbers and all that. I suppose I shall have to face them eventually, with or without your help, although I had not planned to do so this soon."

Philippe possessively wrapped an arm around Sapphira's shoulder and tugged her closer. "You shall not regret this, Father."

A part of her wished to pull away, but a different part liked having this bold young man at her side, while an even bigger share recalled that she could not risk offending any of them. Instead she forced a sweet smile at Count Bohemond. "Thank you, my lord. We welcome your support, and we shall not let you down."

"You had best not. I have been disappointed by crusaders too many times already. And"—he pointed to Philippe and the Cyprian who had dared to challenge him—"we shall only help with Jezeer. I am not risking my troops deeper into the Saracen-held territories."

"Yes, Father," said Philippe.

"As you wish." The Cyprian bowed.

"Enough talk of politics for now." The count clapped his hands. "Let us enjoy some sweet treats. I promise that you have never tasted anything like our sugar cane."

And just like that the most powerful man in the region declared their fate and returned to his meal. Sapphira pressed her lips tight and turned them into another false smile, although she feared smoke might be escaping from her ears and nostrils.

Philippe took her arm and led her back to the table.

Once they were seated again, he leaned close and whispered. "You are angry."

"I am trying not to be. I hope your father did not notice."

"Father notices little, unless it fills his pockets with denarii or adds to his power."

"Oh."

"It is just his way. I am afraid the religious fervor of the crusades holds little appeal for him."

But the man was the head of a crusader state. His sole purpose should have been to promote the cause of Christ, not to fill his pockets or his belly. And most certainly not to promote his own agenda of power. Sapphira's righteous indignation continued to burn.

"Do not worry, though. Father says our troops may not go beyond Jezeer, but we shall see about that. I shall fight for your cause, I promise you, and I shall win the others to our side."

He took Sapphira's hand and gave it a firm squeeze. And for some reason she did not mind one bit.

She liked the way he took control, and the way he spoke of "our" side. Her tension began to drain away, and a warm comfort took its place. This boy would support her. And it seemed others from this region would as well.

A servant leaned over to place a platter of pastries in front of them.

"Try one," Philippe instructed.

She reached out and picked one up, turning it over in her hand to study it. It seemed to be made of grain and crushed nuts, not so different from home. A sticky substance, lighter and clearer than the honey of Britannia, covered the top.

"Go on."

She took a bite into the concoction, which was sweeter and more delicate than anything she had ever tasted in her life. Her eyes grew wide.

"Oh, Sadie, try this." She turned and offered a bite to her friend.

"Heaven must taste like this!" Sadie exclaimed. Finally looking more at ease, she scooped up her own pastry.

Philippe grinned. "I have heard there is nothing like our sugar cane in all of Europe. And few have tried our cinnamon."

"You almost sound proud of your heritage." Sapphira raised a brow to Philippe, who claimed such interest in all things European.

"I suppose it has its merits."

Sapphira let go of the last of her anger and smiled now too. She took another bite of the pastry and savored the sweet and spicy flavor in her mouth. "After sampling this, I can almost forgive your father for being more concerned with his sweets than our crusade."

Almost.

But not quite.

At least Count Bohemond would help them with this first step. Perhaps by then they would be acclimated to this new land and ready to strike out on their own deeper into the area held by the Saracens. Or perhaps Philippe would prevail in his quest to assist them. Either way, this mission was in the hands of God. Ultimately their success or failure would depend on Him.

Chapter 11

After their languid months at sea, the next few days passed in a whirlwind, first heading farther down the coast to the southern edge of the County of Tripoli, then transporting people, horses, supplies, and weapons from the ships and setting up camp.

Before she knew it, Rosalind found herself upon a horse leading the children down a trail behind the Cyprian soldiers as they wove their way through the steep, jagged mountain passages with only a few small tenacious trees clinging to the sand-colored rock. At least the temperature had dropped from sweltering near the coast to merely warm with a cool breeze.

"I cannot believe we are truly on crusade," observed young Garrett from his smaller mount just behind her.

"We have been on crusade this entire time, you dunderhead," Jervais said.

"Not like this." Garrett patted his crusader tunic. They had considered wearing their nondescript clothing for a while longer, but with such a large caravan, they were unlikely to fool anyone, so better to make their intentions clear. The boy sat up a little taller on his mount. "I will feel like it is real when we face our first battle."

"I agree," Philippe said from his self-appointed place next to Sapphira. "I have lived here all my life, but I have never seen a battle."

"We shall not battle," Lillian reminded them.

"But we are ready if we must," Sadie said, concluding the issue.

Rosalind still could not believe it had all transpired so quickly. It seemed that once Count Bohemond made up his mind about something, matters moved of their own accord. Much like Leo had mentioned to her, they did not waste time in this volatile land.

The crusaders had been assured that they would meet little resistance as they crossed through the Christian villages scattered throughout the mountains. And if they were careful, they would reach their first prison at Jezeer before the Saracens found them out.

As they turned a bend in the trail, Rosalind discovered a grinning Leo waiting for her upon his horse. "There you are," he said.

She had barely seen him since the feast at the castle. "I have been basically right here all day."

He chuckled. "I know, but I have not been able to break away until now. I thought we might ride together for a time."

Rosalind scanned her group. All seemed in order. Fifteen-year-old Philippe rode rather close to Sapphira, but she did not seem to mind the older boy's proximity, and Rosalind would not make a fuss over their budding romance when voicing concern might cause an international incident. The others were settled into companionable little groups, and Randel waved to her from where he brought up the rear with young Humphrey.

Taking a deep breath, she turned back to Leo. She did enjoy

his playful banter, and she still had so many questions about this place. He leaned closer and spoke out of the side of his mouth. "It seems we have the all clear from your rear guard."

She reached over and gave him a little shove. "'Tis not like that. Randel trusts me. I just wouldn't wish to hurt his feelings."

"Your *friend* looks perfectly content. So what say you?"

"Of course you may ride with me. But only if you continue to enlighten me about your culture."

"At your service, m'lady."

She grimaced at him, for she had told him repeatedly she was not a lady. "'Twas quite warm along the coast. Is that typical?"

"The summers are our dry season, and a bit warmer here than in France."

"So definitely warmer than Northern England."

"I would think so."

Rosalind was glad they had made the crusader tunics of light fabrics. She wondered how the knights with their chain mail would manage in the heat but imagined crusaders must have been doing so for a very long time. "Why do your soldiers ride horses and not the camels we have seen?"

He patted his steady mount. "Camels are for the desert. Horses do better in the mountains."

As Rosalind continued her perusal, she spotted a village up ahead. She squinted to better make out the simple rectangular stone houses. "Are we certain they are Christians?"

"Yes. Have you heard the story of our Maronites?" The breeze teased Leo's wavy hair over his smooth brow.

"Not yet."

"They are native to this area and have been around since the time of the New Testament. But the Saracen invaders ruled for hundreds of years, and anyone who even remembered the Maronites assumed they had been converted, killed, or perhaps dispersed."

He gave his reins a flick to encourage his horse over a rocky patch. "Then, when the crusaders arrived to Tripoli, the Maronites poured down from the mountains to greet them."

"How did they survive?"

"Most Arabs don't know how to battle in the mountains. The Maronites hid away in the highest regions for centuries. They are a tough people, a resilient people. That is the nature of this area."

By now they had reached the village. Children in loose trousers and long tunics giggled and waved as they dashed between the rectangular stone houses. A few chickens pecked along the side of the trail, undeterred by the great war-horses, and a herd of goats grazed in some tall, sparse grasses not far beyond.

Rosalind continued to ponder the story of the Maronite Christians. "But isn't the Moslem prison we're heading toward located in the mountains?"

"Ah, yes. The Maronite Christians settled in the northern part of the mountains, but to the south another oppressed group, the minority Druze Moslems, learned to survive in the Shouf Mountains. They hold that region as well as the city of Beirut now."

Rosalind paused to really consider the people of this war-torn land. Europeans had first come here over a hundred years ago, and according to their lessons on the ships, there had not been much peace since.

Leo twisted sideways to study her. "What are you thinking about?"

"You always just focus on the grand ideals of the crusades. Never the people."

"If it makes you feel any better, the Arab tribes are a temperamental lot. They always seem to be fighting over something. And in their prime, they slaughtered city after city full of Christians.

I cannot say if the crusaders have done much good here, but I doubt they have done any worse."

A bird swept overhead, reminding her of Randel's quest. A far more pleasant subject. "Have you heard of the Syrian serin?"

He looked at her skeptically. "You mean the bird?"

"Yes. Do you know where we might find one?"

He smirked. "'Tis rather a plain sort of bird. Perhaps we might find a lovely lady like you a peacock instead."

"Randel wished to find one. His grandfather was a crusader and brought home a picture of a serin." But noting the smug look on Leo's face, she did not share the reason, and certainly not the private story of Randel's falling out with his family.

"Randel. I see. Or rather, I do not see. I do not see any evidence of this relationship you spoke of. And I have had several opportunities to observe you together over the last days. I admit that you are companionable, but the very fact that he seems so relaxed back there while I flirt with you is not compelling for your case."

"I need not prove myself to you." Rosalind peered down her nose at Leo. "Randel is not the jealous sort, and he is rather affable by nature. I admire those qualities."

"But, you see, there is nothing to stop me from doing this." Leo reached over and snatched up her hand before she could pull it away. He pressed a kiss to it and wiggled his brows.

Now she did manage to pull it away. "You are incorrigible."

"I prefer determined. And I am determined to woo you. Nothing has changed on that account."

She turned back to find Randel. He watched her quizzically, not quite upset but more confused than she had seen him in some time. With a subtle gesture of her head, she indicated that he should come join them.

It was not that she didn't like Leo. But she had no interest in pursuing a relationship with him. Yet she could not afford to offend this man, who wielded much more power in this land than she had first suspected. Who was to say that she was not part of the reason he had come along for this rescue mission?

She must proceed wisely. Although Leo might not like the fact that she was supposedly committed to Randel, he had not seemed surprised nor offended over the idea. Surely any gentleman, or even a partial gentlemen like Leo, would understand if another fellow had a prior claim.

Randel did not feel certain at first that Rosalind truly needed him. He had been daydreaming of the Templar fort they had passed near the coast. How he wished he might have strayed off the path to meet with them, if only for a few moments, but he would not leave his charges for a selfish reason. There would be time aplenty to become acquainted with the Templars once their mission had finished.

Now that he shifted his full attention to Rosalind, he was struck with an odd urge to wedge himself between her and that presumptuous Cyprian fellow. Even then he was about to ignore the impulse, for he did not wish to stir up trouble, until Jocelyn trotted her horse next to him.

"God give you good day, Sir Randel." The vixen smiled coyly at him. "I thought you would never part from your dear Rosalind."

"How funny that you should mention it, for I was just on my way to her now."

"Oh, please do not rush off. I feel as if we have been growing apart of late. I do so miss our conversations."

All the better, that. "I am sorry to disappoint you, Jocelyn, but she is waiting for me even now."

Jocelyn huffed.

Manners suggested he should offer to speak with her at a

different time, but he would not bow to niceties when dealing with the leader of the she-wolf pack. And although he had intended to stay to the rear of the children and keep watch over them during the journey, an entire English battalion was behind them. Surely they were safer than he was at that moment.

Without further comment, he trotted away from a no-doubt-seething Jocelyn and past the children.

"Ah, and here he comes now. I wondered what had taken him so long." The Cyprian tipped back his head and chuckled.

Randel flinched, not certain if he should be offended. He pulled his mount next to Rosalind's and the fellow she had spent time with at the feast. Randel had presumed the man was only being friendly, but after that possessive scene he just witnessed, he did not feel certain any longer. "I am ready for a break from Humphrey's pining over Bohemond's daughter," he said by way of excuse.

"Randel, have you met Leo?" Rosalind asked.

"Leo of Cyprus, nephew to the king." Leo nodded with confidence.

Wonderful, another nobleman toying with Rosalind. Randel's protective nature soared to high alert. "Sir Randel, son of the Earl of Penigree."

"I see."

The two stared at each other for a moment, taking each other's measure. Randel did not like the Cyprian's arrogance, although he must admit that he appeared to be a jovial sort and a fit soldier.

Rosalind giggled forcibly, as if hoping to break the tension. "I asked Leo about the serin. He said they are quite common to the region."

"So are you a fan of birds?" Leo asked with amusement in his tone. "I personally prefer to collect weapons. But to each his own, I suppose."

"In truth, it is more my mother's hobby. 'Tis something I did with her as a child." Randel immediately regretted defending himself to this man. He need not feel embarrassed over his avian interests. "But it rather took hold of me."

Leo tipped his head, as if in concession. "Well, spending time with one's mother I can appreciate. I had far too little time with my own."

"His mother was a Moslem," Rosalind said. "Is that not fascinating?"

"Oh." Randel tensed his jaw and gripped tighter to the reins, taken off guard by this new information. "I did not realize intermarriage was permitted."

"It happens, although it is rare. My parents were not married, but they were most certainly in love. My mother was killed by an uncle who was determined to save the family's honor while I was still very young."

"Leo! How sad. Why did you not tell me sooner?" Rosalind asked.

He shrugged. "I did not wish to ruin our festive dinner."

"I have heard of these honor killings, but I confess I did not believe it possible." Randel scratched at his chin. Back home in England illegitimate birth was common enough, especially among the peasant class.

"Believe it. Perhaps my father would have married her if he had known what was happening, but he was off fighting near Jerusalem at the time. He took me in and raised me as his own just as soon as he found out. So never fear, I am as Christian as the rest of you."

"I am so sorry to hear of your loss." Randel offered the fellow an expression of sympathy, surprised that Leo had shared so much. He could hardly hate him now.

"It was long ago. The good news is that you need not fear my loyalties. Although . . ." Leo reached over and tugged playfully at Rosalind's dark braid. "Much as you have dreamed of the Syrian serin, I have dreamed of marrying a blue-eyed beauty from Europe. So you might not wish to trust me completely."

Randel jerked in Leo's direction, but Rosalind was yet between them.

Rosalind pushed Leo's hand away. "Stop that, Leo. Randel, I do believe he's testing you. I hope you will forgive me, but I told him of our agreement, and I do not think he believes me."

"If I had such an agreement with a woman like Rosalind, I would keep her close at all times. In fact, I would put a ring upon her lovely finger as quickly as possible to avoid any confusion."

Now Randel had no idea what to think of the fellow. He would not have expected him to be so forthright about his interest in Rosalind. And the realization struck him that if Leo was not precisely a nobleman, he might have honorable intentions after all.

The part of Randel that was committed to Rosalind's well-being paused to consider that this man might be willing to offer marriage and security to this dear friend. Marriage and security that Randel could not give her as a warrior monk. But a different part of him flamed at the very thought. Besides, Rosalind claimed she did not wish to marry. And clearly she had summoned him to thwart off this potential suitor.

So thwart he would.

Randel reached out and took Rosalind's hand in his own. "I do thank you for being so clear on the issue, Leo. I will keep this one close by my side for the duration of the journey to prevent further confusion."

Rosalind smiled at him with admiration and affection. Perhaps it was only an act for Leo's sake, but she seemed sincere, and Randel's heart skipped a beat.

"In that case, I suppose I will leave you both to your bird watching." Leo trotted back toward his troop up ahead of them.

"Thank you!" Rosalind sighed.

"Is he truly so troublesome?"

"Only when he speaks of marriage. You know I have no desire to marry, but I do not wish to stir up problems. He has been one of our most faithful supporters here in Tripoli."

Randel's stomach twisted. Precisely as he had feared. "And I do not think he will be as easily deterred as Rumsford."

"No, I think we shall have to be more convincing with our ruse in the future."

Randel grinned at her. "I do not think that shall be too difficult."

Rosalind's cheeks tinged to a sweet shade of pink. "Nor do I," she said.

Chapter 12

"Lady Brigitte, if you do not plan to eat your stew, send it this way!" Sadie called across the roaring fire.

They had set up camp in a narrow valley between two mountains, but they had nearly reached their destination now, and upon the morrow they would need to better hide their presence. However, for tonight they enjoyed one last relaxed dinner, with Randel and the boys to one side of the campfire and Rosalind and the girls to the other.

Rosalind looked to fifteen-year-old Brigitte as she spooned her stew into the air longingly, then allowed it to plop back in her bowl. Now that Rosalind thought about it, Brigitte had been leaving food behind for days, and the normally curvy young lady looked a bit sharper and bonier than usual.

"I suppose you can have the rest, Sadie."

"Wait." Rosalind held up a hand to stop Brigitte from passing along her food. "You need to eat, young lady. All of us need our strength for what lies ahead."

"If she does not want it, I will take it," called Jervais. "I can be strong for the both of us."

Brigitte shot him a glare, then came to squat before Rosalind where she sat upon a log. Tossing another glance over her shoulder, Brigitte lowered her voice to a whisper. "I have gotten too fat of late. We all know I do not truly plan to fight, but if I do not return home betrothed, my mother shall be sorely vexed."

"What do you mean, you are fat? You've been working harder than you have your entire life. All of you girls have toned up nicely from your training. I wish you would not worry about boys and romance so, but trust me, men do like a few curves in the right places."

"Not Humph—" Brigitte slapped a hand over her mouth.

Rosalind turned to Sadie, who never had patience with such silly girlish games.

Brigitte pled with her eyes.

"Well, you brought it up, not me." Sadie shrugged. "'Tis well known amongst the girls that Brigitte hopes to catch Humphrey as a fiancé before we return home. But he seemed quite taken with Bohemond's daughter back in Tripoli, and now she's worried."

And said daughter was as thin and tiny as a waif, not to mention dark-haired with pale skin. Quite the opposite of the buxom, robust, blond Brigitte.

Rosalind sighed.

How could she convince these girls that they could be strong on their own and let romance and marriage come if and when they might, that they should not sell their souls for a man?

Rosalind had thought she was that sort of strong girl, yet she had let Sir Hugh take her virtue so lightly, had given herself to him and nearly destroyed herself in the process. Surely no one could blame her for wanting better for these girls.

She took Brigitte's hands in her own. "Brigitte, you are not

Bohemond's daughter. You shall never be, but you are beautiful the way God made you, and the right man shall find you perfect."

Now she gave Brigitte's hands a firm shake. "And if you do not finish your dinner, I swear I shall send you packing back to Tripoli and far away from Humphrey. You must be strong and battle ready, else I shall not let you travel with us."

Brigitte's gaze fell to the ground between them. "Yes, of course. I know you are right. Only it is hard to see him admiring another."

"Now is not—"

"I know," Brigitte cut Rosalind off with her voice raised to a degree that the other girls might hear. "Now is not the time for romance. Easy for you to say when you are naturally as slender as a reed and the man you admire most cannot take his eyes off of you."

"That is not true," Rosalind protested. But when she peeked across the fire, surely enough, Randel's wistful gaze was fixed upon her, and he offered a little wave.

All the girls giggled.

"Rosalind, you know that I am truthful above all things," Sapphira said. "And the truth is, on this issue, Brigitte is absolutely right."

And the giggles rose to a new pitch.

"Shh . . . ," Sadie shushed them all. "We sound like a bunch of little girls."

"We are a bunch of little girls," Lillian said.

"'Tis not as if you have been lacking for male attention either, Sapphira." Brigitte headed back to her seat with her stew still in hand.

Sapphira did not answer, and although it was hard to tell in the flickering light, Rosalind suspected Sapphira's cheeks had flushed pink.

"You have not said much about Philippe," Rosalind prompted. "Do you enjoy his company?"

Sapphira took another bite of stew and seemed to be weighing her answer. "He has excellent manners, and he is quite kind."

"And quite nice to look at," teased Issobelle with her red curls sparkling.

"Is he?" asked Sapphira coolly. "I had not noticed."

Which of course elicited yet another round of giggles.

"So you don't mind that he has been spending so much time with you," Rosalind pressed, for she knew the girl would go to great lengths to do her duty, even if she was not feeling comfortable about it.

Sapphira bit her lip. "I suppose I do not mind, but I wish he would not show me such particular favor. I am concerned about his intentions."

"Surely his intentions are honorable." Issobelle leaned forward with excitement. "He has been courting you right in front of his own family."

"I realize that." Sapphira squirmed upon a rock. "But I have made it clear that I wish to join the church. Although he has not mentioned marriage or the future in a forthright manner, I fear he does not take my plan seriously."

Rosalind had made it clear to Leo that she was attached to Randel, but he did not seem to take her seriously either.

"You know," said Brigitte, who despite her flighty nature was quite smart concerning issues of romance, "many girls claim an interest in the church before fully reaching their womanhood, and of course before meeting the right man."

Now Sapphira's blush grew obvious. "I do not wish to discuss it further."

"As long as you understand that if you ever do change your mind, that would be acceptable," Rosalind assured her. "There are many different ways to serve God and fulfill His purposes."

Sapphira just nodded. She had reached her womanhood early on their voyage, but she had spoken to her sister about it rather than Rosalind. In fact, she seemed quite shy about such issues. But at least she did not seem truly distressed by Philippe's attention, more so confused. Rosalind would give her time to work that out on her own.

Perhaps that was the problem with Leo. He thought Rosalind might be persuaded to change her mind now that they had met. Rumsford had been deterred easily enough, but he knew he had little to offer a girl like Rosalind. However, Leo had made it clear that he intended to marry her. And in any normal sort of circumstances, she would be a fool to turn him down.

But her life had ceased to be normal on a fateful night a year and a half ago.

Although Rosalind feared she was not worthy, perhaps she must consider joining the church like Sapphira, elsewise these pesky suitors might never give her a moment of peace. Why did Rosalind always seem to draw such bold and charming men?

First Sir Hugh, then Lord Rumsford, and now this Leo. She had had her fill of them. She would take a mellow, faithful, and genial sort of fellow like Randel over any one of them.

Glancing behind her, she noted that Leo watched her from across the way. Unlike Randel's companionable wave, Leo sent her a searing look along with a sensual toss of his dark, wavy hair. He wiggled his thick brows her way, as if to say, *Just you wait.*

Utilizing every ounce of strength within me, I somehow managed not to fling myself across the dark valley and wrap my hands about Randel Penigree's throat. Oh, how they ached and burned to plant themselves in his gullet and squeeze tight. My hatred had naught but burned and strengthened over the past month.

He nudged one of his boys playfully. I could not say which, for I could not have cared less about the group of obnoxious youngsters. They clawed upon my nerves. In fact, I had rather grown to hate the lot of them, for they had helped Randel in his rise to glory.

Was I the one given leadership in this campaign? No, Randel was. Was I the one who feasted in the count's castle? No, Randel. Randel and his passel of rowdy children and that awful Rosalind who was ever glued to his side. Meanwhile, I languished in the background, in the tedium and the boredom of this horrid crusade I did not even believe in. And meanwhile my brother, the only person I had ever truly loved, lay dead in a grave in England.

Perhaps I should find myself a romantic distraction, as seemed to be the course of the day on this ridiculous mission with its women and children. In fact, I just might. It would take my mind off my troubles, but only for a short time.

Matters like a dead brother were not easily dismissed. And my brother would be avenged. The more I dug, the more I pressed, the more I suspected Randel Penigree had been more involved with his death than even I had guessed. Something horrible had occurred at Gravensworth Castle. That I knew for certain. And Randel Penigree was to blame. From that I would never be dissuaded. I yet lacked evidence of foul play, but the very fact that he survived while every soldier beneath him perished was condemning enough in my mind.

Once battles started and soldiers were wounded and disappearing, then I could strike. Oh, it would be easy to send a sword or an arrow flying his way, but would he suffer enough? Not likely. No, I yet needed the perfect plan.

That Rosalind woman stood and approached Randel now. She laughed at something he said. Perhaps I would take her down as well. I had liked her well enough in the beginning, but much like the children, she had chafed my nerves raw due to her continual fawning over the imbecile.

I took a deep breath and braced myself. I picked up my dagger and pressed my thumb against the sharp blade. But now was not the time. And perhaps I would not do the deed myself. It all depended on which strategy would most likely bring Randel Penigree down for good and destroy his name and reputation along with him.

"Please, one more story," whined one of the twins, as Randel moved toward the exit flap of the tent.

"It has been a long day. You boys should rest."

"I am too excited to rest," said the matching twin. "Tomorrow is the day we have been waiting for all these months."

Randel yet held the flap open over his head. "And it might be a difficult day. So you will need to be fresh and ready."

"Go ahead," Humphrey said. "I shall tell them a story they shall not soon forget."

"Keep it appropriate." Randel shook his finger at him.

"Oh, it shall be." Humphrey assumed the cherubic expression of an angel.

Randel grimaced, but he let the flap fall closed behind him.

Through the fabric he heard Humphrey say. "Appropriately . . . scary!" Humphrey's shadow lunged at the younger boys, and they all squealed.

Randel chuckled and headed to the groups gathered near the fires. He really should not hide out with the children night after night. Tomorrow they would head into battle, and he would do well to become acquainted with more of the others. After his defeat at Gravensworth, it had seemed easier to stay hidden away at home, and then with the children, to avoid tough questions and suspicious stares. But he was ready to put all of that behind him.

Lady Honoria and Lord Haverland trusted him now. They had given him a place of honor on this crusade. And he had even managed to befriend the commander of the Tripolian forces.

He skirted his way past the she-wolves as they flirted with a group of Tripolian soldiers, being careful not to draw Jocelyn's notice.

There was the commander now, an engaging young man with light brown hair and a trim beard, dressed as a proper European crusader. Randel headed his way and noted that Lord Rumsford and several knights from his ship were conversing with his new friend.

"Randel, come join us!" the commander called. "I assume you all know each other."

"Sir Randel and I go far back, ever since he stole my first love." Rumsford jostled Randel playfully with his shoulder.

"So that is it!" Randel suddenly recalled a young woman named Elizabeth with flowing chestnut hair. "I never could remember why you hated me so much. But neither of us ended up with the girl. So I suppose it does not matter now."

"I am quite over her. And you have rather grown on me during this trip. Although you do tend to keep yourself hidden away with those children."

"What can I say? I am just a child at heart."

The commander wrapped an arm around Randel's shoulder and gave him a shake. "That is why he is so much fun, I tell you."

"Well, I have not made his acquaintance" came a surly voice from the shadows.

"Sir Manfred, allow me to introduce you to Sir Randel." Lord Rumsford pulled the man closer to the firelight.

Randel vaguely recognized Sir Manfred as one of the knights who had been aboard his ship. A rather short, broad man with a craggy face, but strong looking, and evidently trusted enough to be near the women and children.

"Sir Manfred is a fine soldier. You should test your sword arm against him someday."

"I might do that," Randel said.

But Manfred just sneered at him and pulled back again.

What was the man's problem? Perhaps he was jealous that Randel had grown in favor on this crusade, while he had stayed in the background. But it was not as if any of the other knights had been jostling for an opportunity to serve as glorified nursemaid to the children. Randel had earned his new place through hard work and faithfulness.

"So did he truly steal your first love?" asked the commander, attempting to steer the conversation in a more pleasant direction.

Rumsford laughed. "I had been working up the courage for weeks to approach Elizabeth and ask her for a dance."

"Yes, our fathers had been spending quite some time together, and I had grown tired of hearing about the elusive Elizabeth. Mind you, I was only twelve, and Rumsford already a randy sixteen."

"And that night I must have pushed Randel too far."

"Indeed. No less than five times you headed in her direction, and no less than five times you turned back." Randel shook his head at the memory. "I thought you quite the besotted fool."

"Then this one says to me that if I will not ask her, he will do it himself. For a moment, I thought he meant to ask her on my behalf, so I said for him to go right ahead. And the next thing I knew, he had the fair Elizabeth twirling in his arms, and all my future hopes and dreams came crashing down around me. And the pup was not even as tall as her!"

"Ha ha! Crashing down. Surely you exaggerate." The commander gave Rumsford a shove.

"Perhaps not," Randel said, "for he has barely spoken to me these last seven years."

"I was but a lad, and losing one's first love can leave a fellow quite forlorn. Although, I must say," Lord Rumsford gestured beyond Randel, "tonight it looks like someone else is in jeopardy of losing his love."

Randel turned to observe Leo pressing near to Rosalind and chucking her on the chin. She grimaced at him and pulled away, but Leo only scooched closer. Rosalind appeared a bit annoyed, but Randel's heart thumped hard in his chest and pounded in his ears. In no uncertain terms Rosalind had told Leo that she was not interested in him. A gentleman of honor should respect a woman's wishes, but Leo did not seem to concern himself with such niceties. He went after what he wanted with full abandon.

Well, two could play at that game. Randel would put a stop to this once and for all.

Chapter 13

Once again pushing Leo away, Rosalind noted a flash of ivory moving her direction. Randel, no longer so mellow, strode straight at them with stark determination, and if she was not mistaken, even a bit of anger.

"Leo of Cyprus, you push the lady too far."

"You see, Rosalind, even he thinks you are a lady." Leo just chuckled devilishly.

"This is not a game. I must ask that you unhand her."

"All is well, Sir Randel. 'Tis just Leo's way." But Rosalind took this opportunity to stand and move apart from Leo.

"If you wish to spend time with her, by all means do. But if you plan to leave her alone in the moonlight . . ." Leo wiggled his brows. "I cannot be held responsible for my actions."

"In fact, I was just heading this way to ask Rosalind to walk with me."

"What a wonderful idea." Sincere joy bubbled in Rosalind's chest and burst into a smile across her face.

"Come." Randel wrapped an arm over her shoulder, and not for the first time, she noted how snuggly she fit against him. She reached up to place her hand over his, and tossed a triumphant look over her shoulder at Leo.

"He is still watching us," she whispered close to Randel's ear.

If she was not mistaken, he shivered as her breath tickled his skin.

"We shall give him something to watch."

Randel led her between two tall tents to a narrow area that only Leo could see. Then he twisted her in his arms and pulled her to him. As Rosalind gasped and turned her questioning gaze up to Randel's dark eyes, she spotted something there she had never seen before. An intensity. A strength. And a yearning. As her mouth still gaped in shock, he caught it with his own.

Something about the all-too-familiar sensation caught her off guard, and her body responded, even as her mind struggled to make sense of it all.

Fire shot through her, and old feelings she had thought long buried surged to life. Precious seconds passed before she found the strength and the shred of intention needed to pry her mouth away from his. She buried her head against Randel's sturdy chest. Wanting to hide her reaction. Ashamed of her ardent response.

She did not wish to be that girl again.

Dear God, help me. What had he done? Though not quite a saint, Randel had never let his instincts overtake his rational mind in such a manner before. "It was just a kiss," he whispered over her head. "Merely a kiss," he repeated, for both of their sakes.

But he knew it had been much more, and surely she felt it too. Rosalind and Randel, both committed to remaining unmarried for their own reasons, had tangled their hearts during those brief moments. That was not how a warrior monk behaved. "I am sorry," he said, "I did not mean it to go that far."

Yet he clung to her as if he had been tossed into the sea during a shipwreck, and she were a beam of wood that might float him safely to shore.

"No, it was my fault," the pain in her voice stabbed deep into his chest.

He grabbed her precious face in his two hands and pressed his forehead to hers. "Do not say—"

But he was cut off by a boisterous pounding. Leo banged his metal cup against the rock beneath him and cheered. "I concede! Enough already. You win. I am quite convinced."

Of course, Leo, the reason Randel had found himself in this situation. He had been determined to set the man straight and drive him away from Rosalind once and for all. Yet the minute he pulled Rosalind into his arms, his anger had shifted to a different sort of intensity.

"Go away, Leo." Randel let his hands slip down her arms and fall to his sides in defeat. He closed his eyes.

Leo must have acquiesced, for a chuckle faded into the night even as Rosalind continued to press her face into his chest. Good, for he did not wish to see the haunted eyes that would surely match the raw pain in her voice.

This was not supposed to happen. And yet it felt so right. As if the stars had finally aligned and his life at long last made perfect sense. Except that it made no sense at all. His path had been planned. He had reconciled himself to becoming a Templar. It was what he wanted, or so he had thought until just a moment ago . . .

This could be so simple.

He could gladly marry the girl. Except that he would lose his family and his place in the world. And beyond that, he reminded himself, she did not wish to marry him either. That pain he had heard when she spoke . . . Oh, how he hated himself for being the source of it.

"Leo is gone. I do not think he will bother you again." He tipped up Rosalind's chin and found the courage to face her troubled gaze.

"But . . ." she said.

"Shh . . . all is well. Forward, ever forward. Remember? I am sorry our kiss got a bit beyond my intentions, but I think it served its purpose."

"But . . ." She turned to see that Leo had gone, then back to Randel, then pressed her head to him again. "I suppose you are right."

There was no point in bringing up all the bizarre and mystical things that had passed between them in that addlebrained instant while their lips met.

"Nothing has changed," he said, although he knew the words were not quite true. But he said them for her good. He would do anything to soothe the misery in her eyes.

"Nothing has changed," she murmured hopefully against his tunic.

"Nothing has changed," he assured her, attempting to mean it this time.

"Ever forward, never back."

"Precisely," he said, although quite how he could move forward from this moment, he did not know. At least tomorrow would bring their first skirmish. Right now he needed the immediacy and danger of battle to drive these confusing feelings far from his mind.

Silent tears streamed down Rosalind's face as she tried to sleep, replaying the unfortunate kiss again and again in her mind. After losing Sir Hugh, she had assumed she would never experience such sensations again. She had been wrong. Perhaps she had allowed herself to heal too much. She should not let herself enjoy life to such a degree after what she had done.

The waves came again, the pain rose up within her.

At the time the decision had made so much sense. "Just take the potion," her mother had said. "It will be simple," she had assured Rosalind.

She had known Hugh would never marry her. Although she had not protected her virtue zealously enough, neither did she wish to be a nobleman's kept woman. And she needed to provide for her mother and siblings. She'd determined that never again would she watch them starve the way they had after her father passed away.

But from the moment the awful act was done, she'd known what a tragic error it had been. And Hugh had made sure to crush her into the ground with his words, so much so that she had thought she might never rise again.

"Thief, harlot, murderer!"

Those names yet haunted her, ringing all too true.

Did Randel know?

He and Hugh were the best of friends. But somehow she suspected Randel would not judge her so harshly even if he did. He would recognize her intense regret, partake in her pain, and shoulder her weighty guilt alongside her.

Still she could not bring herself to utter such awful words to her dear friend. As far as she was aware, only her mother and Hugh—and of course every priest who had graced her confessional—knew the truth.

Father Andrew had assured her again and again in that shadowy place on shipboard that her penance had been long paid, but she could not bring herself to believe him. She would continue attempting to earn her forgiveness, until at last her own heart ceased to bleed.

But that kiss . . . the kiss had been a dreadful error. She must never let it happen again! At the time of her indiscretion with Hugh she had been of the prevailing mindset that only nuns, monks, and priests were called to holy lives. That it was only natural for regular folk to give in to their passions and desires.

But she knew better now. And she would never give way to such temptations again. Especially not with another nobleman—no matter how superior his character might be. No matter how different her heart told her that his kiss was from Hugh's.

She took a deep breath and attempted to slow her racing thoughts. How she missed the mother of her early years in moments like this. How she longed to press her face into her mother's nurturing shoulder and cry upon it. She felt adrift, alone, despite the many sleeping girls surrounding her.

On so many occasions, she still needed the wisdom and guidance of a parent herself. However, it was her mother's poor advice that had gotten her to this point. And she dared not speak of her sins to any of the righteous women on this crusade. Somehow she must trudge forward on her own.

By tomorrow morning she needed to put all of this turmoil behind her and be strong for the children. She could not let them down at the moment of their first battle.

The next day, about the time the sun was highest in the sky, Randel led the children to a ridge overlooking what would be the site of their first battle. Lady Honoria and Sir Ademar had led the women to a similar ridge slightly farther to the south. A vast valley spread before them with a large walled prison fortress tucked in the center. Beyond it on the next rise lay a village—an enemy village.

As they lined up the horses, they took the opportunity to

drink deeply from their skins of water. The entire army of crusaders—Englishmen, Tripolians, and Cyprians alike—had pushed hard all morning to get here without being detected.

Waking and packing before the dawn, they had moved hard and fast from the southern border of the crusader-held area of Tripoli into the Saracen territory. These mountains had once been held by the Europeans, but they were overtaken some twenty years earlier during the time of the legendary Saracen leader, Saladin. Now, through a tenuous peace agreement with their fellow Moslems, the minority Druze Moslem group, who mixed Islam with several older religions, held the southern portion of the Shouf Mountains, the city of Beirut, and the prison before them.

Randel watched as their troops moved stealthily and quietly down the hill toward the sprawling prison, which reportedly held many of the Europeans caught during the push to take back the Kingdom of Jerusalem during the last attempt in 1217.

His sword hand twitched. He remembered well the battle fever that overtook a man as danger grew near. A part of him wished to be following the army down the hillside. But war did dark, horrible things to a man's psyche, and he was still recovering from the battle at Gravensworth Castle.

He yet kept Humphrey nearby each night to wake him in case he began screaming in his dreams. Only once had he frightened the children in his care, but they had managed to make a joke of it. He supposed there was some benefit in having an older, less naïve boy among the group.

And although Randel might miss out on some valuable battle experience this day, he would be gaining leadership experience instead. He had been trusted not only with protecting the children, but with communications and distance defense as well. If anything went wrong, he and Sir Ademar would need to think fast and set matters straight.

"Sir Randel." Rosalind rode up beside him. "Perhaps now you can tell us of the plan."

"Of course." He alone had been trusted with the details, but now that the moment was upon them, it was for the best that everyone be apprised.

"As I am certain you deduced, the crux of the plan for this first attack is stealth and speed. With any fortune, the Saracens have no reason to suspect our approach. We do not wish to turn this into a full-scale war, for the enemy has hundreds of supportive cities at their backs, and we have only the Mediterranean at ours, with most of the crusader troops currently occupied in Egypt."

Their army, which had swelled to over five hundred men with the addition of the Tripolian and Cyprian troops, should be able to take a prison, but they were no match for the huge armies native to this land. Not at all like when the tens of thousands of Europeans had flooded to this area like a swollen river of people in the early days of the crusades.

Randel gazed down at the prison as he spoke. "So we must strike quickly. They keep a full troop of guards at this prison fort to help protect the area, but to our knowledge, there are no large Saracen armies within fifty or sixty miles of here. There is one sizeable village about a half mile to the east. But unless a guard escapes, there is no reason to suspect they will find us out and send reinforcements."

"So this should be easy." Jervais sat back in the saddle with an arrogant grin.

Randel glared at the boy. "War is never easy. Hundreds of things might go wrong. We might have underestimated our enemy. We might have been monitored by spies. There could be traitors among us. We must be ready for anything."

"So what is our part?" Philippe asked from his place next to Sapphira. He had decided to join their special troop to help guard her rather than heading into the thick of battle, although he seemed well trained and bursting with courage.

But Randel was happy to have him, and with Philippe, Humphrey, Rosalind, and some of the children who had grown quite adept at fighting, he had not felt it necessary to ask for more guards to watch over them. They should be safe enough on their ridge.

"Our part is mostly to support in prayer," Sapphira answered Philippe's question with confidence.

"Of course," Randel said. "We will pray. I have done my study of these crusades, and I believe some of the most successful battles were supported by troops assigned specifically to prayer. Sapphira, would you like to lead us when the time comes?"

"I would be honored."

He continued, "But we must also be at the ready for whatever might occur. Particularly with archery support. We are in an excellent position here."

"They are getting close," Garrett whispered, as if worried he might reveal their position.

Sadie stared straight ahead and nodded stoically. "I am ready."

"We are all ready," Rosalind confirmed.

"One more thing," Randel said. "We are not to be heroes. If matters do go amiss, we will meet up with Lady Honoria's troop and rush back to crusader-held territory. It will be our duty to get word to Tripoli if, heaven forbid, the others fall into enemy hands. And once the battle is over, we will help tend the wounded."

If at all possible, the children grew more serious as the weight of their responsibility washed over them. But they could not even begin to comprehend the heavy weight Randel carried. For he alone of this group understood the reality of war, and he would do anything in his power to keep them safe. He could not, would not, fail again.

Glancing across a shallow ravine, he squinted to better see Lady Honoria's troop. Sir Ademar would keep them safe, and many of her women were quite capable with the bow. Plus Father Andrew and two of the lesser knights accompanied them. He spotted Jocelyn, looking misplaced in this weighty situation.

Out of nowhere, the memory of his shocking kiss with Rosalind washed over him. But there was no time to think of romance now, and he was somewhat surprised to realize he had not thought of it all morning, even with Rosalind at his side. He had thought of her simply as a trusted comrade. Thank goodness, for he would need reliable allies this day.

He assessed his troop one last time, even as foot soldiers began to stealthily spread through the nearly barren valley below.

Meanwhile the knights galloped full speed toward the prison entrance about a furlong away. With any fortune, by the time the guards inside saw them, they would already be battering down the door. They did not want a siege situation. Rather, they wished to overtake the place before the enemy was prepared. But already Randel saw a frantic scurry within the outer walls of the prison.

They had been spotted, and Saracen guards flooded the courtyard of the prison. Again his sword hand twitched to join the battle, but again, he turned his thoughts to his own mission.

Chapter 14

Rosalind gasped as she watched the crusaders thundering toward the prison and the enemy preparing to face them. But she could do nothing about any of that. And so she surveyed her own troop. They looked impressive in their crusader surcoats on their fine steeds.

Only Randel, Philippe, and Humphrey wore the heavy, encumbering chain mail of a knight, but they all sat at the ready. Eyes determined. Weight shifted forward on their horses. Even Lillian and Brigitte, the most girlish of the females, appeared intense and focused with their bows and quivers strapped across them.

Sapphira, the slenderest and frailest of them all, seemed to be imbued with some celestial power as she began to lead them in the Lord's Prayer. The others took up the chant with a sense of urgency, and Rosalind joined them.

After several minutes of prayer, Rosalind dared to look again at the frightening sight below. A group of soldiers were battering the gate with a giant cedar trunk, and it seemed the doors were buckling beneath the weight. Apparently the enemy had not had time to reinforce them, although a crowd of men provided counterweight at the other side, and she saw others running toward the doors with support beams.

A few of their men climbed up ladders and quickly overtook the guards who had been standing watch on the walls, but again, more seemed to be moving that way.

At that moment, the huge cedar trunk shattered the gates with a reverberating crash that could be heard clear across the valley. That sound awoke something deep within Rosalind. A fierce exhilaration she had never experienced before. Her pulse thudded hard, and her blood seemed to race through her veins at an astounding speed.

It jolted her to her core. All fear melted away. She felt oddly tethered to the world around her, every sense awakened to high alert. Time seemed to slow. This must be it. The battle fever she had heard of. And in that moment she understood.

The children's prayers around Rosalind took up an even louder volume, a greater fierceness, for others must have sensed it as well.

Knights poured into the prison gates, and soldiers continued scrambling over the walls. The courtyard was filled with guards now, and as the knights could only enter a handful at a time, many of them tumbled from their horses and fell to the ground.

But the enemy guards were not wearing armor. They did not have shields or horses, and soon the tide seemed to shift.

Rosalind pressed her hands tighter together and continued to shout her prayers. At this distance she could not see blood, could not spy the horrid sort of injuries they had been warned to be prepared for. But she could watch the general ebb and flow of the battle. Their crusader forces now seemed to be taking the upper hand, and hundreds were yet awaiting to reinforce them from outside the fortress walls. Men were moving across the court-yard now and beginning to break through to the actual prison.

Surely within moments a new flood of prisoners would be freed to help with the battle from within.

And just when she thought their cause was secure, Sapphira shrieked from down the line. "Sir Randel, look!" She stood in her stirrups and pointed to the far distance.

A giant cloud of dust headed their way from the Druze village beyond the fortress.

The soldiers on the ground had no way of seeing it, for it would be blocked from their view by the broad prison walls.

"Dear God in heaven, no!" slipped from Sapphira's lips, even as she pressed her hand against them.

She must not show fear, could never despair. She must remain strong for the rest of them. But what could she do to help? What could the dust cloud mean, except that many men from the city were rushing their way to support the enemy?

Even the women on the other ridge likely could not see the threat approaching. At least not yet.

Ice-cold fear sliced through her. All this morning she had managed to keep it at bay, but now the truth struck her all over again. Hundreds could die. Her friends, her sister, and now dear Philippe, all because of her vision. Her so-called gift, which on most days she doubted she even wanted.

But thanks be to God, Randel took over, even while she stood frozen in the stirrups.

"We must warn them. Humphrey, Philippe. Go. Go now, and go fast."

By the time he had uttered the final words, the two oldest, bravest boys in their armor upon their large war-horses were already crashing down the hill.

A sick lump settled its way into Sapphira's belly—different, more soul crushing, than the shiver of fear that had struck her moments ago. As Philippe rushed into danger, she felt as if a piece of her went with him.

How? When did that happen? Surely it was just that she had come to lean upon his support. She sat down in her saddle now. Felt her body withering, crumpling, beneath the weight of this war. And this was only the first battle.

She closed her eyes. No, this was not right. Of course she could never do this in her own strength. None of them could. Chants from her visits to the convent of St. Scholastica came back to her. A desire welled up within her to sing them. To surround this battle with sounds of praise. But she had not thought to teach them to the other children. A wretched failure on her part.

"My grace is sufficient for thee: for my strength is made perfect in weakness."

The words floated up from that place deep within her, although she had lost her way for a moment. They came as if they were not conjured by her own devotion, her own prayers. Rather as if they were given as a free gift. And then she felt more words welling up.

"For when I am weak, then I am strong."

That was it. Within her mind, the two simple lines began to morph into a lyrical chant. She prayed through them three times, loud and clear, before the others caught on and joined her.

The cloud yet thundered closer and closer, and the shapes of men on horses became clearer and clearer.

Sir Ademar galloped toward them. "Quick thinking, Sir Randel. We did not see them at first, but when the young men went flying down the hill, we spotted the source of the trouble."

"I think they will reach them in time."

Sapphira did not stop the chant, but she lowered the volume that they might better hear their instructions.

"Keep praying." Sir Ademar waved to them. "It is working.

But move down the hillside into archery range and ready your arrows. Whichever side of the prison they pass by on, we must offer support. I love you, son," he called to Garrett, with what could well be his final farewell.

Garrett nodded bravely.

Then Sir Ademar hurried back to the women under his care on the other ridge.

They all continued the chant as they moved their horses carefully, stealthily closer. They were more exposed now. But looking down the line, Sapphira saw that they all remained focused and determined. She had thought some of the flightier girls might have floundered. But they appeared ready.

A special sort of charge. A certain hum and crackle. Odd little shimmers of light seemed to surround them.

Sapphira found the courage to look for Philippe and Humphrey. They had made their way down the hillside and were swallowed into the vast throng of the army. Which, in the next moments, turned outward in two directions as if preparing for the new threat.

The riders from the Druze village were nearly to the prison now, but approaching from the rear. They parted in two directions. There were more than she might have expected. Perhaps as many as two hundred, although it was hard to say. How had they known? Had someone betrayed them? But it mattered not now. Soon half the enemy reinforcements would pass their way.

"At the ready," Sir Randel called.

Finally, she silenced their prayer. She pulled out her bow and notched an arrow in the string. Thank goodness Rosalind had taught them all so well. As yet they were somewhat hidden by small scraggly trees and a bit of brush. But Randel led them yet closer so that they might fire without impediments.

Sapphira tensed her muscles and pulled back her string. The men rushing helter-skelter about the side of the prison did not seem to look up and notice them, although they were not far off. She could make out individual warriors now, fierce with their baggy trousers and native head wraps. They wore no armor. Were likely just the regular men rallied at the last moment from their fields and businesses.

Yet she must do this thing. All of them must, before their own men were destroyed. Before they could reach Philippe or Humphrey or any of their soldiers. They had come this far, and there was no turning back now.

"Ready, aim," called Randel, "fire."

Sapphira pointed her arrow to the center of the mass thundering their way; she did not focus on faces, only the threatening mob, and she let her arrow fly. Then she reached back and grabbed the next arrow and repeated, again and again, just as she had been taught. Until not a single projectile remained.

Finally she paused to survey the aftermath. It seemed that perhaps a fourth of the men had been taken out by the arrows before they ever reached the crusader army. That meant dozens of their soldiers might be spared.

The knights and well-trained soldiers appeared to be quickly mowing down the group of villagers. Looking to the south, she could see that Honoria's women had admirably dispatched with a good portion of the enemy fighters as well, and their soldiers were taking care of those who remained.

Sapphira took up the prayer again, but something had shifted. She could sense it. For a moment they had been in true danger. But now she felt a peace, an assurance deep within.

The battle would be theirs.

Her thoughts turned to Philippe. There was no way to find him in the midst of the throng, and she did not sense the same peace and rightness when she pondered his name. While the others continued their chant, she quietly turned her prayers to Philippe alone. The boy who had not been afraid of her gift.

The boy who had made her feel so safe and so treasured. Who had showered his affections and compliments upon her in a way her tough, coldhearted sister had never thought to.

If the battle was won but Philippe was lost, would it even be worth the while?

Of course it would, she told herself. Today they would fulfill the call of God and free the prisoners. She must think like a warrior, a leader. Except she was not at all sure she believed herself.

Not long after, Sapphira again leaned forward on her horse. The battle was now over, but this time she anxiously awaited any report from the front. Sweat beaded on her forehead and trickled down her back in the searing afternoon sun. Her horse flicked its ear and tossed its head, chasing away a buzzing fly. She pressed her face into its neck despite the heat, and drank in its soothing, familiar scent. Not only did she fear for Philippe's safety, but for the fathers of many of the children, and even for Humphrey, pest or not.

"They will be fine, just you wait and see," said Garrett gently from beside her.

"And if they are not, you must not blame yourself," Sadie whispered from close to her other side.

"Why ever would she . . ." Then looking closely at Sapphira's face, Rosalind seemed to realize. "Oh, dear, dear Sapphira, you must not take such a burden upon yourself. Every person on this crusade made their own decision, of their own volition."

Of course Sapphira knew that, in her head, but a part of her would simply not be convinced. That assurance she had felt deep in her spirit yet warred with emotions that were weighed down by such a heavy sense of responsibility. They had all begged Randel to let them proceed to the valley now that matters had settled. But he had only allowed them to go as far as the path to meet with the ladies and Sir Ademar, who had insisted they wait until he assessed the situation.

That had been nearly an hour ago, and with each passing minute, Sapphira's shoulders tensed into tighter and tighter knots, despite how many times she whispered to herself to have faith.

"Sapphira, please tell me you do not take the pressure of this crusade upon yourself." Rosalind pulled her horse closer and peered at Sapphira with concern etched across her features.

Sapphira pressed her lips together.

Sadie laid a hand upon Sapphira's back. "She will not lie just to please you, Rosalind. You must realize that by now."

Rosalind grimaced but seemed not to know what else to say.

"They will be fine," said Garrett again, taking Sapphira's hand this time.

She smiled. Garrett had avoided her for much of the trip, choosing the company of the boys instead, but her stalwart childhood playmate understood that she needed him in this moment, even if their changing bodies had created a new shyness between them.

At long last a few horsemen broke away from the mass of humanity in the valley and headed up the hillside toward them. She made out Sir Ademar with his brown beard. And then Humphrey with his head of dark curls leaning heavily against his horse. Then finally, yes, a knight removed his helmet and she spotted Philippe's blond hair and even spied his incorrigible grin.

She blew out a long deep breath she had not known she was holding. Her muscles began to unknot. At last, all would be well. Not that she wished to hear of death tolls among the soldiers, but if the boys were safe, she could survive this.

However, as they came closer, her feelings shifted once again. For Humphrey gripped his side. His face appeared pale and his lips tinged blue, as if he were freezing upon this hot day.

Chapter 15

With a kick, Randel thrust his horse forward down the hill. "Is he well?" he shouted, but was still too far off for them to hear.

Sir Ademar lifted his hand and gestured for the rest of them to proceed.

Randel arrived first, and despite the lad's haggard appearance, Humphrey managed a weak smile.

"I did it, Sir Randel. I survived my first battle." But he looked halfway to death's door.

Randel shot a questioning glance to Ademar.

"He lost much blood, but we've staunched the flow. And the wound itself seems clean and not too deep. I believe he shall heal. He just needs time to regain his strength."

Randel gripped tightly to the reins and closed his eyes for a moment as relief washed over him. Sending the boys into the fray had been the right decision, he knew that and had reminded himself again and again over the past excruciating hour, but he sent up a silent prayer of thanks that they had not paid with their lives.

Opening his eyes, he took a closer look at the others. Philippe was covered in dirt and blood, but the healthy glow upon his cheeks proved the blood was not his own. The commander of the Tripolian forces sat beside him, also a mess but otherwise hale and healthy. "And the rest of you?"

"We are all fine." The Tripolian commander nodded. "Our losses were not heavy thanks to that warning and the excellent archery support."

"You call this fine?" Leo displayed a slash across his cheek. "What shall the ladies think of me now?"

"I hate to admit it," Randel said, "but I fear it shall only add to your roguish charm."

Everyone shared the first chuckle after this their first battle. Randel smiled as he realized his worst fears had been allayed to the point that he might now jest. It was always an important moment when life began to return to normal. Only Sir Manfred loomed behind the crowd with a scowl upon his face, which seemed to be his singular expression.

The rest of the children approached now and made appropriate fusses over the injuries while congratulating them all. He noted that Rosalind kept her distance from Leo. Rosalind. Whatever would he do with that woman? But if today had proven anything, it was that he did indeed possess the heart of a soldier, and he wished to continue on his path to become a Templar and protect Christians in the Holy Land.

Lady Honoria nodded to the commander and to Leo. "You all did a fine job. Thank you so much for your part." She turned to Lord Rumsford. "So how do matters stand?"

Rumsford came forward, less grubby than the rest, for he had been leading the troops. "We shall not have the final reports for some time, but Sir Manfred estimates we lost about twenty men, with a similar number seriously wounded. Of course many of the soldiers have bumps and scratches, but taking all into account, a resounding victory."

"Excellent results," said Father Andrew, not wearing his syrupy smile for once. "Not long ago my brother's entire troop was lost back in our very own England."

He glanced to Randel, for the priest knew of the tragedy of Gravensworth from the confessional.

Randel nodded, although he had never before realized that Father Andrew shared a similar pain. Unease washed over him.

"I am relieved that our losses were minimal." Honoria sighed.

Taking all into account, of course, those truly were excellent results. Still, Randel's heart clenched for those who would never return home to see their wives and children. How much better to be a warrior monk, without such earthly ties.

"Some of the villagers fled," the Tripolian commander said, "but I do not think they shall cause us further trouble."

"But they will spread the word that we are here," Sir Manfred grumbled, glaring directly at Randel, as if that were somehow his fault.

"That was bound to happen eventually. We did not expect to maintain the element of surprise for long." Honoria lifted her gaze and surveyed the scene before her. She seemed to be searching for something. "Tell me of the prisoners."

Of course, her husband and cousin.

Rumsford grimaced and shook his head. "They are not here, my lady. We found about a hundred prisoners, but most are weak and sickly. It seems they have not been well fed, and disease festered in the prison. They will need time to recover before we can move onward."

"As will our injured soldiers," Ademar reached out to lay a reassuring hand on Humphrey's shoulder.

"Only one hundred, you say? I had hoped for more, especially after finding so many guards." Honoria held herself firm and straight, though Randel could see the pain in her eyes.

"The guards kept watch over the whole region. Many of the

149

prisoners have perished over the past two years, and some have been moved to the prisons near Beirut," Rumsford said. "But I am sure we will learn more as the days go on."

"So what do you advise?" Honoria asked Sir Ademar.

Ademar gestured toward the prison. "We have the perfect defensive fort right here."

"I agree." The Tripolian commander turned his horse in that direction. "I doubt the Saracens will try to regain this area. 'Tis at the very edge of their holdings. Even if they do, it would take weeks to move an army here. Most of their soldiers are occupied in Egypt, as are ours."

Honoria sat silent for a moment. Randel could only imagine her inner turmoil. But surely she did not expect to find her husband or Richard DeMontfort at the very first prison. Then again, given the divine nature of their mission, perhaps she had dared to hope.

"Let us set up camp in the courtyard and around the walls. But not inside the prison itself. At least not until we can thoroughly clean it. And isolate the prisoners until we assess their illnesses," Honoria said.

Then she turned to the women and children, who had hung back quietly listening to the official exchange. "Ladies, get your herbs and poultices ready, we have much work ahead of us. And children, watch and learn the healing arts. We all must be ready for whatever might arise."

Seemingly bolstered by her own speech, she lifted her chin again. "I thank you all for your valiant service today. We saved many of our men by exposing the enemy before they arrived. Now on to the next step. Let us keep the prayers flowing and determine to lose none of the wounded in our care."

She shifted her attention to the Tripolian commander and Leo. "And will you stay with us here?"

The commander lowered his head. "I am afraid only for a

short time, my good lady. We have found the majority of the Maronite prisoners. Though your cause is just, I am afraid we do not share it."

Leo shifted uncomfortably in his saddle. "We promised to return after this battle. We dare not anger the count."

"I dare anger him!" Philippe nudged his horse closer to the leaders of the group. "He is naught but a bully and a blowhard. We should do what is right and not worry of the consequences."

"Philippe, enough!" Leo shot a glare at his young relative. "You should not speak of the count in that manner, even if he is your own father. We shall talk of this in private."

An uncomfortable silence filled the space around them.

"Well, what are we waiting for?" Honoria started down the hillside, and her ladies followed.

"Children," Randel said, "let us proceed to our new camp."

His children. In his care. All of them safe and well. Randel was grateful for this opportunity to play the parent, for once established in his new life, he would never have the chance again.

After their long morning of travel and tense midday of battle, Rosalind spent an exhausting afternoon cleaning and preparing what had been the guards' quarters for the women and children. She wiped her moist brow, no doubt brown from a mix of dirt and sweat, and leaned on her broom as she examined the area.

Dust seemed to be everywhere in this place. With little vegetation to hold the dirt down, it filled the very air. But the room smelled fresh and appeared tidy. She supposed that was the best they could hope for. Her duties as lady's maid had rarely required such physical labor. She had been primarily responsible for keeping Gwendolyn's personal chamber neat and laundering her fine gowns.

But many of the noble women along for this crusade had no

idea where to even begin with such tasks, and so Rosalind had taken charge as everyone who was not tending the wounded, including the boys, had worked like scullery maids to make the place shine.

"That should do it, children. You can bring your packs inside. Remember that the girls are in the room to the rear and left, and the boys to the front and right."

"Keeping us as far apart as possible?" Jervais winked.

"Always."

"But Humphrey is not here." Brigitte sighed.

"For that I am sorry." Rosalind wrapped an arm about Brigitte's shoulder, which yet felt bonier than usual. "But the physician said he should be fine as long as no unexpected infection sets in. He will be well cared for."

One by one the children ventured outside, and Rosalind took a final survey of their new quarters. She had felt odd emptying the place of the belongings of the Saracens, especially the prayer rug. It seemed somehow irreverent, despite the fact that they were infidels. Rosalind had tucked it in a corner to save as a memento of this trip. She picked it up and surveyed the fine stitching and colorful pattern. Someone had put much love into making it.

But the leaders of their group wished for as many of the troops to stay inside the walls as possible, and as they did not wish to use the disease-ridden prisons—except for their own newly taken prisoners—some had been assigned to the garrisons while others would camp in the courtyard. Only a portion of the foot soldiers of the Cyprians and Tripolians, who would be leaving soon, camped beyond in the valley.

With the prayer rug under her arm, she headed out to fetch her own belongings. That surly Sir Manfred growled at her as she passed him by. No doubt he disapproved of the prayer rug, but she held little regard for the man's opinions.

Along the way to the horses, a familiar voice called her name.

"Rosalind, Rosalind, please wait. I wish to speak to you." Leo jogged toward her across the bustling courtyard. He took her hand and pulled her into the shadow of one of the buildings.

"What is it now, Leo?"

"It is nothing like that. You need not sound so leery." He grinned at her, then winced and pressed a hand to the inflamed cut upon his cheek.

She could not help but feel compassion for the fellow. He had come along to aid them, after all. "You should have that taken care of."

"In good time. It is only a scratch, and many are still in dire need of medical attention."

She smiled. He was a good-hearted sort, even if an irrepressible rogue. "What did you wish to say?"

"I just wished to apologize that we must leave so soon. Philippe and I tried to convince the commander otherwise, but he was insistent that we do as the count instructed."

"No apology necessary. I understand."

"I just did not want you to think . . ." He raked his fingers through the thick waves of his hair.

"You did not wish me to think it had anything to do with me rebuffing your romantic advances," she finished for him.

He took a deep breath. "Exactly. I might not like that you came here previously committed to another, but I want you to know that I would never seek to punish you over such a petty matter."

"You know, there are other single European women along. And some of them have blue eyes."

"Yes, I met a few lovely ladies just last evening, although might you explain why some call them she-wolves?"

Rosalind giggled, feeling at ease with him again. "Just use caution and sound judgement with that lot. Several are quite on the prowl for a husband."

"Well, I have no complaints there."

"In truth, most of them are nice enough. Just beware of Jocelyn."

"I came to that conclusion on my own." He reached over and tapped the rolled rug beneath Rosalind's arm. "Do you know what this is?"

"Yes. We know little of Moslem culture, but even we have heard about their prayer rugs."

"Moslems pray five times every day. One cannot help but admire such devotion. But I do not think the Druze recite the prayers or use the prayer rugs, so perhaps there were other Moslem forces here to support them."

"I do not understand how the Druze differ from the other sects."

"To be honest, no one knows much about them. The Sunnis and Shiites differ on issues of Mohammad's successors and certain finer points of doctrine. But it seems the Druze mix in a number of other ancient religions with Islamic teachings. They are very secretive about their beliefs. Their fellow Moslems do not consider them to be Moslems at all."

"I suppose that is not so different than our Christian sects." She shook her head. "It always befuddles me that we began these crusades to support our brothers in the Byzantine church, and then turned on them and took their lands in the fourth crusade, claiming they were not true enough Christians."

Leo half chuckled. "'Tis funny yet 'tis not. Rome is fickle—that no one can deny." He nodded toward the rug. "Did you pause to wonder if the owner died today?"

Rosalind pressed her lips together and nodded. "Likely he did. Only a small percentage were imprisoned, and from what we could see on the ridge, few of the enemy fighters fled."

"What do you plan to do with the rug?"

"We gave most of their possessions to the soldiers to do with as they wished, but I could not part with this."

He nodded. "It is good that you honor your fallen enemy."

"Thank you."

"I enjoyed our time together, Rosalind."

"I did as well. And I so appreciate all you taught me about this people and this land."

"I shall miss you when I leave."

"And I you," she said, realizing it was true. His romantic pursuit aside, Leo had been a good friend.

He gave her a small bow. "My lady."

She just shook her head at his persistence in using the incorrect address. "If you insist."

Leo offered one last irrepressible grin and walked away.

Once he was gone, Rosalind could not help but wonder. If she had been open to a relationship with him, might he have fought harder for her cause?

But it did not matter. She was no longer a young woman who would sacrifice what was right for what was expedient. The last time she had chosen expediency at the prompting of her mother, it had nearly destroyed her. She was learning and growing and would never make such a mistake again. No, her resolve to remain single aside, she did not love Leo in that way, and she could not pretend she did merely to court favor with the powerful man.

In a few days, two-fifths of the soldiers would return to Tripoli, and their English troops would be left to press deeper into foreign territory alone. It pained her to think she might have prevented that, but if indeed God had called them on this crusade, their job was only to remain faithful.

Victory would depend upon Him.

Chapter 16

By their second night at the prison in Jezeer, life was falling into a new sense of normalcy. Sapphira leaned her head against Sadie's shoulder and gazed into the flickering campfire. It was nice to have a friend, a sister almost. Her own sister had always been more of a mother to her.

They all had worked hard over the last days to tend the wounded, bury the dead, and prepare their temporary home. Sapphira's muscles ached in ways that she had not experienced during her training upon the ship. But she felt great satisfaction in her hard work and all that they had accomplished.

Already the former prisoners were rallying with a new glow to their cheeks as they spoke wistfully of home, and most of the wounded were well on the mend. Sapphira had learned much about healing from the ladies of the group. Though it broke her heart that men had been injured due to her vision, it mitigated her guilt to be actively assisting the injured, and she never would have expected to be so enthralled by the healing arts. She could hardly wait to learn more.

Philippe grinned at her from her left. He took her hand and pressed a quick kiss against the back of it before letting it go.

Sapphira repressed a smile and tucked her face deeper into Sadie's safe and sturdy shoulder.

Sadie snorted, but then another giggle from farther away caught Sapphira's attention.

Rabia, the young daughter of one of their guides, covered her mouth and giggled some more.

Sapphira sat up straighter and motioned to her. "Rabia, come and join us."

Rabia offered a polite little bow. "Oh, no, I could never impose upon your hospitality." The girl's French was a bit stilted and heavily accented, but overall it was quite good.

"You are welcome anytime."

"Thank you, but I must take this water to my father." She lifted her bucket higher for them to see.

"Might I ask why you laughed?" Sapphira said.

Rabia shuffled her foot a bit. "I was surprised. Unmarried boys and girls do not touch in my culture. But it was funny to see your reaction."

Philippe chuckled. "She is a bit of a shy one."

"Not shy, just reserved," Sapphira corrected.

Rabia pulled her Moslem head scarf tighter around her face, as if for protection from such foreign ways.

"Someday I would love to hear the story of how your family came to be a guide for the crusaders." Sapphira tossed out the suggestion as if tossing crumbs to a frightened bird in hopes of luring it closer.

And it worked. Rabia, with her fathomless dark eyes and tan skin, took a few steps in their direction. "That is simple. We are of the Sufi Moslem faith. There are very few of us in this area, and our lives were threatened. The crusaders have offered us safety in exchange for our assistance, for we know this land quite well. And we have discovered that we have more in common with them than we might have expected."

"Well, now you must certainly come and tell us your stories sometime," Sapphira said.

"Perhaps another night." Rabia offered a hesitant smile, and Sapphira returned it. Then Rabia scurried off.

"I could have told you about her family," Philippe said. "They have been with us for many years. They are quite trustworthy. We never would have brought them otherwise."

"But it is so much more interesting to hear it from her own lips."

At that moment, Rosalind, Randel, and the rest of the children came and joined them. "There you all are." Sapphira had an idea she wished to share with them.

As they sat, Jocelyn, dancing with a sheer Oriental scarf at a distance in the firelight, called out, "Come back. Sir Randel. The fun is only starting." But Randel paid her no heed.

"It seems the Cyprians brought wine to celebrate the victory, and matters have gone quite wild," Sir Randel said. "Jocelyn's dancing has passed the point of appropriateness, and Rumsford, along with about half of the soldiers, is quite intoxicated. We thought we would all be better off over here."

"I suppose we should not judge them for celebrating. It has been a difficult few months to get here." Rosalind sat down. "But I don't think Honoria is pleased, and we didn't want to be a part of it."

"And that Sir Manfred fellow looks as if he wishes to strangle you," Jervais said to Randel. "Whatever did you do to him?"

"I have no idea." Randel shrugged.

"Sir Manfred hates everyone," Garrett said. "'Tis just his way, but he is an excellent soldier. He served under my father back home."

"Well, I am glad everyone is here. I had been hoping to catch you all at once." Sapphira patted her knees to get their attention. "And what I have in mind will be a nice respite from the carousing. I want to teach you all some of the songs I learned while visiting the convent of St. Scholastica. It did not occur to me before the battle, but there are several places in the Old Testament when praise is employed as a part of warfare."

"Rosalind has a beautiful voice." Randel gripped Rosalind's shoulder, his admiration obvious to them all.

"I love to sing!" Lillian said.

"What of you boys?" Randel asked. "We know that Garrett can play a drum."

"I can sing a fair bit." Jervais shuffled his foot back and forth with false modesty.

"And Garrett has the voice of an angel," Sapphira said, for he used to sing to her when they were younger.

"Thank you so much." Garrett grimaced. "I was going to keep that fact to myself."

"Well, I think it is wonderful." Rosalind mussed Garrett's wavy brown hair. "This is something we shall do together. 'Tis like praying, only prettier."

"Precisely!" Sapphira smiled, glad that they were accepting her suggestion so readily.

"And while we're learning new things," Sadie said, "I've been meaning to ask Randel and Rosalind if they ever learned the secret bird calls used as a code by the Ghosts of Farthingale Forest."

Rosalind laughed. "No, but I heard of them from Lady Gwendolyn."

"Indeed I did." Randel sat down by the fire now. "We used them to excellent effect when rescuing the Lady Merry, and then again when we needed to stand up to the council and stop Sir Warner from attacking the city."

"So what do you say? Shall we teach them?" Sadie beamed with excitement.

"That is a most excellent idea." Rosalind took a seat beside Randel and gave him a playful slap on the arm. "And it reminds me of your Syrian serin. In all the excitement I had nearly forgotten. Have you seen one yet?"

"Not yet."

"Do you know what sound it makes?" she asked.

"My grandfather never mentioned it."

"Then we must determine to find out and add it to our secret calls." Rosalind laid her hand upon his shoulder companionably.

Sapphira always enjoyed seeing them together. That must be how a happy married couple appeared. She had never really had much opportunity to observe that with her parents deceased so soon and her sister's husband away in the Holy Land.

Randel nodded. "Interesting. The serin's call could be a special battle strategy just for us."

"Rabia might know the sound it makes," Sapphira said.

She glanced at Philippe again, and he was smiling warmly at her as always. "I cannot wait to learn your songs, Lady Sapphira."

"I cannot wait to learn the birdcalls." Garrett hopped from foot to foot with anticipation.

"Is there an owl call?" asked one of the twins.

"Indeed there is," Sadie said. "A barn owl."

And so they all settled in for a pleasant evening of learning and playful teasing. When Philippe reached over and took Sapphira's hand, she did not jerk away. For he would be leaving all too soon, and she still had much to unravel about her feelings for him.

On this, their third day in Jezeer, Randel watched the children working hard at their sword training once again. Though the Tripolians would be leaving on the morrow, Philippe insisted he would stay with them. And so he had offered to train the children in special sword techniques used by their army and particularly helpful against the Saracens' curved weapons.

Randel crossed his arms over his chest. Philippe seemed to have matters in hand. He was well on his way to making himself invaluable to their troop, as he no doubt hoped to do in his quest to remain with the lovely Sapphira, who had clearly captured the young man's heart.

Rosalind sat near the girls, awaiting her turn to spar with Philippe. They had put off discussing their disastrous kiss for far too long. The children would be fine without them for a few moments.

He walked to her and squatted down beside her, tugging at the sleeve of her tunic. "Might I borrow you for a while?"

"Borrow me?" She turned and smiled. "Well, I suppose you must ask the girls that question."

"Go." Sadie gave her a shove. "Philippe is doing a fine job. I'll assist if he needs any help. You two deserve a break."

Randel stood and offered Rosalind a hand to help her up, then just as quickly released it. He led her across their practice field, which lay to the north of the prison, and directed her toward the shade of a gnarled tree. It offered them a comfortable and semi-private place to sit.

Perhaps it would be better to take her somewhere that they could truly be alone, but this conversation would be challenging enough without adding the temptation of more kissing to the mix. They would both be safest here.

He watched the children for a few more minutes without saying a word.

She nudged him with her shoulder. "Did you wish to speak to me about something?"

He lowered his head and shook it as he chuckled. "I did, but now I find it rather hard to begin."

"Is it about the . . ." Now Rosalind faltered.

He swallowed. "The kiss."

"I thought we had put it behind us." She bit her lip.

"Yes. And I want us to go forward with our friendship as if nothing is amiss."

She nodded, letting her lip slip back through her teeth. "I think we have managed to do so these last few days."

"We have. Quite admirably. But the kiss brings up a related issue. A deeply personal issue I have been meaning to discuss with you for some time."

Rosalind sighed. "We do tend to keep our conversations to light pleasantries. 'Tis not that I don't trust you . . ."

Then they both sat in silence again for a few moments.

Finally Randel blurted the issue that had been pressing upon his mind. "I plan to remain here and become a Templar. After we complete our mission, of course. I would not abandon you all. I should have told you earlier, but I do not wish the children to know. Not yet."

Her head snapped up, and her eyes registered shock. "A Templar? As in a warrior monk?"

"Yes. That is why I shall never marry. And why I had no right to kiss you so."

"Please do not apologize for the kiss again. And you do not owe me an explanation—although I'm glad you told me about your plans. I want us to be true friends and not to feel we must hide things from each other."

She clasped her hands and rubbed them together. "But a Templar? Randel, are you certain? I have come to notice that while you are quite adept at warfare, you have a gentle heart and you take hurting others rather hard. What draws you to it so?"

Her words stung him, although he knew she did not mean them in that way. They rang too similar to the reasoning he had heard throughout his life.

"I told you I had a falling-out with my parents. They wished me to join the church, but I have always wanted to be a knight. Finally, with this decision, I found a path that might please us all."

She stared at him quizzically for a few moments. "I am not certain that I see you as a priest either, but you are intelligent and very sincere in your beliefs. Perhaps it would be more fitting. Are you sure about this plan to be a Templar?"

So many thoughts warred within him, but he had said too much already. He steeled himself against further questions. "I am sure."

"Jocelyn shall be disappointed." Rosalind nudged him playfully.

"Thank goodness I have not seen her all morning." Randel would be perfectly happy if he never saw that woman again.

"She always sleeps late, especially after a night of carousing. I assume the Tripolian and Cyprian soldiers enjoyed the show."

"They all shall no doubt be following us home to Europe," he chuckled.

"Or kidnapping the she-wolves to marry them and keep them here."

"You see, there are advantages to being a monk. But what of you?" he asked, staring deep into the pools of her blue eyes. For so long he had put off this question, but now that he had shared his own reason, he wanted to know. "Why do you not wish to marry?"

She looked away over her shoulder as she answered. "I made some horrid mistakes with Sir Hugh." Her voice grew breathy as she spoke and faltered completely for a moment before she whispered, "I no longer deserve marriage and family."

He reached over and gently pulled her chin back toward him. He was not shocked, for he had already suspected something along those lines. Rosalind was a passionate young woman, and she must have fallen to Hugh's seduction, but she had a good and pure heart beneath it all.

"That is ridiculous," he said. "Whatever you have done, God can forgive and restore you. He would not wish you to consider your life ruined."

"But what man would want a woman so damaged? I do not wish to enter a marriage under false pretenses."

He tucked a stray strand of hair behind her ear with all the brotherly kindness he could muster. "Rosalind, I realize this is a somewhat useless point, but *I* still think you worthy of marriage."

"You do not understand. I have not told you everything." She bent over and hid her face against her knees.

He waited to see if she might say more, but it was clear she did not wish to proceed. And he would not push her, for he saw the pain that even this discussion had stirred. Truth be told, he had not shared the full depths of his sorrow either. "If you ever wish to share your burden, I am here for you."

"Thank you," she whispered with tears choking her voice. "'Tis good to have a friend."

In that moment he almost wished he could be more. That he could prove to her how worthy she was. How capable she was of love. What a perfect mother she would make.

But that honor must go to someone else. And perhaps not for quite some time, as she was not yet ready. For now he would pray that her heart would heal, and that she would be prepared for love when the right fellow came along.

Chapter 17

"Wait here," grumbled a battle-scarred man in broken French.

I glanced about the dark alleyway in this Druze village, not so far from the prison of Jezeer. My heart thudded wildly in my chest. The moonlight barely reached into this shadowy place. Danger lurked around every corner. Enemies resided in each home. But I would not turn back.

This was my chance. The one I had been waiting for throughout this long and worthless crusade. I finally had concocted the perfect plan to bring Randel the most shame and humiliation possible, and likely see him killed in the process. But even if he was not killed, his life would be shattered, and he would never dare show his ugly face in England again.

I pressed myself against a stone wall and gathered my courage. I had faced my brutish father on countless occasions—stood up to him to protect my brother, although in the end I had not been able to save him from Randel Penigree. Surely I could face whatever this night might bring.

Another Saracen rounded the corner and held out his hands. "There you are, my friend." He was surrounded by the fellow

I had sent to fetch him and several burly guards, one of whom held a torch that sent a flickering glow across the area.

This new man, supposedly the chieftain of the village, appeared relaxed and welcoming. "I hear you have important information."

"I do. You shall not regret meeting with me."

"Why do you wish to betray your people? I see your skin is as white as any European, and your French flawless."

"I came on this journey for my own purposes. I do not wish for you to harm my people. Merely thwart my enemy and send the rest of them on their way. They do not belong here. In truth, I am not terribly attached to the Christian faith. Some might feign devotion, but do we not all just want to thrive and serve our own purposes? I believe you Saracens should have the right to live your own way in your own land."

The man stroked his long dark wooly beard. "Hmm . . . it is usually unwise to trust a traitor, but you have captured my interest. I will at least hear you out."

"This crusade his been sparked by the vision of a certain young woman. A child, really. 'Tis silly, if you ask my opinion. I believe if you capture this child along with the group of children who have traveled with her, you will do away with the heart of this mission, and the rest of them shall quickly retreat back to Europe where they belong."

"And how would I go about *capturing* them?"

Something in the Saracen's tone told me that he did not have mere capture on his mind, but I could not trouble myself with such technicalities now. I had come too far.

"We have not yet left the prison at Jezeer."

"I suspected as much, and could have confirmed this on my own."

Desperate to impress him, I spoke the first thing that came to my mind. "The Tripolians and Cyprians will be leaving on the morrow, depleting our troops nearly by half, and the prisoners are not yet recovered to full strength. Now is the perfect time to strike."

His eyes sparked with interest, and so I continued.

"I have noted that every day around midmorning the children train in the field north of the prison. They are the only youngsters with the group, and should be easy to spot. If you approach from the hillside, I believe you could take them with little resistance. The rest of the troops will be training on the far side of the prison at that time."

"Hmm . . . Also outside of the walls?"

I did not like the question. I had not intended to say so much, for though I did not support the crusaders' cause, I yet had friends among the group. But I could not afford to lose his trust. I swallowed hard and said, "Yes."

"And what is in this for you?" He stared into my eyes. For the first time I spotted something harsh and fierce behind his congenial smile. However, it was too late to turn back now.

"Only that you protect me and destroy my enemy. I require nothing else."

He chuckled, low and deep. "Good, for you have already given me your information, and if you had demanded payment now, I could have easily dispatched with you."

Cold fear flooded my senses, but I did not let it show upon my face. If he thought me weak, that would be the end of me. "I have not yet told you which girl, but I believe my terms are fair enough. Do we have a deal?"

He bowed. "Quite fair."

"She will be the slender one with white-blond hair and blue eyes. Her name is Sapphira."

His smile stretched even wider.

"And be sure to kill the leader of their troop. A tall, thin man with short-cropped dark hair. A Sir Randel. He's a tricky one.

This shall be of the utmost importance to your cause. Once you have the children, the rest of the English crusaders will be gone soon enough. I guarantee it."

He nodded. "It has been a pleasure doing business with you, my friend. If matters go well, perhaps we shall meet again and you shall dine in my home. I would be most honored."

"Perhaps." Although I hoped not. All I wanted was to destroy Randel Penigree and return to England just as soon as possible.

But now I couldn't help but worry. Would I bring the entire army down along with him? Nonetheless, sometimes one must do what one must, and consequences be blasted.

Surrounded by the other girls, Sapphira picked at her breakfast of fruit, cheese, and nuts as the Cyprian and Tripolian forces prepared to return home. She knew that beyond the fortress walls they were lining up in formation to leave at any moment, and the thought had stolen her always-fickle appetite away.

Philippe yet remained in the guard house with some of the boys. He hoped that somehow in the shuffle his relatives might not notice his absence. But she spotted Leo storming their way.

"Where is he?" Leo demanded of Randel without breaking his stride.

Randel just inclined his head to the guard house, and the angry man marched inside.

Not a moment later, she heard the struggle, the shouts, and then, "No. You cannot do this to me!"

Leo ducked back through the door with his smaller, fifteen-year-old relative flailing and kicking over his shoulder like a troublesome toddler.

"Stop!" shouted Philippe. "This is not fair! This is not right! It should be my decision."

Leo never faltered. Never deigned to respond. Several soldiers surrounded them now. Philippe must know he was beaten. Finally he ceased struggling.

Lifting his head, he sent a heartbroken look Sapphira's way.

"Be safe," Philippe called as they whisked him away. "Come back to me. I wish to make you my wife someday." The last words filtered to her from beyond the prison wall.

Sapphira's mouth dropped open. Though her heart ached to see him leave in such a manner, she could hardly believe he would broach the subject of marriage so soon.

Sadie reached over and patted Sapphira's hand. "I'm sorry. I know this must be hard for you."

"Oh, it is so romantic." Issobelle squealed and pressed her joined hands to her chest.

Sapphira moaned. "Do not be ridiculous."

"Right," Lillian said. "You wish to be a nun."

"Well." Sapphira felt obligated to speak the truth, no matter the inconvenience. "I confess I have had second thoughts of late. But for goodness' sake, I am only thirteen years of age. And I shall not be much older by the time we leave."

"'Tis not unheard of." Brigitte, at fifteen, tossed her yellow hair in a worldly-wise manner. "Some girls marry as young as twelve. My cousin did."

"That's ridiculous," Sadie scoffed.

"I am not 'some girls.' I would never consider marrying until I was at least eighteen. I yet have much learning and growing to do." Sapphira frowned.

"If I turned eighteen and was unwed, my mother would think me a pathetic old maid indeed." Brigitte sighed, no doubt still stinging under the loss of a chance with Humphrey.

This whole matter had been almost too much for Sapphira's heart to bear. She did not need this sort of romantic confusion at her young age. Perhaps it was for the best that Philippe had been dragged away, even if it was against his will.

"So we will be all alone in foreign territory soon." Rosalind brought the conversation back around to the true issue at hand.

She was right. Sapphira must let Philippe go and focus upon what mattered. Their mission.

"Not for long." Randel tossed aside a stick. "We are sending a troop of scouts to Beirut even now. And soon the prisoners and wounded shall be ready to move. I would say another week at most."

And then they would press onward, to the next challenge and the next battle. Without local support. Without the element of surprise. With only a few native guides to lead them.

Yes, Sapphira needed to focus upon what mattered and turn her heart from thoughts of Philippe to thoughts of God.

Rosalind awoke with the same sense of unease that had stalked her mercilessly the day before. It jolted her so suddenly from her sleep that she knew she would not return to the warm, hazy world of her dreams, although the sun was only now beginning to tinge the sky with a predawn glow.

The girls around her slept quietly. That heart-full nurturing sensation she always felt when she watched them in repose encouraged her for a moment, but it was soon crowded out by the unease once again. Perhaps it had first arrived as the full ramifications of Randel becoming a Templar had finally struck.

In the beginning she had thought only of the possible consequences for him. But as she further considered the matter, she was forced to admit that she had grown quite attached to him, and although she had never allowed herself to think in terms of marriage, perhaps the smallest part of her . . .

She did not even let herself finish the thought. Perhaps Randel was not the source of her unease after all. They were thousands of miles from home and living inside enemy territory with depleted forces. Surely that was reason enough to feel concern. Stealing from her bed, she pulled her tunic over her shift and donned her leggings. She splashed off her face with water from the basin and combed her fingers through her hair. Good enough for what she had in mind.

Rosalind headed outside and climbed the stairs to the parapet. A guard nodded her way, but otherwise paid her little heed. She looked out past the Druze village in the distance with its stone buildings. The first ring of muted sunshine met the horizon. She remained still as it crept upward and painted the sky with streaks of yellow and orange. Midnight blue seeped to lighter and brighter shades.

How amazing that wherever one might travel, the sun still circled the earth in the same way. God still held the heavens together. Some matters did not change.

A warm arm wrapped about her shoulders with such pleasant familiarity that she did not even flinch.

"I did not expect to find you here," Randel said. "'Tis a lovely surprise."

She rested her hand over his where it gripped her shoulder and stroked it with her fingers in the most natural sort of way. "I awoke with a start. I have felt uneasy this past day. Perhaps since the local forces left."

"I have not felt quite right either. We should talk to the children and address this issue in prayer."

Good Randel, with his good heart. She might not have thought of prayer, but he was precisely correct. She whispered up a prayer even then, as she stood with him watching the sun decorate the sky.

Chapter 18

Sapphira sat up with a gasp. She had been communing with God while yet in her bed when the certainty overtook her.

We are in danger. We should not be here. We must not remain!

Though the reason remained hazy, she suspected a large enemy army might be moving this way.

She threw off her covers and dashed to Rosalind, but Rosalind was not in her bed.

Not even wasting time to grab a tunic, Sapphira ran outside in her shift to search for her friend. "Rosalind! Rosalind!" she called.

It occurred to Sapphira that, now outside, it would be more natural for her to call for her own sister, but Rosalind was the name her heart shouted. The person she needed to soothe her fear. And so she called again.

In the early morning light, she finally spotted Rosalind, scurrying down the stairs from the parapet followed by Randel. Sapphira rushed their way.

A panting Rosalind grasped her by the arms. "What is it? What is wrong?"

"Danger. . . . headed this way . . . Must leave!" Sapphira had not even realized she was in such a dither until she attempted to speak.

Rosalind shot a significant look sideways to Randel.

"Slow down, please, Sapphira," said Randel.

She gathered her thoughts and started again. "I was praying when it came to me so clearly. I believe danger is headed this way. We must leave this prison, this valley. And we must do so at once."

Rosalind pulled Sapphira into her arms and shushed her, as Randel encircled them both.

"All will be well," Rosalind whispered into her ear. "We believe you, for we had sensed something was not right and were praying upon the parapet. But we must speak to your sister and the leadership council before anything can be decided."

"I shall go find them," Randel said.

Sapphira rested her head against Rosalind. Clung to her. Drank of her strength. She had begun to wish that Rosalind might be her guardian rather than her coldhearted sister. But at least she could have Rosalind as a mentor and a protector.

In a matter of minutes Randel waved them to Honoria's large tent, which had been set up in the courtyard of the prison. Rosalind yet kept an arm around Sapphira as she led her through the flap. Once inside, she faced her sister, Haverland, Rumsford, Sir Ademar, and several other noblemen. All the leaders of this crusade.

"What is it, child?" Honoria seemed perturbed with her already, and she had not yet said a word.

Stepping away from Rosalind's fortifying support and finding her courage, Sapphira spoke. "I believe danger is headed our way. I suspect it is a huge enemy army. We must leave. Hurry back to the crusader-held territory. It is our only chance. If the men are not battle ready, then let us recoup in Tripoli for a time."

Sir Manfred smirked. "I see. She misses young Philippe. How typical of a maiden."

Sapphira's mouth fell open in shock.

Sir Manfred eyed her with disdain. What was he even doing here with these esteemed leaders? He only commanded a small troop of men, but he seemed determined to gain power and position through demeaning others.

Sapphira tamped down her indignation. Her pride was not the issue here, and she could not let emotion cloud her thinking and prove them right. "Philippe is not the reason. Not in the least. You trusted my vision to bring us here, now trust me in this. If not to Tripoli, then at least to the coast, where we will have quick access to the ships."

"We trusted your *vision*," Rumsford corrected kindly but with firmness. "Did this message come to you in such a powerful, supernatural way?"

"Well . . . no. But I am well accustomed to detecting God's still small voice. As Brother Francis mentioned, it is far more reliable than any dramatic vision. And I feel so certain in my heart."

"The heart is fickle, sweet girl. 'Tis likely a bit of fear has overcome you," said Rumsford. "This place would test anyone's nerves."

"We should not dismiss her too quickly." Sir Ademar stared at her as if trying to detect something. "She has never misled us in the past."

"The Tripolians felt confident that there were no armies within traveling distance," Honoria said. "And that the Saracens will not risk a full-scale war over a few released prisoners."

"And if we wish to have any hope of meeting the crusaders from Egypt this summer in Jerusalem, we cannot afford to waste time," Sir Ademar conceded.

"You all keep mentioning Jerusalem, but it was never a part of my calling." A sick sort of dread circled in Sapphira's belly.

They credited her with being the inspiration for this crusade, but would she be held responsible when these esteemed adults steered it off course?

Her sister stiffened and leaned forward with a glare in her eye and a sharp edge to her voice. "Your call was to set the captives free. Is not the Holy City of Jerusalem being held captive by the Saracens?" Honoria pounded the table before her.

"But I did not see that! I did not feel that!" Sapphira heard her own voice growing shrill and desperate. "You must believe me. You say I am the spark of this crusade."

"My dear." Sir Ademar crossed to her and placed a soothing hand upon Sapphira's shoulder. "Though I have great respect for you, I must side with your sister. The children's crusades were led by fiery vision alone, and just look at what happened. This crusade is different, for we temper vision with wise experience and leadership. I think we should remain here and move forward as soon as possible. Not backward to Tripoli. If we lose ground now, we might never regain it."

"Is it wise leadership, or is it my battering-ram of a sister set upon her own stubborn way once again?" Sapphira slapped her hand over her mouth, unable to believe she had said as much in front of this group. She had not wanted to let emotion cloud her thinking, yet her stupid, childish nature had gotten the better of her.

Honoria bristled. "I think we can all see who is being stubborn here, and I think we can all see why we cannot let a changeable thirteen-year-old make decisions for an entire army."

General grumbles of assent came from the group.

"That is all," Honoria nodded to dismiss her.

"That is not all." Sapphira pulled herself as tall and straight as possible. "Will you not even pause to pray about this?"

"Prayer is always advisable," Father Andrew said, pressing his hands together.

Honoria pressed her fists into her hips. "I feel confident in my decision."

Though Sapphira wished to throw a royal fit, she would not be accused of behaving like a child again. She lifted her chin and forced her voice to remain calm. "At least let me take my own troop back toward the coast. Surely you will grant me authority over them, if nothing else. And we will do our best to rally the Templars at the fort near the sea to join our cause."

Finally, that seemed to break through Honoria's stubborn shield and capture her interests. She leaned one ear in toward Sapphira. "The Templars are faithful to Count Bohemond. I doubt they will support us."

"But perhaps if they hear from me in my own words. It has worked before."

Randel and Rosalind moved forward to flank her on either side. "My lady," Randel said, "allow us to do this thing. We have faith in Sapphira's ability to hear from God. If there is the smallest chance that danger is heading this way, would it not be better for the children to be long gone?"

Honoria looked to Ademar and then Haverland and shrugged.

Meanwhile Sapphira noticed silent messages passing from Rosalind to Rumsford and back.

"I see no harm," Rumsford spoke up. "If they feel strongly about this, they will only bring fear to the camp, and none of us needs that. Allow them to go on their mission. Surely they can pray for us wherever they are."

"This is true," Father Andrew said. "And fear would only serve to weaken their faith."

"But even if they rally the Templars, there are only thirty or so knights at the fortress," Haverland said.

"Thirty or so of the best trained, most highly experienced knights in all of the Outremer," Randel countered. "And if we can draw them to our cause, perhaps more Templars shall join."

"I, for one, would be happy to have Garrett safe along the coast," Sir Ademar said. "'Twas harder than I had expected to see him here during the fighting."

"True enough." Haverland relaxed from the tense and combative way he had been holding himself. "I almost wish Humphrey was well enough to travel on horseback."

Honoria twisted her mouth as she considered this. "Fine. Go. But this had better not be about that boy Philippe. I reared you better than that." She glared straight into Sapphira's eyes. Into her very soul.

"I swear it is not."

"They should take some of the guides," Ademar said.

His words reminded Sapphira of her new acquaintance. "Can we please take Rabia and her father and brothers? I should like to keep them safe with us."

Honoria shot her a warning look. "I wish to hear no more about this supposed danger. Do I make myself clear? I will send you on this mission with your requested Sufi guides, and in return, you will keep your mouth closed until you leave this place."

Hot anger filled Sapphira, threatening to burst from her chest in an unladylike bellow. But it was clear she could not protect them all. Utilizing the diplomacy she had been taught from birth, she clenched her teeth and said, "Fine. I agree to your terms."

At least she could keep her friends safe. 'Twas better than nothing. The rest would be in the hands of God.

"'Tis not fair," grumbled Brigitte as she stuffed her belongings into her pack. "We have just gotten settled here."

A part of Rosalind felt the same, but the unease plaguing her had lifted the moment the decision to leave had been finalized.

"War is not about being settled." Sadie crossed her arms over her chest. "It is about playing one's role and doing one's duty. It is about keeping one's comrades safe and defeating the enemy."

Tears slid down Brigitte's cheeks. "I realize that. But despite all our instructions, despite all our training, it did not become real until I saw Humphrey and Philippe racing down that hill toward an enemy army. 'Twas all just play and make-believe until that moment. And now I just want to stay hidden away in these walls, where we can be safe."

Issobelle gave Brigitte a squeeze from the side. "'Tis harder than any of us understood. But we fought well under pressure. Even you. Now we have been tasked with an important mission, and we must accomplish it." The younger girl seemed to lend Brigitte a bit of strength.

"I do not understand why it must be us!" Brigitte insisted, stomping her foot.

Rosalind wished she could share the real reason they were leaving, but they had promised not to stir up trouble whilst in the camp. "I cannot explain why, but I believe we will be safer by traveling to the Templar fort."

"We are always safest in the center of God's will." Sapphira tied her sack up tight. "And I believe this is what He wants for us." She pressed her lips together, clearly wishing to say more, just as Rosalind did.

But her simple words seemed to hearten all of the girls. Though they oft found Sapphira trying, they trusted her ability to hear from God. Elsewise, none of them would be on the crusade.

Rosalind could not quite register that the leaders of this crusade had dismissed Sapphira so quickly. Were they daft? Why had they not felt the same unease Rosalind had? Might God have a purpose even in their stubbornness?

She did not understand nearly enough about such matters. All she knew for certain was that she must follow God's leading in her own heart. And she thanked God that she had not been denied that right. She would take the children far away from this place. But they would be alone with little defense for the next few days. And who knew if the threat Sapphira felt so strongly might yet chase after them.

Lillian and Issobelle joined Rosalind near the door. They stood strong and straight with their bows and quivers upon their backs.

"We are ready," Issobelle said. "Good thing we left most of our fripperies on the ship."

Sadie and Sapphira strapped their swords around themselves in final preparation. Rosalind was likewise armed. And they all wore their plain tunics, for they would try to remain inconspicuous while traveling in such a small group.

Rosalind hated to leave everyone else behind. They should all be heeding Sapphira's warning and heading back to crusader-held territory. But she had no power, no authority on this trip. And Randel and Sapphira had leveraged all of theirs just to save this small group.

"Come, girls." She led them all outside into the bright sun.

Clearly the boys viewed this new adventure in a different light. The twins were bouncing about in their excitement even as their mother attempted to hug them good-bye. Not knowing the danger, she had wished to keep them with her, but the energetic duo would not miss out on the fun. Garrett and Jervais, who both sat polishing their swords, beamed with anticipation.

Garrett looked up as they approached. "We are going to visit the Templars!"

"I know," Rosalind said, attempting to smile.

Randel held extra sacks full of provisions, and their Sufi guides were preparing horses for everyone. At least they could move swiftly if needed and would not be slowed down by hundreds of foot soldiers.

Rumsford approached. For all she had thwarted his advances, the man had defended her admirably this day. She walked to him and offered him a hug. "I cannot thank you enough for your support."

He patted her back and then let her go. "I hope you know what you are doing."

"I hope so as well."

He turned to face the group. "Godspeed to all of you. Take good care of one another."

In just a moment they would ride out of this place. A small part of Rosalind hoped that they had been mistaken. That the army full of Englishmen would be fine. That they would find them still here and intact when they returned a week hence with a troop of Templars.

But the odds of that seemed impossibly small.

Chapter 19

About an hour into the journey, Randel steered the entire group beneath the shade of a lone, gnarled olive tree. They were well away from the camp, and 'twas high time to tell them the truth.

They looked to him with anticipation. For leadership, for instruction. A mixture of pale and tan faces, blue and brown eyes, males and females alike. Even their Sufi guides.

He braced himself for the speech he must deliver. "I need to share with all of you the true reason that we left. Sapphira believes she heard from God and that our army is in great danger. Rosalind and I agree with her. It was not safe in Jezeer, and so we convinced Honoria to send us on this mission."

The children gasped. Sick looks crossed their faces.

"But my father . . . " Garrett whispered.

"Our father and our mother," Lillian cried, guiding her horse closer to her twin brothers.

All playful excitement was gone from their faces now, as the boys grasped their sister's hands.

"We cannot just leave them!" Issobelle shouted. "We have to go back!"

Sapphira moved to Randel's side. "We did everything we could to warn them." She took a moment to share the specifics of her warning and their encounter with the leaders of the crusade. "I tried to convince them, and Randel and Rosalind supported me, but they would not listen."

A very flustered Brigitte pulled herself up and adjusted her hair. "Wait. If they did not believe Sapphira, then we should not despair. She might have misunderstood."

"I hope I am wrong," Sapphira said, her voice trembling, "but I do not believe I am."

Randel reached out and placed a hand on Sapphira's shoulder in a show of support.

Sadie, always stalwart and prepared, clasped her sword by the hilt. "Either way, we should stay focused and rally the Templars."

"I agree." Jervais looked ready to battle as well. "If this is true, they shall need us more than ever."

"We shall all take care of one another," Sadie said. "We can do this."

Randel nodded to them all. He watched and waited as they continued registering this challenging news.

"We felt uneasy in the camp as well," spoke up Abu-Wassim, their Sufi guide. "My daughter had a dream of an impending threat and awoke in a fright."

Rabia shyly glanced up.

"We will do all in our power to keep you safe," said the eldest son, Wassim, for whom the father had received his own title. "But we should not tarry here long. If trouble is approaching, we should be as far away as possible."

"I agree," Randel said. "Children, you are stronger than you think. You are well trained and ready to face this challenge. More than that, you are strong in the spirit, as you have demonstrated on more than one occasion. I have full confidence in this group."

Randel turned his horse and headed up the winding mountain passage. Soon they would reach the crest of this path and start down the other side.

Rosalind caught up with him. "You did well. I know I do not say it enough, but you are a fine soldier and an admirable leader."

That warmed his heart, as kind words always did, but Rosalind's most especially. Again, he felt that tug toward her. That desire to be the man she needed. To give her the love she feared. But he could not.

Finally they reached the peak of the trail. The rock wall that had enclosed them opened and allowed them to look over the expanse of valley far below them.

And that is when he saw it.

He held up a hand to halt the group. Only Rosalind shared the shocking view.

Hordes of soldiers filled the valley, at least four times more than the ones they had brought from England. Smoke rose from odd places. He could no longer spy the red flag of his homeland waving over the prison walls.

And then the barren terrain of the valley of Jezeer melted from his vision.

For a brief moment darkness seemed to engulf him. And then he was in that other place. The one he only visited in his nightmares.

Smoke surrounded him. Screams met his ears. He slashed his sword again and again. Stumbled on a slick pool of blood, although he knew not whose it might be. He was responsible for his men, his troop, this castle.

And he was failing miserably. It seemed all was lost, but he continued to fight. His enemy in the black surcoats came at him one after another. Sweat and soot filled his eyes. He could hardly see. Then, in a flash, it was no longer black before him, but the ivory and crimson of his own soldier. And before he could stop, his sword pierced deep into the man's belly.

He froze. Struggling for breath as his blood turned to ice. He watched the man collapse onto the battlement. The young face crumpling and contorting. The hazy, smoky world swirled around him.

"Randel. Randel!" Rosalind tugged at his arm hard, dragging him from that awful place.

He could not find his voice, but focused on the valley below, teeming with dark enemy soldiers much like ants mobbing food upon the ground. Each fighting to take their piece of the spoils. He felt the pull as if they fought to take a piece of his very soul.

The responsibility now fell upon him to save his entire army.

Rosalind did not understand the war that waged within Randel—only witnessed the devastating aftermath playing across his face. This was not merely about the army crowding into the valley below. That much was clear. At one point she feared he might lose his breath and all consciousness along with it. But the children were yet at his back, and they had not witnessed his panic.

For now, she must find her own courage and take charge. "Abu-Wassim," she called in a light voice. "Could you and your sons please join us? Children, stay put for a moment longer."

They did not appear entirely deceived by her ruse, but perhaps they were not yet ready to see what lay beyond, for not a single person protested.

The other adults joined her and Randel.

Abu-Wassim wiped his face with a loose end of his head wrap. "I did not expect it so soon. There must have been an army passing by as they traveled from Arabia to Egypt. Both sides have been calling for reinforcements."

"We left just in time. Allah be praised," said the elder son, Wassim.

"But look." The younger brother pointed to the valley far below. "They are not fighting. A white flag waves over the prison."

"Are you certain?" Rosalind squinted and attempted to discern the scene below her. They had traveled many miles already through the winding mountain paths. Although she suspected he was correct, she could not make out the details clearly enough.

"He has the eyes of an eagle," Wassim assured her. "He is certain."

Randel no longer appeared ready to collapse, but he remained still and quiet.

"Let the children approach," Abu-Wassim whispered to Rosalind. "It will be easier for them to comprehend if they see it for themselves."

Rosalind had not had opportunity to become acquainted with this man during their brief hours together, but she spotted peace, wisdom, and strength in his eyes. He was a father. And far more of an adult than either she or Randel. She must trust him in this. "Of course."

With a simple wave, she gestured for the children to approach. They did so with trepidation and spread out silently upon the rise. The sight before them was not unexpected but was difficult to digest, nonetheless. Sapphira pulled her horse close to Rosalind and the other adults.

"We must . . ." Sapphira's voice emerged soft and breathy, then seemed to catch in her throat entirely. She tried again. "We must pray."

Sapphira slid from her horse, and the rest followed suit. Garrett and Sadie took either side of Sapphira and clasped her hands, much as they had that day Rosalind spied them in the armory. Then the other children joined the chain of support, rounding off with Rosalind. Randel finally seemed to rally

himself and came to them as well, taking both Rosalind and
Sadie's hands and linking them all in a circle.

Only the Sufi family stood to one side. Then Abu-Wassim
fell to his knees facing east, their standard prayer posture, and
his family followed his lead and sent up petitions as well.

Rosalind knew not what to think. They did not worship the
same God. Or did they? Rosalind was not even sure. Certainly not
their Jesus. But Sapphira caught Rabia's eye and nodded her way.
Perhaps at a time like this, one should not bicker over character-
istics of the Divine. Only pour out their hearts in sincere prayer.

Sapphira began to lead their group in one of the songs she
had taught them around the fire. "'The Lord is my Shepherd; I
shall not want. He maketh me to lie down in green pastures . . .'"

As the soothing words of the psalm washed over Rosalind, she
sensed a holy presence filling their clearing upon the mountain.
It flowed over and around her with comforting warmth. And
for perhaps the first time, she understood what drew Sapphira
again and again to prayer.

In that quiet, peaceful place, she saw herself as if from a
distance and realized she had not allowed herself to feel, barely
to breathe, since the moment they looked down over the valley.
Fear should have overtaken her, despair crushed her, but she
had thought only of the children and had thus stayed in control
of her own emotions.

And now she needed no longer control them, for she sensed
her heavenly Father would take over for her in the very same
way. She need not win His approval, nor even His forgiveness
in this moment. Only rest in His love.

Sapphira switched from the song into a sincere and heartfelt
petition for their families below. Then several of the children
joined in with their own pleas. But Rosalind just rested in God's
almighty hands. A piece of her heart screamed that she did not
deserve this, yet she received it nonetheless.

Did Randel feel it too?

She squeezed his hand and peeked up into his handsome face. It had regained its color, and his breathing had steadied. But he seemed to be coming back into himself rather than lost in the presence of God.

She closed her eyes again and melted back into that heavenly sphere, resting in the calm silence that now surrounded them like the softest blanket.

Finally, she heard Sapphira draw a deep breath. They all opened their eyes and stared at their young spiritual leader. "I sense God saying the same thing He did during the battle. 'My grace is sufficient for thee: for my strength is made perfect in weakness.' I know not if Honoria followed the Lord's will for our army today, but I know those of us here are in the center of it now, and He is strong enough to redeem this situation and see us through this trial."

"I have never felt such peace," Sadie whispered in awe, speaking the words that all of them seemed to be feeling.

"Nor have I." Abu-Wassim stood to his feet and wiped a tear from his cheek. "Indeed the God you worship has been with us this day."

Bright surges of energy tingled through Rosalind. To think, that even this Sufi Moslem had sensed the hand of God. She could not begin to fathom the ramifications.

"So what do we do now?" Garrett asked.

Randel let go of her hand and stepped forward, rising again to his position of authority with a newly regained confidence. "Abu-Wassim, you know this army and this region much better than I do. Will you take charge for now?"

Abu-Wassim, with his warm brown eyes, bowed his head in humility. "I would be honored. I believe the enemy will next sweep the area to look for any stray scouts and guards. We could try to outrun them, but we have been through quite a shock. I think the wiser course would be to hide in a nearby mountain cave for the next day. Then we can slowly make our way toward the Templars, staying off the main path, of course."

Randel nodded. "I agree. If they are under attack, we cannot bring reinforcements in time. And if they are captured, as I believe and as we all hope, then we yet have time to save them."

Rosalind watched the strain pulling at Randel's features, and for the first time she understood what must have struck him in that initial instant. The fate of the English army was in their hands, and he was responsible not only for the safety of these children, but also for every soul on this crusade.

She tangled her hand through his again and gripped it hard, determined to help him carry his burden. He would not be in this alone. She was strong enough to help him shoulder this weight—along with Sapphira, and Abu-Wassim, and all the rest of them. They must do this thing.

Together.

Chapter 20

The afternoon sped quickly by as they climbed through rough rocky terrain and made camp in a cave.

Rosalind paused to glance about their new shelter. The place was large and cavernous. They'd lit only a few torches and had to hope that any smoke would be well diffused by the time it reached the opening fifty or so yards away. How she would have loved to cook a hearty meal, as they had been able to in the courtyard at Jezeer, but they had ample dry provisions to get them through these next days.

She sent heavenward a silent thanks for their Sufi guides. Her group never could have found such a place on their own. Surveying the sleeping area she had set up for the girls, satisfaction filled her—although she would be cautious to watch for the poisonous vipers of which their guides had warned them.

Surely they would be safe enough, if only for a time. The rest and peace from earlier that afternoon yet echoed through her heart, but she wondered how long it might last, for already pressure and fear were threatening to crowd it out. Those moments in God's presence had reminded her of swimming deep in the pool near her home when she was a child. So serene, so wondrous. Sparkling lights and bubbling swishes.

Yet being human, she always had to surface for air once again.

The children seemed subdued as they sat in a circle listening to Abu-Wassim telling tales of this region. He seemed to understand that what they needed more than anything was a parental figure, for all but Sadie had at least one family member at risk in Jezeer. Although she had done her best to nurture the children, they needed the steadying hand of Abu-Wassim.

Finding no other work with which to busy herself, Rosalind scooched her way into the circle between Sadie and Sapphira. Sapphira smiled and took her hand. Rosalind noted that Sapphira likewise held Rabia's hand to the other side of her. She had never expected to trust these Sufi Moslems so completely, but as Sapphira clearly felt the same, Rosalind could find no reason to second-guess her instincts.

Randel sat quietly in a shadowed corner with the armor and weapons they had brought along. As Abu-Wassim continued his enchanting tale, Randel checked over every piece of equipment. Rosalind considered joining him, but he appeared enthralled in his task, and he likely needed this time alone with his thoughts.

A scuffle in the long tunnel leading toward the mouth of the cave caused them all to freeze in silence. The men, Sadie, and Jervais stood and readied their weapons.

"It is only me," came a vaguely familiar voice from the tunnel.

Abu-Wassim and Hassan relaxed instantly, which told them all that it must be Wassim returning from his time at guard. The Sufi family spoke French well and communicated with ease.

Wassim's smiling face appeared from the dark tunnel as the flickering torches illuminated it.

"All is well?" his father asked.

They had climbed a good way from the trail, but their lookout point not far away allowed them to keep a distant eye on the passage. Wassim nodded and grabbed for a skin of water, drinking deeply before answering. "A small contingent of enemy scouts passed by but detected nothing. Hassan, can you relieve me for a time? My eyes were drifting closed in that smoldering sunlight."

Hassan jumped up and grabbed a few supplies.

"I imagine they will come back this way before nightfall, so keep a careful watch for them."

"Of course." Hassan headed out.

Wassim took another long draught of water and then said, "I did sneak in close enough to overhear one thing that caused me concern, though."

"What is it, son?" asked Abu-Wassim.

Randel joined the group.

Wassim wiped his mouth with the long rough sleeve of his woolen tunic. "One of them mentioned the girl with the white hair and blue eyes. I fear they might be looking for us specifically. How would they know about Sapphira? Do you think someone betrayed us?"

Rosalind's heart clutched in her chest, and she wrapped an arm protectively about Sapphira.

Randel's eyes squinted in contemplation. "Surely not. Perhaps the story has reached them from Tripoli. Tales of our arrival must be spreading."

Sapphira bit her lip but said nothing.

Randel turned to her and smiled briefly. "There is no need to fear. We had already planned to stay out of sight. And they cannot know anything for certain."

"Of course not," Rosalind said.

"Nothing needs to change."

"But perhaps you can all wear head coverings when we travel, so that if we are spotted from a distance, we shall not draw notice." Rabia sucked in a sharp breath, as if she had surprised herself by speaking.

"Do not be shy, daughter. That is an excellent plan." Abu-Wassim smiled to her. "It will be especially helpful to hide the blondes, and your Issobelle with her hair of fire. It is always best to cover the head in this climate anyway."

Issobelle tossed her curling locks. "I suppose it would be hard to miss us here." But she sounded rather pleased with that fact.

"Tell us more of the Saracens, Abu-Wassim." Randel lowered himself cross-legged on the floor with the rest of them. "How do they think? What do they value?"

Abu-Wassim shook his head. "Not many Europeans ask such questions, but it is wise to understand one's opponent—to see them as real people with real hopes and desires. I applaud you, Sir Randel."

Rosalind felt such pride in Randel, although she knew she had no real right to such an emotion. Despite the game they had played along this trip, he did not belong to her.

"No need for praise," Randel said. "Just share with us all that you can."

Abu-Wassim rubbed his bearded chin for a moment as he considered the questions. "From what I have witnessed, most crusaders fight for power, or money, or fame. Some of the better ones fight for honor and religious ideals. But all of these motives are quite different than the typical Saracen."

"So tell us, please," Randel said, "why do they fight?"

"Many are fueled by hatred, a powerful force. Most Europeans grow disenchanted after a time and then leave. But the Moslems have nowhere else to go."

A sadness washed over Abu-Wassim's features. "You have stolen pieces of their homeland. It is a matter of honor and pride that they keep it. It is a religious command that they take over the whole earth. The crusaders have ruined everything they worked for centuries to accomplish."

Their group glanced about at one another, clearly as surprised by this information as Rosalind was.

Abu-Wassim cleared his throat and continued, "And the early crusaders sinned greatly against my people. Rivers of Europeans flowed here. Not just well-trained knights and soldiers. Poor peasants. Starving, desperate people. They raped and pillaged. Some claim even . . ."

"Even what?" Sadie asked, her eyes wide.

"It hurts me to speak of such things, and I know not if it is true. But perhaps even . . . cannibalism." Abu-Wassim bowed his head. "The Saracens believe these stories, and they hate you with a fierce passion."

The cave grew very quiet. Several of the children shifted uncomfortably. They had all been so proud to join the grand tradition of the crusaders. But no one had ever told them such stories of atrocity.

Given the circumstances that Abu-Wassim had described, circumstances that generally matched details Father Andrew had taught them, Rosalind feared the rumors might be correct. Hordes of desperate peasants had indeed reached the Holy Land, likely without enough provisions, likely without enough leadership.

Anything might have happened.

"That is beyond horrible, and if it is true, I am so very sorry for it," Sapphira said. "But I cannot help wondering something. Our Christian faith tells us that hatred is wrong. Jesus commanded us to love our enemy. I am sure many of us fall short, but do the Moslems not share this conviction?"

Abu-Wassim frowned. "Hatred of one's enemy is permitted. Everything comes back to honor and purity, which they believe the crusaders have stolen from this land by polluting it with infidel influence. That shame must be avenged."

Rosalind's mind reeled.

Randel picked at a rock by his foot. "Bohemond calls them his Saracen neighbors. He wants to coexist with them. Is he wrong to think so?"

The son Wassim spoke up now. "My father speaks of lofty religious ideals. The average Moslem just wants to prosper and live at peace. But in many cases that hatred burns beneath the surface."

"Do you hate us?" one of the twins squeaked out, speaking the question they must have all been wondering.

"Of course not." Abu-Wassim's smile was sincere and serene.

"Why are you so different?" Garrett asked.

"Most of the Saracens are of the traditional Sunni and Shiite Moslem faiths. We are of the minority Sufi Moslems, and we are nearly as hated as you yourselves. Although we adhere to basic Islamic teachings, we focus on the inner realms and seek to connect our hearts with the Divine. In this way, we have found a path of peace and love, and we believe that this is the truest form of Islam."

Sapphira sat up onto her feet. Her eyes sparked with that special fire. "That is it! I knew you had searching hearts. Perhaps we are not so different."

"I sense the same about you, dear child." Abu-Wassim pressed his hand to his heart.

She bounced as she spoke now. "Have you ever stopped to wonder if perhaps the God you seek is in fact the God of the Christians? All Jesus taught about was peace and love."

The same question had flashed through Rosalind's mind.

But a flicker of hesitancy crossed Abu-Wassim's face. "We do believe that *Isa*, as we call him, was a great prophet and an example of love. But our traditions are firmly based in Islamic teaching. The Quran is Allah's final word to mankind."

Rabia patted Sapphira's hand. "One of our early leaders, Rabia al Basri, a poetess for whom I am named, might have wondered the same sort of things. She said, 'In my soul there is a temple, a shrine, a mosque, a church that dissolve, that dissolve in God.' I do not think she made strong distinctions between the religions."

"Perhaps." Abu-Wassim cleared his throat as if uncomfortable with the direction the conversation had taken. "And I do not mean to imply that Sufis are the only Moslems with good hearts. I have met others among different traditions. Whatever our faith, I think we all know somewhere deep inside that the path of love is best. But many harden their hearts to that truth."

He gazed slowly about the circle, looking them each in the eye. "I am blessed merely to know that we all seek God with the same sincerity. And if we truly seek Him, I believe we shall find Him."

Sapphira's smile stretched wide across her spritely face. "Our Scripture says so as well."

"Now, did I tell you the tale of the wisest jinn?"

"What's a jinn?" Sadie asked.

"Ah, they are supernatural creatures. Very powerful, sometimes good and sometimes evil, but responsible for much of that which we do not understand."

"I want to hear!" shouted one of the twins.

"Tell us another story," his brother said.

Abu-Wassim obviously wished to close the subject of religion, but the conversation had awakened something within Rosalind. Both a sorrow and a hope.

"I will pray for you," she heard Sapphira whisper into Rabia's ear.

"And I for you," Rabia whispered back.

Chapter 21

Dusk had come, which Sapphira only knew from Wassim's report to the group. The cavern remained dark, with only the flickering dance of torchlight to illuminate their play. Their storyteller, Abu-Wassim, now stood watch outside, and the children seemed to have found their spunk again. The boys practiced swordplay nearby with Hassan and Wassim, while the girls chatted quietly and braided each other's hair. They had tucked Rabia deep into the corner so that she might remove her head scarf out of sight of the boys and join the fun.

Though Sapphira had always shirked elaborate hairstyles, she had to admit there was something soothing and companionable about playing with one another's hair. It calmed her frayed and snapping nerves after the long, difficult day. Even Sadie had played along and now wore a coronet of honey-colored braids. Sapphira relaxed into Lillian's delicate ministrations upon her own head as Brigitte worked at Rabia's raven-black silken tresses.

"I wish Humphrey had come with us." Brigitte sighed. "We might have kept him safe."

"I'm sure you all wish your families were safe as well," Sadie said. "But wishes shall only serve to sadden us. We must stay focused and determined to rescue as many as we can. Besides . . ."

Sadie did not finish the statement, and Sapphira glanced her way to determine why. Though she could not see her friend clearly in the shadows, the many compassionate eyes now resting upon her told her that Sadie had somehow reminded them all of her presence.

"Thank you, Sadie, for thinking of my feelings. But for once, I am free of guilt. Yes, my vision sparked this crusade, but if others have taken it from my hands and continued in their own stubborn directions, I cannot be responsible for that." At least she was free of guilt in her logical mind, although her heart still troubled her a bit.

Lillian sighed from behind her. "I had thought to say as much but feared you would not believe me. You did everything that you could."

The girls went back to chatting about Humphrey and the other males in the group. Rabia shared that she was already arranged to marry a distant cousin when she turned sixteen. And of course, as it did so often of late, Sapphira's mind turned to Philippe. She had managed not to think of him most of the morning, but now—surrounded by nothing but dark and quiet and time—she had too much opportunity to dwell on him.

And on the fact that her interest in him had been turned against her by the leaders of their army.

This was why a young girl should keep her heart focused upon God alone. Especially a girl who wished to be a nun. Especially a girl with such a unique gift. Surely she had no right seeking after earthly pleasures when she had been offered the riches of the spiritual realm. Yes, if she did have some guilt, her feelings for Philippe were the source. Yet she could not quite bring herself to regret her time with him.

Suddenly, Rabia broke through the gentle lyrical chatter with a sharp command. "Freeze!"

Something about the tenor of her voice demanded that they all obey.

That is when the hissing to Sapphira's left became clear. She could not determine the distance, but it could not be far. Abu-Wassim had warned them they might encounter snakes, and that the snakes in these caves were deadly.

Sapphira feared that one of the flightier girls would scream and thrash and doom them all, but their training had instilled each of them with self-control, and they sat immobile.

"Wassim," Rabia called out in that same calm yet authoritative voice. "Viper. Hurry."

Sapphira had her back to the boys. But hearing the hiss grow closer, she could not resist turning her head ever so slowly to spot the creature slithering just a few feet away.

It raised its diamond-shaped head high off the ground and stared directly at her with its narrow eyes as its long forked tongue continued to hiss. It moved forward inch by inch, clearly with her destruction in mind. Its eyes shouted that she had stepped into enemy territory, and for it she must die.

Sadie looked about to jump on the snake.

"No, Sadie!" Rabia commanded.

Sapphira did not even have time to form words into prayers. Only cried out the precious name of Jesus in her heart.

And in that instant, so many thoughts flashed through her mind. She could not die this way. Not now. Not after coming so far. Not with her sister and her entire army in danger.

And then she heard a *whoosh* and felt a cool breeze tickle past her neck. The head of the viper flew free even as a dagger clattered into the wall. The snake's body fell limp to the ground.

Across from Sapphira, Rabia collapsed against Brigitte.

Sadie moved into a defensive stance in front of Sapphira.

Randel and Rosalind ran over to comfort them as Wassim collected his dagger and tossed the snake's carcass into a sack.

During that moment, lasting an eternity, when Sapphira had stared into the eyes of the snake, it had been as if she'd stared into the eyes of Satan himself and understood for the first time that she was invading enemy territory, spiritually as well as physically. She was safe, for now, but never before had she felt so vulnerable. It was too much, all too much for one young girl to bear.

As Rosalind's arms encircled her, she at last unfroze and broke into sobs, sobs she had been holding at bay for months. But there was no holding them back any longer.

Beneath it all, Sapphira was just a normal girl who at times needed to bury herself into a soft motherly chest and cry all her sorrows away.

I pressed against the cool prison wall, putting as much distance as possible between myself and the others. I did not want comfort, did not want the companionship of the many surrounding me. I only wanted out of this dreadful, stinking, disease-ridden place.

It was not supposed to happen this way. I could not fathom where I had gone so wrong, or why I was being held with the rest of the Englishmen when the chieftain had given me his word that he would protect me.

I had still been asleep within the walls that morning when the Saracen army invaded. By the time I heard the screams, rallied myself, and climbed up to the parapet, the prison had already been surrounded by a sea of the enemy.

Perhaps they had nothing to do with my plan at all, for they were not dressed in the fashion of the local Druze but rather a foreign style I had not yet seen. There were scores of them, over a thousand at least. This could not be the small local force I had expected.

Even as I leaned out over the scene, I heard shouts of, "Surrender. Lay down your weapons." White flags rose to replace the golden Plantagenet lions on their field of red.

Though I hated weakness of any sort, surrender had been our only chance. The Saracen horde had raced toward us from every side, blanketing the very earth while most of our soldiers were outside of the wall training.

Even if they had made it inside in time, we would not have long survived a siege in this foreign land with our limited provisions. No, surrender had been our only option.

This is not what I had wanted, not what I planned. Would it help that we had been kind to the enemy prisoners who survived—that ridiculous Honoria even insisting they receive medical treatment? I had loathed her for it at the time, but suddenly I saw the wisdom. Perhaps it might win us some mercy.

But why had the chieftain not followed my plan? Why had they followed their own agenda? By the time I had looked out over the valley, the area where the children practiced was already swamped by the enemy. Surely they had been taken.

Where was the chieftain? Why did he not come for me?

I rubbed my hands over my sleeves, not cold but exhausted and troubled and frustrated beyond belief. Had he forgotten about me? Did he not know where to find me? Or did he have no power within this vast army?

Just as I was about to despair ever getting out of this nightmare, a burly guard shook the door loose. He pointed directly at me. "You, come."

I stood and brushed myself off. No need to look a fright, even after my ignoble treatment.

I followed the man through the dark passageways of the prison and out into the starry night. He led me to several imposing-looking fellows, including, thank goodness, my co-conspirator, the chieftain.

"Greetings," he said to me in heavily accented French.

"I thought you had forgotten me."

"Of course not," he snarled. "But your words have not proven true."

Fear cut through me. "I spoke nothing but truth. Why did you abandon our plan?"

He laughed as if my question was the funniest thing he had ever heard and nudged one of his companions. The stern-looking fellow sneered more than chuckled.

"It was your plan," the chieftain said. "Never ours. Do you think we would just send your army away to come back and attack us from a different angle? *Bah!* We are not fools. But I do thank you for so much valuable information."

"You said my words were not true."

"We cannot find this girl you spoke of. The heart of this crusade. We have found no group of children at all. Only a few older boys among the fighters. But it matters not now, for we have your entire army."

His words struck me like a blow to the gut. If he did not have Sapphira, my plan might have failed completely. Already Randel's death and even her own would be considered more of a sad consequence of this attack than the complete disgrace as I had hoped. But what if he was not dead at all? Everything would be for naught. "Surely you jest?"

"I swear I do not."

"Then go after them. What are you waiting for? I told you they are the key to defeat. They were here when I returned. They cannot have gone far."

"Hmm . . . you are the only person in this place who seems to have heard of them at all." The second man, who appeared to be an authority over even the chieftain, glared at me. "But as

I assume everyone would wish to protect such children, I will believe you . . . for now. Stories have come to us from Tripoli of a visionary young woman. So perhaps you speak true."

"Then will you free me? As you promised? I can help you to look. Or spy among my own people, if needed."

The chieftain laughed again, his large, round belly bouncing above his loose trousers and wide black belt. "Your boldness is charming. But since you did not quite keep your word to us, we shall not quite keep our word to you. We have our own plans for you now."

The burly guard clasped me by the elbow and dragged me away.

"Rosalind, could I speak to you alone?" Sapphira whispered from where she crouched over Rosalind, shocking her from the warm haze of sleep.

"Goodness, you frightened me." Rosalind rubbed her eyes and fought to make sense of the situation. Sapphira wished to speak to her. It must be important, for Sapphira rarely requested anything.

"Please," Sapphira pled.

"I'm coming." Rosalind struggled to her feet, wrapped her blanket around herself to cover her shift, and followed the girl to the edge of the cave, far away from the others, where they could see a bit in the moonlight. As they walked through the long tunnel, the crisp, still air filtered together with the warm evening and herbal scents beyond their enclosure.

Sapphira sat down upon a boulder and Rosalind tucked in close to her, covering them both with the blanket.

"What is it? I know you had a difficult night. I'm sorry for that."

"It was awful, and afterward I was determined to be stronger than ever. But instead here I am . . . here I am . . ." Sapphira gulped down a sob.

"Here you are what?" Rosalind asked.

"Missing Philippe." A tear trickled down Sapphira's cheek. "I did not expect it to trouble me so."

Rosalind spied Randel on watch duty beyond the opening of the cave as he stared back over his shoulder at them. She waved his gaze away. He should be on the lookout for the enemy, and Sapphira would want her privacy.

"That is fine, darling. You grew quite close to Philippe while he was here. We all need friends in our lives."

"But what does this mean? Have I been lured astray from my true calling by this distraction? Should I give up my desire to wed Christ? Maybe I do not want to be so special. Maybe I just want to be a regular girl who marries a regular boy and has a regular family."

Rosalind chuckled. "I am not sure that anything about Bohemond's family is quite *regular*."

Sapphira sniffled. "You know what I mean. I never imagined I might do such a thing, but I never imagined feeling this way about a boy . . . a young man, I suppose."

"Have you talked to the other girls about this?"

"No, they would tease me. I spoke to Sadie a bit, but she knows less about boys than I do."

"Well, these feelings are right and natural, but only you can know what God is speaking to your heart."

"But what of the . . . you know. . . ." She dropped her whispered voice even lower. "The intimacies of marriage? St. Augustine thought them base and animalistic. I always wished to rise above such matters, like the ascetics."

"That is ridiculous! Is that what you were taught in church? Is that what your sister taught you, or what your aunt, the Duchess Adela, modeled in her marriage?"

"Well, no, but I have been exposed to many theological writings . . . and as for my sister . . . I have always gotten the impression that she did not much enjoy that aspect of marriage."

"Sapphira, I promise you that it is beautiful and natural and God-ordained. And when it is with a man you love, it is quite pleasurable."

"Are you certain?"

"I am." At least Rosalind was certain about the natural and pleasurable parts, although she had never experienced such intimacy in a God-ordained setting. But she supposed that would change everything. Make it beautiful, rather than leaving her feeling full of shame.

It almost made her wish that marriage was not so far out of her reach.

"The subject frightens me," Sapphira whispered and closed her eyes tight.

"You are young yet. There is no need to rush. But I think you should remain open to the possibility that God might change the desires of your heart in this area of marriage."

"Oh."

"And I promise you that we shall get out of this safely and you shall see your Philippe again."

"You do not know that." Sapphira sighed.

"True enough, but we must keep our faith."

Sapphira nodded, even as her eyelids drooped.

Rosalind placed a kiss on the girl's smooth forehead. "Do you think perhaps you can get some sleep now? We have a long day tomorrow."

"I shall try." Sapphira headed back into the cave, but Rosalind remained for a few moments to think.

It seemed that once again Rosalind could be wise for others but not for herself.

What would she have said if it had been fifteen-year-old

Brigitte rather than Sapphira who had come to her with such questions? And what if the girl had confessed that she had already sullied her virtue and rid herself of a child?

Rosalind supposed she would tell such a girl that God is loving and forgiving and longs to give her a second chance. Much as Randel had said to her. But it was not Brigitte who had done such horrific things, nor anyone else. It was Rosalind who had committed the atrocity, and she was not so quick to forgive herself.

At least not yet. Though she must admit, her time spent in God's presence was shifting something deep inside of her. Awakening her to new possibilities.

Perhaps through this crusade she could yet find her redemption and offer herself a fresh start.

How sadly ironic that when she was finally beginning to open herself to the idea of love again, the one man she might desire to share that love with was determined to become a monk.

Chapter 22

Randel glanced over his shoulder once again. This time Rosalind sat alone, illuminated by cool moonlight in the mouth of the cave. A part of him wished to call her over. The enemy was unlikely to travel at night, and this cavern was well hidden from the trail below. He needed the listening ear of a friend. Today's events lay heavy upon him.

But if he shared his burdens with her, he might say too much. No, he should not risk it. Nor should he risk being too close to her so far from watchful eyes. Instead he focused on the rippling silhouettes of the rocky mountainside and the rich sky flecked with light.

Over these last few days, so much had happened that he had managed, for the most part, to forget about their kiss. But out here, alone in the moonlight, it had haunted him. He must not allow a woman—no matter how good or beautiful or ideal a fit for him—to tempt him away from his goal.

If all went well, he would meet the Templars within the next few days and be that much closer to joining their ranks.

Yet . . . as he heard the soft crunch of gravel behind him, he did not stiffen. He did not warn her away. He merely raised a welcoming arm for her to slide beneath.

And Rosalind did, fitting perfectly, as always. She snuggled deep into his side and rested her head against his shoulder in a friendly manner. Yet the feelings she stirred in him went far beyond friendship. They were feelings of family, of home, and of much, much more. They sat quietly on the rock, overlooking the rugged terrain and the passage at a distance.

Although he could have sat like that forever and never grown bored, after a time he broke the silence. "Is Sapphira well?"

"She's fine. Only putting herself through unnecessary angst over her feelings for Philippe. Young girls tend to do such things, you know."

He chuckled. "Young girls, young boys. Older men and women. I think many of us suffer from this affliction."

Rosalind glanced up at him from the side of her eye.

Only a few sentences had escaped his mouth, and he feared he had already said too much.

"Perhaps," she said. "Sapphira had always planned to be a nun, but now she isn't sure. I suppose you would understand that more than I would. But I fear the girl puts too much pressure on herself. This gift of hers . . . Well, I can see how that might confuse her. But she should remain open to wherever God might lead her."

Randel removed his arm from Rosalind's shoulder and put an inch of space between them. Was God leading him to be a monk? He had never heard the voice of God as Sapphira claimed to. "How do you think one knows when God is leading them?" he ventured to ask.

A smile tipped the corner of her lips. "You've got me there. I thought the guilt that overtook me so oft must be God's admonition. But today when we prayed, I sensed His tangible presence for the first time, and I felt no guilt. No condemnation at all.

But I do not yet claim to know much about such issues. I was speaking of Sapphira. Not myself."

"Do you think you might change your mind about your own future?" he asked. "Might God lead you in a different direction? Perhaps to marriage and family someday?"

"I have begun to wonder." She wiggled a bit on the rock, as if wishing to close the space between them.

He surrendered to her unspoken request and gathered her beneath his arm once again. "Good. For you deserve that. More than any woman I have ever known. You will make the best mother in the world."

A little gasp escaped her. "It still pains me to think of motherhood. But I believe you are right. The path that has brought me here was awful, but despite it—or perhaps, through it—I am beginning to find my strength."

For the first time understanding dawned. He wished to turn away from the harsh light of truth, but he had already seen it too clearly. If motherhood pained her so much, perhaps she had done more than lose her virtue. Perhaps she had done something to rid herself of Sir Hugh's child, which would be awful indeed.

Some might say unforgiveable, but he believed God could forgive any sin. And surely she had learned from her error and punished herself long enough. He would not probe deeper into this wound for the sake of his own curiosity.

He gave her shoulder a brotherly squeeze. "You see. I knew it. You shall meet a fine husband and rear a fine family. What about that Leo fellow? He rather grew on me."

"Leo is not the sort of man I'm looking for," she said, then sat quietly again.

When he turned to look at her, the moonlight glimmered against her wet cheeks. "Oh, Rosalind, do not cry. What is it now? Have I said the wrong thing?"

"No . . . you have done everything right." She sniffled.

"Then why are you crying?"

"It just seems so unfair."

"What is unfair?" His heart broke for her.

"It is unfair that the one man I might wish to open my heart to . . . is not available to me."

She hung her head low so that he could not see her expression.

He caught her chin with his finger and lifted her face toward his.

Surely she did not mean . . . But who else . . . ? And did he not feel . . . ?

When at last he caught her gaze, he could no longer deny her meaning. He had never been in love before, had never witnessed true love in the eyes of another, yet he recognized it when he saw it now. Their friendship had grown and strengthened, and the bond between them had become deep and steady. It was warm and companionable, full of trust and understanding, yet there was a spark that simmered beneath it all.

What more could he ever want?

And in that moment, every possible answer to that question fled his mind.

He wanted Rosalind as his partner in life, as his other half. Nothing had ever been so obvious to him.

Longing to close that slight space of otherness between them and lose himself in her very being, he lowered his lips toward hers. This kiss was nothing like that regrettable one for Leo's benefit. It was gentle, searching, questioning. It joined their very souls. He wanted nothing more than for his lips to melt into hers and connect them for all eternity.

But he also desired to look again into her sweet, intoxicating eyes. He pulled back just an inch, in wonder, in delight. But the confusion swirling in her gaze brought him back to reality and hit him like a punch in the gut.

She could not be his. He had just told himself as much.

Using every ounce of self-control that had been drilled into him by his firm, cold mother, he placed his hands upon her shoulders and pried them farther apart.

"I am . . . I should . . . I never . . ." But he knew not what to say. It felt somehow wrong to apologize for such a tender, pure sort of kiss. But it should not have happened. And now he could never unknow the truth that he had fallen in love with Rosalind of Ipsworth.

She touched a gentle finger to his lips. "Please. Do not say anything. I know we cannot be together. But somehow it brings me comfort to know this is not easy for you either."

"I wish it could be different."

"Just promise me this," she said, resting her forehead against his. "Remain open to what God might place upon your heart."

"That is fair enough," Randel said.

She seemed to float away like an angel and disappear into the cave.

Her request was fair enough. But what he did not tell her was that his heart was far too muddied by shame to ever hear God clearly. He would always second-guess himself.

And so he had little choice but to stick with his plan. And to find that inner strength and toughness that he so desperately needed in order to survive the life of a soldier.

The next morning Rosalind squinted against the sun, peered behind her, and then scanned the rocky hills all around. Though they were far from the beaten path, chills ran up and down her spine every time she thought of the sea of enemy fighters they had spotted yesterday. She wiped the sweat from her brow with the corner of her makeshift Moslem veil and pressed onward.

Her small horse, which Abu-Wassim had hand chosen for this mission, picked its way nimbly over the shifting terrain, around boulders, and through deep ruts in the earth. The steep incline did not seem to concern the animal. Suddenly she realized how silly she had been to even consider a camel for this journey. From the little she had seen of the animals, they were large, clumsy, and top heavy.

She patted her horse's black, wispy mane in appreciation. "You're a good boy, Rafiq. I could never do this without you."

But again, she glanced around. They had all woken before dawn to get an early start. As Wassim suspected, the same search party that had passed them in the afternoon had come by again in the early evening, heading back to Jezeer. No one else had come their way, so the route to the crusader-held territory should be clear.

Except that the exhausted, heart-weary children had dawdled and bickered and moaned all morning.

They had resisted packing their bags and seemed to have to stop every few minutes to relieve themselves behind the large boulders or fill their skins with water once again. The children had never fought her and Randel like this. No doubt it was hard for them to first leave their parents behind and then abandon the relative safety of their cave. But they must move onward if they hoped to have even the smallest chance of being reunited with their captured loved ones.

Finally, Abu-Wassim had taken over with the firm tone of an experienced father who would allow no argument, and for the past hour they had moved as swiftly as the narrow, rugged trail—used only by a few stray goat herders—would permit. This route took them high up the side of the mountain rather than skirting around the edge like the main path. And so far they had not come across a single encumbrance, although she had heard some of those goats bleating at a distance.

She surveyed the children, also in makeshift Moslem garb. Thankfully their simple tunics and leggings were not too different than the native attire, and they had all grown tan in the bright summer sun. With the addition of veils and *kaffiyeh*s, they could almost pass for Saracens from a distance.

The girls had been instructed to sweep their veils across their faces if anyone approached, and the boys to lower their headgear and hide their eyes. Though some of the Maronite Christians had blue and green eyes, they were not common among the Saracens and might raise suspicion.

But hopefully in this remote area they would encounter no one at all. They continued picking their way toward friendly territory as the sun rose high in the sky. No one spoke—whether because of fear of detection or exhaustion from the draining heat, Rosalind could not say. Although they were high above the level of the sea, the summer had continued to grow hotter. Even the mountain temperatures were far warmer than anything she had experienced in northern England.

If they had stayed on the main path, they might already have been safely to crusader-held territory by now. But in the same time that they might have covered five or six miles on the worn, winding road, she doubted they had gone more than one.

"Everyone remain calm with eyes forward," Abu-Wassim barked his command.

Rosalind recognized the tone as the one Rabia had employed yesterday when the snake nearly attacked Sapphira.

Danger was afoot.

"A small troop of enemy soldiers is moving in this direction," Abu-Wassim said. "They are scouring the mountainside and moving quickly."

"I told you boys to hurry!" Lillian shouted at her brothers. "Why do you never listen to me?"

"Cease." Abu-Wassim took command again. "We have no time for blame. Do your best to appear a group of Saracen nomads, and do not draw undo attention. Rosalind and Randel, move closer to me."

Without appearing to hurry, Rosalind urged her horse forward and around the children. She schooled her features to remain calm but could not convince her pounding heart. Tugging her veil farther over her face, she caught up with the men.

"What do you suggest?" Randel asked.

"We could do all of the talking and try to pass you off as our family," Abu-Wassim said, "but if they are looking for a group of children, as Wassim overheard, that is not likely to work."

"We could try to outrun them." Hassan gripped his reins tightly. "But I saw them too. They were expert horsemen, likely Druze."

"The men yesterday were from a foreign troop. But if these are Druze, they might know these passages as well as we do," Wassim said.

"Perhaps we should hide again and hope they are in too much of a rush to stop and search." Abu-Wassim took a deep breath and let it out slowly. "Each of the options comes with some risk. Sir Randel, you must be the one to decide."

That haunted look flashed through Randel's eyes only for the briefest second, and then the strong warrior Rosalind admired filled his being. He sat forward on his horse and scanned the area with a keen eye. "Are there any caves nearby?"

"I know of a small one." Wassim pointed ahead and up the mountain. "We can get there in a few minutes, if we can get the children to hurry."

"I say we hide there," Randel said. "If they find us, your family will go meet them while the rest of us remain hidden. How many did you see?"

Abu-Wassim clenched his jaw. "Less than ten, I would say."

"Those are reasonable odds." Randel turned to the children. "We must hurry. All of you, stay close." He yanked at his reins and kicked his horse. In one fluid motion they lurched in the direction Wassim had pointed.

"Trust your horses," Abu-Wassim said. "Just hold tight and let them lead the way. Do not fight for control."

Rosalind gave Rafiq another pat and urged him forward, gripping tightly with her legs and loosely with her hand. She gave the horse its way, and sure enough it hurried up the mountain at nearly a trot.

"I am so scared," she heard Issobelle whisper behind her.

"Shh," said Sapphira. "Just hold on and pray."

A good reminder. Rosalind resisted the urge to close her eyes as her horse skid on the loose rocks, but the animal knew its own limits, and after a few minutes, gained her trust. Looking back, she spied a glimpse of an enemy soldier. And she suspected he had caught a glance of her as well.

Chapter 23

Randel peered from the cave out into the scorching sun. They had managed to make it this far safely, but the enemy search team had definitely spotted them and closed the gap. He drew in slow deliberate breaths to keep himself calm and battle ready.

As the group of Druze crested the hill, he winced and clenched tighter to the hilt of his sword. "Everyone, try to appear relaxed. Do not stare at them," he said in a low voice.

With his free hand, he pulled loaves of pita bread from the sack and passed them around. "Remember, we just stopped here to eat in the shade." This cave was barely recessed into the side of the mountain. Although they were deep in the shadows, they were not out of view.

His group responded admirably. Despite the fact that they had behaved like a group of spoiled children that morning, when faced with true danger, their training took over. He used the excuse of distributing food to turn and watch the encounter about to unfold.

Abu-Wassim nodded to Randel as he and his eldest son stood and leisurely walked toward the invaders.

"Rabia and Hassan, chat in Arabic. And the rest of you. Make some noises, but only murmurs and grunts and Arabic words that you have learned."

"What of you?" Jervais whispered.

"I will only speak if I must command you. Here they come."

The men were now within earshot, and the children ate and chatted. Sapphira and Rosalind had evidently picked up the most Arabic, for they mumbled comments about the food and the weather. Hassan kept up a running monologue, a story perhaps, and Rabia responded at regular intervals.

They would appear a group of Saracen nomads, just as they intended. Randel only wished they had more animals along to complete the ruse. But Abu-Wassim planned to say that their goats had escaped while they slept, and that they had climbed the mountain to catch them.

It just might work.

Abu-Wassim greeted the enemy strangers warmly with his hands outstretched. He talked to them for a few minutes. But the man in charge kept pointing to the cave. Several times he went to step in their direction, and Abu-Wassim blocked his path with more animated chatter.

"They want to see us," Hassan said under his breath. "They have been commanded to check every person for white hair and blue eyes. Father is arguing that we are mostly women and he must preserve our modesty. Rabia and Garrett, come with me."

The three of them, who would best pass as nomads, stepped out of the cave. Hassan held up his hands, clearly asking what the problem was. Perhaps they would waylay suspicion, but Randel would not count on it.

"Sadie, Rosalind, Sapphira, and the rest of you boys, ready your swords but do no more." He kept his voice low and spoke in English.

Beyond the cave voices raised to shouts. Men on both sides of the confrontation gestured wildly. Their group had clearly formed a defensive line now to block the cave, but the others were growing more aggressive.

Abu-Wassim punched the leader of the enemy group in the nose, but as yet swords had not been drawn. For now their ruse as a group of nomads protecting their women persisted. But the Druze seemed determined to complete their mission.

Randel counted nine enemy soldiers. Not the best odds, as they only had four actual men, but they had seven more trained fighters and the rest of the girls to provide archery support. "Archers, stand one by one and move slowly to the rear. Prepare your bows."

Sapphira nearly froze with fear. Ever since the Druze had begun chasing them up the mountainside, she could not shake the image of the snake from her mind. His evil, narrow eyes seemed to follow her everywhere, bent on her destruction. His hiss resounded in her ears. The enemy of her soul sought her destruction. She had angered him, and now he was determined to remove her.

But her logical mind yet knew truth. Her God was bigger than the enemy of her soul. He was bigger than the entire Saracen army. He had created each of them, and this mountain that held them, and the earth and sky and sun. He held the whole world in His hand, and she was His own dear child.

With greater determination than ever before, Sapphira sought to still her mind, to calm her breathing and slow her heartbeat. She sought that kingdom of God deep within her, and all the peace and beauty and joy that dwelt there. She was not strong enough on her own. She did not have the courage to continue, but she knew where she could find it.

The children remained huddled, immobile.

Randel watched and waited. Could they handle such an imminent threat? They had done well enough in Jezeer from a distance, but this was a different situation entirely. His battle training had kicked in from the first moment of threat, but would theirs?

Then Sapphira began a prayer, and they all shifted to the positions he had given them. With the shouting outside, no one hesitated to take up the whispered chant along with Sapphira. Thank the good Lord. They might yet have a chance.

"Rosalind, Jervais, Sadie, and I will attack first, and only if swords are drawn. The rest of you be ready to protect yourselves." He glanced about. Sapphira and the twins did not weigh a hundred pounds each. "On second thought, maybe the rest of you should start with archery."

"I do not wish to sit here and wait for all of you to die." One of the twins stood now, his face bright with determination.

His matching brother joined him. "We shall never survive on our own. Our best chance is to attack all at once. I want to join you."

"Me too," Sapphira said.

More blows erupted between the men from behind Randel.

"Fine. All of you, but be careful. And girls, do not shoot unless you have a clear view of the enemy or they are coming at you. We do not want anyone caught in the crossfire."

Everything was ready. The prayers continued.

And then an enemy fighter drew his sword.

"Now!" Randel shouted.

Before the enemy could register the threat, the entire scene shifted to a battlefield. Seven of them rushed at the Druze fighters before they could even think to draw their swords. Abu-

Wassim, his sons, and Garrett had all been on high alert, and were fighting before most of the soldiers could even respond and find their weapons.

Determination filled Randel as he struck at a man who was unsheathing his sword. Blood pounded through Randel's veins at a frightening speed. His vision grew sharp and focused. He managed to slice deep into the fellow's arm. The man pulled out his sword with his left hand, but Randel quickly dispatched him.

Responding to the faint swish behind him. Randel caught a blow coming at his side, and engaged another fighter. With the quickest glance he spotted several enemy soldiers on the ground. Others fought the men of their group, but seemed confused by the extra swords coming at them from low angles.

Another man came rushing at him, but he managed to side-step and give him a shove. As the man stumbled apart from the fray, an arrow struck straight and clean into his chest.

Randel spun to survey the scene. Five fighters remained, but they were fierce. Swinging and slashing with the desperation of men who knew they were outnumbered. He dove into the action and managed to draw a fighter away from the smaller Hassan.

Although she was barely an adequate swordsman, Sapphira fought with all of her might.

Their attackers seemed confused by the presence of so many women and children circling about like a swarm of pesky insects, and so focused on fighting the men.

But Sapphira watched for strategic opportunities to distract them and to offer supportive strikes. Even now, she noticed a tall man knock Abu-Wassim to the ground. Before he could harm her friend, Sapphira ran at the Druze. He turned toward her, but was caught off guard by her left-handed swipe of the sword.

Her weapon cut into his side, not deep enough to kill the

man, but enough to double him over in pain. She would not stop, could not stop to think about the feel of her sword meeting human flesh.

Abu-Wassim jumped to his feet and continued the fight.

Sapphira glanced about the chaotic scene. Her head grew swishy and her stomach heaved. But lives were at risk, so she pressed on.

There. Wassim appeared to be struggling. But just as she dashed his way, the enemy soldier plunged his sword deep into Wassim's chest. All she could do was call out to God yet again for strength and mercy.

After a few moments of dodging and parrying, slashing and striking, Randel managed to disarm his opponent and send his sword flying across the clearing. As the man tried to run away, Garrett tossed his weapon like a javelin and brought the man down, then quickly fetched his sword.

Randel took a breath as he debated his next move. That is when he spied the blood covering Jervais's arm. The boy continued to fight bravely, but his opponent stood several inches taller and had a clear advantage. Randel intervened, pushing his way between them.

This fellow was tough. He bandied sword strokes with him, taking his measure, but saw no clear weakness. Meanwhile at least two more bodies littered the ground, but Randel could only pray they were not his people.

Their swords tangled. The large man shoved Randel back, but he was prepared. He rolled over his shoulder and back to his feet with his sword at the ready. Lunging again, he flew at the man, but the fellow sidestepped, managing to catch Randel's free arm and swing him around.

He kept his sword firm in his hand, and the next thing Randel knew, he was face-to-face with Jervais—his sword hurtling toward the boy's unprotected belly. Having not a second to spare, Randel tossed his sword aside with a groan. He slammed into Jervais, and the boy lost his sword as well. They tumbled to the ground together.

Rosalind gasped as she registered the horrid sight of Randel and Jervais upon the ground, with a Druze looming over them, sword raised. The man she loved and a child she had come to view as her own. Both unarmed. She could not bear to lose either of them.

Without thinking—without so much as breathing—she grabbed the dagger from her boot and threw it straight and sure.

As Randel scrambled to his feet to face his attacker, the man's face suddenly went pale. His mouth gaped. He grabbed at his chest and crumpled to the ground, revealing the dagger in his back. Then Rosalind, her own face covered with dirt and blood, stood in the man's place.

Randel and Jervais both grabbed up their swords and dropped into low defensive stances. Abu-Wassim disarmed the last man and pinned him to the ground. At last, no enemy soldiers remained on their feet.

"Children. Back into the cave. Now," Abu-Wassim commanded.

They ran to obey.

Only four adults remained in the clearing. Four? Randel scanned the ground and found Wassim lying flat on his back and staring up at the sky with sightless eyes.

Tears trickled down Abu-Wassim's face, but he otherwise appeared stoic. "Make sure they are all dead."

Rosalind gaped in horror. "But Lady Honoria said to use mercy whenever possible."

Randel understood. "We cannot afford mercy now. There is no time to drag prisoners along, and if we leave them, they will betray our position. We must keep the children safe and get word to the crusader forces. It is our only choice. Rosalind, go to the cave and distract the children."

The rest of them would do what they must. That was the lot of a soldier.

Randel delivered a death blow to two more men, then sunk to his knees upon the ground. They had won. And only lost one person. An adult fighter at that. He should be so thankful. He should be so relieved. But the close call with Jervais had been too much for him. Far too similar to . . .

Images of Gravensworth washed over him, and he doubled over, no longer having the will to fight them.

Rosalind tried to think of a way to distract the children but instead took the easy route and instructed them all to face the back wall. Rabia was crying for her lost brother, but the rest of them stood in shocked silence as they no doubt relived the past five minutes.

She had been so scared, yet so determined to protect these children. And as she had prayed a supernatural sort of fierceness had washed over her. Beyond that, she did not remember much. Mostly dashing about and striking at anyone who came too close to the youngest fighters.

Knowing she had limited strength, she had relied on speed and cunning and used several of her tumbling maneuvers to evade flashes of steel. But her body that had felt so centered and strong moments ago, now quivered and went cold. She feared it might turn to syrup and ooze across the floor of the cave.

That is when it hit her. She had killed a man.

The instinct of a mother wolf had overtaken her, and she had done what was needed. It was the second time she had been responsible for taking a life, but on this occasion, she had no regrets.

"Can we look now?" one of the young twins asked in a squeaky voice.

Rosalind braced herself, tensing muscles that threatened to collapse. "I suppose we must."

But no one turned.

"Perhaps we should take a moment to thank God for delivering us," Sapphira said.

"But he did not deliver my brother." Rabia wailed, and Sapphira gathered her friend into her arms.

Finally Jervais turned, and then Garrett and Sadie. Rosalind needed to be brave as well. She needed to dig down deep inside herself and find whatever courage remained. But as she swiveled about to face the scene, her body grew cold and tingly once again. For the first time she noted the metallic scent of blood. Flies had already begun to buzz around some of the corpses. Randel was right.

War was not glorious. It was ugly and horrible.

So why did he say he did it? She must remember. Must find some meaning in this. Yes! He said he did it to protect the innocent. To fight evil. She had protected the children. And she felt no remorse for that. But she was struck with the complexity of the situation. Nothing was as clear-cut as she had assumed when she had set out on this crusade. The Druze were only obeying orders. And their leaders only doing what they believed to be right. Why did men fight so? Suddenly, she had no idea.

Then, in the midst of the bodies, she spied Randel crumpled to the ground.

What on earth?

She ran to him, though her legs wobbled beneath her. She threw herself at his side. He knelt low to the ground with his face pressed to it. She felt the warmth of his back and sensed the slow rise and fall.

Alive.

But as she pulled his face from the ground, she was not so sure. It was pale and covered with terror. His eyes did not focus on her. He tugged away and wrapped his hands around his head. "No, no!" He shouted. "It cannot be!"

She took him by the arms and shook him hard. "Randel! Randel, it is me. Rosalind. Look at me. Come back to me." Still not succeeding, she grabbed his face in her hands and stared straight into his haunted eyes. "Look, Randel. Look at me."

Finally something broke through the haze in his eyes. "Rosalind!" He collapsed against her and buried his head in her chest. "Oh, Rosalind, thank goodness you are here."

She cradled him to herself. "Shh. Shh. Do not despair. The children are well. We lost Wassim, but he fought valiantly until the end."

He shivered against her, although he did not cry. Only trembled in shock. He had also fought valiantly until the end. She wished she understood what demons from his past had reduced him to this shell of himself.

But they must gather themselves together and move on from this place. It had been hard enough to lose a single friend today. They could not lose an entire army.

Chapter 24

"There it is!" Garrett stood in his stirrups and pointed to the Templar fortress made of tan stone, still a good quarter mile away.

"I want to be a Templar!" one of the twins said.

"Me too!" echoed his brother, bouncing in his saddle.

"They are the toughest warriors in the world!" Jervais proceeded to fake a sword fight with Garrett.

Sapphira slowed her pace a bit and beckoned Rabia to follow her to the far side of the wide road, away from the commotion. Sadie looked back with a questioning glance, but Sapphira nodded her forward. Rabia liked Sadie well enough but seemed to trust Sapphira the most.

She smiled to her friend in encouragement. "We shall be there soon."

But Rabia only nodded without showing any expression.

Sapphira wished there was some way, any way, to go back in time and save Rabia's brother. Her mind wandered to memories of the skirmish on the mountainside. If only she had seen Wassim faltering sooner . . . then again, she might not have helped at all. They might both be dead. Overall the battle had been a resounding victory and had helped to restore her faith, but Rabia had been shattered in the process.

Sapphira noted the scent of saltwater and fish tinging the air. She had always loved that aroma, but never before had it brought her so much comfort. Soon they would reach the Templars and send word to Bohemond. Surely all was not lost.

Now if only she could think of a way to ease Rabia's pain. After Abu-Wassim had led a short service of Moslem prayers and they had buried Wassim, the girl had stuck close to her father. At least today she had ventured to ride alongside Sapphira and Sadie. But Sapphira could think of little to say. None of the platitudes she would normally use in this situation seemed to work. Finally she hit upon something.

The Sufi family could easily have turned on them, but they had remained faithful to the end. "Your brother died a hero, Rabia. You should be very proud of him."

"You believe he burns in hell."

Rabia's bitter words struck Sapphira like a slap to her face. She jolted and gasped. "Oh, Rabia! Is that what you think of me?"

Rabia's face softened. "I know that you are a compassionate person, but you are still a Christian. You must believe he is in hell."

Sapphira paused to consider her answer. Of course there was truth to Rabia's words. That was the very reason she had not known how to comfort the girl. "Do you believe that Christians go to hell?"

Rabia bit her lip. "We work very hard to keep the commands of Allah, and Christians do not keep those commands at all."

"Rosalind once told me that Moslems have no assurance of heaven."

"Allah must decide if we have done enough to earn eternity

in *Jannah*, paradise." Rabia sighed. "My brother was very good and devout, though, and of all of us, he had the most profound experiences with the Divine."

Sapphira pressed her lips together. Though she was commanded to preach the gospel, was now the right time? She did not wish to be cruel, but something in her heart bid her to proceed. "I believe that Christ died on the cross to pay the price for the sins of every person who will accept Him. He alone is my assurance of heaven."

"And do you believe your Christ is the only way to heaven?"

Sapphira gulped down a lump in her throat. "Yes. And so it is imperative that I share this news with others."

"Then you *do* believe my brother is in hell."

Sapphira reached over to take Rabia's hand. For a moment the girl flinched away, but then she allowed the comforting touch.

"Is it fair to say that I hope there is something I am not accounting for? That your brother perhaps found Christ somehow during those divine experiences, or even at the moment of his death? I do believe that Jesus is the only way, but I hope from the bottom of my heart that your brother is happy in heaven right now."

"I suppose I can accept that."

"I leave the final judgements to God."

"And you would wish to see me accept your Christ." Rabia peeked up from under her veil.

"Of course. I love you. Would you expect anything different from me?"

Rabia cracked half a smile. The most Sapphira had seen since her brother passed away. "No. Given your beliefs, I suppose I should be offended if you did not at least try."

Sapphira chuckled. "I have prayed for you every night since we met."

"For my soul?" Rabia sounded concerned and tugged her hand away.

"And for your safety. And now I pray that God will restore your peace and joy. I was very young when I lost my parents, but I still remember. I suppose a brother must be similar."

"My mother died giving birth to me. Wassim was like a second parent." Rabia drifted back into the depths of that sadness again.

Oh, how Sapphira's heart broke for her friend.

The Templar fort was now close enough for her to make out the guards posted on the walls. She did not wish to even think of what they would do if the Templars would not help them.

And she could not help but wonder if she might see Philippe again soon. But their recent battle had put her relationship with the boy in a more rational perspective. Right now she must take matters one day at a time.

She did not even know if she would survive to make long-term plans. If she did, her sister's fate and the future of this crusade would also play a major role in any decision she might make about Philippe. Her confusion over the matter had lessened as she rediscovered her courage during the battle.

And she would need that courage to face whatever might come next.

Randel's head buzzed with excitement. He knew he should remain focused on his mission. Focused upon saving his army, protecting the children, and comforting the mourning family with him. But in this moment he could think of nothing beyond meeting the Templars.

Their flag featuring a bright red cross waved regally over the fort, and he stared in wonder at the sharp eagle eyes with which the knights watched them approach, their stoic faces without a flicker of concern or even curiosity.

The group had brought along the English and crusader banners, and so the fortress gate was raised high to let them pass. A sign overtop read, in French, *Poor Fellow-Soldiers of Christ and of the Temple of Solomon*. Randel's hands trembled, and he could barely keep a grin from spreading across his face as they passed under it. But then his past failures crept in to dampen the moment.

At least on the mountainside he had won the battle. He had protected the children and had not fallen into that dark place until every last enemy fighter had been destroyed. He could be proud of that.

A tough, battle-scarred group of Templars stood waiting for them in the courtyard. They wore long ivory tunics with their red-cross emblem, not so different from the battle tunics the North Britannians had brought along.

"Greetings." A high-ranking man stepped forward and held up one hand, as much to halt them as anything. His short-cropped hair shined silver in the sunlight and stuck straight from his head like so many needles. Deep grooves covered the portion of his tan, weathered face that was not hidden by his long beard. His Norman French lineage was apparent in his features, as was the case with many of these men.

Randel slid from his horse. "Greetings. I am Sir Randel of North Britannia in England. We have come seeking refuge and assistance. We are with the army that recently fought alongside Count Bohemond's men in Jezeer."

"They sent word as they traveled each way. But on their return they claimed you had won." Though the man still largely masked his emotions, his eyes grew more wary.

"Matters have turned. The Tripolians assumed we would be safe enough in Jezeer, but they were incorrect. A huge Saracen army descended in a horde and took our men off guard."

The man made a sound somewhere between a snort and a laugh. "So much for Divine guidance. The fools. I grow weary of idealistic Europeans complicating matters."

Sapphira gasped. Randel could almost feel her bristle with indignation.

Meanwhile Randel's heart clenched in his chest. Would they refuse to help them?

"So, how did this motley group escape?" sneered the Templar. "Women *and* children. You amateurs have outdone yourselves this time."

Randel was still stinging from the verbal attack when Sapphira approached the Templar leader.

"Perhaps you are hasty in assuming we are not guided by providence. I am Lady Sapphira of North Britannia, cousin to the Duchess Adela. My vision led us to this place. And I had a message from God that warned us away from Jezeer. If our army had listened, they might be safe right now."

Somehow she managed to stare down her nose at the much taller man in a manner that bespoke both breeding and authority. For a moment Randel worried that the fellow might take offense, but Sapphira had been reared for such a time.

The Templar studied the girl. "I have heard of you. You are as angelic as the rumors say. But I put little stock in words from God. It sounds to me like you grew scared and ran away, like one might expect of a young girl."

She stared straight at him without wavering. "I had permission to leave. This is my troop, and I wished to protect them. We were coming here to request support. Since Bohemond's army left, our ranks are depleted. On our way here, we saw the devastation from a distant mountain, and without us, it might have been months before anyone even learned of this tragedy."

"Unfortunately for you, we do not support random crusaders on rogue missions."

Sapphira planted her feet wider and pressed her fists into her hips. "But you do protect Christians in the Holy Land. Our mission was to release prisoners. And now our own men need rescuing. That is certainly within the duties of the Templars."

The man nodded to her with a touch of respect. "You know of the Templars, I see. But we are only thirty men. I will send my swiftest horseman to Tripoli to apprise Count Bohemond. I can promise you nothing beyond that right now."

"And if you will, please remind him that at least ten of his Maronite Christians were too sickly to travel and have now been recaptured along with the others." Sapphira phrased it as a request, but the command in her voice was clear.

"Of course."

"Will you allow us to stay here while we await word?" Randel asked. Though their ships were not far off this shore, it would be better to spend time with the Templars and win them to their cause.

"You, yes. But not them." The Templar nodded to Abu-Wassim and his family.

"But they are friends of the count, and the oldest son died defending us," Sapphira said.

"They may camp on the beach, but they will not defile our fortress." The man crossed his arms over his chest.

Randel was about to argue when Abu-Wassim cut in. "That will be quite acceptable." He laid a hand on Randel's shoulder to prevent any further trouble.

"Then we have a plan." The Templar leader waved to one of the soldiers. "Sebastien will show you to the guest quarters." Without so much as a good-bye, the man strode away and the soldiers dispersed.

Sebastien eyed them all suspiciously as he approached. He had a jagged scar running down the side of his face, and he walked with a limp. Randel could not guess his age by his weathered face, but his hair and beard were yet brown.

"Right over here." Sebastien led them to a simple building

against the wall of the fortress. "Sir Giles may have given you permission to stay, but I warn you, keep those brats out from underfoot."

Randel tensed. These men certainly were a hard lot. "The children are all trained fighters, but we will keep to ourselves. I would not wish to disturb the order here."

The man just grumbled.

Perhaps Randel would not mention his desire to join the Templars straightaway. He must win their favor first. And that would be no small task.

As the girls noisily unpacked their belongings and set up their room, Rosalind made her way to the common area in the center of the building, hoping she might make the stark area a bit more like home. It would take at least two days to get a response from Count Bohemond. They might as well take advantage of this quiet respite—for one way or another, it would not last long.

Passing through the doorway, she found Randel sitting alone on a bench at the long trestle table filling the room. His hands were clasped in front of him and his head dipped low, but his eyes were open and fixed on the bare wall across from him. He did not appear to be in prayer. More like deep contemplation. And he looked a bit downtrodden, although he had been in good enough spirits upon the ride here.

She slid onto the bench beside him and placed a hand on his back. "So . . . did you dislike them as much as I did?"

"Who?" He blinked a few times, as if rousing himself. "The Templars? They are a gruff lot for certain, but I expected as much from hardened crusaders. Did you really dislike them so much?"

She kept her voice low so that the children would not hear. "Gruff is putting it mildly. Rude. Arrogant. Mean, perhaps. Are you certain this is the path for you?"

He shrugged his shoulders. "They must be all those things to survive here. I am more concerned that I will not be up to their standards. I was watching them train just a moment ago. I have never seen fighters so fierce nor so disciplined."

"Nor so jaded," Rosalind added with a frown.

He looked up at her, hurt blaring in his eyes.

"I am sorry, Randel. If this is truly what you want, I will support you." She rubbed his taut back with small circles now. "But despite your bad experiences with war, you have not grown callous like these men. You still have emotions. You still feel pain and sorrow."

"And fear. A career soldier cannot afford fear nor even pain. I need that sort of toughness, elsewise . . ." He paused for a moment. "I have been meaning to talk to you about . . ." His voice drifted off again.

But she knew exactly what he referred to. The incident after the battle. "There is no need to explain, Randel. Abu-Wassim told me of the haunting spells that soldiers sometimes suffer after a battle. It is not a weakness. Only human."

"It makes me wonder if I have what is required to be a Templar."

"You do. Never doubt that." She leaned into him with a sort of side embrace, resting her chin upon his shoulder. "You fought admirably and did not allow yourself to give in to your demons until the danger was gone. Still, I wonder what a life like this would do to your heart."

"Perhaps my heart is the problem. These men seem to have harnessed their hearts."

"More like murdered them," Rosalind whispered. She took his cheek in her hand and turned him to her. "Look at me, Randel. You can do whatever you put your mind to. But still I ask you, I beg you to consider, is this God's path for your life?"

"Shh!" Randel said.

At that moment, one of the girls entered the room, and Rosalind jerked away from Randel. She had not even given thought to how close they were. It always felt so right and natural, like coming home, but she did not wish to confuse the children. Nor did she wish to give away Randel's secret plans before he decided to share them with the others.

And she must respect his plans for his life, even if she was not convinced.

Sapphira, dressed for the first time since the feast in a proper girlish kirtle, came and sat across from them, concern plain upon her dainty features. "How can we persuade them?"

"To help us?" Randel asked.

"Yes." She pulled at her whitish tresses that now hung free. "Perhaps if I recounted my vision to them. It worked with Brother Francis and at least some in Count Bohemond's court."

Rosalind looked to Randel. Politics was not her world. Until the crusade, her world revolved around face paints and fancy gowns, but hopefully he would have a plan.

"They did not seem likely to be swayed by anything that cannot be proven to them," he said. "I imagine they have heard far too many stories like ours."

"True."

"What they did respond to was your strength. We must be on our best behavior. Let them see how well trained and disciplined you children are. That is more likely to win them to our side."

He reached out and brushed Sapphira's rose-colored kirtle. "A bit of feminine charm might not hurt. A few might miss sisters and mothers. But be careful on that count. Some monks come to see women only as evil temptresses. And be sure that the girls do not touch them in even an innocent manner. It would be an offense to their vows."

"Good thinking." Sapphira pursed her lips. "I will warn the other girls. Especially Brigitte."

"And of course we can pray." Rosalind reached out and covered Sapphira's hand with her own. "Perhaps God can work a miracle, even in these hard hearts."

"Agreed. Tonight we shall all be on our best behavior for dinner. Our new mission shall be to convince the Templars that we are true soldiers for Christ, and afterward we shall meet back here for an extended prayer time." Sapphira stood and returned to the girls, lost in her own thoughts.

Randel chuckled. "I suppose there is no point in reminding her that I am in charge here."

Rosalind smiled. "She will obey you in logistical matters, but I think we all know who is truly running this crusade."

He nodded.

They hadn't finished their conversation from earlier, but Rosalind knew not how to pick it up again.

Randel had much to consider, and pressuring him would not help. Hopefully his time with the Templars would give him the perspective he needed. It would not be fair to lure him from God's plan because of her own selfish desires. She had been that type of girl once before.

And she had left that girl far behind in England.

Chapter 25

Rosalind leaned against the crenellated wall of the parapet along with several of the children. Word of the horseman finally returning from Tripoli had traveled like wildfire through the fortress. She watched as he galloped the last stretch of shoreline.

Along the beach she spotted Abu-Wassim and his family, likewise turned toward the approaching rider. How strange to think of him as Abu-Wassim, which translated to *father of Wassim*, now that his son was gone.

Beyond the sand lay the frothing Mediterranean with their ships bobbing at a distance like pretty toys. It would be so easy for them to sail away to somewhere safe. But they could never leave the rest behind. Images of Honoria, of Sir Ademar and Humphrey, of the sweet convent-bound Anna and Margaret, even of Rumsford and of Jocelyn had haunted her these last days.

So many lives depended upon them.

As the rider drew near, they all hurried down the stone stairs to hear the answer they had been awaiting—while feigning patience the best they could—for the last four days. Judging by the speed with which the rider traveled, Bohemond must have dallied extensively before making his decision.

Four days of leaving their people to rot in that valley. Four days of trying to reassure the children that their family members would be well, when she was not at all certain that was true.

The rest of the children and many of the Templars had all gathered in the courtyard. Rosalind found Randel and secured her arm through his.

He patted her hand and smiled. "The news will be good. It must."

But Rosalind knew an empty promise when she heard one, having delivered so many herself this week.

The rider galloped through the gate and hopped down from his horse. The winded fellow handed a missive to the leader of the group, who she had learned was named Sir Giles, though the man had never bothered to introduce himself.

Sir Giles broke the red wax seal and unrolled the parchment. As usual, his face registered no emotion as he read. Then he rolled it back up and tapped it a few times against his palm.

They all waited quietly, remaining on their best behavior to impress these men, or at the very least, to not annoy them. Rosalind felt an eternity slip by as Sir Giles pondered the missive.

At long last, he spoke. "Count Bohemond will not help you. He gives a list of reasons, but as none of them are worthwhile, I will not recount them. Suffice to say, he puts his own comfort before the lives of those he claimed as allies."

Rosalind's stomach tied into a knot. Bile rose in her throat. But she tried to keep up a stoic front, as she knew they expected in this place. The children also made valiant attempts to remain still, but she noted ashen faces and tears trickling down cheeks.

"Please forgive the children their grief." Sapphira took a step forward. "Many of us have parents among the captured."

The briefest flicker of compassion passed through Sir Giles's eyes. "I see."

"And I understand that the count will not help us, but . . ." Sapphira clasped her hands and pressed them to her chest. "Will you?"

Sir Giles considered her quietly for a moment.

Rosalind grew agitated. The man must say something. Anything!

"Perhaps you would allow me to share my vision with you," Sapphira ventured.

He waved the suggestion away. "I have no faith in visions. God, yes. His Word, certainly. The decrees of the Pope, of course. But not mystical nonsense that no man can prove."

"Oh." Sapphira's face crumpled.

And if possible, Rosalind's stomach twisted even tighter.

"But I have been watching you," Sir Giles said, eyeing Sapphira keenly. "Your group is disciplined and courageous. The children have been surprisingly well behaved. And I have been moved by your commitment to prayer."

He looked to his men, and several of them nodded the affirmative to his unspoken question. "As you said, it is the Templars' mission to protect travelers to the Holy Land, and I have already sent for backup from some nearby Templar forts. Once they arrive, we shall consider our next move. We will help you, but we shall be sorely outnumbered."

His words did not bring as much comfort as Rosalind might have hoped, but at least all was not lost.

As was his habit, Sir Giles turned on his heel and walked away.

Three days after Count Bohemond's refusal, Randel stood on the beach with warm waves lapping at his ankles. He rubbed the tension from his neck. In North Britannia, the shore was on the east coast, and he could watch the sun rise over the sea. But here in Tripoli, the sea stretched to the west.

Nonetheless, he had come here early this morning as the sun lit the sky from over the mountaintops so that he might think and pray. They had now been at the Templar fort for an entire week, and he could hardly wait to set out again.

The beach was now filled with several troops of Templars. Sir Giles did not expect any more to arrive. He had only sent word to the forts within a few days' travel. This morning the leaders, Randel included, would meet together to form a plan.

Though deep in his heart he believed that God could give them the victory, his logical mind could not fathom any possible way. He and Sir Giles had already talked extensively about the logistics and options. At this point the best idea they had come up with was to camp in the mountains and wait until some of the massive Saracen army departed for elsewhere. But that could take months. And the longer their people languished in those prison walls, the more would perish.

All this was assuming the enemy had even let the English army live. But the white flags of surrender Hassan had spied gave Randel hope. Although the Saracen troops were a mixed lot, much like their crusader counterparts, many were known to be honorable men after the tradition of the famous Saladin, who had retaken Jerusalem for the Moslems during the third crusade.

Randel and Sir Giles both held out hope that when they put the minds of so many military leaders together, they might come up with a viable plan.

Abu-Wassim approached him and laid a fatherly hand on Randel's shoulder. "Has anything been decided?"

"Not yet, but soon. How is Rabia doing?"

"She remains listless, but it will take some time for her to adjust. Hassan and I have known loss before. We understand one must go on, but she does not recall her mother's death."

"Perhaps once we leave this place she might enjoy bedding down with the girls."

Abu-Wassim managed a haunted smile. "I think that would cheer her."

The patter of feet behind him caught Randel's attention. He turned to see Sapphira frantically dashing in his direction for the second time in as many weeks. Again she wore only her shift, and this time her gangly legs were clearly illuminated in silhouette.

"Hurry," Abu-Wassim said. "Before they notice."

Randel ran to meet her before the newly arrived Templars, who were now cooking their breakfasts over campfires between the tents, could observe her inappropriate attire. He caught her and pulled her to a semi-private area behind some rocks that dotted the shoreline. "You really must learn to dress before you come looking for me."

The girl panted and collapsed on a smooth rock. She bent over double for a moment, in an attempt to catch her breath. "I had another message . . . from God. . . . Rosalind thought I might find you out here. . . . She . . . she shall join us as soon as she dresses."

Rosalind was a wise woman, for the sight of her running in her shift would have elicited a far different reaction than Sapphira's slight, coltish figure.

Randel waited until Sapphira's breathing slowed to normal. The girl took a last deep breath and pressed her hand to her side.

"So then," he prompted, "tell me of your message."

"Gideon. I have been hearing this name for the past few days every time we pray. I thought perhaps it might be the name of a soldier or some ally who could help us. Then early this morning as I prayed again, it welled up from deep within me, the story of Gideon from the Bible. I do not know it well, but it all came back to me with stunning clarity."

"I remember that there was a Gideon . . . but little more," Randel confessed.

Sapphira stood now, grabbed his arm, and began tugging with a force he would not have thought possible given her small size. "Come. Let us hurry to the chapel. We must find it and read it together. In Judges, if I am correct. I believe we shall find our answers there."

Randel waited until all the Templar leaders made their way into Sir Giles's office. He peeked around the corner of a nearby building to watch the last of them file inside.

Then he turned back to Sapphira. "I hope you are certain about this."

"More certain than I have ever been of anything in my life," she assured him.

He rubbed at his temple and the gnawing pain that was developing there. "Well enough, then."

During the breakfast hour, he, Sapphira, and Rosalind had pored over the story in Judges. But he still was not quite convinced. He had come up with ample arguments against the plan, and he feared these seasoned crusaders would not be impressed.

Nonetheless, he led Sapphira the rest of the way to the office. At least now she wore a proper kirtle and a wimple that hid most of her ethereal hair. She looked every inch the noblewoman rather than the wild fairy-child she had appeared earlier that morning. He poked his head through the doorway and rapped on the wooden support beam as his eyes adjusted to the dim light.

A shadowy figure lifted his head. "What is it, Sir Randel?" asked Sir Giles.

"The Lady Sapphira requests to join us. I realize this is unorthodox, but she has provided much guidance and leadership to our army. I hope you will allow her to share her thoughts."

Randel could now make out Sir Giles's craggy features. He glanced about to the other men. Several of them shrugged.

"I see no harm," said one of the warrior monks from a different troop. "I have heard tell of this Sapphira, and I should like to meet her."

"Fine, then." Sir Giles beckoned them. "Let us get on with this."

Randel nodded to Sapphira. She nodded back as she stiffened her spine and lifted her chin in a most regal manner. He stepped aside, and she glided into the room like a queen holding court. Resisting the urge to bow, he followed her.

"Greetings, Lady Sapphira," said Sir Giles.

Employing just the right blend of confidence and femininity, with which her sister had ruled their region for the past six years, Sapphira nodded to the group of Templar leaders. "Greetings to all of you. My sincere thanks for allowing me to take a part in this meeting."

"Of course," Sir Giles said.

A few of the new Templars eyed her with curiosity, and at least one young fellow with something far more predatory, but she did not so much as flinch beneath their appraisal.

"You may proceed," Sapphira ventured to say with a flick of her wrist in Sir Giles's direction, in that subtle way establishing herself as an authority in this room. Honoria had taught her all the tricks a woman needed in order to wield power.

She glanced up at Randel to gauge his reaction, and he raised his eyebrows in surprise. She responded with a quick smirk for his eyes only.

"Ye-es," Sir Giles stumbled over the simple word. "We need to make some decisions. You all know the mission—to rescue the English army from the prison at Jezeer. The question is how."

Randel stepped forward. "We only saw the enemy army from a distance, but there must have been at least a thousand men."

"They appeared like ants swarming the prison," Sapphira said.

"But we know not if they remain. We assume that, for such a large army to have gotten there so quickly, they must have been redirected while en route to Egypt." Sir Giles rocked back and forth on his heels. "Nor do we know the state of the prisoners."

"I say we move toward Jezeer and send scouts ahead to assess the situation," said one of the Templar leaders.

"We can plan little until we do," another added.

"Still," Sir Giles said, "it would be good to have some contingencies in mind so that we might bring the needed supplies."

"The main question is how to get inside the walls." The young man with the predatory eyes stared at Sapphira. "How did you breach the defense the first time?"

Randel moved between her and the man and answered, "We had the advantage of surprise. The gates were not barricaded when we rushed down from the mountain, and we far outnumbered them, bolstered as we were by the Tripolian and Cyprian forces."

"We shall have none of those advantages this time." Sir Giles stroked at his long beard.

"What about some sort of Trojan horse approach?" suggested a man in the back of the room.

"They will not trust any gift from us." The predatory fellow sneered.

"But perhaps a supply wagon. We might solicit help from the Sufi family I saw on the beach. Some of my men speak Arabic quite well and have passed as natives before."

"It is an option," Sir Giles said. "And perhaps we could free the army within to help us. But we only have two hundred men. Even with the English army's three hundred—assuming they are well and can aid us—the odds remain two to one, if the full force is still there."

"Two to one are acceptable odds for Templars," one of the men spoke up. "But we know little of these English fighters."

"They are well trained," Sapphira said.

"But not at the level of the Templars," Randel admitted. "And while the children are safe with us, there are nearly two dozen women among the captured. A few of them can fight, but most would need protection."

"What other ideas do we have?" Sir Giles asked.

Sapphira's plan threatened to bubble from her lips, but it was not yet the right time.

"Well, we could wait for some of the forces to leave. Every available soldier on both sides is being called to Egypt as matters escalate," said a calm and rational-looking older man. "But we would need to head that way to know when the time comes."

"We would need extensive provisions," Sir Giles said.

"We could send word to the Knights Hospitaller at Crac de l'Ospital," suggested yet another Templar. "They could be here in plenty of time, and they might be able to double our forces."

Sir Giles shook his head. "Count Bohemond hates them. He might not let them pass by Tripoli, and even if he did, that could prove the end of our relationship with him."

The predatory fellow swept his hand in disgust. "I am sick of appeasing that fool."

"Nonetheless," the wise older fellow said, "we cannot afford to anger our local leader."

Though Sapphira shared the younger man's disgust that they would risk her people for matters of politics, her plan did not require more soldiers. Only courage and daring that even the Templars might not possess.

"Any other ideas?" The slightest hint of desperation made its way into Sir Giles's voice.

The moment had come.

Sapphira lifted her chin and stepped a slippered foot in the man's direction. "Might I share an idea?"

Chapter 26

All gazes immediately rushed to Sapphira. She felt the weight of their stares but had grown used to being the center of such attention over the past months.

"What is it, Lady Sapphira?" Sir Giles eyed her skeptically.

"I have had the name of Gideon on my heart these past days. Sir Randel and I looked up his story in the chapel this morning. Are you familiar with it?"

"Only vaguely," Sir Giles admitted.

Others shrugged, so she continued. "Gideon was a judge in Israel. He had the option of using a huge army, but God led him to use only three hundred men against ten thousand. Far worse odds than we face now. And He gave them a creative plan to confuse and rout the enemy."

"The enemy fled in terror before anyone ever lifted a sword." Randel put a hand on her shoulder in support.

The older fellow inclined his head. "I recall that story. But it was not just the plan that succeeded. God sent a dream to the enemy that added to their fear."

"That is true." Sapphira said, but did not waver.

"What are you not telling us?" asked the fellow in the back. "You see visions, do you not? Your fame has spread throughout Tripoli."

"I believe I receive messages from God, though not often in the form of visions." She forced herself to remain relaxed and imperious, though her heart beat fast in her chest. "But Sir Giles gives my ability to hear from God no credit, so I do not wish to argue that here."

The man pushed to the front of the room, and Sapphira took note of his sincere blue eyes. "Well, I do. Please, tell me more."

"I have heard the name Gideon whispered to my heart for several days now during my prayer times."

Sapphira pressed her hands together in a maidenly fashion to keep them from trembling. "However I did not remember his story well, having only read it once before. Then early this morning it came to me so clearly. The strategy of Gideon's battle. The lamps, the trumpets, the enemy army fleeing in terror, and I pictured us in the role of the Israelites."

"It is the best plan we have heard so far," said the Templar with the blue eyes.

"Humph," Sir Giles said. "I do not like the source of this idea."

"It is not for you to decide alone," the older fellow said.

"I recall the story now too," the predatory man spoke up. "It could have merit. But if it doesn't work, we would have to face the enemy without the support of the English prisoners."

"I agree," said Sebastien, who never had seemed to like her or any of the children. "It could turn disastrous. I do not like it one bit."

"But," the blue-eyed man said, "you are not taking into account the guidance of the Divine."

"I agree," said the older fellow. "I stand with Lady Sapphira."

The men about Sapphira bickered amongst themselves. Many

for her, but many against. Sapphira steeled her heart and began to pray silently.

Finally, Sir Giles clapped his hands to gather their attention. "Enough. It is clear that there is no obvious path to victory. Every plan holds merits and dangers."

"What is the merit of this Gideon nonsense?" shouted Sebastien.

"You know I am quicker than anyone to dismiss supposed messages from the Divine," Sir Giles said. "But I have witnessed the Lady Sapphira in prayer, and I cannot completely discount the possibility that it might be true. Especially when so many of my esteemed colleagues are inclined to believe her."

"Surely you jest. I will not stand here and listen to this any longer." Sebastien stormed from the building.

But the others remained and waited for Sir Giles to continue.

"I realize this is an odd thing to say." Sir Giles stroked his black beard streaked with silver once again. "But I think the children should decide. It is their people, their families who need rescuing. And they know the Lady Sapphira better than any of us. Sir Randel, will you gather them outside?"

"Of course," Randel said. With one last squeeze of Sapphira's shoulder, he ducked out the door.

"And have your men join us in the courtyard," Sir Giles said to the leaders. "If we take Lady Sapphira's unusual route, we must all be in agreement."

The men began to file out. The predatory one frowned at her, but the older fellow and several others smiled warmly her way. Only the blue-eyed man stopped to speak with her. He had soft blond hair and a smooth, tan face with a crooked nose, which added character rather than detracting from his pleasant appearance.

"Lady Sapphira, I am honored to meet you. My name is Sir Etienne. I would like to kiss your hand, but . . ."

"I understand." She smiled back to him. "It is not allowed."

"A lifetime of manners is hard to break." He grinned sheepishly. "I have heard that you are from North Britannia. Am I correct in assuming you are the cousin of Richard DeMontfort and the niece of Bernard Saint-Germain?"

"You have heard of them?" Her previous act left her entirely. Suddenly she was a wide-eyed little girl again, and there was nothing she could do to hide it.

"They are fine crusaders, the both of them. And their forces were some of the most honorable men I have had the pleasure of meeting in the Holy Land."

She pressed her hands to her lips. "Oh, Sir Etienne! Might you have any idea where they are now?"

He frowned at that. "Not for certain, although I heard tell they were captured by Druze forces."

"We have heard the same."

"I take it they were not at Jezeer."

She shook her head.

"Likely they are at the prison near Beirut, for that is where the higher-ranking nobles are held. All the more reason that we must set your people free to search for them."

"Precisely." Her heart soared at this unexpected support. "And Richard DeMontfort is the rightful heir to the recently deceased duke. His sister, Adela, now rules in his stead, but the entire region prays for his return."

"Then I thank the good Lord that He has spoken through you, and that you have listened."

Though he could not reach out and touch her, she felt his gaze as a comforting embrace. "And I thank you for your kind words."

"I will fight for your plan."

"May God bless you," she said, and together they headed outside to face the gathering crowd.

Rosalind whispered up silent prayers as Sapphira shared her plan with those gathered. Sadie clung tightly to Rosalind's hand for the first time ever. The girl must be more nervous for her friend than she had ever been for herself. Even Abu-Wassim's family had been allowed back in the gates for the event.

Glancing about at the children, she suspected that many of them were sending up petitions on Sapphira's behalf. Over these last days, they had spent much time in prayer and were developing into that army of spiritual warriors just as Sapphira had envisioned from the start.

Of the other plans mentioned, the only one that held any possible merit in Rosalind's mind was calling for the Knights Hospitaller, and mostly because she wished for Randel to meet them. From the moment they set foot here, she had not liked these Templars, although some of the newer additions seemed less jaded. Perhaps the Hospitallers, with their focus on providing care to the sick and injured, would be different.

But of course Sapphira's plan was the best one, and the only one with any divine inspiration. They had worked hard at perfecting it this morning, with Randel asking the tough questions and she and Sapphira reasoning out their arguments.

"They have to listen," she whispered to Randel, who stood only inches to her left.

He twisted his neck and covered his mouth before whispering back. "She has many supporters."

Rosalind continued to pray as the Templars argued amongst themselves. Many of them seemed leery of Sapphira's suggestion.

"As we already concluded in our planning session," Sir Giles bellowed above the other voices, "each plan has merits and disadvantages. But I would like to hear what the English youngsters have to say. It is their families we seek to save."

"We have followed Lady Sapphira thus far. She has never let us down. And we would follow her in this as well!" Jervais called with confidence.

"Agreed!" shouted Garrett with a surprising amount of fervor.

"I will follow Sapphira!" said Lillian.

"Me too!" her brothers called as one voice.

All of the children nodded and cheered their support.

"But why are we putting this decision in their hands?" A younger Templar with sharp, wolfish eyes spoke up. "They are all in a fragile emotional state. A decision like this calls for wisdom, experience, and logic."

"If I may speak." Randel pushed through the crowd and stepped onto the raised platform next to Sir Giles. "The Lady Sapphira is quite unique. I have observed her this entire trip, long after the initial excitement wore off. And I would follow her anywhere."

To Rosalind's surprise, Sadie climbed up onto the platform as well. "I have no family in Jezeer. I have no real family at all. But my troop has become my family. I believe the Lady Sapphira hears from God, and I would trust her with my life. With all of our lives."

"If you will forgive me." Abu-Wassim now stood in front of the platform and bowed to them all. "*As-salamu alaykum*. I come in peace. As you can see, I do not share your religion. Yet even I will attest that there is something very special about the young lady, both in character and in vision. I trust her plan."

"But do the Moslems not know the story of Gideon?" asked the troublesome young dissenter. "They share many of our biblical accounts."

"I am not familiar with the tale which Sapphira just told, and I know the Quran well. The part at the beginning about testing the army is similar to our account of Talut, but not this name Gideon nor the battle plan."

The Templars began bickering amongst themselves once again.

Sir Giles held up a hand to quiet them. "I think we have heard enough. Perhaps we should take this to a vote."

Rosalind saw Sapphira approach him and speak, but she could not hear the words. She redoubled her prayer efforts on behalf of the young girl.

"Lady Sapphira has one more thing she would like to say."

Sapphira closed her eyes for a moment, then opened them and gazed over the crowd. "If we can learn one thing from the story of Gideon to guide us in this decision, it is that God wants men committed to His plan. And just like Gideon sent home the soldiers whose hearts were not in the battle, I do not wish to drag any man along against his will."

Rosalind felt a shift in the atmosphere around her. Demeanors softened. Men stared at Sapphira with respect. Some even with awe. As she focused on the girl, she could almost spy a halo of light surrounding her, not with her physical eyes, yet she sensed more than saw a glow about her.

"I charge each of you to search your own hearts," Sapphira said. "What does the Spirit whisper to you there? Quiet your minds and your emotions and all the distractions about you. God is always speaking, if only we are still enough to listen for His soft voice deep inside."

Now Sapphira radiated. The peace and joy upon her young angelic face were palpable. Only the hardest of hearts could ever deny it.

The place was quiet for several moments. Yet the silence was not uncomfortable. It was contemplative. It was powerful.

"I believe in Sapphira's plan!" said the kindly blue-eyed Templar who had spoken on the girl's behalf earlier.

"I believe!" came the call, once, twice, then three times from random places throughout the crowd.

Then the Templars took it up as a chant, all together. Only a few bitter-looking men yet protested, including that Sir Sebastien who had been so rude to them from the start.

"Then I believe we have a decision," Sir Giles said. "We will need to gather a large supply of lamps and horns before we can leave. And of course we will send scouts ahead and revise our plan as needed. I confess that I too sensed the presence of the Lord today, but we shall be wise as serpents and innocent as doves, as Scripture mentions."

Rosalind let out a breath she had not known she'd been holding.

Sapphira had succeeded. Rosalind could hardly believe it was true. But she should not be so surprised. She too was learning to sense God's presence. To war in prayer and to rest in His almighty strength.

Two hundred men against a thousand. The odds were not good, and her stomach plummeted as she thought of the situation in that light.

The success of this plan depended on God stirring up fear in the hearts of the enemy. Could anyone be certain that He would carry out that part? Sapphira never mentioned hearing anything specifically on that count. They could hardly dictate their plan to the creator of the universe.

But they must trust that if He was in this plan, somehow He would see it through to completion.

Chapter 27

Randel poked at the campfire with a stick. Though they needed the light, they most certainly did not need the heat on this steaming night. But something about the undulating flames calmed his nerves.

They had made good time today as their fully mounted troops moved back toward Jezeer. And he had begun to make friends with the kind Templar, Sir Etienne. Perhaps before long he would be ready to broach the subject of joining their ranks.

Yet much tension still brewed. There was his own apprehension about his ability to join the Templars, not to mention his mounting feelings for Rosalind. And in addition to the upcoming battle, Sir Sebastien and a few other rabble-rousers had come along to stir up trouble, in spite of Sapphira's instruction that any dissenters to their plan stay behind.

Even now the man glared over at the children from the opening of his tent.

But the children paid him no heed. Out in the open air, they had begun to grow boisterous once again, and the boys enjoyed a rowdy game of chase. The girls sat to one side, singing one of Sapphira's Scripture songs while playing with each other's hair. Rabia appeared almost happy as she braided Issobelle's bright red locks, although he knew she could easily fall into tears at any moment.

Rosalind plopped down beside him cross-legged on the dusty ground. She held an ancient-looking ram's horn trumpet in her hand and studied it in the flickering fire light. "'Tis a wonder they found so many so quickly."

"Well, Bohemond seemed much more inclined to lend us instruments than soldiers," he chuckled.

Still, it had taken another two days of gathering supplies before they had been able to leave. He could hardly believe their army had been prisoners for nine days now. So much could have happened in that time. Tomorrow they would send scouts ahead to assess the situation, and hopefully the ordeal would be over soon.

"You did a good job of rallying the Templars," she gave his hand a squeeze. "Lady Honoria could not have asked for more. You have been an exemplary leader at every turn."

"I hope you are right."

"Of course I'm right. And Sir Etienne said the same."

A true smile played at Randel's lips. "Sir Etienne gives me hope."

"Speaking of hope, have you spied your Syrian serin yet?"

"No, oddly enough, though the Templars say they are common in this region."

"Soon, then, I suppose. Shall you send word to your mother?"

"She would like that. And hopefully by then I shall have good news about my future. Perhaps when this is over, you might deliver the bird to her for me."

"I would take most excellent care if it." Rosalind smiled.

"I have no doubt."

Rosalind pressed the horn to her lips and attempted to blow, but nothing came out. Last night they had all tried the instruments to see who might blow the charge. Randel had done well enough, being acquainted with a number of musical instruments, but Rosalind had not succeeded.

No problem there, though, as not everyone would have a trumpet. They had not been able to acquire a full two hundred horns in this remote area, but Sapphira seemed certain that the result would be the same.

Trying again, Rosalind puckered her lips and blew hard. The horn emitted a wailing mewl, like a cat in pain.

Randel put his hands to his ears. "For the love of all that is holy, Rosalind, spare us."

She lowered the horn to her lap. "I shall master it yet. And you promised to teach me the lute, remember."

"Someday. When matters are less tense."

"And when shall that be? Once this is over, you shall head off with the Templars."

"With the Templars?" came a disgusted voice from behind them.

Sir Sebastien stomped over. He must have crept closer while they spoke, elsewise he would not have heard Rosalind's soft voice. Stealth was among the Templars' many noteworthy skills.

"What do you mean? Sir Randel a Templar. Ha! Not in this lifetime."

Wincing against the rebuff, Randel focused on the more pressing issue. "Please," Randel whispered loudly. "I do not wish the children to hear."

They all still played noisily and did not seem to notice anything.

He motioned Sir Sebastien closer, though he regretted it the moment the man's sneering face loomed over him. Randel was sick of this fellow's bad attitude, which had hovered like a cloud over this whole trip.

"Is it true? Do you wish to be a Templar?"

"I have considered it. My mother always wanted me to join the church. But right now I must remain faithful to this mission and these children."

Sir Sebastien scowled. "I knew you were a fool, but this tops everything."

Randel stood to better face the man. "*I* am the fool? You are the one along for a mission you do not believe in."

"A mission spawned by your brats. But the Templar brotherhood comes first. I could not stay behind and betray my fellows."

"Perhaps I long for such a brotherhood." Randel relaxed his stance.

"Trust me, you would not be welcome." Sir Sebastien's hands fisted at his sides.

"Sir Etienne might feel differently."

At that moment, the young twins came flying by. One tripped and tumbled straight into Sebastien, nearly knocking the arrogant coxcomb off his feet.

Before Randel could think to intervene, Sebastien stood and backhanded the boy across the side of his head.

The boy wailed and grabbed for his ear. But Sebastien showed no mercy. He grabbed up each of the twins by their collars, pulling them so far off their feet he nearly choked them. Then he tossed them roughly toward Randel.

The world seeped to red as anger welled within Randel. He helped the boys up and checked them for injuries.

"I told you to keep these brats out from under feet."

As Rosalind pulled the boys to her chest, Randel flew at Sebastien. "Never! Ever! Touch one of my children again."

"Or what?"

Randel's fist twitched at his side. His head felt about to explode.

Sir Sebastien swiped a hand his way. "Coward. You will do nothing."

Unable to take it any longer, Randel pulled back his fist and drove it deep into Sir Sebastien's gut.

The man doubled over.

"Who is the coward now?" Randel took a step back, but the violent action had only sparked so many frustrations from these past weeks and months. He longed to pound the scoundrel's face into one of the many hard rocks surrounding this place.

"Why, I ought to . . ." Sir Sebastien ducked low and plowed Randel to the ground.

Fury exploded within Randel, and his fists flew as they tumbled again and again over top of one another.

The next thing Randel knew, several men were pulling them apart.

"I did not expect this of you, Sir Randel." Sir Etienne frowned at him. "But, Sir Sebastien, you have been itching for a fight these last few days. I suggest you both go back to your tents and cool off. Sir Sebastien, one more outburst like this, and I shall speak to your commander about sending you home."

Randel's anger seemed spent. Already he regretted being lured into the man's trap. He did not wish Sir Etienne to think poorly of him. He shook off his aching fist and headed to his tent.

Once there, he collapsed onto the ground. What sort of leader had he just been? What sort of example to the boys? But Sir Sebastien had pushed him too far. By harming the boys, of course, but—if truth be told—more so by mocking his desire to become a Templar.

Rosalind slid into his tent and let the flap close behind her.

"You should not be in here. The Templars might misunderstand," Randel said.

"Everyone saw what happened. They will know I have only come to comfort you."

She left space between them, no doubt to leave two distinctive shadows if anyone attempted to spy. But she reached over and clasped his hand.

Fire zapped between them. Much like the fire he had stared into earlier this evening. Molten. Blazing. Fire that gave warmth and light, but could just as easily devour and leave one with nothing but ashes.

Rosalind. His best friend. His closest ally, yet the most pressing reason he questioned his ability to become a Templar. How could he stay here in the Holy Land without her when she needed him so?

He clutched tightly to her hand. "I apologize. I behaved horribly."

"Surely you jest," she whispered. "If you hadn't punched him, I would have."

They both dissolved into laughter. Rosalind. No wonder he loved her so.

Sapphira surveyed the dark and quiet valley surrounding the prison fortress in Jezeer. A half-moon offered its light so that she could see the outlines of hundreds of tents encircling the main structure. Only a handful of guards upon the walls appeared to be awake and alert. The rest had given way to slumber.

And somewhere in the bowels of that prison—hopefully, for the alternative was too awful to consider—her sister was locked away, along with so many who had become important to her during this trip.

Was it only this morning that the Templar scouts had set off to spy the valley?

By noon they had returned with the report that the army

remained and, from what they could assess, the prisoners were likely still alive. But they had not risked getting close enough to speak to anyone, for the element of surprise was paramount. Everyone had spent the afternoon preparing and rehearsing their plans. Then they had headed in this direction at dusk.

Fortunately, they had not run into any perimeter guards along the way. Although these tough, hawk-eyed Templars would have easily dispatched with them, their absence might have alerted the enemy to their presence.

"I think the time is close," Sapphira whispered to Randel, although they were positioned partway up a mountain several furlongs from the prison and surely no enemy could hear her.

"You tell us when. Everyone should be in place now."

Although she could not see the Templars, she knew they spread in groups of twenty or so throughout the semicircle of mountains surrounding the prison and even hid in their own stealthy way throughout the edges of the valley. It was a slight deviation from the biblical story, but she had felt a peace about the plan. They wished to leave only a narrow passage for retreat—for their strategy depended on the enemy escaping in a panic, and they wished to drive them directly east, back into the desert from whence they came.

But would the plan work? It seemed foolish to assume that an entire army of a thousand men would run in terror.

"Randel." She tiptoed closer and whispered so that no one else would hear. "What if it does not work? I wish we had a way of knowing if God has stirred up fear among the enemy."

He gripped her shoulder. "We cannot risk detection to find the answer, but we have been praying the whole way here. You must trust what God has shown you in your heart."

She glanced about at the children. They had decided to stay together for this momentous occasion. Even now, many of them prayed.

Rabia stood nearby Rosalind. They had spoken of Jesus more and more over their trip here, and Sapphira could only hope that this experience might inspire her friend to turn to the God of love.

Assuming, of course, that it worked.

The lantern was close by and prepared. Jervais, who had a way with tinder, was ready to spark it. Of their group, Garrett, Lillian, Hassan, and Randel would blow the horns, for they all could do so loud and true.

And Sapphira would choose the moment. She still could barely fathom that Sir Giles had granted her the honor.

But if not her, then who? This entire plan had been her idea. Well, God's idea, she hoped with all of her being, but spoken through her own frail vessel. Her stomach clutched tight, and her shoulders tensed. But she pushed past the physical sensations and sought out that peaceful place within.

Seeming to sense her need, the girls surrounded her and laid their hands upon her. She felt a surge of the Spirit within her. Sadie prayed fervently beside her. And in that moment she had clarity. The time had almost arrived, but not quite.

She led them in a song. Rosalind, Randel, and the children all joined along. They sang it once and then twice. Midway through the third round, a voice spoke strong and clear within her heart. *Now!*

Chapter 28

"Now!" Sapphira spoke the word aloud.

Almost instantly, Jervais lit the glowing lantern and the trumpets blasted out the call. Those not blowing shouted their agreed-upon cry, "For the cause of Christ and for freedom!"

More of the children lit lanterns from Jervais's flame and ran in both directions. Light and sound rippled outward like a wave, and within a matter of seconds, to all appearances, a giant army, battalion after battalion, surrounded the prison.

They continued blowing and hollering. Their shouts bounced between the mountains, until they became a single thunderous roar, ominous in its tone.

For a moment, Sapphira dared not peer into the valley below. What if the Saracens retreated within the walls? Worse yet, what if they gathered their arms and came out to fight? Their group could never withstand such an onslaught.

But cracking open her eyes, she took in the scene again. Their crusader forces appeared by both sight and sound to be a mammoth fighting force. And surely enough, the Saracens below scrambled about, crazed and confused in their fear.

At first the Saracens seemed to stumble over and atop of one another, unable to devise a plan. Then a flood of them headed to each side of the prison walls. A few seemed to fight the current, but to no avail. They all ran helter-skelter, a mob moving toward the east without their tents or supplies. Some grabbed horses, but most dashed away on foot.

As the crowd thinned out, she was able to see that the prison gates had opened, and men poured from the fortress as well. Several even scurried down the sides in their rush to escape.

Finally the crusader army ceased their shouting. Few of the enemy soldiers remained below, yet running away in the night. Only a cloud of dust rose to the east, blocking sight of the Druze village beyond.

Then all grew still and quiet once again.

God had been true to His word. Sapphira had heard Him correctly, and the Templars had done well to trust her instincts. They all had employed a monumental amount of faith this night. And they had prevailed.

But now they must find their people.

"Come," Randel called. "To the prison!"

Because their forces had been spread in such a large ring throughout the mountainside, nearly ten minutes passed before they were able to meet with all of the Templars in the valley outside of the prison.

Rosalind fought off fear. Not a single soul appeared to remain. The tents lay empty as they passed between them, ghost-like shells in this forsaken valley. Not so much as a breeze stirred within the prison walls.

Sir Giles awaited them as they reached the entryway.

"Has anyone gone inside?" Randel asked.

"We thought we should wait for you." Sir Giles looked directly at Sapphira.

Sapphira froze in place as her eyes grew large and she reached for Randel's hand. Rosalind would have loved to do the same, but instead she clamped a young girl to each of her sides.

Then Sapphira nodded. "Please send in your men to open the prison and see if they are inside."

Good thinking, for Rosalind doubted any of their group could bear facing a prison full of empty cells.

Sir Etienne lifted his chin, and a troop of Templars disappeared inside the walls.

Rosalind watched in the moonlight as they made their way across the courtyard to the prison door, as they opened it and disappeared into the pitch black.

How many minutes passed as they waited?

How many prayers flew through their minds? How many fears did they all repress as they stood staring into the black maw of the prison door? Seconds or hours? Rosalind could not say, for it seemed as if an eternity passed.

Finally the muffled shout came from the dark interior, "They are here!"

A *whoosh* of air escaped Rosalind, and her stomach unknotted. Sapphira collapsed against Randel in tears. In a moment, their group melded into one giant hug. Then they dispersed as the first prisoners began straggling into the courtyard.

"Mum!" one of the twins shouted. He, his brother, and Lillian tripped over one another racing toward the woman.

As dazed and confused prisoners continued filling the courtyard, their group rushed forward to greet them.

Sapphira spotted Honoria and headed her way. But she did not see the strong, tough woman she was accustomed to. Instead, a haunted female ran toward her holding out her arms. "Sapphira, you are safe!"

She knew not what to do as her sister pulled her to her chest. Her body remained stiff, unused as it was to such outbursts of emotion from the cold woman who had served as her mother. But something else held her back as well.

Then it hit her. Resentment. If Honoria had heeded her warning, this would not have happened at all. They would have been spared these last tense ten days. And of yet, she knew not how many lives had been lost.

But Sapphira forced her body to soften. To relent into the hug. She could not afford to hold on to bitterness, for nothing would chase God's spirit far from her presence more quickly. She nestled her head into her sister's shoulder. A place of refuge she had longed for but rarely found. "I am so glad you are alive."

Lord Rumsford made his way to them. Then Sir Ademar limped over with Garrett secured to his side.

"What happened? Are you up to telling us?" Randel asked the assembled group of leaders.

"Sir Ademar never did feel right about our decision to stay in the valley," Honoria said. "When the enemy descended like a flood, he had the white flag flying within a minute."

"But I was not quick enough." Sir Ademar lowered his head. "Sir Manfred and most of his troop were lost before the enemy paused to note our surrender. I am sorry for that."

"How many?" Sapphira asked.

"About fifty in all."

"The women?" Rosalind joined them now.

"All captured safely alive," Honoria said. "But Jocelyn disappeared somewhere along the way. We fear the Saracens might have taken her as a . . ." Her voice dwindled away.

"As a what?" Sapphira asked.

"As a harem slave." Rumsford softly supplied the answer.

"Dear God, please no." Sapphira pressed a hand to her mouth. As much as the woman had stirred up trouble along the way with her forward manner and her provocative clothing, no one deserved that.

"But who do we have to thank for our rescue?" Honoria asked.

Sapphira pointed to the Templars joining their ranks. "The Templars offered tremendous help and support, but truly you have God to thank. It is a long story. We shall explain later."

Randel stood on his toes and scanned the courtyard. "Where is Lord Haverland?"

They all checked the area.

"He was tending Humphrey when last I saw him," Sir Ademar said. "The boy's wounds were not healed when we were taken."

And that is when they caught sight of a lone figure stumbling from the prison. He held a smaller, drooping form in his arms.

As the moonlight at last hit his face, his expression said it all.

Sapphira hurried with the other leaders in that direction.

Lord Haverland fell to his knees, still holding his limp son. Each word came out tortured and twisted. "Humphrey did not make it."

Sapphira's first thought was that perhaps God would heal him. Surely they had seen miracles aplenty on this trip. God could most assuredly raise the dead. He had done so several times in Scripture.

But as she paused to seek her heavenly Father, a faint whisper in her heart said, *Not this time. My grace is sufficient.*

No! It could not be. Humphrey could not be gone for good. It was not right. Not fair. They could have prevented this.

At that a wall of bitterness threatened to rise up in Sapphira again. If only they had listened to her. But again she pushed it down, for no one was suffering at this moment more than the broken father before her.

"Oh, God in heaven, forgive me!" Lord Haverland cried. "Would that I had listened! Would that I had pushed past my pride and given heed to your warning, Lady Sapphira. I should have at the least sent him with you. How will I ever tell my wife? It is all my fault."

He broke into a sob, laying the boy on the ground and pressing his face into the too-still chest.

Compassion welled from some supernatural place in Sapphira's heart. She knelt beside the man and placed a hand on his shoulder. "There is no use casting blame. What is done is done, and I am sorry for your loss."

"War comes at a high cost. Too high sometimes." Father Andrew moved to Humphrey and began mumbling the last rites.

True words, every last one of them. Yet they would not bring back her friend. Nor Rabia's brother, for that matter. War came at a high cost. Perhaps they had all failed to count that cost.

Randel harnessed every ounce of his self-control to keep from hurling himself at Lord Haverland. Thank goodness he had vented some of his frustration on Sebastien the night before, for Haverland had clearly suffered enough already.

Yet anger fumed and steamed within Randel.

And behind the anger . . . yes, that pinch in his gut was guilt. For he had sent Humphrey into the battle fray in the first place. Not that he had any choice, and yet . . . The awful sensations threatened to rise up again, but he managed to push through them and surface back to reality.

Randel pressed his fingers into his aching temples. At least they had saved most of them. All might easily have been lost.

Sir Giles and Sir Etienne came and joined their small leadership council.

Sir Etienne clapped a supportive hand to Randel's shoulder. "So, have you asked how it happened?"

"How what happened?" asked Rumsford.

"How the enemy was moved to fear. Our plan depended on them giving way to panic, but we had no way of planting those seeds without risking detection."

"I do not know for certain, but I have a guess," Honoria said. "I heard the guards talking. I have not picked up much Arabic, but I heard the name Sapphira uttered in horror. Something about her terrifies them."

"Yes, they questioned me about her," Rumsford said. "I denied she existed, but it was clear they had heard of her and that rumors were spreading."

Sir Ademar hugged young Garrett closer to his side. "They thought she had disappeared like a spirit into the hills. And when their troop was discovered slaughtered, their fear grew."

"Our God is truly amazing," Sapphira whispered in wonder. They all stood quietly for a moment.

Then Sir Giles cleared his throat. "I know this is the last thing you want to hear, but we must move quickly. We are not safe."

"The question is," said Sir Etienne, "do you wish to return to Tripoli or head on to Beirut? If you wish to look for your men in Beirut, I fear this is your only chance. Right now they believe all is well, but once they receive word of this"—he gestured to the prison—"they will be on high alert."

Randel knew what his choice would be—to get these children far away from danger. But it was not his call to make.

Lady Honoria's glance darted about, as if she were confused. "We have saved so few. Less than a hundred people, and many of those not even our countrymen. We have not yet found my husband or my cousin, who might be our future duke."

"If we do not go on," Rumsford said, "then what was the point of all of this?"

The man was correct.

"But we are all so tired and worn already." Sir Ademar nodded to Lord Haverland, who yet wept over his lost child.

Somewhere during the discussion, Randel's anger with Haverland had drifted toward compassion. Although his own guilt still ate at him.

Sir Ademar continued, "We need time to rest and recoup. Perhaps back to Tripoli then onward to a new area, closer to Jerusalem. We know not where our people might even be."

Sir Etienne let go of Randel's shoulder and stepped forward. "We do not know for certain, but as I told Lady Sapphira and Sir Randel, most high-ranking nobles captured by the Druze are taken to Beirut."

"And as some of the Jezeer prisoners rallied, they made the same claims," Lady Honoria added.

"But . . ." Ademar looked to Haverland and the sad form of Humphrey again.

Lord Haverland struggled to his feet now, though he did not leave the side of his dead child. "We must push onward. Just tell us the plan and we will do it. This cannot be for nothing."

"What is to keep them from following us?" asked Rumsford. "Or from sending messengers to the city?"

Sir Giles lifted a brow. "The Templars can handle this. Some of them shall be returning, but Sir Etienne and I, along with our troops, plan to stay with you and see this through."

"We shall spread out over all the passages between here and Beirut, traveling at top speed," Sir Etienne said. "No messengers will get by us. As for the rest of you, stay until the morning and refresh your people, but you must travel quickly as well. By the time you have arrived, we will have assessed the situation and devised a plan."

"God willing, we can strike before they ever know we're coming," added Sir Giles.

"I shall send a message to our ships to move farther south, but still out of sight of Beirut." Lady Honoria seemed to be coming back to her normal confident self.

"Excellent plan." Sir Giles nodded. "For once our task is accomplished, we shall need to get away swiftly."

Chaotic caterwauling snapped me from my sleep. I did not understand the source. But I tiptoed to my door and saw men dashing around the hallway in a panic, screaming about jinns and armies. The guards assigned to my room were nowhere in sight.

I could not waste time to discover the details. This was the chance I had awaited during my ten-day nightmare in this silken prison. My fellow captives began to stir, but I did not waste breath on good-byes. I needed to slip out immediately and alone.

Pressing myself tightly into the shadows along the wall, I hurried through the hall and ducked through an archway. I rushed through the main room, but no one was looking for a lone escapee.

As steps passed my way, I hid behind a table. Two men were arguing. Based upon the few words of Arabic I had picked up and their erratic arm movements, I suspected they were terrified and considering if they should run far away. But who wished to run? The leader of the Saracen army? The entire village?

Once the area was clear, I snuck through the front portico and out into the frantic streets lit by moonlight and torches. I so badly wanted to understand what had happened, but I heard again shouts of crusaders, armies, and jinns, along with a word spoken in both terror and awe.

Sapphira!

The fools. I had been the one to create the fear of the young woman in their hearts. I had called her a powerful blue-eyed jinn and had stirred up every ounce of panic I possibly could, hoping they would go after Sapphira and Randel at all costs.

Not so they would run away like scared children. Although after the traumatic week I had endured, I was glad for any respite.

A small part of me wished to linger and learn what had happened, but I would find out soon enough. Once I was safely returned to my own people.

The mass of Saracen soldiers seemed to be heading through the Druze village and toward the desert to the east, but I pressed upstream against the throng of bodies in the direction of the prison. Soon I would be far away from this place. And if by some chance Sir Randel had survived this ordeal, heaven help that man!

For if such a thing were possible, I hated him more now than I had for being responsible for my brother's death. Why, I would not be at all surprised if I learned he had killed the boy with his own two hands.

Chapter 29

Though he was as tired as any of them, Randel gladly took a turn upon the wall to make sure none of the Saracen army attempted to return. Unlike those who had spent the last ten days imprisoned, at least he had been fed properly and had not feared for his life.

Many of the Templars were already flying off toward Beirut, but Sir Giles had done well to give the prisoners a few hours to recoup.

The Englishmen had little clothing and no weapons when they left their prison cells, and were even now searching out their belongings. What they could not find, they would have to requisition from the abandoned Saracen tents. They still needed time to adjust to their new situation and the loss of so many. Besides, their foot soldiers could never travel at the pace of the mounted Templars.

He peered through the dark at the distant Druze village. It was too far away to spy any details, but there seemed to be much movement for this early morning hour. So far he had not spotted anyone heading toward the prison, but like the other guards along the parapet, he remained on the highest alert possible.

He could not believe that Humphrey was gone. The boy had been like a younger brother to him. And though Humphrey had his annoying side for certain, he had helped guard the secret of Randel's haunting dreams and spells. Randel had owed him much for that. Guilt settled deep inside him now. Perhaps he should have gone himself to warn the troops and never put the boy in danger. Yet the safety of the other children had also been at stake, and Sapphira had needed protection at all costs.

Sometimes in war there were no right answers.

Just death and destruction wherever one turned.

A flash of sword. A splash of blood. A body crumpled against the battlement . . .

No! Calling forth every ounce of strength that he possessed, he fought through the memories. He must stay alert and protect his people. He could not bear to be the cause of one more lost soul.

That is when he saw a figure running his way. It seemed to be wrapped in loose robes of the Moslem style, although it wore no headgear that he could tell. From this distance he could not tell if it was a man or a woman. Either way, he would not allow any enemy to breach their defense.

He pulled out his bow and notched an arrow along the string. Glancing to his right and left, he noted Hassan and several other guards doing the same. Whoever this unfortunate soul might be, they would regret ever heading their way.

But the figure had not yet come within range. Though it had been moving at a run, it now seemed to stop and double over, as if struggling for breath. Then it continued at a walking pace. Closer and closer.

Almost within the range of his shot.

Closer . . . and then . . .

"I know her!" shouted Hassan, the man known for his sharp eyesight.

"Who is it?" Randel asked, unable to make out the face.

"The one you called she-wolf."

Randel squinted harder. He held his bow, still quivering in his hand, but raised the arrow over the head of the figure. Could it be?

Soon he saw the whipping black hair. He realized the fabric was a wrapped sheet rather than a robe, and he managed to make out Jocelyn's features.

"Hold your fire!" he called to the other men. And then, "Fill the line."

It took several minutes for him to run down from the parapet, across the courtyard, and through the gate. He dashed around the side of the prison and hurried to Jocelyn just as she reached the wall and sagged against it.

The first light of dawn had begun to fill the horizon, and he could make her out more clearly now. She looked up at him with tears streaming down her face, leaving pools of black makeup in their wake. He spied a bruise upon her cheek and another upon her shoulder.

With great tenderness and a bit of trepidation he pulled her to himself. "Oh, Jocelyn, I heard the news. I am so sorry."

"But I escaped. I am here now."

"Thank the good Lord in heaven for that." Though he was moved to great sympathy for what she must have undergone, still, the feel of her against him caused him discomfort, and he put her gently away. "And just in time. We will be leaving soon."

She fell back against him and clutched his tunic in her fist with desperation. "Oh, Sir Randel, you will never know how glad I am to see you."

He took her under his arm and led her toward the prison gate. He had no idea what to say to her. No idea what sort of horrors she might have endured. Certainly the native soldiers had shared stories about the Saracens' harems of slaves and of their many wives. To think that any of their English women—even Jocelyn, who was most assuredly not a woman of virtue—had been subjected to that made his stomach churn.

Humphrey gone. Jocelyn beaten and violated. So many of their people had now perished.

How many horrors would they be subjected to upon this journey? And why on earth was he so determined to stay in this place and continue to fight? He could no longer remember.

But one thing was certain, they must complete this mission. They must find Sir Richard DeMontfort and return him safely to North Britannia. Rumsford and Haverland had been correct. If they did not find their people and set them free, then all of this would have been for naught.

Late that afternoon, Rosalind rubbed at her aching back as they finally slowed the horses in a hidden valley along the path to Beirut.

It had seemed this day would never end, blending as it had with yesterday. She and the children had managed only the briefest nap after their conquest in Jezeer before they had been roused to start on their way once again. Even that little bit of sleep had been troubled by dreams of Humphrey's limp form and the dark mouth of the prison, which threatened to suck her in.

Much like the children, she had wilted against her horse the entire day. Randel had given the youngest members of their troop turns riding with him when they looked as if they could not keep their eyes open one more minute. But Rosalind was a leader now, and she had pushed through her exhaustion.

Finally the Templars along their route had pointed them to this sanctuary. Thank goodness they had not pressed them forward until sunset. They were hours from the prison now, and the Templars had left scouts along the path to watch for any messengers. If even a single member of the Saracen army headed this way, they would all know soon enough. But if Jocelyn's stories proved true, the Saracens would not be following them.

Far too tired to dismount gracefully, Rosalind slid from her horse and landed with a thump on the dry, rocky soil.

She spied Jocelyn nearby and attempted to smile her way. Jocelyn scowled back. There was a new hatred, a new anger in the woman's dark eyes—surely the result of her horrific week. And yet . . .

Rosalind beckoned Randel and pulled him behind her horse. She lowered her voice to a whisper. "I still do not understand why Jocelyn was the only woman taken. Do you not find that suspicious? And she escaped so quickly once we returned. I feel bad for the woman—I do. But I do not think we should trust her so blindly."

"Although your point is valid, if you had seen her when she returned, I do not think you would question her so."

"Lady Honoria did not seem to suspect a thing. Perhaps we should warn her to be on her guard."

Randel rubbed his temples, a gesture that had become too typical of late, as if his head were always troubling him. "Let us keep an eye on her ourselves for a while."

"Think about it. The Saracens seemed to somehow know the precise best moment to attack our people."

He glanced over top the horse in Jocelyn's direction. "But what motive could she possibly have? It makes no sense."

"I'm not certain." Rosalind had asked herself the same question over the duration of the journey today. "But I do not trust her. I've always felt she was up to no good."

"On that I can agree. But she is so terribly broken right now."

"Yet she seems more meanspirited than ever."

"I am more concerned about that awful Sir Sebastien." Randel jerked his head in the man's direction. "I cannot believe he was assigned to travel with us. Talk about up to no good. I fear the man came along for no other reason than to taunt me."

"You should not let him bother you so." Several times today the two had sparred verbally. Rosalind hoped they would not come to blows again. "Besides, Sir Sebastien could not have betrayed us at Jezeer. We had not even met him yet."

"We will watch Jocelyn, but I do not feel comfortable casting baseless allegations."

Rosalind swiped a hand down her face. "I suppose that is best. Perhaps my sleepy mind is playing tricks on me."

"Let us set up the tents. You are all in desperate need of rest."

"What about you? You've gotten no sleep at all."

Pain flickered across his face.

"What is it, Randel?"

He just looked at the ground and did not answer.

"Is it Humphrey?"

Randel pressed his lips tightly together. "I doubt sleep shall come easily anytime soon." He turned to head toward the children.

Rosalind grabbed his arm to stop him.

He gently loosened her grasp. "First things first. We shall talk soon enough."

Surely he did not blame himself. Then again, he likely did. Even she had struggled throughout the day over the memory of her tiny, dead child. The loss of Humphrey had hit too near that nerve. How she wished she and Randel could comfort each other during this time. But perhaps they should not. For each time they were alone, matters grew more and more complicated between them.

◇ ◇ ◇

Randel emerged from his tent just before sunset. The last of the boys had roused from their naps and headed out in search of dinner. He himself had kept his eyes open as he rested, dreading the nightmares that would be sure to come if he allowed them to drift closed.

When he stepped into the open air, the most glorious sight met his gaze. A sky streaked with gold, orange, and the brightest pink, even as the bright orb of sunshine settled itself between the mountain ranges. Such beauty did nothing but mock his state of mind. Surely God should not permit such splendor upon this tragic day.

Humphrey's death weighed upon him, dragging him down, as if he carried the boy's limp body across his own shoulders, although he knew it had been buried in Jezeer. Father Andrew had given a brief but heartfelt mass in Humphrey's honor. There was nothing to do now but move forward so that the boy's death might mean something.

Randel joined the children at the campfire. Rosalind scooched over on a large rock to make space for him. She offered him some dry meat and pita bread. "Here, eat. You must be hungry."

He was not, but he took the food and bit into the stringy meat nonetheless. Though his stomach protested, he forced himself to swallow. He would need his strength for the battle ahead, even if his heart was no longer in it.

He glanced about at the children. Who would they lose next?

Rosalind gazed at him with concern. She rubbed small circles upon his back. "I had hoped sleep might improve your mood. You cannot take this burden upon yourself. You did everything you could to get Humphrey away from there."

He would not argue with her. They both knew all the points, on both sides.

"Perhaps you should speak with Father Andrew," she suggested. "He is very wise about such issues."

"There is nothing to say."

He attempted to wipe the frown from his face and choke down a few more bites. Rosalind did not know everything. And it would hurt too badly to recount the tale.

Randel twisted away from her. To his left, a small group of Templars were sparring with their swords. Those men never wearied. They felt no pain. No sorrow. Yet more than ever he questioned whether he could ever be one of them.

One thing he knew for certain, he could not continue on his current path.

Either he must give up warfare, or else he must—as Rosalind had put it—murder his heart like these hardened men. The second option seemed entirely preferable. A part of him yet loved the battle, yet loved protecting the innocent. He merely needed to become better. Stronger. Tougher. And he was tired to death of his heart aching so bitterly.

That awful Sir Sebastien noticed him watching and strutted over. "Please do not tell me that you still wish to join us."

At least he had not punctuated his comment by calling Randel a fool this time. "Shh! The children still do not know."

Sebastien jerked his chin toward the children. "They have lazed about long enough this day. What sort of leader are you? Boys!" He raised his voice to beckon them. "Come with me. Training time. We did not let you stop early so that you might waste your time with stories and games."

The boys looked to Randel, confused.

"For goodness' sake, man," Randel said. "At least let them finish eating. The twins just woke up."

"But those older two have been awake and causing trouble for a while now." He pointed to Jervais and Garrett, who indeed appeared wide awake and had finished their meal. Although Randel had no idea how playing a game of chess might stir up any trouble.

"I want to train with the Templars." Jervais jumped up now.

"I can give it a try." Garrett stood and stretched, but he did not look as anxious to join the surly lot.

"Fine," Randel said. "But do not tire them over much. They shall need their energy when we reach Beirut."

Sebastien smirked. "As if the Templars would let children fight for them. But perhaps with proper training they might turn into decent soldiers someday, unlike other people around here."

Randel felt once again as if he might explode. Someplace deep inside of him was growing dark and twisted, but he knew not how to fix it.

Chapter 30

As they continued their meal, Jocelyn approached them. She was no longer the arrogant seductress, but rather a quiet, angry young woman. Randel braced himself for the encounter.

"Might I join you?"

"Of course." Randel moved closer to Rosalind to make space for Jocelyn on his other side.

Rosalind leaned forward to see past him. "Is something wrong?" she asked Jocelyn, with good reason, for the girl had never joined them at a meal before.

"I cannot stand to be around them one more minute." Jocelyn glared at her friends and spat out the words. "They think I am ruined now. As if I have a disease and they might catch it."

"I am sorry to hear that," Rosalind said. "'Tis not right that they have added to your pain."

"You know nothing of my pain," Jocelyn spat the words. "Do not make assumptions about me or about what happened while I was gone."

"I am sorry." Rosalind reached across him to pat Jocelyn's arm. "I do not know the right thing to say. But you are welcome to sit with us."

That was generous of Rosalind, especially as she did not trust Jocelyn. But it was clear the girl was hurting. Compassion stirred in Randel's heart as well. He gave Jocelyn's hand a squeeze. "Just let us know if there is anything we can do."

Sapphira ventured closer from where she had been sitting with the girls. "Jocelyn, I want you to know that I am praying for you. As Randel said, if there is anything we can do . . ."

Jocelyn managed to gather her features into something akin to a smile. "That is kind, Lady Sapphira. I do not know if I deserve your prayers, but I appreciate the sentiment."

They all grew quiet at that, and both Randel and Jocelyn continued to eat.

A few moments later, their relative peace was broken by Sir Sebastien's hollering. "Get up, you maggot. Warriors do not weep upon the ground!"

As the man poked his blunted practice sword at Garrett, pressure filled Randel's head. The boy held his side and tears trickled down his cheek. Whatever on earth?

"Stop that!" Randel ran their way.

"Hold!" Sir Sebastien held out a hand to halt Randel's progress. "I can handle this. I am the Templar."

"You are the bully," Garrett said, scooching backward away from the man. Clearly Sebastien had grown overzealous in his training.

"How dare you!" Sebastien pulled Garrett up by his tunic. "I know how to deal with insolent pups. Come with me."

The impudent fool began to drag Garrett away toward a copse of trees, an evil gleam glinting in his eye.

Randel grabbed him back. "Not a chance. Let go of the boy. Now!"

"Or what? We shall squabble in the dirt again? How could I ever bear it? Easily, you weakling!"

Randel wrestled Garrett from Sebastien's grasp, and the boy dashed to Rosalind's waiting arms.

"You have gone too far this time, *Sir* Randel."

Randel had had quite enough. He would not suffer this man to hurt his children ever again. He moved close to Sebastien until their faces were inches apart.

Through gritted teeth he ground out, "You need not like me, for I do not like you one whit. But I swear to you, if you harm so much as a hair on one of these children's heads ever again, I will kill you with my own bare hands."

"Try it," Sebastien said.

A fist came flying Randel's way so quickly, he barely had time to duck, and the blow exploded against his ear.

The pain awakened something within Randel. A fierceness, a passion to protect, and to fight. A need to vindicate Humphrey. A need to prove himself worthy. All of it welled up in him at once, and before he knew what happened, they were rolling on the ground again. Randel delivered blow after blow, but no longer felt the pain. Numbness overtook him and his blood pumped hard.

He knew not how much time passed before someone trapped his arms behind his back as another man pulled Sebastien away. But he continued jerking himself in Sebastien's direction and attempting to fight. Someone needed to teach that arrogant oaf a lesson.

"Do not ever touch my children again!"

"Your children? Oh you poor, delusional idiot. I suppose you convince yourself that they are yours and your fair Rosalind's. Ha! You are not worthy to shine a Templar's boots, let alone be one."

Red hazed Randel's vision.

The man behind him shook him. "Sir Randel, collect your-self." It was Sir Ademar's voice. "Cease this at once, or I shall have to lock you in chains for the night."

But no one chided Sir Sebastien. Of the handful of Templars surrounding them, he was the ranking soldier.

Randel shook off Sir Ademar. "I will go to my tent. That scoundrel is not worth my time. Just watch the children. He hurt your son and might have done worse."

As Randel stomped toward his tent, he heard Rosalind defending his actions to Sir Ademar. But none of that mattered right now. The pain in that dark and twisted place in his chest had overtaken him. How he longed to be in the throes of battle, where everything would grow numb once again.

Sapphira strolled hand in hand with her friend Rabia in a circle around their hidden mountain valley. It felt amazing to walk off the stiffness of the day's long ride and take in the beautiful evening.

Rabia wore a relaxed smile upon her face.

Sapphira felt a matching one making its way across hers. "You seem to be in good spirits today."

Rabia winced. "Perhaps I should not be. Wassim has not been gone long."

"You must enjoy life when you can. Moments of sadness will come for certain, but you need not dwell in them."

"I was thinking about the battle. About your Gideon. The trumpets and the thundering shouts. It was amazing. I cannot believe I am friends with such a hero as you."

Heat crept up Sapphira's face. "I am but a vessel. I know not why God has chosen me."

"You are quite special."

"Only in my willingness."

Rabia stopped now and gazed out over the mountains. "Do you think your God could use any willing vessel so? Even a girl like me?"

"I cannot imagine why not."

Rabia just nodded.

Sapphira wrapped an arm around the girl's waist and tugged her closer. "I am glad we are friends. Before this trip my only friend was Garrett, and we had grown apart. Now I have Sadie and I have you and the other children. That is special indeed."

"I have been thinking a lot about the things you shared with me. About your God of love. And no one could deny the power of your God after witnessing the spectacle at Jezeer."

Sapphira held her silence. She did not wish to push the girl.

"Truly I have never seen anything like that," Rabia said. "Everyone seems to fight for something called religion, something unknowable that flits in the air. But in that valley I saw a very real God. A God who fights for us, not the other way around. And I have enjoyed your songs and prayers."

"I still pray for you every day."

"Thank you."

Rabia visibly shook herself, as if from some sort of trance. She began to walk once again. "You have not mentioned your Philippe in some time. How are you feeling about that?"

Sapphira clasped her hands behind her back. The question surprised her, for she had not spoken to Rabia about her feelings, but she supposed they had been obvious to everyone. "In truth, I have not had much time to think about him. He crossed my mind while we awaited word from his father, but not much since then."

"That is good, I suppose, since you long to be a nun."

"Yes, it is very good. He was the excuse Honoria and Haverland used for not heeding my warning in Jezeer. It is better to remain focused on God and prayer. Especially for a person like me."

285

Though her feelings for Philippe had been natural enough, they had brought her nothing but trouble. For certain she was too young for romance. But looking toward the future, she would do her best to escape its entanglements. She should not allow such weakness into her life ever again. As much as she liked Philippe, she was determined to remain focused on heavenly matters for the remainder of this crusade, and hopefully beyond.

As they made their way around the circle, they passed by the Templars, who were now saying their evening prayers.

"I hate that Sebastien fellow," Rabia whispered. "I cannot believe he was so awful to Garrett."

"I aspire not to hate, although I admit, I do not like him either." She especially had not liked the wicked look in his eye as he pulled Garrett away. "I sincerely hope Sir Randel does not get himself into any trouble over the fellow, but I cannot say I blame him for his anger."

"It will just be another day or two now. I doubt we shall delay for long once we reach Beirut. Hopefully the Templars will go home after that."

"But if we do not find my cousin and uncle, who is to say? We might keep fighting together."

Rabia sighed. "I hate war. I do not understand why we cannot all live in peace."

"Sometimes we must fight for what is right. Do you not believe it is right for us to free our people?"

"That is a worthy goal. But I hope with all my heart you do not continue to Jerusalem. It is far too messy a place. I do not wish to go there."

Sapphira took Rabia's hand again. "Your family should go home after this. I will see to it that you are sent back to Tripoli. You all need time to mourn."

"Thank you. But I shall miss you when you are gone."

"I shall miss you too."

If someone had told Sapphira a month ago that she would make friends with a Moslem infidel and dread losing that friendship, she would not have been able to fathom such a scenario. And yet here she was. Truly, life was full of the most amazing twists and turns. She could not begin to imagine what might be coming next.

Rosalind awoke to a keening sound in the next tent. She jumped up and scurried in that direction, bumbling in her drowsiness.

"Randel, Randel, wake up!" she heard Jervais say through the thick fabric.

When she pulled back the flap, she saw the boys gathered around Randel, who held his head in his hand and shouted, "No! No! It cannot be!"

"'Tis only a dream," Garrett said gently, as he shook Randel by the shoulder. "All is well."

Randel appeared to snap into the present. "Oh, boys, Rosalind, I am so sorry!"

She knelt down beside him. "Do not apologize."

He dropped his head into his hands again. "I promised myself I would not sleep."

"Boys, try and go back to sleep," Rosalind said. "Randel, you and I need to have a conversation, whether you like it or not."

"I suppose I can put it off no longer." Randel hauled himself to his feet with a huff and followed Rosalind outside into the moonlight.

She led him away from the tents and to a rocky outcropping with a pleasant view of the dark mountains. They both sank onto the rock.

"I know you are haunted by past battles," she said. "But it seems to be worse when you take guilt upon yourself. You must let this thing with Humphrey go. 'Twas not your fault. Lady Honoria and Lord Haverland blame themselves, and quite frankly, I am inclined to agree with them. Humphrey's injuries were not that dire until he was imprisoned."

"But I gave the command that saw him injured."

"You sent him as a messenger. A perfectly respectable duty for a boy of his age and training. We might have lost the battle otherwise."

"I know." He shook his head. "I know with my logical mind that you are right. But it is too similar. It is too strong a reminder."

She reached over and took his hand. She traced the line of his vein with her finger. "It is clear that you bear a deep pain. Although I have never pushed you to share it, I think the time has come that you must."

Randel rubbed at his temple with his free hand. "It . . . was . . . Gravensworth." He spoke the word as if it were a curse.

"What happened at Gravensworth?" she prompted. "I know you lost the battle."

"Battle, ha! It was a slaughter. I had been charged with leading the men and protecting the castle. No one expected the Scots to attack. Though it was near the border, the Duchess Adela had recently signed a treaty. But there are too many tribes and factions among the Scots. And we did not have the manpower to withstand them."

"So there was no way you could have known, and no way you could have won."

"There is always a way. As you so often tell the children, no excuses." His head drooped. "I lost all eight of my men that night, and those inside the castle were taken captive. I should not have survived, except that I fell from the parapet and stumbled into the woods during the fray. It was a humiliating failure, and my parents did not let me forget that."

"Randel, you must let it go. You must forgive yourself. These things happen all of the time."

"But I have not told you the worst."

Rosalind's heart clutched and bled for her friend. Good heavens! It was worse? She longed to pull him to her chest and comfort him, but their history told her that such a move would not be wise. Instead she clung to his hand with both of hers.

"One of my men . . . the youngest . . . a soldier named Anslem Sollers . . ." Randel paused and cleared his throat. "He died at my own hand."

"What?"

Chapter 31

Randel pulled back to watch Rosalind's reaction in the dim light. He spied the shock on her face.

"'Tis true. My sword killed him. It was an accident, of course. The night was dark and foggy. I turned to strike at the enemy, and there he was."

Her features softened.

The words were nearly too difficult to speak, yet he pressed on. "There was nothing I could do to save him. As I stood in a stupor, I was knocked from the parapet. I stumbled into the woods, where I lost consciousness and did not awaken until late the next day."

"Oh, you poor, poor man. I am so sorry for you. I cannot even imagine. No wonder you collapsed after so nearly hurting Jervais."

She took his head between her hands and pressed her forehead to his. "But you cannot carry about this burden. You are a good man. A wonderful soldier. You must find a way to let it go and move on. You must forgive yourself."

She made it sound so simple. Far too simple. "The way you have forgiven yourself for whatever sins you have committed?"

Rosalind sucked in a sharp breath and pulled back. "That is different."

"Why?"

"Because it was no accident."

"Will you tell me about it?" he finally dared to ask.

She sighed. "As I fear you might have guessed, I lost my virtue to Sir Hugh. I thought I loved him at the time. Perhaps I did, but that does not matter now. Then when I discovered I was with child, I was terrified I would lose my employment. I could not let that happen, for after my father died, my siblings had nearly starved to death."

Tears trickled down her cheeks. "During the time I worked for Lady Gwendolyn, everything changed and my family was well. When I discovered I was with child, I knew what I needed to do to protect them."

Just as he had feared. His heart ached for her.

"I arranged to get away. I even took money from Hugh's room. But I feared I could not go through with it. My mother encouraged me to do it. She promised it would be quick and easy."

"Was it?" he asked, being careful to keep any judgement from his tone. He knew she had punished herself enough for this decision already.

"No, it was long and painful and horrible. I took the awful potion, and the wise woman poked at me with a huge needle. Hours and hours of cramps wracked me. I thought I might bleed to death. And at the end . . ." Now her choking sobs kept her from speaking at all.

He drew her to himself. "At the end?"

"It was . . . so tiny . . . so perfect. Fingers and toes. I didn't know. I swear to you I didn't know. Elsewise I never would have . . ." And she dissolved into sobs once again.

"Shh, shh, let it all out." He rubbed her back as she continued to cry.

A few minutes passed before she collected herself enough to speak again. "Hugh said he would never forgive me. He called me a harlot, a thief, and a murderer. Those words yet haunt me. They echo in my head. I fear they are true."

"You are forgiven, Rosalind. I promise you. For surely no one could have repented her sins as thoroughly as you. You must accept that." Oh, how he wished he could convince her of that truth.

"As you have accepted God's forgiveness and redemption for your mistakes? As you have accepted that Gravensworth was not your fault?"

But he could not accept that. "We are quite a pair."

She clutched his tunic. "We are. Can't you see that?"

But as soon as she said it, she winced. It must hurt her to think such thoughts so soon after reliving the memory of her child.

He pushed her shoulders gently away from him. "Do you understand now why I need so badly to prove myself? How desperate I am to win my family's approval?"

She considered that for a moment, then proceeded slowly, as if cautious to get the words right. "I do understand, but I do not believe God is leading you in this direction. It is guilt and pain and desperation."

"Perhaps, but that is how I feel right now." He lowered his head, for he no longer wished to look into her haunted eyes.

He could not give her what she wanted. If today had proven anything, it had proven he was far too lost for that. All he could hope now was that Sir Etienne could toughen him and turn him into a proper Templar.

Elsewise he knew not how he might survive.

I could hardly believe my good fortune. When I followed Randel and Rosalind to the rocky outcropping, I had hoped I might pick up a tidbit or two to help my cause. That perhaps I might hear some detail of Gravensworth or learn of some impropriety between the two.

But I had never expected to stumble upon such a treasure trove of indicting information! It was the sweetest balm to my revenge-hardened heart.

Slinking back between the tents, I hid deeper in the shadows. On some deep level I had always suspected Randel had killed my brother, but I had never thought I would hear him speak the words aloud.

My brother had changed his identity when he ran away from our brutish father, but he had sent me word of his new position and his new name. Anslem Sollers, soldier under Sir Randel Penigree at Gravensworth Castle. The very fellow Randel had run through with a sword before slinking off into the night.

Randel had no right to be alive. I did not even feel anger anymore. Nor pain. Hatred had so saturated my soul that it had become essential to my very nature. I lived and breathed for my revenge. And soon I would have it.

Between this conversation and tonight's earlier debacle, I finally had the perfect plan in mind to destroy the man for good. Randel Penigree would be brought down. He would be brought down hard.

At the hand of a woman no less.

The next evening Randel scanned the area as he led his troop into yet another mountain valley, this one only a few miles from the Druze-held prison in Beirut. The Templars had already spread out in their tents, and the passage was carefully guarded from both directions. He had intentionally kept the children behind the foot soldiers today, so that he might be able to allow the others to set up camp before them and thus avoid his enemy.

"Rosalind, take the children and set up in that area over there." He pointed to a shady spot near some trees. "As far from Sir Sebastien as possible."

"Good thinking." She headed that way.

Meanwhile, Randel searched for the leaders. He spotted Sir Giles and Sir Etienne speaking with Lady Honoria and Lord Rumsford. Perfect. Lord Haverland was nowhere to be seen, but he had kept to himself these last days, no doubt grieving his lost son.

"Ho! Sir Randel. How was your trip?" Sir Giles asked.

"Excellent." No need to bring up his squabble with Sir Sebastien. That was over now, and he would be careful to keep the children far from the man so that they would not repeat the situation.

Honoria quirked a brow his way but did not correct him. She turned her attention to Sir Giles. "The more important issue is what you and your men have discovered."

"Yes, we were getting to that. You are just in time, Sir Randel." The man gazed to the east, although a foothill impeded his view of the city. "We have successfully blocked any communications. They do not suspect a thing. And according to my spies, the prison is full of Europeans right now. Nigh on three hundred, many of whom are reported to be Englishmen."

"And of my husband and cousin?" Honoria asked.

"Nothing specific," Sir Giles said, "but we have confirmed Sir Etienne's information that most of the high-ranking nobles were brought here after a major skirmish two years ago."

She sighed. "That is good to hear."

Sir Etienne nodded. "Indeed. The bad news is that the prison is well defended. But we have enough men to overtake them. Our plan is to sneak up on them at night. My Templars can scale the walls and neutralize the guards on the parapet. Once they have opened the gates, we should have ample forces to take the prison."

"How near is it to the city? Might we face opposition from there?" Randel asked.

Sir Giles rubbed his beard. "Too near. But we have spotted your ships just a few miles up the coast. We must keep matters stealthy and quiet and hurry all of the troops and the prisoners to the ships straightaway to make a quick escape."

"That sounds possible." Honoria grabbed to the hilt of her sword.

"What shall you do after this?" asked Sir Etienne. "Recoup in Tripoli and onward to Jerusalem?"

"I do not know." The Lady Honoria's mask of stoic strength slipped, and Randel caught a glimpse of her more vulnerable side. "Sapphira has no peace about moving forward, and I must confess, this has been hard on all of us. Perhaps once we find our people, it shall be time to return home. If not, I think we shall keep most of the women and children in Tripoli where it is safe."

"I understand," said Sir Giles. "This fight is not for everyone, certainly not for the long term. That is why God has called some of us to a lifetime here in the Outremer."

"So when shall we attack?" asked Honoria.

"As soon as possible. This must be a surprise in order to work, but it is late to prepare for tonight. Tomorrow would be best."

Indeed, the sun was close to setting already, and most of the troops had just arrived.

"I would like to go in with the first round of fighters tomorrow," Randel said. Not only because he wished to prove himself to the Templars, but because he itched for his next fight. For the fierceness and numbness of the battle lust. Although something about that frightened him.

"Sir Randel, you must stay with the children. They depend on you," Honoria said.

Of course she was right, but disappointment washed over him nonetheless.

"I agree," Sir Giles said. "You have a special bond with them. You have been an admirable leader to those youngsters."

Sir Etienne gripped Randel's shoulder. "But I do commend your desire to fight."

Their praise filtered like sunshine into his dreary heart. The time had come.

"You know, Sir Etienne, Sir Giles, I have been meaning to speak with you. When the English leave, I would like to stay and join your Templars. I feel especially drawn to Sir Etienne's troop."

Sir Etienne slapped him on the back. "Splendid plan, my boy. We would love to have you."

Sir Giles just studied him. "I can see you as a Templar, but I will not argue with Sir Etienne over you. Sir Sebastien has been with me many years, and he yet holds a grudge against you. I think he blames you for bringing the children here. They stir up something rather ugly in him, I fear."

Randel's blood began to boil again. He recalled that evil glint in Sebastien's eye as he dragged Garrett away, and he burned to put an end to such a threat. "You need to know that I shall not allow his mistreatment of them. In all truth, I can barely abide the man. I believe him to be a villain, and I will do whatever it takes to protect those children from him."

Honoria shivered despite the hot day. "By all means, please do. Has Sir Sebastien ever harmed them?"

"He was rough with a few of the boys, but I intervened," Randel said. "I have been keeping a close eye on him. I do not think anything else happened."

"Sir Ademar mentioned something about a row between the two of you. That was good of you to protect the children." Honoria smiled at him, although the expression appeared forced.

"Well, I suppose we have some big days ahead of us. I shall rally the troops for instructions after they refresh themselves. Thank you all for your input." She turned to leave.

Randel scanned the area with the Templars but did not spot Sir Sebastien. He would do his best to keep his anger in check. Just two more days, and then they might all leave Sir Sebastien behind for good.

Sapphira and Sadie put the last touches on their tent as the other girls tended the horses and helped prepare dinner. It was a strenuous job but quickly finished, allowing them a few quiet moments. Sapphira ducked out of the smoldering sun into the comforting shade of the tent. Sadie followed, and they both plopped themselves down on their makeshift beds.

Sadie stretched out with her hands behind her head as if readying for a nap. The girl smiled at Sapphira, then closed her eyes without uttering a word. That is why they made such good friends. Neither had much use for superfluous words. More and more Sapphira found herself longing to save her words for God alone.

Sapphira pulled out a piece of paper from her sack along with a small vial of ink and a quill pen. She had not found much time to write since arriving in the Holy Land, but a poem had been burgeoning in her mind as she prayed for the last several days. Scratching her quill against the paper, she began to transcribe the words before she forgot them.

After a while Sadie cracked open an eye. Then she sat up and watched Sapphira until she finished and laid the pen down.

"What is it?" Sadie asked.

"A love poem."

"To Philippe?"

"No, silly. To God."

"May I read it?" Sadie crawled over to join Sapphira on her blankets.

"Can you read?"

Sadie grinned sheepishly. "In fact, I can. Lady Merry taught all of the Ghosts to read."

"Well, here then." She handed her friend the paper.

Sapphira watched over Sadie's shoulder, still surprised that the peasant girl could read. She followed along to review her latest work.

> Who would have thought
> that simple acceptance of a cross,
> of a paradoxical three in one,
> could be the beginning
> of human completion?
> Yet something within
> me always knew,
> always yearned,
> always cried for that to come.
> The man I sought was man
> no more, but purest divine entity
> who would saturate my soul.
> I rest in His matchless love.

Sadie sat for a moment in quiet contemplation.

Sapphira pushed down her insecurities. The words were so intimate. No one had ever read her poems before, but if she could not trust Sadie with her most private thoughts, she could not trust anyone.

At last she could restrain herself no longer. "What do you think?"

"I think you are over Philippe." Sadie elbowed her in the side and chuckled.

"Seriously?"

"Seriously . . . I think . . . 'tis far beyond lovely. I'm having a hard time finding the right words. Unlike you, I am not a poet."

"Then, you like it?" Sapphira took the paper back into her own hands and lovingly stroked the words.

"Very much," Sadie assured her.

Sapphira rolled the paper and tied a string around it. "Rabia says that her namesake poetess wrote love poems to God. I wonder sometimes if they are similar?"

"Have you noticed that she seems very open to our Christian beliefs?"

"I have."

"And do you plan to do anything? To . . . I don't know . . . to convert her, I suppose?"

"I don't know either," Sapphira admitted. "A part of me says not to let this chance slip by. But a part of me keeps focusing upon the hindrances. It would be hard for her. For her family. She would leave her whole culture behind. And she is only a child. I do not even know how that might work."

"I have heard that the Moslems kill their relatives if they convert."

Sapphira's stomach clutched at the thought. "I have heard the same. But Abu-Wassim is a kind and loving man. I could not imagine him doing such a thing. Still, the situation gives me pause. In my heart, I mostly feel led to pray and to love and to be a true friend to Rabia."

"I think that is the best plan possible," Sadie said.

Her approval warmed Sapphira's heart and unclenched her stomach. Sadie was the wisest of the girls by far.

"I will pray with you." Sadie stretched back out on her blankets. "We might not have much time left with her."

"Do not remind me."

Whatever these next days brought, their time with Rabia would likely come to an end soon. As yet, their mission barely seemed worth it. They had lost nearly as many men as they had saved. But Sapphira could not imagine going back in time and never having been to this place, never having experienced this crusade, and never having met her new friends.

As she pondered Rabia's stirring face, something deep inside her said that it was all worthwhile, for Rabia alone.

Chapter 32

I settled myself in with a group of Templars to eat my dinner. Being so near to Randel last night had nearly ruined my appetite. But it had been worth it, for I had learned so much. Tonight I would sit near Sir Sebastien and keep an eye on that front of my plan.

To my surprise, my friends had followed me. Old habits, I supposed, as they still could barely look me in the eyes, and they would no doubt rather sit near marriageable soldiers than these worthless Templars with their insipid vows of chastity.

"Lady Jocelyn," said Sir Sebastien. "What a nice surprise."

"I thought it high time we all become better acquainted," I said.

My friends began to chat with the Templars, but I preferred to watch and wait.

I did not like the intense look in Sir Sebastien's eye. Perhaps a few weeks ago I might have enjoyed the game of tempting a monk. But not after my ordeal in Jezeer. Such attention had lost its appeal.

"Jocelyn!" One of my friends poked at me, jerking me from

my thoughts. "Sir Sebastien asked about your adventure in Jezeer."

They all gazed at me curiously. And why not? I had yet to share a word about it. I took a deep breath. "I would call it more of an ordeal than an adventure."

"Oh, come now," Sir Sebastien smirked. "You were the only female taken. Is that not a bit suspicious? No one would blame you if you struck some sort of bargain for your freedom. Although by the fact that you returned, I suppose it did not turn out as you planned."

I gasped. No one else had dared question me until now.

"'Tis obvious that Jocelyn is the most beautiful of the women. Perhaps a Templar has trained himself not to see such things, but it makes sense to us." One of my friends reached over as if to pat my shoulder, then dropped her hand, seeming to think better of it. "Although I am terribly sorry that it happened to you."

"Thank you," I whispered to her and shifted on the log where I sat.

"I see just fine," Sir Sebastien said with a roguish quirk of his brow.

If only this Templar knew precisely what I had bargained, he would think far less of me than he already did, but I did not care one whit about his opinion. Tears welled in my eyes as I recalled just how much matters had not turned out as planned.

I should dwell on the future and the bliss I would experience when at last Randel was brought low and my dear brother's life was avenged. I must harden that last wounded place in my heart to pure steel.

"Look at that! You have made her cry now. Leave her be," one of my friends came to my defense.

The wicked Templar just chuckled. "Well, someone had to ask. A harem slave? Why, it is the story of a lifetime!"

Then he paused with an odd expression on his face and

sniffed his stew. Whatever his concern, he shrugged it away and continued eating.

"Hush!" another friend said. "Enough of that. She will speak of it when she wishes."

Everyone grew quiet and focused on their food after that, giving me far too much time to think about my ten days in the village near Jezeer.

They had been close to guess a harem slave, for I had met a few. Although the Druze did not keep slaves for those purposes, nor did they marry multiple wives, the Sunni leader of the army passing from Arabia to Egypt had no such scruples. The chieftain had offered me to the commander, and he had been quick to declare me his fifth wife.

But I did not want anyone here to know that I was someone's misused wife, even if Father Andrew could likely annul the infidel ceremony. And I most certainly did not want any of them continuing to question why I had been the only one taken.

I had suffered far more than I'd ever expected, but I had grown up with pain aplenty . . . and knew how to harden my heart to it. I could not say I felt good about Sir Manfred's lost troop, although if Randel had been successfully eradicated, that part would have been worth the price. Now I was left to scheming all over again.

I noted that Sir Sebastien's face appeared pink, and he shifted about uncomfortably. He pulled at his collar as his eye twitched.

"Has anyone heard of the plans?" one of the women asked, clearly hoping to break the uncomfortable silence, and having no idea she would cause me tension over my own nefarious plans.

"Likely we will attack tomorrow after dark," Sir Sebastien said. But then his face contorted with pain.

Matters proceeded quickly from there. His face flushed red.

He clawed at his neck as if he could not get enough air. He began to spasm and convulse.

A woman screamed at the top of her lungs, piercing the air with her terror.

And Sir Sebastien collapsed to the ground.

"What in the world?" Rosalind said as the screaming and commotion from across the camp met her ears.

"Come, hurry." Randel grabbed for his sword and ran in that direction.

"Children, stay here," she said. Although she doubted they would listen in this instance.

She took off after Randel and heard Abu-Wassim enforcing her order behind her. Thank God for the precious man.

A crowd had already gathered in the area of the problem, but Rosalind managed to squeeze her way through to Randel. When she reached him, his face was pale and stricken. She took him by the arms. "What is it? Please tell me."

Randel sank to his knees and said not a word. He hid his face in his hands.

Then Rosalind managed to weave in closer and see the horrid sight for herself.

Sir Sebastien. Dead upon the ground. Frozen in a grotesque contorted shape.

"Murder!"

"Poison!"

"Betrayal!"

The chaotic shouts now began to make sense to her.

Jocelyn climbed up on a log, and called out in a loud voice. "Sir Sebastien is dead. Murdered. And I know just the man who did it."

People began to step back now in fear. The confusion waned

as everyone surely must have come to the same conclusion. Had not he just last night said that he would kill Sir Sebastien with his bare hands?

But that was ridiculous, Randel would never . . .

The crowd thinned out, leaving Randel kneeling upon the ground. He looked up.

"He did it!" Jocelyn pointed directly at Randel. "Sir Randel Penigree is the murderer."

Randel scrambled to his feet. "I am not. I am innocent. I swear I would never do such a thing."

Jocelyn glared at him with pure hatred in her eyes. "Everyone heard your threats."

Randel rushed at Jocelyn, but a Templar jumped between the two and held out his arms. "We should make no assumptions."

"This is not an assumption. I know for a fact," Jocelyn persisted.

Sir Giles pushed through the throng of people that now surrounded them. Then he spotted Sir Sebastien. "No! I did not believe it." He covered his mouth with his hand to stifle a sob.

Running to the man upon the ground, he gathered him into his arms. "Sebastien. My poor, dear brother Sebastien." He rocked the younger man. "What happened?"

"It appeared to be poison." One of the Templars said. "A very fast-acting poison. By the time we realized what was happening, it was too late."

Lady Honoria, followed by Lord Rumsford, Lord Haverland, Sir Ademar, and Sir Etienne, now made their way over as well. Each with a look of horror on their faces.

"It was Sir Randel, I tell you," Jocelyn shrieked now. "Clearly one of our own has killed him. The Saracens do not even realize we're here. And we all know who held a grudge against Sir Sebastien. I watched them fight just yesterday, over nothing important, and Sir Randel came right out and threatened to kill the man."

"'Twas not over nothing," Sir Ademar defended.

"And Sir Randel would not be foolish enough to kill him after a threat like that," Lady Honoria said.

"But if he was truly worried about your children . . ." Sir Giles continued to rock his fallen comrade. "I do not wish to rush to conclusions, but it is possible."

Rosalind had stood frozen, taking it all in for these last minutes. Now the reality stabbed her in the heart. Sir Sebastien was dead, and Randel, the kindest, gentlest man she had ever met, was being blamed.

"Poison is a woman's weapon," Sir Etienne said. "A knight like Sir Randel would never stoop to such underhanded machinations. This makes no sense at all."

"He would never do it!" Rosalind wailed in desperation.

Lady Honoria lifted her chin and gazed at the gathered group. Rosalind followed her example and noted that even the stunned children had joined them now.

Then Lady Honoria spoke. "This matter must be dealt with swiftly. One of our own, a man who risked his life for our soldiers, is dead. Sir Etienne, take Sir Randel into your care for now. Sir Giles, Lord Rumsford, have your men look into this at once and gather what evidence you can find. We shall reconvene in two hours. Whatever decision we make, you shall all abide by it. Do I make myself clear?"

The gathered assembly mumbled their consent. Even Jocelyn got down from her log. But she did not look at all defeated. In fact, quite the opposite. She appeared a woman on the verge of her greatest triumph.

Randel could not believe he was being dragged in front of the assemblage with his hands tied behind his back like a common criminal. He knew not whether to laugh, scream, or crumple to the ground in despair. Whatever could these fools be thinking? Of course he had been angry with the man, but murder? Poison? It was too ridiculous. Nothing made sense. He feared he was losing his mind.

The sun was now low in the sky, and the cheerful colors streaming from it mocked him once again. He felt numb to the beauty of it. Numb to the hope of it. Even if he was acquitted, his chance to be a Templar would be gone.

Sir Etienne respectfully led him to Lady Honoria and the other esteemed members of their group, who would serve as a judicial council.

"Sir Randel, I am sorry to put you through this," the lady began. "But we must be thorough. These are harsh allegations that have been brought against you." The compassionate look in her eye said she wished to acquit him and be done with this. "Has the cause of death been confirmed?"

Sir Giles stepped forward. "One of my Templars is quite skilled at the subject. He assures me it was poison. Most likely nightshade. A huge dose, based on the speed and the symptoms reported."

"And no enemy soldiers might have sneaked into our camp?"

"Not on our watch," Sir Giles said with finality.

Lady Honoria sucked in a sharp breath. "Did anyone else have a quarrel with the man?"

No one spoke up.

Randel's chest began to tighten. There no longer seemed to be enough air. Still, there was no real evidence against him.

Sir Rumsford came to the forefront now. "My lady, I am sad to be the bearer of this news, but my men searched Sir Randel's tent and found this vial." He held up the small yet earth-shattering container of dark glass sealed with a cork. "We believe it is nightshade."

Randel could no longer hold his peace. "This is ludicrous.

Why would I . . . Surely I would hide . . ." And even as the thoughts collided in his head, he realized.

It must have been one of his boys. He pressed his lips together as his throat constricted, unable to speak even a single word that might indict them.

"Perhaps you were too blinded by hatred to think straight." Jocelyn sneered. "You are a murderer, plain and simple. I know for a fact that you murdered my brother and never looked back. You never so much as apologized to my family."

Now Randel's thoughts reeled completely out of control. "But I . . . I do not even know your brother."

"Oh, yes. You know him by his alias. Anslem Sollers."

The name crashed into his head like a battering ram. The images rose up all around him. The darkness. The fog.

He pivots and thrusts his sword. He feels it drive deep into the belly of his own comrade. The younger man's face contorts. A flash of sword. A splash of blood. A body crumpled against the battlement.

"No, No. I killed him. I killed my own man. God help me, no!"

Sapphira gasped and then froze, the air still lodged in her lungs.

Whispers surrounded her. Jocelyn began to shout again that Randel was a murderer. But he could not be. It simply made no sense.

"Hold!" said Sir Giles, raising a hand to still the explosive gathering. "Sir Randel, what are you saying? Who did you kill? This Sollers fellow, or Sir Sebastien?"

"I killed them. I killed them all. It is all my fault." Randel writhed upon his knees with his hands yet secured behind his back.

"You see!" Jocelyn cackled. "I told you."

"Wait." Sir Etienne went to Randel's side. He waved his hand before Randel's face. Then he shook him by the shoulders. "Sir Randel. Sir Randel, can you hear me?"

But Randel continued to moan and double over. "I killed them. It is all my fault."

"'Tis clear he is not in his right mind," Sir Etienne said in Randel's defense.

Sapphira approached Randel now. "May I?" she asked Sir Etienne.

"Of course, my lady."

Sapphira knelt down beside Randel and laid a hand upon his arm. As she began to pray for him, she sensed the murky darkness that filled him and surrounded him. It threatened to suck her in as well, but she battled hard in the Spirit. Soon she felt an explosion of strength and blinked her eyes open to see that Sadie and many of the children had joined her.

She closed her eyes again and continued fighting for the soul of dear Randel—the best, the only, commander she had ever had the privilege to serve under.

Rosalind whispered her prayers under her breath, but she needed to keep her eyes open and her senses alert.

As Randel seemed to be calming, Sir Etienne turned to Jocelyn and asked, "Where did this supposed murder happen?"

"At Gravensworth Castle. He was the commander, yet he killed my brother with his own sword. He lost every one of his men that night, and he alone escaped and ran away like a coward."

"Surely not!" Lady Honoria protested. "The duchess would not have recommended him so highly if this were true."

Gathering her courage, Rosalind stepped to the front of the gathering. "May I speak?"

"By all means," Lady Honoria said.

"Some of what Jocelyn says is true. Randel's troop was taken off guard by a huge group of Scots. They had no chance, but they fought valiantly nonetheless. The death of this Sollers haunts him at all times. It was an accident, pure and simple. He turned to strike at what he thought was the enemy on that dark and foggy night, but it was the boy, his own man. The only reason he survived the massacre is that he was shoved from the parapet and by some miracle awoke the next day. He then ran to get help for the people inside the castle."

Randel blinked her way a few times, as if he were starting to come back to himself.

"That makes more sense, and sounds more like the man I know." Lady Honoria sighed with relief. "And if your brother used an alias, of course Randel would not know to whom he should apologize."

Jocelyn huffed in outrage and crossed her arms over her ample chest.

"Randel was horribly troubled by the loss. He tried to be pleasant and lighthearted, but I have seen the darkness of his memories overtake him again and again." Rosalind clasped her hands in petition. "Sir Randel Penigree has the purest, the gentlest heart a knight could ever possess. He threatened Sir Sebastien to protect the children, but I know he would never murder anyone. Let his guilt over the accident at Gravensworth be proof enough that he is not capable of such an intentional act of evil."

Where was Father Andrew? Surely he knew the truth. He would confirm her story.

"Why would you believe her?" Jocelyn turned her venom Rosalind's way. "She is no better. *Thief! Harlot! Murderer!*"

She hurled each word like a dagger. Slow and sure. Straight to Rosalind's heart. "You might have fooled the rest of them," Jocelyn said, "but I know exactly what you are."

Chapter 33

The world began to spin around Rosalind as Jocelyn's accusations echoed in her head. She wheezed in and out but could not seem to fill her lungs. Sir Ademar caught her from behind by the elbows and kept her from falling.

Through blurry vision she took in the horrified faces all around her. Every person in the crowd gaped her way in disgust. Even Honoria. Even the children.

Only Randel gazed at her with compassion and understanding.

But it was not enough. Those words pierced through her again and again. *Thief. Harlot. Murderer.* She had been a fool to think she could ever outrun them. Pressing a hand to her side, she struggled again to find her breath.

But perhaps she had only imagined the disgust. For as Lady Honoria spoke, she sounded confused, taken aback, but entirely unconvinced. "That is madness. What on earth is she talking about?"

"She—" Jocelyn was about to pour out more of her poisonous accusations over the crowd, but Rosalind held up a hand to stop her.

"'Tis true. I killed my own unborn . . . child." As she said the last word, she collapsed into tears and could say no more. Sir Ademar lowered her to the ground, where she sat in a defeated heap.

More voices swirled around her, but she could not take them in. Only recall her tiny, fully formed child in her palm. *Dear God, no! No! Please take this pain away.*

The next thing she knew, the children came and surrounded her much as they had surrounded Randel just moments earlier. Their prayers wafting about her like incense. Their innocent light seeping into her darkest places.

Light like water rushing into her heart, filling each crack, and pushing out every last bit of the darkness that had threatened to destroy her.

Randel could not stop staring as the children prayed over Rosalind. He could almost, but not quite, see the shimmer of light around her on this dim evening. The sun had set during all of the commotion, yet the sun in his heart had dawned for the first time in so many long months.

He could not explain the new hope, the new lightness that surrounded him. The new eyes with which he saw the world. The new perspective that changed everything he thought he had known.

He was forgiven. He was free. And he needed please no one but Christ. Facts he knew, words similar to those he himself had spoken to Rosalind, yet they had never made it past the darkness in his own heart.

But the trouble was not over yet.

"I do not understand the complication nor the hesitation." Jocelyn's bitter tone turned every word into a weapon. "They are both guilty of murder. Kill them both and be done with it."

"Wait!" Randel stumbled to his feet with his hands yet trapped behind him, then strode to Lady Honoria with confidence.

"Sir Randel?"

"Rosalind did rid herself of a child conceived out of wedlock. Sadly, it is true. But she was young and confused. Her family relied on her income, and she did not wish to lose her position and leave them to starve. Her mother convinced her it was the right thing to do, but she has mourned her decision every day since. Her repentance is more true and real than any person's I have ever witnessed. Is not God's grace sufficient? Can she not be forgiven?"

Lady Honoria yet looked shocked and confused. "I put my innocent young sister in her care. I . . . I . . ."

Father Andrew pushed his way through the crowd to the center. "What is going on here?"

Lady Honoria turned to him. "Did you know about Rosalind's child?"

The priest clasped his hands together and looked to the ground. "I did, but I was told in the sanctity of the confession. She committed a grievous sin, and there is no way to undo the loss of the child, but she has been forgiven."

Father Andrew gestured to Rosalind. "No one in the history of the earth has ever repented of any decision so thoroughly. I personally believe that Christ paid the full price for Rosalind's sin upon the cross, but even by the prevailing views of the church, she has done penance aplenty this past year and a half."

"And do you believe Rosalind is trustworthy to lead our children?" asked Lady Honoria.

"Indeed. For no one understands the destruction caused by poor choices as thoroughly as Rosalind does. Since the first day we set sail, she has been a paragon of virtue and a fine example to these young ladies."

Then he shifted his gaze to Randel. "And for whatever it is worth, my son, you are forgiven your mistakes as well." The priest smiled to Randel, and this time he felt its warmth to the core of his being.

Randel noticed that Rosalind had ceased her weeping and now focused on the proceedings.

He must say all that was on his heart, both for her, and for every soul gathered here. "The Rosalind who is before you is a new person. Perhaps once she took money without permission, once she relinquished her virtue too easily to a man who did not deserve it. And yes, unfortunately, without fully understanding the ramifications, she ended the life of her own dear child."

Jocelyn cried out again. "But she—"

"Let him finish." This time Lady Honoria interrupted her.

He paused and looked Rosalind straight in her piercing blue eyes. "But Rosalind of Ipsworth, I say that you are no longer a thief, a harlot, or a murderer. God has given you new names. *Precious. Righteous. His.* Accept these. They are His free gift to you."

"And will you accept . . ." Rosalind hiccupped through the remnants of her tears. "Will you accept that you were never a murderer and that you did your best? Will you stop trying to prove yourself and accept the person that God made you to be and His plan for your life instead?"

Her words reached deep into his heart. A heart that he had wanted to render dead, that now coursed with rapid, pumping life. "I will."

"Enough," Jocelyn shrieked. "I have had it with your pretty speeches. Sir Sebastien is dead, and Sir Randel poisoned him. That is why we are here."

"I am not yet convinced of that," Lady Honoria said. "Is that what you meant, Sir Randel? Did you kill Sir Sebastien to protect the children?"

"If I would have been called upon to fight Sir Sebastien to

protect them, I would have done it in an instant, but I did not poison him."

"Then explain the vial in your tent," Jocelyn demanded.

Drat! In all that had passed during these short but eternally long minutes, he had forgotten the vial. He would not wish to implicate the boys, but the fury in Jocelyn's eyes gave him a different idea.

He turned and pinned Jocelyn with a glare. "Perhaps you planted it there. We now know that you have ample reason to hate me. Perhaps you are the one who killed him in order to implicate me."

"And why has no one ever investigated why Jocelyn was the only woman taken by the Saracens?" Rosalind added. "Is this not suspicious?"

"'Tis highly suspicious," said Sir Etienne. "I have thought so many times, but as I could think of no possible motive, I had not brought it up."

"The Saracens seemed to know exactly when and how to attack to find us at our weakest," Sir Ademar said. "I have wondered about that."

"This is . . . this is . . . You can't think . . ." Jocelyn sputtered.

"I've seen the vial!" one of the she-wolves shrieked, then clamped her hands over her mouth.

"What?" Lady Honoria, stalwart woman that she was, looked as if she could not handle one more surprise this evening.

"I've seen the vial. Lord Rumsford, if I may?" The young woman held out her palm, and Lord Rumsford deposited the evidence there.

She studied it closely. "Yes, this is it. Jocelyn takes it out and strokes it when she believes we are all asleep. She whispers to it. Once, I think she might have kissed it. 'Twas quite alarming. Has anyone else seen this?"

The pack of she-wolves whispered and jostled among

themselves. Finally, the only noblewoman of the group stepped forth. In a quiet, remorseful voice, she said, "I have seen it too. But perhaps we misunderstood . . ."

"I think we all understand quite clearly now," said Sir Giles.

Lady Honoria nodded her agreement. "I am ready to make my ruling. Jocelyn, I believe you are guilty of not only the murder of Sir Sebastien, but also of trying to implicate Sir Randel and Rosalind unfairly. Randel and Rosalind, you will not be held guilty by this court for your past mistakes. Lord Rumsford, have two of your men escort Jocelyn to the ship. Soon we shall try her properly under the local magistrate in Tripoli and allow justice to prevail."

I struggled against the bindings on my hands, unable to believe that matters turned so rapidly against me. A knight lifted me upon his horse and climbed up behind me. I wanted to scream, to thrash, but my only hope lay in a show of docility.

"Are you comfortable?" asked the knight, chivalrous even with a known criminal. It almost made me sad for what I must do. Almost, but not quite.

"I am fine. Thank you." I turned and batted my eyelashes at him. "You are quite kind."

I feigned a few sniffles, though in truth I was too livid to cry.

Another knight mounted his horse, and we headed off toward the coast on this dark night with only a sliver of moon to light the way.

Although I attempted to keep my features even, I seethed and boiled with rage. I would show them. I would show all of them. Not only Randel, not only Rosalind and the passel of annoying youngsters—I would see every last one of them destroyed for this.

I yet had weapons at my disposal. I yet knew how to seduce

and use my womanly wiles. I simply must harden that last soft place in my heart that had so recently ached from my ordeal. But my hatred would see me through. It would give me the strength I needed.

And I yet had my dagger hidden away in the folds of my kirtle. This was not over.

"After the battle we shall all gather here." Sir Giles pointed at the map in the firelight as he spoke to the assembled leaders. "Where the ships will be waiting for us."

"From there we will return to Tripoli, at least for a time, and decide whether this crusade will continue or if we should set a course for home," Lady Honoria said.

Randel paused to consider that. Of course it would be best to head home, but if they did not find Honoria's husband and Richard DeMontfort, matters might yet be delayed. This crusade had proven harder than any of them ever suspected, the territory more brutal, the situation more complicated. If he had ever wished to head onward to Jerusalem, he had lost that desire along the way.

And now with his new bright perspective, he questioned if he would become a Templar at all. The prospect of priest no longer sounded like a second-rate job, but rather a great honor. And then there was the possibility of . . .

"Wait!" Lady Honoria pressed a hand to her head. "What are we thinking? We cannot do it this way. Have we learned nothing?" Her breathing seemed to turn shallow.

"I do not understand," Sir Giles said. "I thought we had all agreed upon this plan together."

Lady Honoria seemed too stricken by panic to respond.

Sir Giles glanced about to Sir Etienne, Lord Rumsford, Sir Ademar, and even to Randel.

Randel was about to shrug his shoulders, when understanding dawned. "She is worried that Sapphira has not been consulted."

The lady nodded vehemently from her doubled-over position.

"But surely Sapphira would have spoken up if she had a concern." Sir Giles yet appeared confused.

"Perhaps not after we dismissed her warnings so glibly the last time," Lord Rumsford said with humility.

"I shall get her, then. Try to take deep breaths, my lady. All will be well." With due haste, Randel rushed off to find Sapphira with the rest of the children.

"Come with me!" he said.

Seeming to sense the urgency, the fairylike child stood and followed. He brought her back to the leadership group in less than a minute.

"Here she is." Randel laid his hands on Sapphira's slim shoulders. "Ask her what you wish."

"What is it?" Sapphira questioned with concern.

The Lady Honoria yet panted slightly and appeared uncomfortable, but managed to find her voice. "Is God in this plan to attack the prison? I do not blame you if you do not wish to speak to me of these matters. I have not earned your trust. But please, I beg of you, tell me true."

Sapphira blinked a few times. "I . . . I am sorry. I did not realize my approval was so important to you."

"Neither did I . . . until we went to proceed without your blessing."

Sapphira pressed her lips tight for a moment. "I confess that after Jezeer, I have not sensed much concerning our direction. But I have felt no specific concerns or warnings about this plan."

"Please, give us a yes or a no," her sister pled.

"I sense . . ." Sapphira stared out into the night sky for a moment. "I sense . . . that it is our decision to make. That is odd, is it not?"

"You tell us, for you are the one who hears from God."

"'Tis just that I felt so strongly that this crusade was dire," Sapphira said. "Yet now the urgency is gone. Perhaps our mission has been . . . fulfilled?"

"But what of the attack?" Desperation flooded Honoria's voice.

By the intense look on her face, Randel could tell Sapphira was seeking the spirit's prompting, as she so often did.

"I believe God is leaving that choice up to us. It will not be without a cost, but if it is important to us, we may proceed."

"It is so very important to me—" Honoria's voice caught on a sob, but she held herself in check—"to know if my husband is there."

"And it is even more important for North Britannia to know if our rightful duke lives," said Rumsford.

Sapphira nodded. "Then you have your answer. However, I would remind you that I do not believe we should head to Jerusalem to fight."

"But if we learn that they are still alive elsewhere?" Honoria asked.

Sapphira reached out and took her sister's hand. "Then we shall seek God's guidance—together."

"Perhaps we should do that right now." Honoria held her free hand out to Sir Ademar.

Randel gladly took Sapphira's other hand and Sir Etienne's as they all joined in a circle.

Sapphira gave her sister's hand a tug. "You lead us, Honoria."

Honoria's cheeks turned pink. Randel had never seen her blush before. At first she spoke with hesitation. "Father God, we humbly come before you. We need your wisdom; we need your guidance. This crusade means nothing if it is not your will."

Then her demeanor shifted and she grew more confident as she continued to pray for forgiveness and direction with true fervor.

At the end, Randel opened his eyes along with the others. They all stood silently for a moment.

"Does anyone sense anything?" Sapphira asked.

But they remained quiet as they all pondered the situation. Finally Honoria spoke. "If God is giving us a choice, I believe we must move forward."

"I agree," said Rumsford.

Ademar and the Templars all nodded their assent.

"Lady Honoria, Lady Honoria." A knight stumbled toward them in his hurry.

One of the fellows who had escorted Jocelyn to the ship. Everyone stared at him with concern.

He panted as he stopped before them. "She has escaped."

"Surely you jest." Honoria's mouth gaped.

"I suppose we failed to search her person. While I was gone to . . . relieve myself, she must have convinced my comrade to free her hands. When I returned, his chest was stained in blood, and she was nowhere to be found."

"Did you search at all?" asked Sir Rumsford, the man's commander.

"I looked for a trail but could detect nothing in the dark. I'm afraid I was gone quite long."

Rumsford looked ready to strike the man but controlled himself.

Randel empathized with the dreadful feeling the man must be experiencing, but thankfully, he relived none of his own memories of failure.

"I humbly apologize, but I have been ill since Jezeer. The water there did not agree with many of us."

Rumsford sighed and raked his hair through his fingers.

"Many of the men are sick with dysentery. We must hurry with this campaign before they grow too weak to fight."

"Where could Jocelyn have gone?" Randel spoke the question they must all be wondering.

"I have no idea, but that girl is volatile." Sir Giles looked around at all of them. "If Rosalind's suspicions are correct, Jocelyn might have betrayed us before. There is no guessing what she might do in her bitterness. I believe we must move up the strike to tonight."

Lord Rumsford brightened at the idea. "The plans are in order. We have the supplies, and the men have been resting all afternoon."

"I say we do it!" Sir Ademar said and clapped his hands together.

"Then what are we waiting for?" Honoria quirked her brows, and the decision was made. "Gather your troops and be ready in an hour. We move tonight!"

Randel headed for the children with a new buoyancy in his step. Not dread, nor fear, nor even numbness. They were ready for this battle, and he was ready to lead the way.

Chapter 34

Rosalind pulled her horse next to Randel's. Once again they would watch the battle from a nearby rise, but this time in the hazy, moonlit darkness. The sprawling prison before them proved quite a sight, perhaps three or four times larger than the prison in Jezeer, with an expansive courtyard and a multi-level construction. Just to the right of the building, the Mediterranean shimmered, and beyond it pinpricks of light flickered at a distance from the city of Beirut.

The Templars would do most of the work. The English army would hide close at hand, ready to support them.

Although a small part of her missed being involved in the action, Rosalind would be glad to keep the children safe at a distance—praying, as they were always meant to do. Although they had now proven themselves in battle as well. At least they were not on the ship with the sick and wounded, the prisoners released from Jezeer, and the rest of the women, many of whom moved too slowly for this mission. Only Lady Honoria was with the troops tonight.

The children spread out in a line, but Sapphira hopped down

off her horse. "Come, let us gather and hold hands the way we have been doing. I feel God's presence so strongly when we join ourselves thus."

The rest of them followed suit, and their well-trained mounts stood patiently by.

"Good plan, Lady Sapphira," Randel said, "but the adults shall keep watch over the situation."

Abu-Wassim and Hassan joined Rosalind and Randel, but to Rosalind's surprise, Rabia moved to the circle of children.

Rosalind reached out and gave Randel's hand a little squeeze. She had barely found time to process the events of the evening before they headed out again, but she could not help wondering if things might change between them. If Randel might open to the idea of a relationship.

For her heart now felt whole and well and ready to love again. She would give him up if he yet felt the call to be a monk, but with much sorrow. For she had never loved any man the way she loved Sir Randel Penigree.

To the tune of Sapphira's worshipful songs, she watched the eerie scene unfold before her. Shadowy Templars dressed all in black scaled the prison wall hand over hand, like some sort of insects scurrying up the side. One by one, the Saracen guards seemed to disappear into the inky darkness.

All was still for a moment, then the gates burst open and more Templars rushed inside.

Rosalind bit down an overwhelming mix of thrill and fear. Unable to do anything else to help, she joined the children in their song. Then something in her gut clenched in warning, though matters seemed to be going well from her vantage point.

Not terribly long after dispatching my captor, I stood awaiting my introduction to a new chieftain in Beirut.

Having been raised by a brutish father, I was a quick runner and skilled at disguising my footsteps. Once the knight was dead, I had stripped off my shoes and dashed directly to the coast, following it south toward the city. After a week in Arab captivity, I knew enough of the language to make my request understood. Not that the city guards required much explanation from a lone European woman in the middle of the night.

I straightened my thick, dark hair and my bright red kirtle, willing once again to use any weapon at my disposal to achieve my goals. For a moment I wondered what would happen to me in this place . . . after. But any fate they had in mind would be better than the death that awaited me in Tripoli. Suddenly fifth wife to a wealthy Moslem sounded quite satisfactory.

"Why do you awake me?" a short, surly man asked in French as he meandered into the room while still rubbing at his eyes.

"You are the leader of this area?"

"Yes. Beirut is under Druze control, and I am the chieftain." Several other men followed him.

"I have come to tell you that the crusaders from England are planning an attack on the prison at Beirut."

He yawned. "We knew this might be a possibility. We have doubled our guard. But your main forces are now captured in Jezeer."

I shook my head vehemently. "No, the Templars retook Jezeer."

He studied me as if unconvinced. "I have heard no report of this."

"Because they have blocked all the passages." Desperation rose up within me now. I wanted to shake this imbecile, but I needed to control myself.

"Why do you tell us this?"

"They have turned on me, and I want to see them defeated."

The chieftain frowned and scratched his rear through his loose pants.

"I swear to you," I said. "They are here. A mere two miles away."

"Impossible."

"You must believe me. The Templars are slaughtering anyone who crosses their path."

"Hmm, the Templars are skilled." He looked deep into my eyes. "When do they attack?"

"The plan was for tomorrow night, but I would not delay in protecting the prison. With my escape, their strategy might change."

The chieftain nodded. He lifted his chin to his men, who scurried into action.

I resisted the urge to sigh with relief and blinked back tears that now filled my eyes. It would happen. I would have my revenge.

"And what do you wish in return, my friend?" the chieftain asked.

"Protection. A fresh start at life. That is all." My knees went wobbly now.

It was done.

"Too bad for you, unlike the weak Europeans, I allow no traitors in my midst." The chieftain jerked his chin again and strode away.

I did not understand. I glanced about, unsure of what was expected of me. But then strong arms gripped me from behind. I called to the retreating back of the chieftain. "Wait! I came to help you. I belie—"

Something sharp and cool slid across my neck. Slick, warm liquid seeped down my skin.

I grabbed at my throat. As my life faded away, I crumpled to the floor.

Randel leaned forward and gripped tightly to the reins. The Templars were through the gate now, yet the battle continued and the prisoners had not been freed. From his vantage point on the hill, he could tell that the Templars were far outnumbered.

Should he do something? Send word? He would not risk one of the children. Perhaps he could take the message himself. But even as he considered that, Rumsford took the English army and headed toward the prison gate. Slowly, a group at a time, they fought their way inside.

His hands unclenched as the tide began to turn. The children at his back yet sang forth their prayers, their voices growing stronger and more poignant in pitch as the sounds of battle filled the night.

Finally, all the Englishmen pushed their way inside. Fifty Templars and nearly two hundred English knights and soldiers fought a similar number of Saracens. Although the prison courtyard was large and sprawling, the pure pandemonium within was clear. Randel could not believe that the prison kept so many guards. But perhaps they had heard about the crusader conquest at Jezeer.

Tension filled him now. This would not be an easy fight, and guilt niggled at him that he sat unscathed while the men below risked their lives. But he was fulfilling his assigned role, and he must be faithful to that.

He glanced over at Rosalind, faithfully fulfilling her role as well. Faithful and good in all things. She prayed every word along with the children, although she remained stalwart at his side. Inspired by her, he took up the prayer as well.

The fight raged on. Clangs and screams poured over the valley to meet their ears.

Randel scanned the city beyond, and that is when he saw it.

A huge mass of torches, blending into one fiery beacon, and heading toward them from perhaps a half mile away.

"Reinforcements?" Rosalind asked, her voice shaking.

"How could they know?"

"Perhaps their guards saw us after all, or perhaps . . ."

"Jocelyn. It matters not now. I must warn them. You are in charge."

Randel kicked his horse forward and hurried down the hill. No longer afraid. No longer filled with false guilt. Yet determined to do his duty and protect his comrades, just as he had always wished to do.

Once to the gate, he realized he would have to fight his way through to find their leaders. Abandoning his giant war-horse, which would never make it through the throng, he slashed and struck, ducking through holes and pressing forward. A swish to his left caught his attention, and he blocked the blow with his sword by sheer instinct.

There—a raised platform. He plowed his way toward it. But an enemy soldier blocked his path and engaged him in one-on-one combat.

Randel remained calm. He drew upon his training as he dodged and parried, struck and spun. He met the man blow for blow, but he had no time for swordplay. In a risky all-or-nothing maneuver, Randel dared to tumble toward the man and knock the weapon from his hand. As he regained his feet, he watched the sword streaking against the night sky.

Much as he hated to, he delivered the death blow.

Scrambling atop the platform, he screamed with all of his might in his native English language. "Saracen reinforcements are coming. A huge mob of them. We must hurry!"

His gaze darted about. They needed to free their people or this would all be for naught. He noticed a doorway that the Saracen guards were particularly protecting. That must be the way inside the prison.

He dashed in that direction yelling the crusader battle cry, "*Deus vult!* Free them! Free our people!"

The energy in the courtyard burgeoned. His men fought

harder, stronger, and many of them stormed with him toward the prison door, roaring in their fervor. Then he saw the Lady Honoria running and bellowing at his side.

Rosalind observed helplessly from the hillside. Though she was equipped with sword, with bow and arrow, with a dagger, and even with a tinder box to light her arrows aflame, she waited patiently with her charges as she had been ordered.

The speckled mass of undulating fire increased its pace. No doubt the Druze fighters from the city now heard the clangs of battle and rushed to help their comrades.

"Should we warn them?" She asked Abu-Wassim as tension and tingling fear both gripped her body at once.

"No. Hold. We should protect the children, especially if the worst occurs. Randel got through. I heard him shouting, and I am certain they are working as fast as they can."

Rosalind spotted a group wearing white crusader surcoats and ramming a door. Surely they were on the verge of breaking the prisoners free.

But the next sight to meet her eyes caused her blood to chill. Men in Druze attire sliding down ropes along the prison wall. What could they be doing? Did they merely wish to escape?

Then someone tossed down a huge wooden beam, and it crashed on the sandy ground.

"They plan to bar our men inside until reinforcements come." Even as Rosalind uttered the horrible words, she pulled out her bow and notched her arrow. But the enemy fighters were too far away. She would have to get closer. Have to leave the safety of her hiding place and leave the children behind.

Now five men worked to drag the beam toward the gate.

"We cannot wait! We must help them now or all will be lost!" Abu-Wassim shouted.

He and Hassan spurred their horses and started down the hill.

Fortunately the men struggled under the weight of the heavy beam and moved slowly, but now more were heading down the wall.

"Children," she called loud and clear, "if things go badly, you must gallop with all your might straight to the ships! Do not stop! Do not look back!" And with that final instruction, she rushed down the hill.

As Abu-Wassim and Hassan began clashing swords with the men on the ground, Rosalind took aim and worked at stopping those on the wall. She hit one, then two, but they were moving quickly through the deceptive darkness, and several of her arrows missed their marks. Others struck their targets, but did not stop the enemy fighters. She managed to hit a third fighter and then a fourth.

Abu-Wassim and Hassan had the advantage over the horseless men, but they yet battled on.

Shooting the last of her arrows, she took out a final man, and he tumbled several feet to the ground. Then she rushed forward to help her comrades.

An idea struck her, and she stopped briefly to pull flint and tinder from the sack at her waist. She scanned to her right. The sea was at least a hundred feet away. She spotted several of her arrows scattered about the ground.

Her plan just might work.

"Ugh! I cannot believe they left us here. We should be fighting." Jervais strained against the hands that held him in their circle and appeared ready to bolt toward the prison.

"A handful of young people would not make a difference," Sadie said practically.

"And they would never forgive us if we got ourselves hurt.

Just look at how Humphrey's death affected everyone." Garrett, always perceptive, saw straight to the core of the matter.

Yet Sapphira ached to be helping as well. She glanced to the dear faces surrounding her on this dark night. "We are doing the best thing we can. Do not cease praying now."

She switched over to the Scripture chant that God had laid upon her heart during that first battle in Jezeer. "'My grace is sufficient for thee: for my strength is made perfect in weakness. For when I am weak, then I am strong.'" They all followed along.

But she could tell that despite their enclosed circle, attention drifted away.

"Ho! She's set it on fire!" Jervais proclaimed.

"The beam to block the door? Rosalind?" Issobelle asked.

"Ha ha! Just let them try to stop us now."

Sapphira continued her chant, but she could not keep from following Jervais's pointing finger with her gaze. Surely enough, Rosalind's fiery arrows had hit the beam and set it ablaze while the enemy fighters were occupied battling Abu-Wassim and Hassan. They would not be able to use it to lock the Europeans inside.

"And I think the tide has shifted. It looks as if our men have broken through and the prisoners are joining the fight," Sadie called excitedly.

But just as quickly, Brigitte cried out, "Oh no!"

They all turned now. A handful of Saracen fighters had rushed from the prison. But instead of heading to the city, they turned directly toward the children. Escaping or attacking? Sapphira could not say.

In an instant Sapphira knew what to do. The idea welled up from deep within her and would not be denied.

"Should we run?" Lillian asked.

"No, the girls could not outrun them, and running will only draw attention. Keep praying," Sapphira hissed in a loud whisper. "Maybe they will not see us. If they do, I shall give the signal of the serin. Get into position."

Not a one of the children questioned her. Even Rabia had memorized the birdcalls Sadie had taught them all thanks to the Ghosts of Farthingale Forest, although they had not yet found opportunity to use the signals. And the serin call had been their own invention, based upon their own strengths for their own purposes.

Several of the children shifted to new locations, and they all subtly prepared weapons, but they remained turned into the circle and continued to pray. Sapphira had the perfect view from her spot as the group of about two dozen enemy fighters headed toward the ten children. The mass of fire from the city had nearly reached the prison as well, and Sapphira could now distinguish individual torches flickering gold in the night.

But she would not lose her faith. Not now. Not ever.

For a moment it seemed like the fleeing group might veer to the right, but then one of the men pointed directly their way and let out a fierce battle cry.

As they crashed up the hillside, Sapphira made the long trilling call of the serin.

Then she counted backward, *five, four, three, two, one.*

With a loud scream, they turned and confronted their enemy with all the fierceness they could muster. The swordsmen dropped low as the archers let loose several rounds of arrows. Sapphira pulled taut her bowstring and let her arrows fly.

Several of the men fell, and many others dispersed in terror. Only two determined fighters with crazed eyes continued their way.

Jervais and Sadie engaged them as Garrett and the other boys got in their strikes as well. Then Sadie fell to the ground clutching her leg. Sapphira dashed in that direction and shocked her opponent with a left-handed strike of her sword to his arm.

He shouted, *"Ya-allah!"* and the last two men turned and ran.

But spotting the children's horses, they grabbed two for themselves and chased the others away before heading off toward the mountains. A sick dread filled Sapphira's stomach as their mounts fled into the night.

Before Sapphira could catch her breath, more chaos erupted down the hillside. This time it was hundreds of crusaders flooding from the prison gates and fleeing toward the beach.

"Hurry!" she yelled. "We must run to the ship with all our might. And we must all be around the bend before the Saracens reach the prison!" For if they saw the fleeing crusaders and prisoners, they might give chase, and the fight would start all over again.

Sapphira could only hope the bright torches would blind the Saracens' eyes to the shadowy movement beyond their goal.

"But Randel and Rosalind?" Brigitte said, frozen in her place.

Sapphira turned to the frenzied mob rushing along the beach. No one broke away from the crowd, and even if they wished to, they could never fight the tide of humanity sweeping down the shoreline.

"We will meet them there. Go! Now!"

Jervais led them, and the well-conditioned children took off at a strong pace. But as Sapphira's feet began to pound the earth, she noticed Sadie struggling to even walk. Blood seeped through a gash in her leggings.

Most of the children were already too far to call, but Rabia had paused, no doubt to seek out her family.

"Rabia! Come, help!"

In a flash, they had Sadie's arms over their shoulders and ran together toward the ship.

Glancing back, Sapphira saw the raging torches a mere furlong beyond the prison. "Faster!" she cried.

Pulling strength from a place deep within, she urged her feet forward at a quicker pace, and Rabia met her stride for stride.

"That way!" Sapphira jerked her chin toward a path that cut over the hillside at an angle and would lead them to the beach farther from the prison.

Most of the crusaders were around the bend now.

But Sadie had ceased to help carry her own weight and sagged against them, hindering their speed.

"No!" Sadie said. "We are too slow. Leave me and save yourselves."

"Never!" Rabia answered for both of them. She hauled Sadie higher on her shoulder so that the girl's feet barely grazed the ground, and Sapphira did likewise.

They finally reached the beach. The last crusaders turned the corner and disappeared out of sight.

The torches seemed to flow like a river of molten fire now, directly to the prison behind them. Soon they would be spotted. They would never reach the bend in time.

Then two figures came back around the corner. Garrett and Jervais!

"We just noticed you were missing." Jervais called as they ran their way.

With surprising strength, Jervais lifted Sadie in his arms. Garrett took Sapphira and Rabia's hands in his own. He seemed to lend them an extra burst of speed, and they all melted around the corner and into the night.

Once safe, Sapphira broke free from Garrett's grasp to peek back around and watch the molten river, still streaming. Into the prison. Not down the beach after them.

She sagged for a brief moment in relief, then sped down the sand once again.

Chapter 35

By the time everyone was safely aboard the ship, the sun was already tinging the sky with morning light in a pale shade of silver. Randel took a moment to lean against the ship rail and breathe in the salty sea air. He whispered up a word of thanks that the Saracens had not given chase up the beach. And he had personally counted each of the children as they had fought their way through the waves and climbed up the rope ladders to the ship. Sadie's injury would require some tending, but only Humphrey would not return to Tripoli with them.

"Sir Randel," Rumsford touched his arm, pulling him away from memories that were melancholy but no longer haunting. "Lady Honoria is ready for us."

Randel followed Rumsford into Honoria's cabin. For the first time in their journey lasting a third of the year, he noted tearstains streaking their leader's cheeks.

She sniffled and straightened herself. "Welcome, gentlemen." She pushed against the table with her hands and stood, although that simple action seemed to require the utmost effort.

Lord Haverland gave her shoulder a supportive pat. "We have been taking tally of who made it safely back to the ships."

Lady Honoria pressed her lips together tight before she spoke. "We rescued almost three hundred prisoners, mostly English, but my husband and cousin are not among them."

Haverland nodded. "We have it on good authority that they died in Beirut during the winter. We never had a chance of saving them."

"But at least we know the truth." Honoria's voice quavered. "The dukedom can move forward. I think they will better embrace Duchess Adela once they realize she is the true heir."

"In a way, the knowledge shall set us all free." Now that his vision concerning his own life had grown so much clearer, Randel understood how a warped perception could lead one astray. "Was that not our primary goal?"

"To set the captives free." Honoria took a deep breath. "I suppose that could have many interpretations."

"And our total losses?" asked Rumsford.

"Less than a hundred men between the various battles," Haverland said. "Considering we saved four times the number that we lost, I suppose we should call this crusade a victory. Yet I can hardly bring myself to feel that way about it."

Lady Honoria squeezed his hand, the hand of the only man who had given his child's life in exchange for their cause.

Randel blinked back his own tears now. He glanced about the room to Sir Giles and Sir Etienne, who had remained quiet throughout the exchange. That is when he realized. "But wait, where is Sir Ade—"

The pained look in Honoria's eye cut him short. "My faithful servant, Sir Ademar, died protecting me at the prison. But I swear that I shall care for his family like my own from this day hence."

Randel's stomach churned. "Does Garrett know?"

"Not yet," Honoria said. "I was hoping you would help me tell him. And we must also tell Sapphira that my husband and our cousin are not alive."

"Before we do so," Sir Giles finally spoke up, "we should decide your next step."

Honoria sagged back into her chair. "I think we are all heart weary."

Although the experience at his makeshift trial had done much to heal Randel's own heart, he had grown weary of this battle as well. "Things are far more complex here than we ever realized."

"And messy," said Lord Rumsford. "So very messy. Other than rescuing our own men, I have lost sight of what this crusade is even about."

"I am ready to return home," Lady Honoria said. "And I believe Sapphira shall agree. I only hope she is not too disappointed that we failed to return the rightful duke to North Britannia."

"Sapphira is a strong girl," Randel assured her. "And she has been in good spirits ever since the rescue at Jezeer."

Lord Haverland pressed a hand to his chest. "Home to my wife and my living children. Though I ache to leave Humphrey here, I am ready to return to the living."

"But we should stop for a while in Tripoli first," Lord Rumsford said.

"That is wise," Sir Giles agreed. "Allow the sick and wounded to heal, and make sure that Bohemond will bring Jocelyn to justice."

"Jocelyn is a troubled woman." Randel of all people should know. "But she is not a stupid one. I doubt she will return to the crusader-held territory ever again."

"And life will not be easy for a beautiful European woman among the Saracens." Rumsford shook his head. "We shall have to leave vengeance in the hands of God."

"Sir Randel," Lady Honoria said, "I would like to thank you for warning us at the prison and for rallying the troops. You are an admirable leader."

Sir Etienne stepped forward. "And I would like to say that we would be honored to have you remain in the Outremer and join us as a Templar."

The offer warmed Randel's heart and buoyed him, as did Lady Honoria's heartfelt commendation. But now was not the time to turn his attention to such matters.

"I thank you both, but if that is all, I will fetch the children. They should know as soon as possible."

"Of course," Honoria said.

He headed across the deck and to the boys' cabin first. Most of them were sound asleep after their overnight ordeal. But Garrett was sitting curled into a tiny ball with his head of wavy brown hair tucked to his knees. At the creak of the door, he lifted his head and his gaze shot to Randel, wary and lost.

Randel sank down beside him upon his pallet.

"My father is gone, is he not? I could not find him anywhere."

"Lady Honoria would like to speak with you," Randel said gently, hoping to allow the lady to explain as she had wished.

"Please! Just tell me." The pleading in Garrett's voice broke Randel's heart.

"Your father was a very brave and chivalrous man. He died protecting the Lady Honoria."

Tears trickled down the boy's cheeks, which appeared wan despite his tanned skin. "That is always the risk with war. But what will happen to us? My sister, my mother, me?"

"Lady Honoria said she will care for you like her own family now."

Garrett nodded and swallowed hard. "That is fitting."

They sat in silence for a moment, side by side. Then the boy spoke again. "My papa is in heaven, with God and all the angels.

And he is so very happy. I shall attempt to be happy for him." He blinked back his tears and swallowed hard.

But Randel could no longer hold back his own tears. "Garrett, I do believe you are the most courageous boy I have ever met." Randel scooped the child into a hug, and Garrett clung to him with all his might.

"I try," Garrett whispered back.

Randel stood and helped the boy to his feet. "Come, we must fetch Sapphira. Lady Honoria wishes to speak to both of you."

Garrett straightened his back and lifted his chin. He had been through much these past months, yet his spirit had grown strong. As much as Randel's heart welled with compassion for the young fellow, he felt confident that God would see Garrett through this difficult time.

With surprising peace in her heart, Sapphira watched the rocky shoreline slip by as they made their way toward Tripoli. She had spent much of the day tending the wounded aboard their ship, but even that challenging task had not burdened her with heaviness.

They would return home. They would not press onward to Jerusalem. Thank the good Lord! She sensed deep within that their purpose had been fulfilled, though that assurance still made little sense.

Yes, they had freed many Englishmen and their ships would be filled near to bursting on their way home. Yes, the dukedom could move forward with Duchess Adela at the helm now. Yes, her own sister could move on with her life knowing the truth, that she was a widow. But was that truly enough?

The lightness that filled her gave her hope that it might be.

Rabia came up along the ship rail beside her. "Sapphira, can I talk to you for a moment?"

"Of course."

"Alone?" Rabia asked.

Something about the shy look upon the girl's face told Sapphira this might not be an easy conversation for her to have. They moved to a shady place on the deck to the side of the cabin. Sapphira sat down cross-legged, and Rabia joined her.

"What is it?" she asked.

"I have been waiting for the right time to tell you, but then I realized such a time might never come." Rabia tugged at her yellow silken head scarf.

"Please," Sapphira said. "You can tell me anything."

Rabia glanced about, then whispered, "I believe. I am a Christian now."

Sapphira faltered. Could it be so simple? Should there not be some special mass, some ritual? A baptism, perhaps? But instead she asked the more pressing question. "How?"

"I had a dream. Your Jesus came to me. He was so beautiful. The most beautiful, brilliant, shining man I have ever seen. And the love . . . the perfect love and compassion in His eyes. . . . When He asked me to be His child, I knew I could never deny Him."

Joy split Rabia's face like sunshine to match her cheerful veil. "I feel so light and free. Fresh and newborn like a babe. It is almost too hard to explain."

And all the questions, all the technicalities faded from Sapphira's mind. She knew it was true, and it was enough. There would be plenty of time to sort through the rest later. She reached out her arms and hugged Rabia. "You are my dear sister in Christ now."

Rabia gave her a squeeze, but then pulled back. "But wait. There is more. Jesus asked me to share the good news with others. To free other Moslems from the heavy chains of their religion. This is my calling, and this shall be my life now."

Sapphira's heart soared. Could Rabia have been the captive Sapphira was meant to set free? "Wait, when did you have this dream?"

"It seems like forever ago, but it was just the night before last. After we talked. The last time we slept in the tent."

And that next day Sapphira had sensed that their mission was complete.

Joy bubbled up inside her and escaped from her mouth in giggles of wonder. She felt like dancing and spinning but satisfied herself with another long hug. Afterward she said, "This is so amazing. This entire crusade was worthwhile—just for you, Rabia."

Rabia's cheeks turned pink. "Oh, I do not know about that."

"Then you shall have to trust me."

Rabia smiled.

"Do you plan to tell people? The others? Your father?" Sapphira asked, then pressed her hand to her cheek. "Oh, goodness, whatever shall your father say?"

"I told him this morning." Rabia surprised her by smiling once again. "He admitted that he had been moved by watching you all during this crusade as well. Though he is not ready to make a change in religions, I believe with time and prayer, I might be."

Rabia peeked around the corner and looked to the other children. "Father does not wish for me to tell people just yet. I had to tell you, though."

"I am so thankful that you did." Sapphira's heart, which had been light and content this last day, now felt ready to burst with happiness.

Then she remembered that Humphrey was not with them, and that Garrett would return home fatherless. This crusade had not been without sacrifice, yet God's purposes had been fulfilled.

"Your news brings me such comfort, Rabia. I have questioned my vision so many times. I have wondered if my sister steered our mission off course. But now I see that no matter the origins of this crusade, God has used it for the good."

"I think it is true that whatever your religion, sometimes God works in mysterious ways," Rabia said, wise beyond her years.

"Still, I wonder if I heard God quite right. If so many needed to die," Sapphira said.

"Do not take guilt upon yourself." Rabia knew her too well already.

"I shall try not to, but I am determined to learn to hear from God more clearly. And I shall commit my life to Him and to that purpose."

"As a nun?"

"That is my fondest hope."

Rabia nodded.

"I think we are almost there now," Sapphira said. "Let us rejoin the other children."

As they turned the corner, Sapphira spotted Brigitte looking wistfully toward the shore.

Sapphira gave her a squeeze from the side. "Are you thinking of Humphrey again?"

"'Tis just so sad. I know we should have expected that not all of us would make it, but I never imagined we might lose him."

"Is your heart broken now?" Rabia asked, for even she knew of Brigitte's desire to catch the boy as a husband.

Sadie, along with Issobelle and Lillian, came and joined them. "I have been wondering the same. I hope you don't mind us asking."

"I must confess . . . not in that way." Brigitte brushed away her yellowish hair that tangled in the sea breeze. "This trip has changed me. I still long for marriage and family, but not with the same desperation as before. I always believed my worth was tied to bringing my parents the best son-in-law, and giving that man the best children."

"And now?" Sapphira prompted.

"And now, I know my worth is in Christ. As much as it is within my power, I will wait for the man God sends to me."

At that moment, Jervais careened toward them, striving to catch a ball that one of the twins had thrown off course. He crashed directly into Brigitte, and the girls exploded into giggles over the timely collision.

"Do not even think it!" Brigitte squealed.

"What? I am sorry. It was only an accident." Not understanding their joke and looking offended, Jervais picked up the ball and huffed away.

Sapphira glanced around her and smiled. She had come on this trip a lonely girl with an odd gift that the others feared. Now she would head home with this group of friends who had experienced God's presence alongside her, and had grown to be like brothers and sisters.

"I realize he is young for you." Lillian nudged Brigitte with her elbow. "But he has grown quite good looking along the trip."

"And tall!" Sapphira agreed, and they all giggled again.

Jervais appeared to have sprouted several inches in the last months, and was now the largest of the children. His body had grown lean and muscled, even his face had taken on a leaner, more handsome appearance.

Sapphira watched as Jervais returned to the boys and tossed the ball at Garrett. Garrett shook his head and tossed it back, far from ready to play at games only hours after learning of his father's death.

"Excuse me please," Sapphira said to the other girls.

She headed his way. Although Garrett was still smallish for his age, he had an inner strength she had always admired. She was more determined than ever to become a nun, but suddenly she realized that a gentle and faithful man was of far more value than one who was arrogant and flamboyant like Philippe.

She took Garrett's hand in her own. "I am so very sorry about your father."

"Thank you," he said but looked shyly away.

"And I will be here for you."

Still he averted his gaze.

She gave his hand a swift jerk. "Enough of this silliness between us. You have always been like a brother to me. And now you will be a part of my family."

He turned to her, his big brown eyes wide with shock. Then he gave her hand a firm squeeze and smiled. "I admit I have missed your friendship."

"And I have missed yours. Let us never let anything stand between us again. Promise?"

He nodded and squeezed her hand tighter. "I suppose I cannot deny an offer of family at a time like this."

Though she had wondered if he might shatter at the news of his father, she could now see the strength clearly shining from his eyes. This crusade had changed every one of them.

Garrett glanced down at their joined hands and then to the shoreline of Tripoli where the noble family awaited them. "Philippe shall be jealous if he sees this. He shall not understand."

At that moment a tall, blond figure waved their way from the shore.

But Sapphira's heart no longer tugged her in Philippe's direction. She was over the boy, and more determined than ever to commit her life to Christ as *His* bride.

"Philippe shall recover." She smiled, ready to move on to the next phase in her life. This crusade might be coming to an end, but she had no doubt that many future adventures awaited them all.

Chapter 36

Rosalind sat with Randel upon the ship's highest deck, patiently awaiting their turn to be rowed ashore to Tripoli. The ship rocked subtly from side to side, and the sun stroked her cheeks with hazy warmth on this surprisingly mild summer day. The children had rushed to shore to meet their Tripolian friends at first opportunity, but neither she nor Randel had been in a hurry to disembark.

Nor was she in a hurry to have the conversation that was long overdue between them. Rosalind was content to just sit awhile quietly in his soothing presence, rocking atop the sea. For after today, he might well leave with the Templars, and she might never see him again.

Forward, ever forward, she reminded herself. She must focus ahead on seeing her family, for she had much to set right with her mother. And she must fervently pray that they would all be well and whole when she returned, for tragedy could easily strike, even in the relative peace and safety of her native North Britannia.

Looking down at her lute, she strummed a chord that Randel

had taught her just that afternoon, then switched to a second and a third. For the first time they had no pressing duties, and the idea of playing at instruments had not seemed a ludicrous pursuit. Her fingers yet felt thick and clumsy, but she was adjusting to the strings and patterns. With her three chords, she could play a simple ballad of a maiden in love with a shepherd.

Finally, Randel spoke. "'Tis good that Lady Honoria has decided to head home soon. It takes longer to fight the winds back toward England, and since it is July already, too much delay would mean waiting for a spring departure."

Rosalind sat aside her lute. Nothing in his speech gave away his own intentions, but a different point caught her notice. "July already! 'Tis my birth month. I suppose I am eighteen now."

Randel grinned her way. "Goodness, you are practically an old maid."

She gave him a playful shove. "That is only among the nobility. We peasant folk are much more practical concerning love and marriage. I am in no rush."

"So are you indeed open to the idea of love now?"

"I find that I am. The trial seems to have provided the finishing touch on the work God has been doing in my heart for some time. Was it only last night?"

"Believe it or not," Randel said. "It seems weeks ago."

Rosalind shook her head in wonder. "People have treated me no differently since they learned of my shame. That is a balm to my soul. And something shifted inside of me when the children prayed."

He sat up straighter. "Truly? I had the same experience. Which brings up something I need to speak with you about."

Here it was. The moment she had been both anticipating and dreading. "Yes?"

"A while back you asked me to remain open to whatever path God might lay upon my heart. What I did not tell you at the time was that my heart was too wracked by pain and guilt to ever hear clearly from God."

"Oh. And now?" She took in a deep breath and held it as she awaited his answer.

"And now everything is as clear as the blue sky overhead. I never felt called to join the church in an official capacity. That was all my parents' plan. What I do feel called to . . . undeniably and irrevocably . . . is loving you, Maid Rosalind of Ipsworth, and spending the rest of my life with you."

Rosalind's mouth gaped open. She could not find her words.

"That is, if you shall have me." He grinned at her with his crooked, breezy smile.

"Of . . . of . . ." She blinked several times at the man sitting on the wooden deck beside her, as she still tried to digest this news. "But wait! What of your family? They shall never accept me."

He grazed her cheek with his hand. "My parents have sworn to disown me if I do not join the church. I cannot see how this is any of their business now."

"What of your legacy? Your fortune? Your future?"

"I am but a fourth son, and I was about to take vows of poverty and chastity. I fear no loss, except the loss of you at my side. I love you, and I want to marry you. We shall face the future with the courage we have learned on this crusade, and we shall make a life together."

Of a sudden, a shyness overtook her. She looked down at her hands, wringing in her lap. She could not believe he would give up so much. For her. For Rosalind of Ipsworth. A woman who had committed unspeakable sins.

He tipped up her face and gazed deep into her eyes. Seeming to read her thoughts, he said, "Forward, ever forward."

Yes, their mantra, more true now than ever.

Then he leaned in and kissed her on the forehead. "You are *precious*."

And on the tip of her nose. "You are *righteous*."

Then his lips met hers in the sweetest kiss she could ever imagine. She waited for him to say you are *His,* as he had at the trial. But instead, he uttered the words, "You are *mine*."

All air swept from her lungs. She pulled back just an inch to see his treasured features and studied them for a moment. "Of course I shall marry you, Randel. And I own a cottage. On Sir Allen's land."

"A cottage." He echoed her words as if a cottage were the most blissful thing imaginable. "And I shall apply to him as a knight."

"We shall make a life, together," she said in wonder, pressing her forehead to his.

A flutter near their heads caused them to jerk apart.

"Oh, my goodness." Rosalind took in the sight of the small yellow-and-grey bird that alit on the rail nearby. "It cannot be."

Randel's grin stretched wide across his face. "It is. The Syrian serin, at last."

He stood and took a step toward it. "What are you doing all the way out here on this ship, you silly little fellow?"

The bird twisted his head and eyed Randel, but did not flee. It let forth its long, trilling call.

"'Tis so lovely," Rosalind whispered. "Shall I fetch a net?"

"That is what I had hoped for. But after all we have been through on this trip, I am thinking that every one of God's creatures deserves to be free and choose their own paths in life. What think you?"

"I absolutely agree." Rosalind stood and joined him, slipping easily under his arm and leaning her head against his shoulder.

"I want to marry you soon," Randel said against her hair. "Aboard the ship. Then there shall be nothing my parents can do to stop us."

"Perfect." And it was. The sky above her seemed to radiate

with God's pleasure. The ship took on a special sort of glow. She was overcome with a wash of warmth and pure joy. A lightness, a cleanness swathed about her. She felt as if she just might float away. She now had a true destiny, a true purpose. She would embrace her future and never again make the mistake of striving to earn her own redemption.

Then they melted back into another kiss. One of many they would share throughout a lifetime together.

Epilogue

Rosalind slid from her horse, nearly teetering as her pregnant belly pulled her forward. Randel caught her in his arms and swiped snowflakes from her lashes.

"What on earth?" A shocked Lady Gwendolyn handed her babe to Sir Allen and ran toward her with all the speed and agility Rosalind remembered. Motherhood had not slowed the woman down one bit.

Gwendolyn nearly crashed into her as she swept Rosalind into a fierce hug. "We heard word from the city that you would be coming, but I had no idea!" She waved to Rosalind's stomach. "What? Who?"

Then her former mistress glanced to Randel's sheepish grin and back again to Rosalind. Her eyes lit with merriment. "No! You two?"

"Married safe and sound aboard the ship nearly half a year past." Randel chuckled.

"We thought we were the ones with a surprise." Sir Allen joined them, holding a baby girl in his arms. "Welcome Randel, Rosalind. And you as well, Sadie."

Sadie bounded toward him for a hug, then stepped back to admire the child.

"Oh, she is beautiful." Rosalind cooed over the pretty babe as well. Soon she would have her own child, and she would protect it with all of her heart, mind, and soul this time.

"But she is not the only surprise," Gwendolyn teased.

"My family?" Rosalind asked. Sadly, they had heard no word from Randel's family at all while they had been in Edendale. Surely they must have heard of the crusaders return. It seemed they did indeed plan to cut him out of their lives.

"Rosalind, your family is safely installed in your cottage," Sir Allen said. "You shall see them soon."

She sighed in relief. Thank the good Lord, for she missed them so and regretted the distance that she had let grow between herself and her mother. She and Randel wanted family about them to help raise their child.

"This surprise is more for Sadie, now that I think about it." Gwendolyn, the fierce knight, giggled like a young girl. "Come out already!" she called.

Lady Merry and Lord Timothy spilled from the castle portal and into the courtyard. Merry held a child as well, a little boy, perhaps a year older than Gwendolyn's babe. And a little girl, three or four years of age, hid against Timothy's leg.

"Merry, Timothy, Wren!" Sadie shouted, and the hugging continued.

"We heard that the ship had passed London, and just had to come and fetch Sadie home," Timothy said.

"It has been too long," said the tiny, dark Lady Merry.

Rosalind took in the scene before her. An entire courtyard of women warriors. Lady Honoria would be so proud.

But then it struck her that if even Merry and Timothy had heard of their return, surely the Penigrees knew of their arrival, likely even of their marriage, and had chosen to ignore them.

Oddly, no one seemed to have any recent word of Randel's family at all, but they did live quite far from the capital.

"Sorry that we lingered longer in Edendale than we expected," Randel said, "but we had much to attend there."

"How fares the capital?" asked Sir Allen.

"Well," Randel said. "Very well, in fact. It seems the people have embraced the Duchess Adela completely now that they know her brother perished in the Holy Land."

"Plus, she had nearly an extra year to win their trust," Rosalind added.

"So was your crusade glorious?" Gwendolyn asked with a wistful expression upon her face.

"It was hard," Sadie replied honestly.

"And complicated," Randel said.

"And worth it," Rosalind concluded. "We have so many stories to tell you all."

"Let us head indoors." Allen gestured to the castle. "'Tis cold out here."

"Ah, the cold is a nice change from the heat of the Holy Land." Randel pulled their sacks from the horses, and they turned toward the steps.

But a clatter of hooves caught them all up short.

A woman followed by several knights cantered through the gates and into the courtyard. The thin, austere-looking lady with greying hair pulled to a stop in front of them and dismounted.

Neither Sir Allen nor Lady Gwendolyn said a word in greeting.

After an awkward moment of silence, Randel sucked in a deep breath. He braced his shoulders as if waiting for a blow and stepped toward the woman. "Mother. What a nice surprise."

Rosalind's stomach clenched. She had come after all.

"Oh, my baby, you are home!" The woman held open her arms to Randel.

A confused Randel moved closer. "I did not know if you would welcome me. I did not join the Templars."

"And I have heard that you married a peasa . . . or I should say, a fellow crusader." She yet held out her arms, and Randel hesitantly embraced her.

"Yes, a valiant woman and a fellow leader," he said.

His mother held him by the shoulders and looked him up and down. "I am just happy that you are safe and well. The rest of that is behind us now. I was foolish to make such demands."

"I do not understand," Randel said.

Nor did Rosalind.

The woman swallowed hard. "I am afraid I have sad news. A pox swept our castle. I have only just recovered and been released from the quarantine. My son, you are now the Earl of Penigree. It was God's grace that you were far away when it happened. And that you made it back home to us so soon."

"What? Father? My brothers? All three of them? Surely not!" Tears welled in Randel's eyes.

"I am sorry. There is no easy way to share such news."

He shook his head. "I cannot believe they are all gone."

"But you are here." His mother cupped his cheek with her hand.

Rosalind's heart swelled with compassion for her husband. The news was difficult. Then again, he had been ready to relinquish his family ties. But she still did not know if they should trust this woman.

"I saw a serin." Randel clearly remained at a loss for words. "But I did not bring it home."

"How splendid. But you are all that I wish to see," his mother said.

He led her by the hand to Rosalind. "I would like you to meet my wife. Lady Rosalind Penigree, I suppose."

Rosalind's head spun as she realized it was true.

"My daughter." The woman embraced her as well, then pulled back in shock. She pressed her hand to Rosalind's bulging stomach. "And my grandchild! The future heir to Penigree."

The woman's eyes filled with happy tears.

"Come inside with us, Mother," Randel said. "We have much catching up to do."

Rosalind clutched tightly to Randel's thick winter cloak. "I cannot believe it," she whispered.

"Well, you must." Randel chuckled. "We shall face this new challenge, together."

Rosalind of Ipsworth, now Lady Penigree, sighed in wonder. Randel would make an ideal leader for his people, and she would lead by his side. Everything in their lives had led them to this point.

She would never have dared to dream of such a future, yet it sat well with her soul.

Historical Notes

Historically speaking, this is the hardest book I've ever undertaken. While there is much research available on the politics of the crusades and the battles fought, there is very little available about day-to-day life in the Holy Land at that time. Everyday issues are often ignored by history because they are taken for granted by the chroniclers. I was able to find little snippets here and there that helped me to picture the clothing, architecture, food, etc. . . . I learned that the crusaders in those areas tended to fuse the native and European cultures. However, the best fact I found was the simple explanation that life in that part of the world changed little from around 1000 AD until today.

Suddenly things became much easier for me because my husband is from Lebanon—which was called Tripoli and was the northern part of the Kingdom of Jerusalem at the time of the crusades—and I have made several extended trips to that part of the world. My familiarity with Middle Eastern customs and religions is a large part of why I chose to write this story in the first place. I have even been caught in Lebanon during fighting between the Muslim group, Hezbollah, and the Israeli forces. So I understand the challenges they face in that part of the world.

Now you might be wondering why I included women and

children on crusades. Of course at this time battle was primarily for men. It was the men's responsibility to protect women, not the other way around. And yet, perhaps because of the religious fervor surrounding the crusades and the pilgrimage nature of them, there is ample record of women and children going along as well. Sometimes even whole families.

Generally women supplied water and provisions and tended the wounded. But it was also considered proper for them to man launching weapons and shoot bows and arrows from a distance. According to Moslem legends of the crusades, there might have been some women disguised as knights fighting on the front lines, although European records do not concur on this issue. Certainly in times of desperation, women throughout history have done what they must and fought for their lives.

"The Children's Crusade" had two waves in the early 1200s. Thousands of children followed visionary young teens and set off on crusade, but there is no record of any reaching the Holy Land. Many died along the way, others turned back, and it seems some might have been lost at sea. I wanted to complete that legend, while still presenting the vast complexities of the crusades.

Bohemond and his family are pretty hazy characters, at least in the available English language research. For that reason I took more liberties with them than I generally do with actual historical figures. I also decided to use the real-life locations of Tripoli and Beirut, since I felt like that part of the world would be very foreign to most readers already. However, the smaller villages and prisons were my own inventions.

Can you imagine my delight when I realized that St. Francis of Assisi was in fact traveling the Mediterranean at the same time as my crusaders? I had to let them cross paths so that the inspirational man could make a cameo. And in case I have any readers who are knowledgeable about Catholic theology, I need to explain that while at this time in history abortion was considered a sin, it did not carry the punishment of excommunication as it did in later times.

As in my other books, I used a slightly archaic, slightly British version of English for ease of reading, rather than attempting to imitate Middle English. And I utilized the King James Version of the Bible, since it is the oldest standard English version available.

Now to the toughest issue: Should the crusades have been fought at all? In the beginning, the Christian countries of Europe were trying to turn the tide of hundreds of years of Muslim invasion and oppression. They wanted to kick the Muslims out of Europe and take back land lost by their Christian brothers and sisters in the Byzantine part of the world. I would contend that those reasons were as solid and justifiable as those fueling any war in history. But war is messy.

From the start motives were mixed. Some wanted power and money, while others had altruistic motives. Sometimes crusaders from different European countries cooperated; sometimes they undermined each other and broke treaties that other groups had made. Some crusades were led by strong, chivalrous leaders, and others turned into riotous mobs. And almost always the new crusaders from Europe failed to understand their enemy and the complex social structure of the Middle East.

Muslims are people just like us. There are many types, both religiously and ethnically, and I am blessed to call many Muslims my friends. While there is, in fact, much violent and negative teaching in the Muslim holy book, the average Muslim person just wants to live a peaceful and prosperous life. They want to be surrounded by friends and family and bring some good to the world. On the other hand, perhaps even more so today than during the crusades, there is a deep religiously based hatred instilled in children throughout the Middle East toward the Christians and especially the Jews. That sad reality cannot be ignored.

But there is one more interesting factor to keep in mind. Much like Rabia in the story, Muslims have been coming to Christ in surprising numbers during recent years. Some through dreams and visions, and many others through the new openness brought to that part of the world by satellite television and Internet.

I hope that in taking this historical trip, you were spurred to think about these same conflicts that are still troubling our world today. And you have seen that, all politics and strategy aside, true freedom can only be found within.

Acknowledgments

I have been blessed with so many partners who have helped me along my writing journey: the ladies of Inkwell Inspirations and Wenches Writing for Christ (oh yes, you read that right), Hampton Roads Christian Fiction Writing Fellowship, a supportive family and church, and many wonderful friends. Thank you to all of you! I would also like to take this opportunity to express my gratitude to all the members of my *Dauntless* and *Chivalrous* launch groups, who helped get this series off the ground. I also recently discovered the added blessing of the British Medieval History Facebook group, which is always ready to answer, and debate at length, any historical questions I might have.

A special thanks to my agent, Tamela Hancock Murray, who stuck with me through the challenging early years. Also to my editor Karen Schurrer, who always provides the right balance of constructive criticism and encouragement. And of course to the whole Bethany team, who have done such a great job with everything from cover design to marketing and publicity. Thank you also to Marisa Deshaies, Darlene Turner, Suzie Johnson, and Angela Andrews, who critiqued this book.

My final and most heartfelt thanks to my writing partner, the Holy Spirit. In God I live and move and have my being. I could never do this alone!

Dina Sleiman holds an MA in professional writing from Regent University and a BA in communications with a minor in English from Oral Roberts University. Over the past twenty years, she has had opportunities to teach college writing and literature, as well as high-school and elementary classes in English, humanities, and fine arts. She lives in Virginia with her husband and three children. She can be found online at www.dinasleiman.com.

More From
Dina L. Sleiman!

Learn more about Dina and the VALIANT HEARTS series at dinasleiman.com.

Born a baron's daughter, Merry Ellison is now an enemy of the throne. Bold and uniquely skilled, she fiercely protects a band of orphans who must steal to survive. Timothy Grey plans to earn a title by capturing "The Ghosts of Farthingale Forest," but will he carry out his mission when he meets their dauntless leader face-to-face?

Dauntless
VALIANT HEARTS #1

Gwendolyn longs to be a knight, not a marriage pawn—and she won't give up her future without a fight. Only the handsome newcomer, Allen of Ellsworth, seems to admire her brave spirit, but will fate keep them apart?

Chivalrous
VALIANT HEARTS #2

⬡ BETHANYHOUSE

 Stay up-to-date on your favorite books and authors with our free e-newsletters. Sign up today at bethanyhouse.com.

 Find us on Facebook. facebook.com/bethanyhousepublishers

anopenbook
Free exclusive resources for your book group! bethanyhouse.com/anopenbook

If you enjoyed *Courageous,* you may also like . . .

No girl has ever become a prophet of the Infinite. Even though the elders warn that she will die young, Ela of Parne heeds the call of her Creator and is sent to bring His word to a nation torn asunder by war. But can she balance the leading of her heart with the leading of the Infinite?

Prophet by R. J. Larson
BOOKS OF THE INFINITE #1
rjlarsonbooks.com

As Princess Una comes of age, a foolish decision leaves her heart vulnerable to an enemy she thought was only a myth. What will Una risk to save her kingdom— and the man she's come to love?

Heartless by Anne Elisabeth Stengl
TALES OF GOLDSTONE WOOD
anneelisabethstengl.blogspot.com

In this highly imaginative fantasy, a reluctant hero undertakes a dangerous and heroic quest to discover his destiny and fight against the dark forces seeking to control The Realm.

Emissary by Thomas Locke
LEGENDS OF THE REALM #1